MARCH TO THE VOLGA

THE EPIC JOURNEY OF CHRISTOPH KARL & JACOBINA MAURER

Novels by **D. Philipp Kaiser**
in this Volga Ancestor series:

March to the Volga

Dreams on the Volga

Courage on the Volga

Escape to the Volga

Freedom on the Volga

MARCH TO THE VOLGA

by

by

D. Philipp
KAISER

Published January 2012
Darrel P. Kaiser

Darrel Kaiser Books
www.DarrelKaiserBooks.com
email:Dar-Bet@att.net
Green Mountain
Huntsville, Alabama

First Printing
ISBN 978-0-9849230-1-4

Dedication

I dedicate this novel to
Mrs. Mildred Kaiser
geb Mildred Karle,
my wonderful mother and
fourth great granddaughter
of Herr Christoph Karl and
Frau Jacobina Maurer.

Her caring love and
inspiration has guided me
to what I am this day.

My eternal love,
My eternal thanks.

A Prayer for Genealogists

*Lord, help me dig into the past
and sift the sands of time,
That I might find the roots that
made this family tree mine.
Lord, help me trace the ancient
roads on which my fathers trod,
And led them through so many
lands to find our present sod.*

*Lord, help me find an ancient
book or dusty manuscript,
That's safely hidden now away
in some forgotten crypt.
Lord, let it bridge the gap that
haunts my soul when I can't find,
The missing link between some
name that ends the same as mine.*
Curtis Woods

Preface

This historical novel is fictional, but is drawn from recorded real life people and events. Where the historical records are missing or incomplete, I have attempted to fill those gaps with reasonable, but entirely fictional, accounts of their lives.

My goal was to spin the tale of their wants, desires, dreams and goals, their successes, failures, and conquests, their whole lives during their move from Germany to Russia to America as they searched for the Promised Land, into a story our children would read.

It is not my intent to damage the memory or reputation of any of my real life characters, and if I have accidentally done so, I sincerely apologize here and now, to all. My only intent is to make all aware of the amazing accomplishments of these people.

March to the Volga is the first of five books spinning the stories of the struggles of five different German families and their many descendants, as the emigrated ever farther and farther away from the old homeland.

This story begins in southern Germany, a few miles north of Löwenstein in the year of 1764. An unnamed man, fleeing his past cruel life in the city, accidentally crosses paths with married couple, Herr Christoph Karl and Frau Jacobina Karl *geb* Maurer.

As you move through the pages of the next 136 years, you will meet more than eighteen additional characters spinning out their lives.

I sincerely hope you enjoy it as a fictional story; I hope you laugh, you cry, you get angry, and maybe sad. I hope that you feel so strongly about what you read, that you write me! Remember, this is fiction and fantasy, it is not a research manual, and you should not assume any of it true. Some of it is, much of it is not! Hopefully, reading it may spark some questions about your own ancestors and roots.

D. Philipp

KAISER

2012

Martin Luther

This book and story highlights the wishes and dreams, the trials and troubles, and the victories and successes of one German Lutheran family line. A driving factor in their lives was their resilient Lutheran Faith, and their following of Priest and Theologian Martin Luther.

His unyielding stand for his beliefs, against the awesome power of those in authority, earns both our respect and admiration.

Woodcut of Martin Luther
By Hans Baldung Grien
Strasbourg, France 1521

Dramatis Personae

Herr Christoph Karl

Frau Jacobina Karl *geb* Maurer

Herr Johann Jacob Maurer

Frau Anna Maria Maurer

Susanna Regina Maurer

Laudema Christiana Maurer

Nobody / Herr Michael Grun / Herr Peter Schwarz

Lt. Von Ditmarr

Lt. Chernyshevsky

Herr Wilhelm Karl

Frau Anna Maria Karl *geb* Grün

Herr Johann Michael Karle

Frau Susanna Charlotte Karle *geb* Michel

Maria Margaretha Karle

Herr Johannes Karle

Frau Christina Elisabeth Karle *geb* Werner

Anna Marguerita Karle

Herr Johann Michael Karle

Frau Elisabeth Karle *geb* Andreas

Herr Johann August Karle

Frau Anna Karle *geb* Steitz

Personae Time Line

	1764	1775	1785	1795	1805	1815	1825	1835	1845	1855	1865	1875	1885	1895	1905
Christoph Karl															
Jacobina Maurer															
Johann Jacob Maurer															
Anna Maria Maurer															
Susanna Maurer															
Laudema Maurer															
Nobody-Grun-Schwarz															
Lt. Von Ditmarr															
Lt. Chernyshevsky															
Wilhelm Karl															
Anna Maria Grün															
Johann Michael Karle															
Susanna Michel															
Maria Margaretha Karle															
Johannes Karle															
Christina Werner															
Anna Margaretha Karle															
Johann Michael Karle															
Elisabeth Andreas															
Johann August Karle															
Anna Steitz															

MARCH TO THE VOLGA

1 MEETING

♠NOBODY♠

Fourteen days ride southeast of stadt Frankfurt, Reichsstadt (Imperial City) of the Holy Roman Empire

It was another early dawn and I had just woken, another bad night sleeping out in the open on the hard ground, at the side of this damned dusty dirt road.

The sun was just coming up, and it was obvious that this was another of those blistering hot days that had tortured me so many times over the past weeks. Even worse than the sun and heat, I had been able to find only a little water and even less food. I must come across water and food soon.

With no idea of what direction to go, I just continued trudging down the road. I lost all track of time, and after walking for what seemed like hours, I found myself in a large valley filled with rows and rows of grape vines, so many that they formed checkerboard patterns as far as I could see.

Desperate for anything to eat, I dove into the vines hoping to find grapes; but no, all the grape berries were still green and hard to the touch, not yet fit to eat. Disappointed, and still thirsty and hungry, I returned to the road to continue walking towards somewhere.

Again, I walked for what seemed like hours, and maybe it was. Off in the distance, I thought I saw someone moving through the vines.

Did I imagine it? Was I seeing things? I desperately hoped it was someone…

Not seeing things, he was real. He was in the rows of vines, and had not seen me. He must be a vine tender.

Would he help me? Would he chase me away? Would he share his food with me, or would he even give me a little water? All these questions raced through my mind as I moved towards the man I had seen, as quickly as my poor weak body would let me.

At hearing my noisy approach, the vine tender looked up from his work. He was startled and stared at me, but did not move. I was afraid he would run and not help me. Frantically, I yelled, "Friend, how are you doing today?"

The vine tender did not run and did not answer, but continued intently staring at me. I thought to myself that I must look a dirty beggar, and then realized that in fact, that is exactly what I am.

Actually, the vine tender had seen the approaching stranger long ago, but was busy with his vines and had no time to waste. As the traveler approached closer, his filthy appearance became visible.... The vine tender mumbled to himself, "Another dirty beggar; what did he want? Would he steal from me? I do not have time for this!"

The vine tender decided he would just ignore the beggar, and maybe then, the filthy beggar would just go away. A small voice inside reminded him that in Heilige Kirche (Holy Church) on Sabbath, they had preached, "We are all the children of GOD."

Dismayed from that revolting thought, and then guilty for feeling it, the vine tender decided that when, and if, the stranger hailed him, he must be as friendly as one would be with any brother. When hailed by the apparent beggar, the vine tender reluctantly answered as a friend, "It is a fine day... and how are you, friend?"

I lied to the vine tender, "I am a lost traveler, and no not where I am. I have not had any food or water for what seems like many days, could you spare a little of either?"

The vine tender again stared, obviously studying me, and then shrugged. He reached down into the vines; I could not see what he might pull out and was fearful.... I almost ran.

As his arm came out of the vines, I expected a knife, but instead his hands held a flask of water and a hunk of meat.

He offered both to me, and without so much as a word, I grabbed at both, gulped down the water and tore at the meat, shoving pieces quickly into my mouth. The vine tender just watched me, saying nothing at all.

For me, time had stopped. Time remained stopped, as I completely quenched my thirst and filled my belly.

When the vine tender realized it was going to be some time before I was finished downing his food and drink, he just returned to working his vines.

After some time, with my hunger and thirst temporarily satisfied, I regained some of my composure and said, "Friend, your charity is much appreciated. Thank You!"

The vine tender asked where I was going, but I had no good answer and kept silent. He asked who I was, and I again kept silent, unsure what would be best to tell them. He shrugged, and simply spoke, "I am *Herr Christoph Karl.* I am a free man, and a follower of our Friar Martin Luther. I am also, as you can see, a vine tender."

Herr Karl told me he was not the owner of all this, but only a poor worker that tends all the vines from sunup to sunset. He also said, "Tending the vines is hard work, but it is good and honest work, and it also good to be out every day among GODs plants and animals."

He somehow realized that I had nowhere to go... and that I was not coming from anywhere, and I was not going anywhere. He looked around at the vines and then asked, "Do you know anything about working with the vines?"

I did not, and lying, I quickly replied, "Of course I do, I have some experience!"

Herr Karl frowned, then shrugged and answered, "All right, there is more to do here than I can handle. If you help, I will give you more food to eat, and a warm place to sleep."

Realizing that this was my best offer in months, I quickly nodded 'yes', and we began to work the vines together. It must have been quickly evident to *Herr Karl* that I had never worked with any vines before, but he did not comment or complain. I closely watched him as he rid the vines of bad new growth, and tried to do as he did.

He taught me that you could just not trim the vine by pulling off any old shoots. You had to be very particular as to which shoots to cut off using a pair of gartenschere (hand pruners). Before too long, I was able to copy his ways, but at a much slower pace.

The vines ripped at my hands, soon they were raw, and I became slower and slower. *Herr Karl* never complained how slow I was, or told me to hurry up; I never complained about my hands.

We both just kept working the vines, and working our way down the seemingly endless rows. Though I was only a beginner and new at this, still we made good progress and made, in my mind, a good team.

After what seemed like many, many hours, I saw the sun was beginning to set. *Herr Karl,* also noticing the dusk, stopped, and said "This is a good days work; now to home for food and sleep. You are a good worker; you may call me *Christoph* from now on."

Christoph picked up his sack of tools and walked out of the vines, and up a gently sloped forest path. We walked for a while up and down, and up and down, the sloping trail.

Eventually, we came to a clearing in the trees; in the clearing was a cottage with white walls and thatched roof. I thought to myself that this must be his home. As we got closer, *Christoph* yelled out, "*Jacobina*, my wife, I have brought us a guest."

A comely, and well-formed young woman came out the door; most likely his wife. She took one look at me and froze; her hands flew to her mouth, in her eyes, I saw fear.

What else could I expect from her? I do look frightful, as dirty and bedraggled as I am. Embarrassed and disgusted at my dreadful appearance, I began to move back and away.

Christoph grabbed my arm and said to *Jacobina*, "This man is our guest. He has graciously offered to help me work the vines, and I have in return graciously offered him a roof over his head, food to eat, and refreshment to drink. He will be with us for a while."

Turning to me he said, "This is my wife, *Frau Jacobina*." I nodded, but was afraid to say anything to her.

Frau Jacobina regained her composure and put a friendly smile on her face, but angrily thought, "Ach mein Gott (Oh my God), what sort of thing has my dear husband brought to our home and table this time. He looks like a disgusting beggar, and smells even worse. There is no way I can welcome him into our home, as stands there now."

Thinking quickly, *Frau Jacobina* replied to both of us, "Of course, as my dear husband has said, you are very welcome. You both must have been working hard for you are very dirty and smell bad. Please wash up, and I will find our guest some cleaner clothing. Hurry now, supper is almost ready." With that, *Frau Jacobina* returned inside and slammed the door closed.

Christoph and I just looked at each other. Not knowing what to say, I said nothing. *Christoph* began to say something, but then did not, and chose to remain silent.

Christoph rolled his eyes, and thought to himself, "She is not happy, and there was something in *Jacobina's* voice about getting washed up now... There would be no discussion."

We both did as told and thoroughly washed up. True to her word, *Frau Jacobina* had laid out some clean, but worn, clothes for me. After washing up and donning my 'new' clean clothes, I felt like a brand new man.

2 THEIR HOME

♠NOBODY♠

Karl home, about four hours walk east of stadt Heilbronn, Reichsstadt (Imperial City) of the Holy Roman Empire

Now that we were suitable to *Frau Jacobina*, it was time to return to the house and hopefully, supper. *Christoph* led the way, opened the door and ushered me into his home. It was as I could see from the outside, very small, with one big square room with a floor-to-ceiling curtain that closed to make two rooms. It was also immaculately clean.

There on the dining table was a basket of brötchen and fleisch and käse (rolls and meats and cheese), and a variety of gemüse (vegetables). *Christoph* was beaming; he was proud of his home, his wife, and the table she had set; it was all wonderful and he had every right to be.

I sat on a rough wooden bench at the side of the table, while *Christoph* took his place at the head. *Frau Jacobina* remained very busy adding even more food to the table, but eventually sat down across from *Christoph*.

All the food looked, and smelled so wonderful, that I just wanted to dig in. I began to, but *Christoph* gently grabbed my arm to stop me. He said quietly, "First, we must give thanks to our LORD by saying Grace."

Christoph and *Frau Jacobina* bowed their heads and closed their hands, while *Christoph* said thanks in prayer to their GOD, "Komm, Herr Jesu, sei unser Gast Und segne, was Du uns bescheret hast. Vater, segne diese Speise Uns zur Kraft und dir zum Preise! Hilf, Gott, heut und allezeit, Mach uns bereit fuer die Ewigkeit. Herr, Du hilfst aus aller Not, Gibst uns unser taeglich Brot, Speisest alle, gross und klein: Lass uns Dir befohlen sein. Segne, Vater, was wir essen Lass uns Deiner nicht vergessen Lieber Gott fuer Speis' und Trank Und alle Guete sei Dir Dank. (Come Lord Jesus and be our guest and let these gifts to us be blessed. Father, bless this meal for our strengthening and to your praise! Help us, God, today and at all times, make us prepared for eternity. Lord, you help in every need, you give us our daily bread, you feed all, great and small: let us be committed to you. Bless, Father, what we eat let us not forget you dear God for food and drink and for all goodness we give you thanks.)"

As I really was not a follower of their Martin Luther, whoever he was, and I really was not sure who their GOD was, and I never had any luck with any religion, I did not ever pray to anyone or anything. However, common sense warned me that if I wanted to eat all this good food, I should join and pray with them on this.

Christoph and *Frau Jacobina* eventually said "Amen," and motioned for me to eat.

I did so immediately. I did little talking, but as we ate, *Christoph* began to tell me about himself and about his wife, *Frau Jacobina.* He told me that he was born around thirty-four years ago here on this land north of Löwenstein. His parents and ancestors had lived on these lands for many, many generations, and even longer farther south of Stuttgart along the Swiss border. He also said that there are rumors that he is somehow related to royalty in Karlsrhue. His parents both passed some years ago, no brothers or sisters have he. He knew of no uncles or aunts or relatives, so there was no one to ask if the royal tale was true, or just a myth.

As *Christoph* had mentioned before, he and *Frau Jacobina* were followers of Friar Martin Luther. He was proud of his work as vine tender, and said that is all he really knew. His father and father's father had all been vine tenders. He repeated what he had said before, that it was a good life to be out among GODs plants and animals each day.

I thought maybe his wife, *Frau Jacobina,* would say something, but she remained silent and let her husband talk. She avoided looking at me, and quietly continued to eat.

Christoph continued, and told me a little about his wife. *Frau Jacobina* was the youngest daughter, of three, born to stonemason *Herr Johan Jacob Maurer* and his wife, *Frau Anna Maria. Herr Johan* was an old man now, being born over fifty-five years ago. As a child, *Frau Jacobina* and her family lived in the village of Kirhart (Kirchardt), a full day walk west of here. Her two older sisters were first born *Frau Susanna Regina,* born four years earlier than *Frau Jacobina*, and *Frau Laudema Christiana*, born two years earlier.

Christoph obviously enjoyed speaking about his wife, and told me that *Frau Jacobina* was born in mid-February around thirty years ago. Her whole family followed the teachings of Friar Martin Luther, and they christened her in the Lutheran Faith a few days after birth.

He and *Frau Jacobina* married in the village of Heilbronn about eight years past. After the ceremony, *Frau Jacobina* joined with *Christoph* in this home, and has been here happily ever since. Sadly, their only son passed after a few months of life, and their GOD has not blessed them with any another children.

While *Christoph* talked, and talked, and talked, *Frau Jacobina* was deep in her own thoughts about this new stranger. She thought to herself, "He cleaned up well and no longer smelled, and he did not seem to be a disgusting beggar, maybe only just a beggar! It was always good when dear *Christoph* brought a hurt animal home to tend for a while, but this was different. Here was a strange man who we know nothing about! Maybe with GODs blessing, this strange man would quickly leave. No, that would probably not be as *Christoph* apparently wished him to stay with us and help in the vines."

Christoph talked about their faith and their following of Friar Martin Luther. He took time to carefully explain what the "following of Friar Martin Luther" meant to them. I think he suspected that I really was not of their faith, and took advantage of this time to tell me about the blessings of their GOD. I suppose he was trying to save me; good luck, many others have tried and miserably failed.

I repeatedly nodded as if I followed what *Christoph* was saying, though I was of full belly and tired, and little of what he said made any sense to me at all.

He politely asked about my life. I replied, "*Christoph*, there is little to tell, and even that little is boring, and in truth, I am very, very tired."

He shrugged, got up and said, "I feel we are friends. You may call my wife '*Jacobina*', no need for using 'Frau'. Yes, I too am tired, and we must get up early to be in the vines. It is time for bed!"

Christoph led me outside to a small covered shed where I was to sleep. I found it warm and cozy with thick straw on my part of the floor. This would make a wonderful bed, so very much better than alongside the road. I wholeheartedly thanked *Christoph,* and wished him and his *Jacobina*, a very good night.

A soon as *Christoph* left, I lay down on the straw. I had a full belly and a soft place to lay my head, and I fell fast asleep and into a deep slumber.

It seemed like I was asleep only moments when *Christoph* was there telling me it was time to get up and tend the vines. As before, we all sat at the table for breakfast and *Christoph* gave blessing. We quickly ate cheese and brötchen.

Over breakfast, *Christoph* said to me, "I must call you some name. Since you have chosen not to tell us yours, we will call you, *Nobody*."

I could tell from his words that he thought this would get me to say my real name, but I did not, and answered back, "*Nobody*, that will do fine." Obviously disappointed that his trick did not work, he shrugged and went back to eating.

Jacobina made a sack with fleisch and more käse and brötchen (meats and cheese and rolls) for each of us for lunch. We said our goodbyes, and went back down the same trail we come up the previous evening.

When we reached the vines, *Christoph* explained, "Throughout the year we must stop bad growth by cutting back extra shoots as they develop. We do that to keep the vines workable, to make the vine give us fruit and not just stems and leaves, and to force the grapes to grow close to the main stem. This way, the sap does not travel as far to produce our grapes."

I nodded I understood, even though it seemed to be an awful lot of attention to give to a plant. The vines were going to grow grapes whether we did all that or not, still we worked the vines from sunup to sunset doing it.

As we worked, *Christoph* would occasionally ask about me, but I steadfastly remained silent. I think he finally understood that I just did not want to talk about myself.

Christoph took my silence as opportunities to tell me more of their Friar Martin Luther, and their Protestant teachings… before long I knew quite a bit about this Lutheran faith and their GOD.

I soon came to understand that *Christoph* and *Jacobina* were just good simple and devout people, and that each day I spent with them, was just a repeat of the day before. Instead of feeling bored by this simple life, I felt good and refreshed, and looked forward to each new dawn.

Late one night at the supper table, *Christoph* announced, "Tomorrow is the Sabbath. We will not be working, but will all be going to Kirche (Church) for the day."

I was tired from working hard all week, and just wanted to lie around and sleep. I did not want to go to Kirche with them, but I did want to see Löwenstein. Both *Christoph* and *Jacobina* were excited about the Sabbath. *Jacobina* even gave me more clean clothes to wear on the Sabbath.

How could I say no and refuse to join with them in the celebration of their faith on the Sabbath? I could not!

3 VILLAGES

♠NOBODY♠

Karl home

Christoph woke me even earlier than usual on their Sabbath morn. I say 'their Sabbath morn' as I am not a believer, but I am not going to let *Christoph* and *Jacobina* learn that, because I have come to enjoy living and working here with them.

The early morning Sabbath meal was smaller than usual. *Christoph* explained that since this was not a day of work, they ate less. That made sense, but I was still hungry and could have easily eaten more of the käse and brötchen. We quickly finished eating, and prepared to leave for the village of Löwenstein, or so I thought.

The three of us began our walk, while *Christoph* explained to me that we would be joining up with a 'better-off' older neighbor family that had an ox and wagon. *Jacobina* and the women and children of the other family would ride on the ox wagon to Kirche. Men would walk.

He continued, as we walked, to say that their Kirche in Heilbronn was a ways to go, but not that really that far. I was puzzled and said, "I thought we were going to Löwenstein."

Christoph laughed and replied, "No, Löwenstein is a Katholische (Catholic) village and Kirche. We are followers of the teachings of Friar Martin Luther, Lutherans or also known as Protestants."

I must have looked confused, and he continued, "Friar Martin Luther was Katholische, but was denounced and expelled from the Katholische Kirche by the Pope because our Luther protested the way the Pope was ruling the Kirche... and so as his followers, we are Protestants or Lutherans." I was still confused.

We eventually came to another farmhouse. It looked just like the home of *Christoph* and *Jacobina,* only larger. Already waiting for us, on the oxen wagon, were the neighbor's wife and two children, a small boy and girl.

Christoph and *Jacobina* gave greetings to their neighbor and his family, and introduced me as their guest, a traveler. They gave no other information to their friends, and nothing more was asked. All accepted me as I am.

Once *Jacobina* and the women and children were upon the wagon, we all started towards Heilbronn with the women and children riding, and we men, walking.

Christoph talked as we walked, "My parents, who are now long passed, told me that Heilbronn was originally called Heiligbronn after a holy spring that came from under the high altar of the Saint Killian's Kirche located there."

He went on, "The Kirche had been Katholische (Catholic) until the early 1500s, when its Reverend Johann Lachmann converted to the teachings of Friar Martin Luther. Reverend Lachmann proceeded to teach and lead the Reformation in Heilbronn against the wishes of the Catholic Kirche. The overwhelming majority of Heilbronn became Lutheran, and the citizens passed laws letting all Catholics and Jews know they were no longer welcome in Heilbronn."

I found this strange, since these Lutherans seemed to welcome anyone. Look how they are treating me! Puzzled and curious, I jokingly asked, "How come all the Lutherans and Protestants dislike the Katholische and Jews so much? Why did they ban them from Heilbronn?"

Both men abruptly stopped. Even the women on the wagon, who had been idly chatting, instantly became silent. All were now staring straight at me. I thought to myself "What have I said?"

Christoph no longer smiled and his eyes narrowed as he sternly answered in a low growl, "those damn Katholische had been killing Lutherans, our relatives and friends, for the last hundred years all over the land around here. My mother and father told me that the Katholische even slaughtered some of my kin because they would not renounce their faith and swear allegiance to their Pope in Rome. In fact, I blame the Katholische for the murders of my parents; so damn them all."

The Other Neighbor added in, "And those Jews do not believe in our Savior Jesus Christ, so damn them too." All in the group said at the same time, "Amen."

Their faces had the look of obsessed fanatics. I quickly added, "Amen," and dropped the whole subject. I would think twice before bringing it up again. It was obvious how they all felt. And with that, the men returned to walking and while the women again began their chatting.

It seemed like we walked quite a ways down the road that wandered between forests and hills, but it was probably only about four hours.

I thought Heilbronn was probably a small village, but in fact, it was a large stadt (city). As we approached from the higher hills, I could make out a large walled area with what looked like a river running through it.

Hesitantly I asked, remembering what my last questions had caused, "Is that Heilbronn?"

The older neighbor who really had not talked much on the way, laughed a little, and then said, "Yes, that is our Heilbronn."

He was still laughing so it must be all right to ask more. I continued with, "It looks like there is a river. What river is that?"

Christoph replied, "That is the Neckar River. It runs through the center of Heilbronn and eventually flows to the Rhine River."

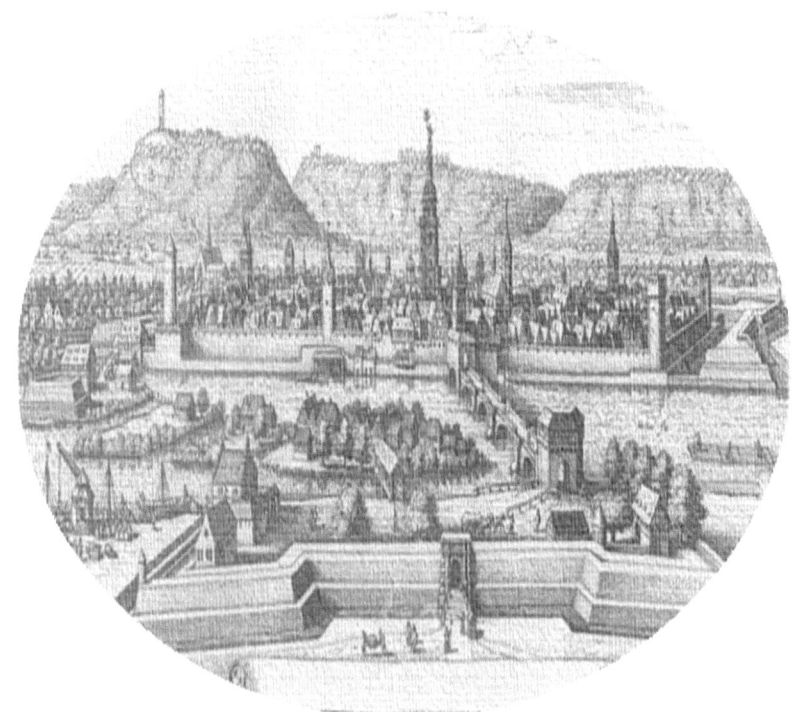

Heilbronn

"And what is that tall building with the spires in the center of the town?" I asked.

Christoph replied again, "That tall building in the center of town is where we are going, our Lutheran Saint Kilian's Kirche."

Their Kirche looked large and imposing from a distance. As we got closer, it dwarfed everything else around it, and I saw that it was very ornate and much larger than I had thought. It was also very beautiful.

As we approached it, we joined many others on their way to the service. In fact, it looked like the whole town headed to Kirche. Everyone was very friendly with hellos coming from everywhere.

Saint Kilian's Kirche

We tied up the ox and wagon, and proceeded to walk the last steps into the Kirche. Someone welcomed us in, I suppose a Kirche official.

Christoph explained, "He is our Pastor, and he always welcomes us when we enter and always blesses us when we leave."

The inside of the Kirche was ornate, but we all sat on wooden pews that were simple and plain... not at all like the rest of the ornate building. I asked *Christoph* why the difference?

He explained," the path for the followers of Friar Martin Luther is simpler than the Katholische way. Because this was originally a Katholische Kirche, they built it very ornate. But for us, the pews have since been replaced with a simpler more plain design."

I do not remember much of the Kirche service, except one passage that went, "Es ist nein Schand zu falle, ist aber da zu bleibe (It is no disgrace to fall, but it is to stay there)!" This message I understood clearly, but I only remember it because I could actually understand what the Pastor was saying. I also remember there was much singing, and the Pastor preaching about their GOD and their Sins and their Savior.

Long ago when I was a boy, I happened to go to a Katholische service, and their Priest spoke in some strange tongue. I had no idea what the Katholische said then, but here with these Lutherans, I actually understood what they said in the worship service, not that I believed any of it.

Thankfully, eventually the mostly boring service was over. I thought we would probably start back home now, and I would still be able to get some rest, I quickly found out I was wrong.

As *Christoph* had told me earlier, the Pastor blessed us as we left. And then, with all the other people, we moved to an area under the Tower filled with long tables and benches.

On the tables were baskets of brötchen (rolls). *Christoph*, his older neighbor, and I sat down. In fact, it looked like all the men sat down.

All women had vanished. The men broke brötchen and talked, instant friends laughing and joking. So many voices, so many discussions about the weather, the vines, money, and even women, that it was hard to follow any of them.

No one seemed to notice, or care, that all the women were gone.

Saint Kilian's Kirche Tower

Just when I was about to ask *Christoph* about where all the women had gone, *Jacobina* appeared with two mugs of bier (beer) for us. As soon as she had given us our bier, she quickly vanished again while other women were also delivering bier all around. The bier was cold and refreshing. *Jacobina* quickly returned with plates of food for us, and vanished again.

Confused, I whispered to *Christoph,* "Where is your wife, *Jacobina?*"

Christoph laughed and replied, "The women eat and drink with themselves, not with us. They want to gossip with each other about women things, and not have to be silent and forced to listen to their menfolk boast and go on and on about men things."

After all of us, the men, women and children, were full and satisfied, it was time to say our goodbyes and head back home. I had so many new friends; I met so many friendly people. This was not like the city I fled from, not at all.

As before, *Jacobina* and the other women and children climbed back onto the ox wagon for the ride back to home. We men walked alongside as before. This time we walked a little slower 'cause of our now full bellies.

We only walked for a short ways when the children had fallen asleep and the women had quietly resumed their chatting. Back up the same road, again through the same forests and hills we had earlier come down. It was all just the same as before, but in dwindling light of the setting sun, it did look different.

Back to the neighbors farmhouse where the women and children climbed down from the oxen wagon and went inside. The neighbors offered water to quench our thirst from the long walk. We drank our fill, and after one last prayer together, said our thanks and goodbyes.

The three of us began our walk back to *Christoph* and *Jacobina's* and now my home. We reached their small cottage by the light of the full moon. It was now already late and had been a long day, and all I wanted to do was to get my shed with its thick straw bed.

Jacobina would have nothing of that. After we all cleaned up, she brought a light meal of brötchen and käse (rolls and cheese) to the table. We were all very tired, and we quietly munched our food with no words.

Hunger quenched, we moved our chairs away from the table and talked about much of nothing. After a while, *Christoph* went over to *Jacobina* and rubbed her back, *Jacobina* reciprocated by gently massaging her husband's feet. I thought to myself that I would have enjoyed that, but alas, I had no wife to rub my feet.

It would be another early morning, and I said my thanks and good night. I could hardly keep my eyes open as I made it to the shed and my thick straw bed. Deep sleep came quickly.

The next morning was early as this was another workday. We tended the vines, as we did each day except for the Sabbath when we did not work, but worshiped in Heilbronn.

The days ran into weeks, and the weeks into months. Our simple daily routine was hard work and devout worship with no time or energy for mischief. It felt good to have a place and a purpose, and be always busy.

During this time with *Christoph* and *Jacobina*, I learned that out here the rules about men and women were much stricter than in my old city. Out here, the men worried about the fields and plantings and the animal breeding, while the women occupied themselves with running the home, kitchen, garden and the education of the children, if they had any. Of course, when harvest came, it was everyone to the fields to get the crop in.

I saw that *Jacobina* actually worked much harder each day than either *Christoph* or me. *Christoph* does not know how lucky he is to have such a good woman to love and take care of him. I envy him, but let me be clear; I am not looking for a Lutheran wife, or any kind of wife. Their way here seems to work out very well, and I will not be sharing my thoughts with either of them. I enjoy being here with them, and am not going to do anything to make me move on...

Village of 𝕷𝖔𝖜𝖊𝖓𝖋𝖙𝖊𝖎𝖓

♠NOBODY♠

Karl home, about four hours walk east of stadt Heilbronn

Some weeks later at an early breakfast, *Christoph* announced that we would not be working in the vines today. We needed vegetables and flour from the marktplatz (marketplace). Today we would walk up the hill to the village of Löwenstein.

Löwenstein

As we walked up a trail that I had never noticed, *Christoph* explained that Löwenstein was a Katholische village with two stone lions near the village entrance. It was not very far to the village, but since it was on the hilltop ridge above the valley, it was a tiring climb.

"My parents told me that the village of Löwenstein has been around for many centuries, and has survived many wars fought over it. It even has what is left of a castle," *Christoph* remarked.

As we passed the entrance stone lions, we entered the village and the marktplatz. While *Jacobina* moved among the sellers tables to find gemüse and brötchen and käse, *Christoph* and I wandered around, and eventually settled on a bench to sit and watch all the people scurry about their business.

Rows and rows of multi-story houses rimmed the marketplace. This was not as large an area as Heilbronn, and the houses were not spread out, but packed together. The people do not seem as friendly either; I wonder why? Could it be as simple as Protestants are friendlier than Katholische? I started to ask *Christoph*, but thought better of that and just kept my thoughts and questions to myself.

More reserved, maybe more aloof. Not a happy place, I decided. More like the city I came from and not like a small village. Yes, certainly more like where I had run from.

I was glad when *Jacobina* returned with her purchases so that we could leave. Löwenstein was too much like what I had just left, too much like the big city!

Christoph turned and asked me, "Before we leave, do you wish to see the Katholische Church. It is only minutes away?"

I just wanted out of here, and strongly answered, "No!"

Christoph looked at *Jacobina,* shrugged, and started walking back down the road past the two stone lions down into the valley. As we made our way down, *Christoph* pointed out in the valley below, their home near the vineyards. From here just below the hilltop ridge, their cottage seemed so tiny, and even the large vineyards looked small.

Soon we were back to their home. While *Jacobina* put away the food, *Christoph* and I idly talked about the day, about the weather, about the vines, and about the future.

"It bothers me that I will always be hired labor, and will never be able to afford my own land and home. I know this is a good life, but might there be an even better life somewhere else for *Jacobina* and me. Do you not worry about your future?" asked *Christoph*.

I shrugged and answered, "No, I never worry about that." As for a better life for them, I did not know, and could not offer him any reassurance, solace, or advice, so I remained silent.

As time went on, the days ran into weeks and the weeks into months. The routine was hard work and devout worship, with no time or energy for mischief; nothing like my former life back in the city.

I felt good to have a place and a purpose. I was satisfied with my life here, though *Christoph* did seem to become more distracted and maybe dissatisfied every day. All this he had, and yet, he seemed to be wanting and searching for even more!

4 NEWS

♠CHRISTOPH KARL♠

Karl home, east of stadt Heilbronn

I am *Herr Christoph Karl.* I am the tender of these plentiful vineyards. My father and my father's father had all been vine tenders. It is a good life to be out among GOD's plants and animals each day.

My *Karl* family has lived in this area for at least a century, and even longer farther south of Stuttgart along the Swiss border. My father told me that we are from royalty in Karlsruhe, but no one ever remembered who the royal was. Now, I am the only *Karl* left; all except me are long gone!

My wife is *Frau Jacobina*, youngest daughter of Master stonemason *Herr Johan Jacob Maurer* and his wife, *Frau Anna Maria*, of the nearby village of Kirhart (Kirchardt). We are simple people and follow the teachings of our Friar Martin Luther.

Even though this is good life, and I know that our Heiliger Vater (Holy Father) will provide for us, still I worry about our future. I must provide more than this for my wonderful wife *Jacobina*, and with the blessing of our LORD, for our future children.

How can I ever provide more for my family in this valley as only a simple vine tender? I own nothing, and as I am now, I will always own nothing! This life will never be enough unless I can own some land to grow my own grapes, and own my own home. I know we shall never see owning land or a home here, as the wealthy Katholische in Löwenstein above own this entire valley and surrounding lands. No, I am a Lutheran, and the Katholische will never allow me to own anything here. I often wonder is there some place where I too could be an owner, but where is that possible? And where would I look?

"The old village women say sarcastically, "The grass is always greener on the other side of the mountain." I wonder.

It was one cold winter day that my neighbor and I again rode their oxen wagon to Heilbronn for supplies. As I was moving through the marktplatz to fill my wife's list, over all the noise I heard a loud voice with a strange accent.

Curiosity drew me toward the voice. As I got closer, I noticed a large crowd around a man that was speaking. A salesman most likely, I joined them to find out what he was pitching. To my amazement, this man was not selling anything, but was speaking of giving land and homes away.

He spoke out loudly to the crowd, "I am speaking of a wonderful place where the land is good and free, and where the government will provide the materials for you to build your own home. And the land and your home and all that you grow on your land will all be yours."

I thought to myself, this must be pigshit, for nowhere could that be true. Yet I continued to listen just as the rest of the crowd did, spellbound with the tale he was spinning. This man swore that not only was all he had already told us true, but that his government would even pay for all our travel and living costs while we moved to his new land.

Some of the crowd yelled out, "Where is this Heaven? Surely nowhere around here."

The man responded, "I am a *Recruiter* for *Johann Facius* of Frankfurt am Main, Agent to the Emissary of Empress Katharina II the Great of Imperial Russland. For those of you that can read, I have handbills for you to take with you. Otherwise, pray listen and I will tell you all you need to know."

The *Recruiter* continued, "This offer is only available for a short time, and is only through the charity of Empress Katharina II the Great. As she was born Deutscher, she offers this for her former people. She has graciously issued a Manifesto that documents this offer in writing. It allows all of you to settle wherever you wish. It guarantees religious freedom to worship where and as you wish. It states no taxes for 30 years for those of you settling on her land. It grants an exemption forever from you or any of your descendants ever having to serve in the Russisches military. And if you are ever unhappy with living in this new land, you'll be allowed to return back here at any time."

While the people in the crowd discussed this among themselves, the *Recruiter* again spoke, "You and your families have all suffered from the endless wars in this area. Your young men have died fighting the foreign armies and the religious zealots. Never again would you face this. How many of you own your own land, or your own homes? We will give all of that to you free. Who among you is not afraid when you worship? In the new land, you will not be afraid as you worship in your own way. How good is the land for farming? The land that we are offering is near the Volga River and is very much like the land around here. It is fertile land with a mild climate that you will be able to grow bountiful fields. In fact, the entire region is a veritable paradise. Now think, what more could you want for your loved ones future? Pray seriously think about this. I will be here for a week to answer your questions and help you prepare for your future. For any of you with more questions, join me in the Gasthaus (Guesthouse) where all the bier and whisky is on me."

Many of the men in the crowd happily followed him to the Gasthaus for the free bier and whisky. The women wandered off in small groups still talking about the

Recruiter's pitch. As they passed by me, I could hear their comments of 'lügen-lügen'(lies-lies), and others words of disbelief. Even so, I asked myself aloud, "What if all he speaks is true?"

I was tempted to join them in the Gasthaus, but thought better of it. There was a lot of truth to what he said, and I would need a clear head to ponder it. Some was true, but how could it all be true? Yet he said that he had it written down for all to see. How could it not be true then? I must think hard on this. Even though I cannot read, I grabbed one of the handbills... I do not know why I took one, maybe just to hold onto part of a pack of lies or a foolish dream.

I rejoined my neighbor and helped pack our supplies on to the ox wagon. I asked if he had listened to the *Recruiter*. He said no, but he did wonder what all the commotion was. I told him it was about a better place to live.

He answered that he was too old for such foolishness. "What could be better than this?" he added. "Be wary, the grass is not always greener on the other side of the mountain," he solemnly warned.

Much of what he said made sense, and yet, what if my neighbor was wrong and the *Recruiter* was right? The rest of the ride home was in silence. I was deep in thought and we were at his house before I knew it. I thanked him for his help and loaded up my supplies, and said my goodbyes.

My neighbor cautioned me again, "Do not worry about what might be. Just make the best of all that is wonderful here in our valley. This is just more advice from an old man."

I was soon home. Supper with my wife *Jacobina* and *Nobody* was unusually silent. Both of them realized that something was bothering me. Luckily, neither asked what was. Even if they had asked, what could I tell them?

Tomorrow is a day in the vineyards, so as usual we all headed to bed early. My mind was full of what-ifs and my neighbor's advice about the *Recruiters* tale; I could not sleep. While lying there next to my soundly sleeping wife, I decided not to tell her anything about this. No good will come from bothering her about something that had no chance of coming true. Maybe I will tell her later, and we can both laugh at this foolishness.

Early the next morning, *Nobody* and I were out working tending the vines. The day seemed twice as long as usual, my mind was not on my work. We finished our long day and returned home. Again, supper with my wife, *Jacobina,* and *Nobody* was silent. Again, neither asked what was bothering me.

It was another night where I could not sleep. Again, laying there next to my soundly sleeping wife, I decided I must go back to Heilbronn. I must know more from that *Recruiter,* and I would leave early in the morning after breakfast.

Next morning at breakfast, I told *Nobody* that he would be working the vines by himself today, as I must return to Heilbronn. I did not explain why to either him or *Jacobina.*

Jacobina did not stop working, but looked at me waiting for me to explain. I did not and she frowned, but said nothing and went back to her work.

I arrived in Heilbronn and immediately went to the marktplatz to see if the *Recruiter* was still there. He was, and today he had an even larger crowd listening to him. Much of what he said was the same as the day before. I needed to know more, if only I could read the handbill, or find someone that could read.

It came to me in a flash, and I remembered that our *Pastor* could read. Within minutes, I was at the church, had found him and explained what I needed. He looked concerned and said he heard the tales the *Recruiter* was spreading. It certainly sounded like lies to him, or at least half-truths. But yes, he would read the handbill to me.

Much of what it said was the same, but in more detail. It told of the Empress Katerina wanting to share her new lands with the people of her birth. It told that all I had to do was sign the contract with the *Recruiter* and he would arrange everything for my whole family.

It went on that we would travel with others north on the Rhine River to Wiesbaden then overland to the Port of Lübeck. We would then sail on a ship to Russland and travel overland to this wonderful area along the Volga River.

It told us that the whole trip would take many, many months, but they would pay for everything, our food, our drink, travel costs, and clothes to wear. We had no need to pay anything at all.

And as the *Recruiter* had said, once at the Volga River they would give us free fertile land to farm and building materials for our homes. The handbill even mentioned that homes were already built and all we had to do was move in. All I had to do was sign the contract to be able to move my family to a fertile land with a good climate where we could grow bountiful crops with great harvests.

Our *Pastor* shook his head and said, "There is no such place. Do not be fooled and believe these lies. There is no paradise but for our LORD's Heaven. Do not risk what you and your family already have. There is no telling what type of Hell awaits you. We are your family and we are here for you always. Where will you worship our LORD in the way of our Friar Martin Luther? Put this foolishness out of your mind!"

He could see that I was still thinking on the *Recruiter's* stories about 'paradise' and sighed, and then shook his head.

Looking disappointed, for he feared he had lost me, our *Pastor* quietly spoke, "My son, this all sounds bad. This *Recruiter*, this stranger who is not one of us, who you do not know, who is not family or Church, is offering to give you all this for nothing. What must you give back in return...? I fear it may be your eternal soul. As the old saying goes, there is never frei brötchen or kuchen (cakes)."

No longer really listening to him, I thanked him for his help and advice. I reassured him that I would do nothing foolish and was just curious about what the *Recruiter* was offering.

As I walked away from the church, dancing round in my head were images of my prosperous lands covered with vines of grapes, and of our new home. I could just not get out of my head that all I had to do to be part of this chance for a new future was to sign the contract.

Still having unanswered questions, I returned to the marktplatz to find the *Recruiter*. As luck would have it, the *Recruiter* had just finished giving his pitch. The crowd had thinned out and I was able to talk directly with him. I greeted him with, "Hello, friend. I am *Herr Christoph Karl*."

He responded with a warm greeting and a wide toothy grin. He asked, "How can I be of help to you, my *Herr Karl?*"

I wanted to appear calm since I had not yet made a decision, but instead, like a silly child, blurted, "When can we leave for the new land?"

His eyes widened as he laughed and replied, "When can you be ready?"

I scratched my head as I realized that I had not considered when *Jacobina* and I could be ready to leave. For that matter, I had not even discussed any of this with my wife. I just expected she would agree, but what if she did not?

"Not really sure yet," I replied. With a little more restraint, I asked, "When is the first group scheduled to leave?"

He shuffled through some papers and pulled out one, and studied it. He looked at me with that wide toothy grin still on his face and replied, "We have room in our first group going north. Plans are for your group to leave here at the river on the morn of Monday 23 July. This group is pretty full, but I can make room for you.... and how many did you say are in your group? Uh, wife, couple of children, maybe, I can make that happen right now. Just need you to sign this contract." He thrust forward a paper to sign.

Very aware that I had not even mentioned this to *Jacobina*, but not wanting to look completely stupid in front of the *Recruiter*, I shot back, "Sounds good, but I really need to talk with my wife one last time before I sign. Oh, and just my wife and I, and maybe my helper man... that is three people." I only now realized that I had not talked with *Nobody*, either.....

That *Recruiter* toothy wide grin again, and then he replied. "Friend, I understand completely, but we do not need your wife's signature on the contract, just yours.... And this is really only informal to make sure I have space for you and wife in the first group. If you sign, and then your wife says nein, well... we will understand that you did not have her permission to sign, and will just tear up this contract."

I hesitated, deep in thought on what to next do.

He shrugged and continued, "No problems. I am here to help you take advantage of this wonderful one-time chance, but if your wife knows better than you and is satisfied with her poor life here and says nein, well then it is, as she says, nein."

Did I hear him right? Does he think I need my wife's permission? No, I never have and never will need my wife's permission for anything, as I am the man of my house. I decide what is right and what is wrong! I was sure that all this was true, and yet, this is an important decision for both of us. I should at least explain this great chance to her and listen to her concerns... and then come back and sign the contract. However, how do I answer this *Recruiter* without losing face by looking like my wife is the real man of the house?

I lied and replied to the *Recruiter*, "That all sounds good, but I just realized I am already very late for another meeting across town. I will be back tomorrow with plenty of time to go over the contract and sign." I shook his hand and planned to walk away.

He kept my hand, and then looking very disappointed with the toothy wide grin gone, replied, "All right my friend, I see you are a careful man in your dealings. It is a big decision and I respect you for that. But do not take too much time to return and sign as the available space is going fast. I hope to see you on the morrow as you have promised. *Herr Karl*, the best to you and your wife." He let my hand go and turned away to another prospective new landowner.

All the way home, I kept thinking about how I would break the news to my dear wife, *Jacobina*. Each time I thought I had a plan, I realized it always ended badly... maybe since I had not originally talked with her; there was no good way out. By the time I reached home, I decided to tell her almost, but not quite, everything...

I met her in the house as she was just starting to prepare our supper. Luckily, *Nobody* had not yet arrived from the fields. I asked *Jacobina*, "Please sit down, as I need to talk with you now." She sat and quietly studied my face.

I said, "I worry about our future here. I am talking with a *Recruiter* that I met in Heilbronn. He has told me of a wonderful opportunity for us. Before you speak, let me tell you about it," and so I told her all the *Recruiter* had told me.

Jacobina quietly listened, but had her arms firmly across her chest. When I finished, there was a frown on her face as she replied, "Husband, I did not know you were unhappy with our life here. I am happy. What makes you unhappy?"

Without waiting for an answer, she continued, "Why did you meet with someone before talking with me? Who is this *Recruiter*? Is he from around here? You did not promise him anything or give him money, did you? Are you saying we are moving? How far away is this place? I do not want to be far away from my family. Is it me, did I do something wrong to make you want to move? Oh… I know it must be my fault!"

She was quickly very, very upset… Now I had another problem in addition to deciding about moving. Now I had an almost hysterical wife. I had to assure her somehow that it was not her fault, and that she had done nothing wrong. She was already sobbing, and I hated it when she cried.

I got up from the chair and went to her, and pulled her up and held her in my arms to comfort and reassure her. I told her that it was not her fault and after some minutes, she stopped sobbing.

She pulled away and emphatically said, "Well then, why do you want us to leave here? I must tell you I absolutely do not want to leave!"

One minute she was sobbing, the next minute she was angry. This was going to be very difficult. I took a deep breath, and then replied, "There is no future for us here. Let me tell you again about all that they will give us for free."

I repeated all the good things I learned about this wonderful opportunity, and about what our Pastor had read to me from the printed handbill. I failed to mention our Pastor's comments that this was a bad idea; telling her that would not accomplish any good… and definitely not gain her approval.

After listening to all my reasons, *Jacobina* replied with loud and angry words, "All right, these strangers who we do not know, say it is wonderful place with a frei (free) home and frei land, and they will pay for all travel to this Promised Land that we can live on without taxation. We will be frei to be Lutherans forever, and they expect nothing in return and we can come back to here at any time. Is that actually what they have promised you?"

I said the only thing I could say, "Yes, they have promised all that and more!"

Jacobina shook her head as if she did not hear the words I spoke, and shouted back, "I do not believe their promises and lies, or that this place even exists. Even if all is as promised and they do not lie, that means nothing to me, as I am very happy here. I will not leave my friends, I will not leave my family, and I will not leave my Kirche!" She was making her stand.

This was the time for me to reassert my position as Man of this House. As gently, but as firmly as possible, I slowly spoke, "Dear wife, I understand you do not want to leave, but I have decided that this is best for our future, and since you are my wife, and I am leaving to take advantage of this wonderful offer, we will leave together. This discussion is at an end." Or so I thought.

No, it was not the end… First, *Jacobina* began yelling, then sobbing and tears, then more yelling, and then wailing about leaving her family. Then cursing at me as she has never done before, then throwing two plates at me, and then wailing that her eternal soul would be damned in that foreign place…… the process seemed to repeat and go on until she just put her head down on the table and sobbed. I hate it when she cries.

I felt horrible knowing there was no way to console her other than changing my decision, and that I would not do. I could do nothing to comfort her without giving in to her demands, so I left the house to let her cry. Outside, I found our *Nobody* just sitting near the fence. In all the turmoil, I had forgotten all about him.

He saw me and then said, "There is no way I was entering your house once I heard *Jacobina* loudly yelling at you."

I replied, "Thank you for not coming in. She is very upset because I told her we are leaving here for a new land on the Volga River in Russland."

Nobody looked shocked, jumped up and asked, "What... where....when.... what will I do?"

I had forgotten I had not told him anything either.... So I repeated the whole story, except of course, I left out any possibly negative words. I also said, "This would be a good opportunity for you also. You could travel along with us, and if you signed your own contract, I believe you would get your own frei land and home. You would not have to work for me! You could be your own man and have people working for you." I even showed him the handbill that I had taken.

I continued, "Or if you choose to stay, maybe my landlord will give you this house and let you work the vineyards for him." While *Nobody* listened, he closely looked at the handbill, almost as if he was reading it.

Irritated that he did not seem to be really listening to me, I mockingly asked, "Can you read that?"

"Yes, I can read some, but it takes me a while. I can also sign my name," he casually answered.

Surprised but curious, I asked, "Where did you learn to read, and will you read what it says to me?"

He told me, "My mother taught me what I know when I was very young," and then he slowly read aloud what the handbill said.

It was just as our Pastor had earlier said. As for whether he would go with us, he told me he would have to think hard on this. Like my wife *Jacobina*, *Nobody* had much to consider.

A more pressing issue had come up, and unfortunately, I had to tell him that I thought our supper might be left to us to prepare. He smiled, and nodded in understanding.

I noticed it was now quiet in the house, and slowly opened the door to see what was happening. *Jacobina* was not in sight in the kitchen; she must be in our bedroom.

I motioned for *Nobody* that all was clear and we quietly moved to the kitchen to find supper. It was cold meat and cheese quietly eaten in silence. As soon as *Nobody* was finished, he gave thanks and left for his shed. I thought about sharing his shed for the night.... But I decided as the Man of the House that is not appropriate.

So instead, I settled into a chair and covered myself with a quilt. I would leave *Jacobina* alone until she felt better. I was sleeping as soundly as one could in a chair, when *Jacobina* gently touched my cheek to wake me. It was still deep in the night.

She whispered, "You should not be sleeping in the chair and should come to our bed. I am sorry for my outburst." She gently rubbed her body against mine, and her soft voice deepened slightly as she spoke, "You are my husband, and I will always support your final decision. But, is there nothing I can do with you tonight that might change your mind about us leaving? Is there nothing at all that you might want from me?

Even though I was still sleepy, my body and mind instantly understood her message. However, my mind also understood the price and conditions of her offer... and so I replied with much regret, "No, my wife, my mind is set and I will not change my decision in exchange for any of your attentions."

Instantly, all changed and her sweetness was gone. She screamed at me, "Then be in your chair for all night. You will not share my bed or body." And with that, she was gone.

An involuntary sigh came from deep inside me, realizing that did not go well, I slowly fell back into troubled sleep.

Early morning came and *Jacobina* did not rise to make our breakfast. I let *Nobody* in and we again shared, as we did the evening before, our feast of cold meat and cheese. We prepared the same for mid-day out in the vineyards, and quickly left.

It was almost a relief to work with the vines... we did not talk about it, but both of us were worried about what would be waiting for us when we returned at the end of the day.

That night, no supper prepared by *Jacobina*. She never came out of the bedroom. Another supper of cold meat and cheese quietly eaten in silence. Again, *Nobody* finished his meal and went to his shed. Another night for me in the chair with a quilt, only on this night, she did not visit me with another offer.

The following few days, or maybe even a week, blurred into a daily and nightly repeat of cold meats and cheese, and my now favorite chair and quilt.

When Sabbath came, *Jacobina* did not come forward to go as we usually did to our Church. Still, there was no way to console her other than changing my decision, and that I would not do. I would just have to give her time to accept our new future; the question was, how much time? I was already over a week past due with my signing the contract. There might not even be space for us in the first group. That might make *Jacobina* happier, but would only delay the inevitable.

We were leaving, if not in the first group on 23 July, then in the next group, whenever that was!

WHY?

♦JACOBINA KARL♦

Karl home, about four hours walk east of stadt Heilbronn

I am *Frau Jacobina*, wife to my good man, *Christoph Karl*. He is of the royal *Karl* family out of Karlsruhe, and his line is from the old ruler Charlemagne. Sadly, he is the last of the *Karl* line. My husband is a vine tender as was his father and his father's father. He is a good and devout man, and is a follower of the simple ways of Friar Martin Luther, as I also am.

I am the youngest daughter of *Herr Johan Jacob Maurer* and his wife *Frau Anna Maria* of Kirhart. I was born and christened in the faith of our Friar Martin Luther in Kirhart around February 15, 1734.

My father was born around 1711 and always lived in Kirhart; four days ride southeast of Heidelberg halfway to Heilbronn. My father was proud to be a stonemason to build many castles churches and public buildings. He would always say," It is hard work, but I leave something for the children of my children to see."

I met my husband, *Christoph*, about eight years ago at a meeting after Kirche in Heilbronn. I might not have ever met him but for the pitcher of beer I spilt on him. Instantly I liked *Christoph*; and instantly my father did not.

My father was a proud stonemason, and did not want his daughter to marry a farmer. I constantly reminded father that *Christoph* was no ordinary farmer, but was a tender of the vines. In my eyes, the two were completely different. My father did not share that vision.

It was only that *Christoph* was also a devout follower of Friar Martin Luther that my father allowed me to continue to see him. With time, all my family and even my father grew to like him. *Christoph* and I married in our Lutheran Kirche in Heilbronn in 1756.

We moved to our small cottage in the north valley below Löwenstein. We have been very happy here with *Christoph* tending the vines and me keeping a home for him. The only sadness in our lives until now comes that our only son passed after a few months, and we are not blessed with another of our own. As my *Christoph* is the last of the *Karl* line, I must somehow give him a son to carry on his good name. I pray the LORD will choose to bless us!

I still do not understand what has possessed my husband to make him want to move us from here and from my family. I had no idea he was unhappy with our life here. He says it is not my fault, but the duty of a wife is to keep her husband satisfied. What could I have done wrong?

I am happy here! I see my family at Sabbath. I am happy with my Kirche! Why, it makes no sense, why did he meet with the strange man, this *Recruiter*, without ever telling me about it? And where is this new land... this Russland or this Volga River? My *Christoph* talks of frei land and a frei home…What nonsense is that? No one gives you anything for frei. What does this *Recruiter* want in exchange? His words cannot be the whole truth, they must be lies, and why does not my husband see this? Does this *Recruiter* have some hold over *Christoph*?

I played the conversation with my husband back through my mind, "….strangers who we do not know, say it is wonderful place with a frei home and frei land, and they will pay for all travel to this promised land that we can live without taxation. We will be free to be Lutherans forever, and they expect nothing in return and we can come back to here at any time. That means nothing to me, as I am happy here. I will not leave my friends, I will not leave my family, and I will not leave my Church!"

I realized that even if I was right, it was not good to challenge my dear husband. I left him no choice, but to speak the 'he makes the decisions' rant. Of course, I did not help at all by my hysterical actions, but I was angry and hurt. I did purposely miss him with the plates, but 'my eternal soul being damned' was probably too much.

I really did think that my nighttime seduction would work. Why not, it has always worked very well in the past. It never occurred to me that he would refuse me, and when he did, I was again angry and humiliated. How dare he refuse my bed and my body! He could enjoy himself forever in that chair. I slept just fine that night in our comfortable bed.

I decided I would just outwait my dear *Christoph*. No food; my mother always told me that the way to a man's heart was through his stomach. I will no longer cook for him; in fact, I will stay here in the bedroom as long he is in the house.

It did surprise me when after a few days; *Christoph* did not come and apologize. This was serious, as he must be determined to do this move. We had never argued this long before. Well, I will just up the pressure. I will not go with him to our Church on Sabbath!

On the eve of the next Sabbath, I had second thoughts and changed my mind, and decided not going to Sabbath only hurt me. I knew what to do. I would again cook his meals and be civil to him. We would both go to Church and pray for Divine guidance. I am sure GOD will agree with me and bring my *Christoph* to his senses. If not GOD, maybe our *Pastor* can persuade *Christoph* to see the truth and ignore the *Recruiter's* fanciful tales.

Then there is always my family, they may be able to convince *Christoph* to forget this moving nonsense. My father can be forceful and intimidating. Yes, my poor dear *Christoph* does not have chance not changing his mind.

Once he does, he will just forget this nonsense and we will go back to the way it was. Just in case my dear *Christoph* does not return to his senses, I will still deny him my bed and my body!

NO MORE TIME

♠CHRISTOPH KARL♠

Karl home

When I felt I could wait no longer, I asked *Nobody* what he had decided to do. I simply asked, "Will you go with us to the new land or stay to work this land?"

He shrugged and said, "I go with you on this new adventure... and yes, I will also sign for my new land and house."

We agreed then that on the morrow we would both go back to Heilbronn to sign with the *Recruiter* to set our future in motion.

Another supper with just the two of us, and our cold food... and another night of fitful sleep in my now favorite chair.

Early morning came and the two of us were on our way to Heilbronn. We made good time, and when we reached there, we raced to the marktplatz to find the *Recruiter*.

We could not find him anywhere, and when we asked around, no one had seen him for at least some days... maybe a week. We searched up and down and all around Heilbronn with no success. Same story all around, no one had seen him for at least some days... maybe a week.

Dejected, tired, and hungry, we stepped into the Gasthaus for food and drink. After ordering our meals, we asked the other patrons one last time about the *Recruiter*. Same story, no one had seen him for at least some days... maybe a week.

From the back, one of the patrons asked, "Did you see the handbill posted on the wall as you came in?"

We looked at each other, looked at the wall and there was a handbill there. I answered, "No, we had missed it, and Thanks, friend."

On the wall, *Nobody* read from the handbill aloud what was printed, "I am traveling to other villages spreading the word about this great and wonderful opportunity of frei land and homes. I will be back in Heilbronn in about two to three weeks if the offer still exists to again talk with any interested, signed *Recruiter*."

Well that was that; we would just have to wait since we had missed our opportunity. No way to tell if this great opportunity would still be available; we would just have to show up and see when the *Recruiter* returned. Disappointed, we slowly walked back up the road to home.

On the bad side, if we missed our chance, the worst that would happen is that we would continue on working and living as we had been before the offer. On the good side, my wife *Jacobina* might return to me as my wife…. and not a stranger. Also, there might be real food for supper and no chair for sleeping.

We made a pact to keep all that we had learned in Heilbronn today just between the two of us until we learned more. No use making things even worse at home, as if things could get worse.

Upon arrival at home, we noticed the door was propped open…. When I looked inside, *Jacobina* was busy cleaning. Something good smelling was cooking.

Jacobina saw me and immediately said, "This does not mean I agree with you or will move. This means that it is time to resume our lives. Tomorrow is Sabbath, and we will all go to Kirche and pray to our LORD for his guidance."

She continued with, "I do not know where the two of you have been, and I do not care. But you are again filthy and smell. You need to thoroughly wash and change your clothes before you come into my home for supper. It would also be good to be clean for tomorrow's Kirche."

I was silently thinking that my dear sweet wife *Jacobina* was back with me when she turned to me and said, "And no, you are not yet welcome on my bed or my body. You will have to make do with your chair." With that, she pushed me out through the door and closed it. We both did as told and thoroughly washed up.

The three of us were up early the next morning. While on our way to our neighbors, *Jacobina* made us promise not to mention a thing about moving to anyone.

When we joined our neighbors, with the women and children on the ox wagon, and us men walking, we talked about everything else. *Jacobina* made up some fanciful tale about being sick the last few weeks, and that is why they have not joined them for Sabbath. Everyone believed her.

When we arrived at Kirche, *Jacobina* continued to act as if nothing was wrong. She greeted and talked with everyone as usual.

Once inside, she pulled me aside and whispered into my ear, "We must pray to our LORD for guidance. We need his wisdom in this matter to know what to do, and must pray that he give us a sign showing us the right direction. Pray with me now, my dear *Christoph*."

And so we earnestly prayed, asking for the wisdom to make the right choice and a sign showing us the right direction. I do not know if *Jacobina* received any Divine guidance, but I know I did not.

After the ceremony, as usual, we for a moment stopped to talk with our *Pastor*. He saw us and smiled, and then said, "*Herr Christoph Karl* and *Frau Jacobina*, I am so glad to see you. I was so afraid that you had left us for the new land with that *Recruiter* fellow. I am glad you did not fall for his promises. Be blessed, the LORD be with you."

I smiled and said nothing. I looked at *Jacobina* and she was glaring at me. I was in for it now, and the only thing that was saving me was that we were in public.

Jacobina had earlier noticed her family in another area in the Church. While we had not been able to sit with them, we were able to meet up with them after the service outside. We all greeted each other warmly, and *Jacobina* seemed to move our group slowly farther away from the other people.

Her mother, *Frau Anna Maria,* asked, "and how is our daughter and wonderful husband, *Christoph,* been doing these past few months?"

Jacobina calmly answered, "Family, this is our helper to *Christoph* in the vineyards. He has never told us his given name, so we just call him *Nobody.* He is also our friend and guest." While all were slightly taken back by his strange name, all warmly greeted him.

Jacobina then still calmly said, "Oh, and we have news. Husband *Christoph* has decided it would be best for our future that we soon move to a new land far, far away." She might as well hit me over the head with a shovel.

Everyone slowly turned and stared at me in disbelief. *Mother Anna Maria* wailed, "This cannot be true. Why would you take my daughter away from me? What good could come of this? What evil are you bringing upon our family?"

Jacobina's older sister asked her, "Sister, what are you talking about? Tell us everything about why you would even think about doing this crazy thing?"

Jacobina then recounted the entire story that the *Recruiter* had brought to this area offering the frei land and frei home in a virtual paradise in a faraway land, and that I had decided that this was best for our future.

Mother Anna Maria would not accept that one of her daughters was leaving, and to her husband she turned and said, "*Johan Jacob Maurer*, husband, you cannot let this, this evil man take our daughter away from us. Do something husband!"

Before I could answer anyone, *Jacobina's* father had roughly seized my arm and pulled me aside. On his face, I could see shock, dismay, anger, and grief. Trembling in anger, he looked at me and in a deep voice growled, "What madness is this. Explain yourself now! Why would you do this? You will not take my daughter from her family! Do you understand? You will not take my daughter from her family! If you hurt her, I will…. My GOD, this all must be Satan's cruel joke."

The whole group rejoined her father and me. Now I am the center of her family yelling at me about how cruel I am, how horrible I am, how wrong I am, how stupid I am, how unfair I am, how much a fool I am, how I do not deserve her, how she must leave me, and finally how little of a Man I am.

I knew there was no reasoning with them so I just remained silent. I looked past their angry faces over at *Jacobina* to see if she was happy with her result, and expected to see that. Instead, I saw that there were tears running down her face and that she was sad.

Suddenly, *Jacobina* quickly moved and pushed her way between her family and me. She turned to them and sternly said, "Do not insult my husband, do not yell at him or berate him. He is a good man and does not deserve this. He has decided that this is best for our future and I am his wife. I will accompany him whenever and wherever he chooses to go. If he chooses to move to a faraway land, I will be at his side each step of the way. We will live together, and suffer or prosper as one as we have sworn to in our marriage vows. That is all we will say on this issue."

With that, my wife *Jacobina* turned to me and took my hand, and led me away from the group. I had no idea where *Nobody* had been, but within a few short steps he had rejoined us. After the three of us had walked a short way, *Jacobina* motioned for *Nobody* to continue on, and to allow us to talk.

She turned to me and said, "Husband, I am so sorry for that. You did nothing to deserve that. No one is allowed to say things like that to you, except of course, for me. As I said to my family, we are one and if you feel that it is best for us to leave, I will happily leave with you. Make your plans and let me know when we leave. Come, let us go home now and be our happy family once again."

We caught up with *Nobody* and enjoyed a quiet calm walk home. In all the turmoil, we have forgotten to the let our neighbors know that we were leaving. Lucky for us, we had caused such a loud commotion that everyone from the church had heard it, and seen us leave.

Our neighbors eventually caught up with us on the road home, and told to us that *Jacobina's* mother and father apologized and said they loved us and wished us the best wherever we were. And that *Jacobina's* father also added that his daughter was welcome to live in their home at any time for as long as she wished…

Jacobina thanked them and said, "All is good. You have been wonderful neighbors, but *Christoph* and I will soon be moving to a new land and new future."

They asked about when and where.... And *Jacobina* spent the rest of the trip telling them all about the wonderful future the *Recruiter* and the handbill had told us.

The next morn after a wonderful night's sleep with my wife in our bed, everything felt perfect. Today we would again try to locate the *Recruiter* and sign the contracts.

Jacobina felt she had chores to do around the house, but gave her blessing on the contract signing. *Nobody* and I made our way once more back to Heilbronn. This time we were in luck, as we found the *Recruiter* back at the edge of the marktplatz talking to people. We worked our way through the crowd and when fairly close, he noticed us and broke away from those he was talking to.

"Hello, friend," he said. He continued with, "It *is Herr Karl,* is it not? I must have somehow missed you a few weeks back when you were going to sign the contract. Are you ready to sign now?"

I asked, "Is there still room in the first group for my wife and me, and this man?" referring to *Nobody*.

The *Recruiter* scrunched up his face, scratched his beard and replied, "Oh, I am not sure I can do that. The first group is pretty full.... But let me look and I will see if I can fit you three in."

The *Recruiter* returned to his table, and picked up and shuffled through some papers. He pulled out one paper, and studied it. "I could cancel some others and make room for you, but are you sure that this is what you want," he asked?

We both instantly replied, "Yes!"

All of sudden that wide toothy grin was back as he replied, "*Herr Karl,* the three of you are in the next group going North. You will leave here at the river on the morn of Monday 23 July. All I need from you to make this final is for you to sign your Contract."

Nobody spoke up and said, "I would like to travel with *Herr Karl* and his wife, but would like to sign my own Contract for frei land and home."

The *Recruiter* studied him, and then replied, "You are a single man... The Empress Katarina II prefers married couples as they are more stable and of better character, but if *Herr Christoph Karl* will swear to your good character, I am authorized to let you sign your own Contract. However, because you are single you will only get one-half the frei land that *Herr Karl* and his wife get, and your house will be smaller. Any questions?"

"No, no questions," *Nobody* replied. However, he did ask to see our Contracts before we signed them. The *Recruiter* looked surprised, but picked up two Contracts and handed one to each of us.

Nobody looked at his Contract and slowly read aloud what it said. I listened intently. The *Recruiter's* mouth had dropped open in shock that my friend could read. The *Recruiter* quickly recovered and his face was again in that wide toothy grin.

Everything that the *Recruiter* told us before was in the Contract. The frei land and frei home, the frei travel and clothes and food and housing were listed, as was freedom of religion and no taxation along with more.

The *Recruiter* patiently waited until we were finished and the asked, "Are you both ready to sign now."

"Yes!" we both said.

I was first to sign, and *Nobody* guided my hand to spell out my name as my signature. On to the next Contract where *Nobody* signed '*Michael Grün.*' The *Recruiter* congratulated us on our decisions, and offered to celebrate with frei bier in the tavern... but we declined. We had much to do over the next two months.

The new '*Michael Grün*' asked, "How will we travel and by what route?"

"By boat, by wagon, by foot, and by ship. As for the route, here is a map that we follow that you may keep. I have many more maps," replied the *Recruiter*. I took the map, and we said our thanks.

As we turned away, the *Recruiter* added, "Also, remember that you may take only what you can carry on your back. You will have no need for anything else as we will provide everything for you."

We nodded that we understood, and began to make our way through the crowd to go back home. Suddenly, over the noise of the crowd, we heard the *Recruiter* shout to us, "*Herr Karl* and *Herr Grün*, do not forget Monday twenty-three July. Do not be late as we cannot make everyone else wait on you."

As we walked home completely satisfied with ourselves and the day's happenings, I turned to the new *Michael Grün* and asked, "Is that your name? How do you say it?"

He laughed and replied, "*Michael Grün* .... I always was partial to the name *Michael*, and when I looked around, I saw all the green plants…. So I signed *Michael Grün.*"

We both laughed… "Ok, from now on, we will call you *Michael Grün,*" I replied.

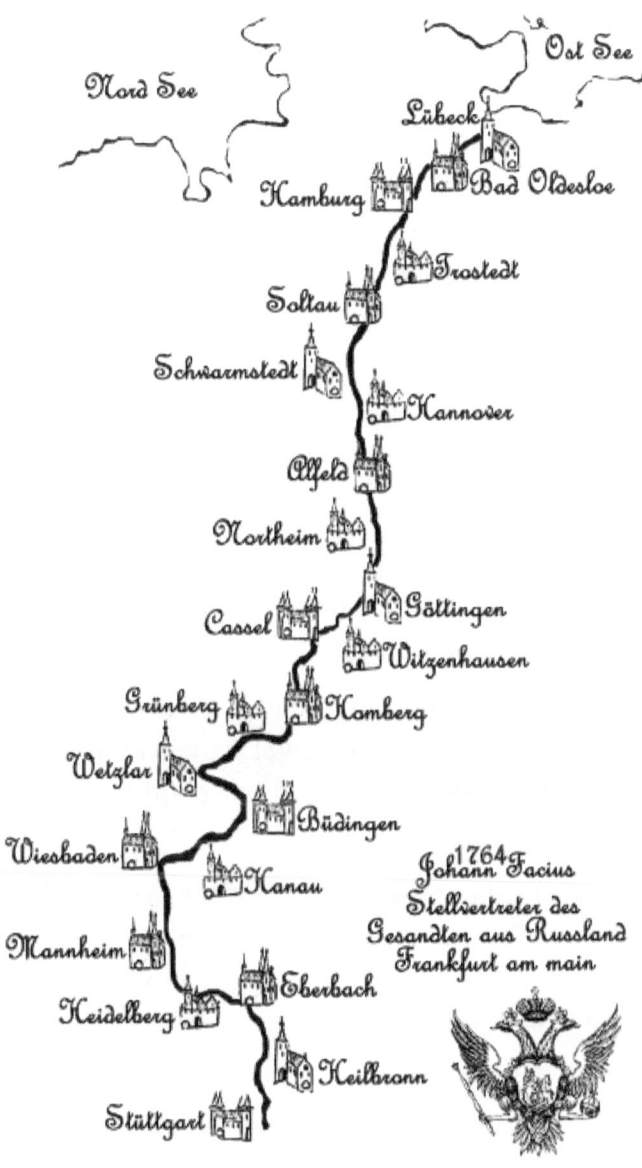

Map of Route to Lübeck

When *Michael* and I arrived home, *Jacobina* was there waiting for us. Her first words to us were, "I know where the two of you have been, and by your smiles you must have been successful. Good, but you are again filthy and smell. You need to thoroughly wash and change your clothes before you come into my home for supper."

Michael and I both laughed. Some things never change, and we both went to clean up as my wife had directed.

Over supper, we recounted the events of the day to *Jacobina*. We brought out the map and she steadied it. And we broke the news to her that our *Nobody* was now *Michael Grün*.

Jacobina looked at the new *Michael Grün* and asked, "Is that your real name?"

Michael snickered and repeated what he had told me, "No, but I always liked the name *Michael*, and when I looked around I noticed all the green bushes. That is how I decided on my new name, *Michael Grün*."

Jacobina laughed and said, "Bless you *Michael Grün*. It will be an honor to travel with both my wonderful husband *Christopher Karl* and our good friend *Michael Grün*."

Jacobina asked, "Just when are we leaving?" I replied, "We leave on 23 July, about two months from now. We have much to do, much to give away as we can only take what we can carry on our backs."

Jacobina slowly looked around the room and sighed. "It will be hard to decide what to give away and what I must take."

"We will do that together," I gently replied.

The next eight weeks went by as fast as the storm winds move through the forest treetops. Before we knew it, we were having our last supper in our home, for early on the morrow we would be making our way to Heilbronn.

Early the last morning, according to our custom, *Jacobina, Michael,* and I just sat for a moment in silence before we left this house for the very last time. It has been a good home to us, but now we move on.

We had only gone a few steps, when I realized I forgotten the few coins of silver that I had saved away for bad times. This was no bad time, but there was no need to give a gift to the next living in the house.

An old custom warns that returning home for forgotten things is a bad omen, and that it is better to leave it behind. I returned anyway and found the coins, but also stopped and looked in the only mirror in the house. The old ways required this, so that our journey would not turn out to be bad.

5 WORK OF SATAN?

♦ANNA MARIA MAURER♦

Village Kirhart, about four days ride southeast of stadt Heidelberg

I am *Frau Anna Maria Maurer*, wife of stonemason *Herr Johann Jacob Maurer* of Kirhart. I am also the mother of *Jacobina*, my youngest daughter and unfortunate wife of *Christoph Karl*.

I am going out of my mind with worry about my daughter and her foolish husband. There is no sense in what they are going to do. To move from our wonderful area to somewhere in a foreign country on a promise from a stranger that no one has ever heard of before, that is ridiculous, absurd, and unthinkable!

I always suspected that my *Jacobina* was a little different, but why could she not be more like her two older and wiser sisters, *Susanna* and *Laudema*. They have never thought of moving far away and leaving our family.

Does my *Jacobina* have no love left for her father and mother, and her sisters? What could we have possibly done to drive her away? Ha, she has no cares for our feelings!

No care at all; Ja (Yes), I mean none! We have always given her our love. We raised her to be better than this. This makes no sense, and makes my head ache. The only possible cause must be her foolish husband, that *Christoph Karl.*

He always seemed a sweet sensible hard working man, and a good mate for our *Jacobina*. How could we know he would do this? He acted like a devout Lutheran and always attended our Church. You just do not imagine this type of irrational action by a good Lutheran, from a Katholische maybe, but not a good Lutheran.

Daughter *Jacobina* mentioned a stranger, a… she called him a *Recruiter*, that came to this area offering frei land and frei home in a virtual paradise in a faraway land. How could have *Christoph* be so stupid to be seduced by these lies? Could this *Recruiter* be Satan, or one of his evil minions in disguise, plying his offer of frei land just to get grasp of their eternal souls?

If he got them to go willingly to this Godless place, would they be eternally damned? If this is what has happened, then they are lost to us and the best we can do is pray to our LORD to save them. Yes, that is what we must do.

We will pray that they come back to their good senses and change their minds, and if that is not possible, then we will pray for our LORD to save their eternal souls.

Yet, what if GOD is testing their faith or, heaven forbid, testing our faith? What sin could we have done to deserve this test? We lead a good clean life and are all devout followers of Friar Martin Luther. We repent our sins and ask for forgiveness in our daily prayers...

Maybe this is as it was in the Old Testament, when GOD tested his people's faith for his own reasons. My every thought makes all this more confusing, and makes my head ache even more. I will never understand why this is happening. The only answer I know is to pray for forgiveness and guidance. Please, pray with me now for them.

KATHOLISCHE FARMER!

♠JOHANN JACOB MAURER♠

Village Kirhart, about 4 days ride southeast of stadt Heidelberg

I am *Herr Johann Jacob Maurer*, master stonemason of Kirhart. I am the father of my youngest daughter, *Jacobina*, wife of the fool *Christoph Karl*.

My wife, *Anna Maria*, believes that praying will solve the craziness that has afflicted my daughter *Jacobina*, and her idiot husband, *Christoph*. Praying will not solve this; the only thing that will solve this is to take *Christoph* behind the shed and beat the holy shit out of him until he returns to his senses! If he does not return to his senses before I beat him to death, then at least my daughter will be free of his lunacy, and be able to remain here with her family, which is where she should be.

I never really liked that farmer, yes, I said farmer! My innocent *Jacobina* was always pointing out that he was not a farmer, but a vine tender. The hell with that, he was, and still is, a farmer! He acted like a devout one of us, devout Lutherans, but I now think he is really a damned Katholische farmer in disguise. I should have never trusted him and let him have my *Jacobina's* hand.

I am the fool now; my *Anna Maria* will not let me handle *Christoph* as I know I must. I am helpless and can just watch it all happen, so what is the use of even thinking about all this?

Anna Maria was very clear when she warned me, "You will not do anything, my dear husband. I know what you think you should do, and that is not something I could ever accept as your wife. Please listen to me, and do as I ask."

I do not believe that this *Recruiter* stranger is Satan or a dweller from Hell, any more than I believe there is free land waiting for my crazy daughter and her husband. And the idea of GOD testing us, who believes that anymore? As the old saying goes, "Suchen für Brot im Hunde Stall (she is looking for bread in a dog house.... the wrong place)." There is nothing I can do now, except hope that they will soon come back to their senses.

Thank the LORD that we have two more daughters that have never shown this foolishness. I just hope that they will consider our feelings, and never threaten to leave us alone. We need them to care for us in our old age.

As for *Frau Jacobina Karl* and *Herr Christoph Karl,* they are in GODs hands now. I pray that he guides and blesses them in these times of their obvious great need. For me, I must go on with my life, and as they say, "keine schreien uber versunken milch (do not cry over spilled milk)."

CALM AGAIN

♠MICHAEL GRÜN (NOBODY)♠

Karl home, about four hours walk east of stadt Heilbronn

I am not sure why *Christoph* has become obsessed with leaving this wonderful paradise. It is a quiet and fertile valley where he most obviously enjoys tending his, well not really his, plentiful vines.

His wife, *Jacobina*, is devoted to him in every way. Her only wishes are to keep him happy, give him children, and to keep a good home for him. While he obviously loves her and is happy here, for some reason, he no longer is just satisfied and thankful for what his GOD has given to them.

Maybe it was the loss of their only son so early in his young life, or maybe it was the seduction of the *Recruiter's* tales about frei land and a frei home.

While I have only known *Christoph* and *Jacobina* for a short time, I know they are a simple, honest couple devoted to family and their Lutheran faith. You could ask for no better friends, and I do believe they are my friends, probably my only friends.

I am by birth of the busy city. I find this rural simple life refreshing and good for my health. That is part of why I escaped from city life, there were other reasons, bad friends, bad drink, bad women, and just my being very bad, but these details are best hidden and forgotten. With the friendship of *Christoph* and *Jacobina* and the Grace of their GOD, maybe I will never fall back into the temptation of my former life.

As I mentioned before, I am not sure why *Christoph* feels they must leave here. I would not, but I am not sure how I would tell him why without my rather unsavory past coming out. Even if I did come clean with who I was and what I did in the city, I do not believe it is my place to tell him he is wrong, even if everything in my being tells me he is wrong!

I, without any question, know there is nothing in this life that is frei! This *Recruiter's* offer of frei land and home smells of a foul city-type swindle, but I know of no way to prove that to *Christoph* so that his mind would change. He did not listen to his dear wife, *Jacobina*, or his old neighbor, or his *Pastor*, or even his wife's mother and father. I can understand not listening to the last two, but why would he listen to anything I had to say?

All my life experiences scream to me 'Nichts ist ausser dem Tod frei, und dann mussen wir es mit unserem Leben bezahlen' (Nothing is free except death, then we must pay with our life), and yet, what if this is that once in a lifetime fabled 'Topf voll Gold am Ende des Regenbogens' (pot of gold at the end of the rainbow). We would be fools not to reach for the pot of gold...

I do not really want to leave because I am happy here, and I do not want *Christoph* and *Jacobina* to leave either. *Christoph's* obsession is just upsetting the good thing I have going here.

After all is thought out, I am not really risking anything by going with *Christoph* and *Jacobina*. I had nothing before I met them; I have nothing now, so, in truth, I have nothing at all to lose.

If the *Recruiter's* offer turns out to be true, I could be a wealthy man. If not, I am still on the same adventure that I started when I ran from the city. Only this time I have a direction, two good friends, and best of all, frei food and travel with no work required. Honestly, what more could a man expect from life? So on 23 July, it is the three of us off to find our futures and fortunes in some strange land.

Even if I forgot about becoming wealthy, which I will not, as *Christoph* and *Jacobina* graciously opened their home and lives to me without question, and for that reason alone, I will stay and travel with them. I will help and protect their dreams as long as they let me, so help me GOD.

From somewhere deep in my memory, a voice rang out a warning I knew as a child, "ein Versprechen schwer zu halten (A promise hard to keep)!"

6 LEAVING HOME

♦JACOBINA KARL♦

Stadt Heilbronn Sammelplatz on the Neckar River

My *Christoph* has decided that our future will be in a far-away land. I am not so sure that is where our best future waits, but as the old saying goes, "Mach dir nicht sorgen über Eier nicht gemacht (Do not worry about eggs not yet laid)!" As his wife, I must go with him and for better or worse, we will make this trip together and meet our destiny as one.

It is the Monday morning, 23 July, and *Christoph* and I and *Michael Grün* are waiting here at the stadt Heilbronn Sammelplatz (central gathering place) on the edge of the Neckar River for our first step towards our new land.

Also with us are the *Recruiter* and four other families, who we do not know. Three of the families are Lutherans as we are; one is *Katholische*. I will not hold that against the *Katholische* family, as they seem nice enough, though my *Christoph* will certainly not be friendly to them.

My family came to see us off. I did not expect to see them again, after my plan to change my *Christoph's* mind created that horrible scene at our Church here.

When I ran away from the scene I created outside the *Kirche*, I left my parents and sisters embarrassed and humiliated, and subjected them to the whispers and stares of the other people. How wrong I was in what I did! Now, other than saying I am sorry, there is nothing I can do… And saying I am sorry just does not seem to be enough, so I am doing nothing, nothing at all.

That did not seem to matter to them, here seeing us off was my vater (father) *Johan Jacob*, my mutter (mother) *Anna Maria*, and my two schwestern (sisters) *Susanna* and *Laudema*.

My mother came close to hug me, and quietly whispered in my ear, "We love you and *Christoph*. You both will be in our hearts for always. Please remember our family and us often and fondly. Come back and visit us if you can. I pray GOD blesses you both."

I saw my father also hug *Christoph*, and heard him whispering something like, "Take good care of her. If she comes to any harm, I will hunt you to the ends of the land, and you will not enjoy it at all when I do find you!"

Thankfully, my *Christoph* did not react in any way to this threat, but only smiled. Thank you, my husband!

My vater moved near to me and proclaimed, "You do not have to go with *Herr Karl*. We will make room for you in our home!"

My mother pulled her husband back, and sharply said to him, "Do not say that, my husband. She must always be at her husband's side. To do otherwise, would be to break the Marriage Vows they both swore to before GOD and before all of us, and to renounce our very Faith. She will stay with *Christoph*, just as I have always stayed with you." My father just shrugged, and remained silent.

My sisters, *Susanna* and *Laudema*, leaped forward and hugged me, and with tears streaming down their faces, gave me their blessings and good-byes.

It was almost time for us to leave, and our boat waited on us. With final waves, my dear family turned and slowly walked out of my life. I watched as they shrunk in the distance, till I could no longer see any of them.

I looked over at my *Christoph* and said a silent prayer, "Please GOD, bless us in our travels and insure we have made the best choice. Protect the three of us as we travel through the land north and on to the unknown. Amen."

Our group going up the Neckar River that morn was to be five families plus ours, but two of the families were late to arrive. We waited for an hour, and then all loaded onto the horse-drawn boat to make our way up the Neckar River.

Still waiting for the others, the *Recruiter* became more and more visibly agitated and upset. My *Christoph* reminded him that they just might have changed their mind and decided not to go...

The *Recruiter* snapped back without thinking, "Not go... I have signed contracts on them. They have to go! I will see to them when I return."

Everyone on the boat looked at each other in shock. Realizing he should not have spoken so, the *Recruiter* quickly added, "*Herr Karl,* you are most correct. I agree that there not being here, is no problem. They were most likely delayed and we will fit them in with the next group."

Horse-drawn Boat

We all heard his words and laughed aloud, but we were all questioning whether we had made a terrible mistake. Too late now, suddenly I was very afraid, and I turned to *Christoph* and said, "My husband, I am afraid. Hold me close so that I can draw on your strength." *Christoph* pulled me to him and held me, and I felt better.

The *Recruiter*, now calm again, told us, "You should all settle down, and get as comfortable as you can. Enjoy the ride, as we will be on this boat for at least all today. We ride this boat up the Neckar River until we get to the Rhein River, near Mannheim. There we will meet up with more families and board a larger boat. In three or four days we will be in Wiesbaden, where we will join with many more families."

I had never been farther north than my birthplace, Kirhart. All this was new to me, and while I was still afraid, I was excited too.

The *Recruiter* seemed to be happy that we were making good time; just before sunset, we arrived in a small village known as Eberbach.

We were all glad to get off the boat and on to land. Preparations had already been made for us, and we were fed supper and provided shelter and beds in a large communal tent. *Christoph* and I, and *Michael* were exhausted, and we quickly cleaned up for bed. Once in our beds, we fell deep asleep almost immediately.

I am normally an early riser, but this morning it was still very dark when they woke us. We ate and packed up, and were ready to again board the horse-drawn boat just as the sun peaked over the hills.

Again, we were delayed from leaving. One of the Lutheran families that had just yesterday left Heilbronn with us, had vanished in the night; apparently, they had changed their minds. The *Recruiter* and other men did a quick search for them, but they were long gone. Another family joined us in Eberbach, so we were again back to four families, plus *Michael Grün*.

Before long, we were again heading up the Neckar River, this time toward the Rhein River and the village of Mannheim.

I was still enjoying the sights along the river and stayed awake, but I saw my *Christoph* and *Michael,* both stretched out on the boat floor, fast asleep.

When the sun was high about mid-day, I saw a large city south of on the river. "What city is that? I asked the *Recruiter*. With tall buildings, it was twice the size of Heilbronn.

Heidelberg Castle

"That is stadt Heidelberg, home of the Academia of Heidelberg. There farther up the hill you can see what is left of the old castle that has been empty and crumbling for many years," replied the *Recruiter*.

We slowly continued up the river. After some time, we passed by, on the right side, what the *Recruiter* called Mannheim.

Only a short time later, we reached the wide Rhein River and tied up at a dock. Dear *Christoph* and *Michael* slept almost the whole way, and missed seeing everything.

We were all more than eager to get off the boat and on to land, even though it was only midafternoon. As before, all was prepared for us and they quickly led us to one of four large communal tents to rest.

Mannheim

At suppertime, we went to what I thought was a communal tent, but was actually a large dining hall. We ate and drank to our fill, and we paid nothing, nothing at all. Our *Recruiter* led us back to our tent to get some sleep.

I noticed something peculiar, and whispered to *Christoph*, "There are men who look like guards around our tent. Is that to protect us from harm, or is that to prevent us from leaving, as that one family did back in Eberbach?"

"What nonsense are you coming up with now?" *Christoph* replied, and then quietly laughed. Later however, I saw him glance around to see if I was right.

It was another very dark morning, when they awoke us to travel on to Wiesbaden. Like the morning before, we ate and packed up, and were ready to again board just as the sun rose. This time it was much larger boat, and riding along with us were at least fifteen families and more single men.

Wiesbaden

There was no horse to pull this boat. The river would take us north with the swift current flow. Even though the boat was larger, we moved along quicker than our horse-drawn boat, because the wide Rhein River current was so much stronger.

While our ride yesterday was relaxing, this boat ride was rougher, and even my sleepy *Christoph* and

Michael stayed wide-awake. Shortly before sunset, we docked at the city the *Recruiter* called Wiesbaden.

We all left the boat, led by the *Recruiter* and a group of other men to an area of more large tents. Many campfires lit up the early night sky and people were everywhere. As I took all this in, I came to an abrupt stop and accidentally exclaimed aloud, "Mein Gott (My God)!"

Husband *Christoph* quickly grabbed hold of me, and with much concern, asked, "What is wrong? Are you hurt?"

"No, just I never saw this many people in one place in my whole life," I self-consciously replied. *Michael* and *Christoph* laughed for quite a while.

Finally, *Christoph* replied, "Yes, all these people are just like us, leaving their old ways and traveling to the new land, to build their better futures."

"May the LORD protect us all," I silently prayed to GOD.

7   LOST TO US

◆ANNA MARIA MAURER◆

Between stadt Heilbronn and Village Kirhart

I had told my husband and daughters, "We will meet them on river dock in Heilbronn, only to say good-bye." This was a lie. I really wanted all the family there for one last chance to persuade them to cancel, or delay at least, their leaving. Sadly, that did not happen, and still they left.

We will never know whether Satan, or pride or greed, seduced my *Jacobina* and her fool of a husband into forever leaving us. All we know is that they did leave.

The walk away from them that morning was almost unbearable; many times, I wanted to rush back to them and plead with them one last time. I could not; as I realized they were already lost to us and were not coming back. I turned to my dear husband *Johann Jacob*, took his hand in mine, and said, "We have raised our daughter *Jacobina* into a strong fine woman, and she will survive and prosper. I hope that we will see them again in the future days, but I fear that all we have left is our memories. Those memories we must save, they must last us for the rest of our lives."

Along the way home, my mind kept replaying the morning. It was good to see my youngest daughter again, and I cherished the chance to talk with her one last time and to give her our blessings; well, at least, my blessings.

I was very angry with my husband for the threat he made to *Christoph,* but I suppose I could not expect anything else from him. My *Johann Jacob* is a good man, but he is stubborn and he does not easily accept ideas that are not his own. He was always stubborn, even when we first married, but has gotten more so as he grows older.

Even so, his remarks were not proper. He knows that our Marriage Vows are more important than anything except our faith in our LORD. I felt horrible rebuking him in front of the family, but I had to choose between embarrassing him or supporting my daughter keeping her vow with our GOD. I could not allow her to disappoint our LORD for any reason! I know it was only the great despair and pain that he felt that made him say such a thing anyway, GOD forgive him.

We walked in silence much of the way back. We were almost home, when I turned to my husband and my daughters and said, "We must dwell only on the happier times with them. Cast out the pain and frustration from your mind, and cradle and enjoy the good times we had. Pray for their eternal souls, their safety, and their happiness. And maybe, with GODs eternal blessing, *Jacobina* and *Christoph* will come back and visit us sometime in the future. If this is not to be in our time, we know that we will be with them again in our eternal life in Heaven."

We all cried and hugged each other for a few moments, even my dear strong husband *Johan Jacob*.

8   OVERLAND WE MARCH

✦JACOBINA KARL✦

North of Wiesbaden on the road to the Promised Land

It was a fitful night's sleep in the communal tent; so many people moving around during the night going out as nature called, or returning from it. Then there were the babies crying, the children whining, a few drunks, a few arguments, and much loud snoring.

My thoughts kept going back to my leaving my family, and our parting at the dock. I already miss them so much, so much pain. I am among so many, and yet, I feel so alone. I looked over at my sleeping *Christoph*, and was tempted to wake him, but that would be selfish of me, as he too needed his rest.

The next morning came early... pitch black, clear with bright stars still out, cool but not cold. Our *Recruiter* gathered us up and led us to meal tent for breakfast. I noticed that other groups also had their own recruiters, and that along with each group was an armed guard. Too protect us or to prevent us from leaving?

Our *Recruiter* stood on a wooden box and announced, "I am leaving you now to go and spread our offer to more villages. You will be guided the rest of the way by *Herr Hess*, who will speak next. Bless you all on your travels to the new land."

We would never see our *Recruiter*, who we had come to put our trust in every word he told us about our future, ever again. *Herr Hess* climbed on to the box and spoke, "I am your new guide. Remember my face and name in case you get lost. I will guide you to the port of Lübeck."

We moved, actually we were herded, to an area filled with oxen wagons. I and other women, and the younger children, were loaded on the wagons. We would ride, and the older children and all the men, young or old, would walk. Where there was once the chaos of a crowd, now suddenly there was order with all waiting for the signal to start the march. Finally, our caravan was slowly on the way.

As the sun rose, I looked around and saw at least fifteen oxen wagons filled with women and children, and a few with supplies of all types. Also in each wagon were the driver, a guide, and the always-present guards. Men, and boys of all ages, shuffled along beside the wagons.

We bumped along the rough paths, trails, and roads. The wagons rocked and creaked, and the women chatted, as best they could, over the noise.

The children soon tired of just sitting, and whined until they had a chance to jump off and play along the trail as the wagons slowly rolled forward. As each grew tired one-by-one, the children would again be loaded upon the wagon next to their mothers.

We passed what some thought was north of a large city called Frankfurt. In fact, when we stopped after sunset and camped the first night, the lights of this Frankfurt lit the sky in the south. It must be a very large city, as it makes a very large glow in the sky.

I, like everyone else was dead tired, though all I had done was ride on the wagon. *Christoph* and *Michael* were tired from all the walking, but did not complain. All we wanted was some food, and a place to lie down and rest. We got both, and quickly fell asleep. Sometime in the middle of the night, I woke to thoughts of my mother and father and sisters. Troubled, I softly cried myself to sleep some time later.

"Time to be up," yelled our guide *Herr Hess*. He yelled again, "We have to get fed and get back on the trail. The boats are waiting for us at the port. Your future is waiting for you. Let us go!"

As usual, it was still dark outside. No stars out, must be cloudy. This was just a sleepy repeat of the day before with the same creaky wagon, same noisy children.... same women. After a while, it was all just a blur.... Time passed as slowly as the wagons rolled forward. I felt sorry for *Christoph* and *Michael* having to walk while I rode, but not too sorry, better them than me.

Actually, I could see them much of the time, and they seemed to be doing just fine, talking and sometimes horsing around with the children and men around them. Maybe they were having a better trip than I was…

We passed west, I think, of another village. "This village was Hanau," someone said. Hanau looked large, but was much smaller than the city of Frankfurt.

Like the night before, we stopped after sunset and camped. The lights of the village Hanau also made a glow in the cloudy night south sky, but it was much smaller than that of Frankfurt. In fact, I could still see the glow from Frankfurt off in the distant sky farther to the southwest.

The night was the same as the previous ones, same early morning anguish from missing my family. Again, there was the before light wakeup call. No stars again this morning, and the wind had come up, making it even cooler. Other than the weather, the wagons, the people, and the landscape were a boring repeat of the days before. There was no excitement in this traveling at all.

Sometime later, I noticed there might have been a difference. Some new faces this morning, and some I remembered were no longer with us. Some must be leaving from second thoughts, and some must be joining to share in our future.

When this day's trip ended after sunset, it was very dark and I knew we were far from any village. It mattered little to any of us, and as on the prior nights, it was eating, sleeping, and then up before sunrise and back on the road. I had never imagined this trip would be like this. I thought it would be an adventure, exciting, and maybe even, fun. No, it is not any of those; it is only boring, and then, more boring.

Riding along with nothing else to think about, my mind again drifted back to my family and to my wonderful life with my dear husband, before we started this trek. In that before time, I never did appreciate what we had and how lucky I was. I especially missed my private time at night to spend with my dear husband *Christoph*.

As we slowly rolled along towards our future, our guide *Herr Hess*, stood up and announced, "We are moving along well. Tonight, we will be in Büdingen. Tomorrow is the Sabbath, and we will have some time to worship and time to rest, and for some of you, time to clean yourselves."

My initial reaction was to be offended, and I heard the other women around me whispering that his comments were improper. To be honest, I had missed my usual personal wash up time, and I, like the others was beginning to have a less than pleasant scent. The men, well, they just stunk, but come to think of it, not much has changed their as men usually stink!

Herr Hess ignored the whisperings and continued, "We will have separate wash areas for the women and the men, and another area for the women to wash their family's clothes. You single men, I advise you make some trade with a married man for his wife to do your wash."

Now the women were no longer whispering, but were yelling at their husbands that they had better not promise them to do any washing for any other man. I, on the other hand, felt that getting away from this wagon and washing my clothes, as well as the clothes of my husband, *Christoph*, and the clothes of our friend, *Michael*, was a good thing. I looked forward to anything, anything at all, to end this boredom!

As we continued slowly bumping along, I wondered what this Büdingen would be like. I so hoped that there was a Kirche where the followers of our Friar Martin Luther could pray. My boredom lessened as I fancied what sights and happenings tomorrow would bring.

True to the *Herr Hess's* word, we arrived on the outskirts of Büdingen in early afternoon. We camped not far away, and I could see that Büdingen was a walled city.

We were immediately guided to separate areas to wash, and to our surprise, were provided clean clothes for us to put on. It was a madhouse, as the women tried to find the clothes that they each wanted. Some even argued and tussled over the very same clothes.

I made a quick choice of clothes, pushed my way out of the crowd of women, dressed, and moved outside to see where my *Christoph* and *Michael* were. I was so glad to be off that wagon, and be washed and into clean clothes. It was such a blessing.

A man directed me to a common area where all were to gather after they cleaned up. Rows and rows of tables and benches were there for all of us to sit on. After some time, *Christoph* and *Michael* appeared, also in different, but clean, clothes. I am not sure how really clean they were, but neither smelled any longer. That was also such a blessing.

I realized that none of us had our original clothes. To the women beside me, I asked, "What happened to our dirty clothes? Should we start washing them?"

She laughed and answered, "They came and took away the clothes. Said they smelt so bad that no washing would ever get them clean. Said they were going to burn them!"

I loudly protested to *Christoph*, "Where are they? Stop them! How dare they, those are my clothes!" *Christoph* just looked at me and shrugged. He was no help. I glared at *Michael*, another shrug, no help. I thought to myself, "What use are these men?"

The women beside me, who I was now not talking to, offered her view, "Your husband can do nothing. Your dirty clothes are gone! You all have clean clothes as we all do now. Were your old filthy clothes so fine that you want to keep them? If not, why do you make such a fuss?"

While I did not like what she was saying, she did make a lot of sense. I was just being silly. Slightly embarrassed, I slowly sighed, and then answered to both her and my husband, "You are so right. I did not have to wash the old dirty clothes and we now have fresh clean clothes for the Sabbath. Let them keep all those clothes."

The women beside me, said nothing in reply, but just shook her head.

After they led us to our area in the communal tent, we were able to just rest and talk. They called us for supper later, and after eating, *Christoph* and I slowly strolled around the camp area.

It was nice just being together again, and even with all the people around, it seemed like just the two of us were here. No idea where our friend *Michael Grün* was, and to be honest, at this minute I did not really care.

We heard that we would be going in to Büdingen to worship tomorrow, and would have plenty of time to stroll around the city. Today, it was still overcast and cloudy, and I hoped that tomorrow the weather would clear, and it would be a sunny warm day. We also learned that we would not be traveling at all tomorrow, but would get back on the move the next day after tomorrow.

Eventually, most all headed to their beds for a good night's rest. I tried to sleep, but was too excited about attending church and seeing Büdingen. Thoughts of what we might find drifted through my mind as I finally fell to sleep.

Again, in the early morn, I awoke with despair from leaving my beloved family and a yearning for our life before. I questioned myself, "Was it really too late to change our minds and go back home? Would my husband *Christoph* even consider returning?" I knew in my heart the answers to both. Yes, it was too late. No, he had his heart and mind on this better future.

Büdingen

♦JACOBINA KARL♦

The camp outside the Jerusalem Gate of Büdingen

The sun was well up when they woke us. It was a clear and sunny day. It was good to sleep in, but now all hurried to clean, dress, and eat.

Büdingen

They divided us into three groups, one our Lutherans, one of Katholische, and one small group of unbelievers who did not honor the Sabbath. I felt so sorry for the unbelievers as they would never know the Grace of our LORD, only the eternal damnation of Hell. So sad...Might there be something I could do?

I turned to my husband and said, "This trip is so long. Maybe we will have chances to honor our faith, and help these poor lost souls find the right path. We might help them much like we did with *Michael.*"

Christoph was frowning as he looked at me and replied, "My dear wife, you are so right, but we must be careful and patient with all these strangers. Like us, they too want to worship or not worship, as they choose. We owe it to our LORD to help them see the way to salvation, but we will best do that by example, and not by preaching."

"Of course, you are so right, my husband," I replied while silently thinking how I could go about helping all the lost souls.

As they guided our group down the road, we passed a number of houses outside the walls. Our guide explained that those that lived outside were mostly religious extremists, Huguenots, sectarians, and separatists.

I turned and whispered to *Christoph,* "What are those? I only know of Lutherans, Katholische, people called Jews, and the damned unbelievers."

Christoph shrugged and whispered back, "My dear, I know not of those, either. But since we know we are of GODs faith, they must all be the wrong faith as are the Katholische. *Jacobina,* do not embarrass us by asking our guide *Herr Hess.*"

I remained silent and nodded in agreement. I have no idea why he would think I might do that.

Herr Hess led us over a bridge and through an opening between two small towers. He called this the Jerusalem Gate. Someone loudly asked, "Is this named for our LORDs Holy city of Jerusalem?" *Herr Hess* did not answer with words, but nodded yes.

As we slowly walked down the cobbled streets, I was able to look into the street side shops. I was amazed at all the interesting things that were for sale. More than once, I grabbed my husband's arm and dragged him to the glass window, and asked, "What is that? I like that one, do you? Have you ever seen that before?"

His usual reply was, "No, never seen that before now."

As we continued to walk, I noticed many colorful frogs on the walls of the shops and homes. Curious, I thought to ask my *Christoph*, but since he, as usual, did not feel talkative, I instead asked our guide, "What do those frogs mean?"

Herr Hess laughed, and as we slowly walked on, replied, "You have noticed the large frogs on the buildings. The frog is Büdingen's town symbol from an old legend. The legend tells that around 1522, I believe, Count Anton of Ysenburg (Isenburg) and Büdingen married a girl named Elisabeth. His wife turned out to be very demanding. On their wedding night, Elisabeth became upset by the hundreds of croaking frogs outside down in the castle moat."

Herr Hess continued with the local legend, "The unruly bride cried that her husband did not tell her about the frog noise, and so she wanted a divorce. She threatened to withhold marital bliss from the Count unless he did something immediately about the noise. Of course, the

Count did not want that, so he woke-up court council and decreed the city should immediately drive out all frogs."

"The bailiff woke the sleepy people of Büdingen and they were required to start on a wild frog chase. Children invaded the nearby marshes and groves with nets, baskets, hooks and rope to wrangle up all the frogs in the neighborhood. In no time, the baskets were overflowing and the frogs were all caught and put under guard in the marktplatz. Back at the castle, with the frogs' croaking much diminished (although it was deafening in the marktplatz), the princess bride gave an appreciative kiss to her suffering count," our guide recounted.

"What do you think they did with all the frogs?" *Herr Hess* asked us. No one in our group had any idea or guess.

He answered, "The smartest in the town came up with the idea to drown them in the river. The Count and his new bride came to witness the great Büdingen frog-drowning spectacle. The people dunked the frog-filled baskets in the river until the frog frenzy noise had stopped. That evening, very few croaks could be heard, but those came from way downriver. Since that time, people here and nearby say this is the most beautiful town, and with the fewest frogs. Everyone lived happily ever after, but for the frogs."

We all laughed at such a silly story... Our group eventually made it to the marktplatz, where even though it was the Sabbath, open-air vendors were hawking their goods. This was a surprise to me, for where I was raised, this was never allowed on the Sabbath.

The town folks here were friendly, greeting us with, Hallo or Guten Tag, Guten Morgan, or Gute Wünsche (Good Day, Good Morning, Good Wishes).

As we came around a corner, we got our first close look at the church. We had seen the Kirche tower early from our camp, but of course, there it looked much smaller. Once again, I grabbed my husband's arm and whispered, "Look at it! I think it is much larger than our Lutheran Kirche in Heilbronn."

Like everyone, he was looking up with his mouth open. He closed it, turned to me and whispered back, "Yes, it is much, much larger." In awe, our whole group was quiet. Being so close to the Kirche in the narrow streets, and then looking up, made it even more immense and awesome.

We patiently waited outside the Kirche entrance for a while. It would have become boring, but everywhere I looked, there was something of interest. Eventually, the church doors opened and the worshippers streamed out.

I recognized some of them as Katholische that had been traveling with us. That made no sense, as this is a Lutheran Kirche, not a Katholische Kirche. Disturbed, I asked *Christoph*, "Why are those Katholische coming out of a Lutheran Kirche?"

Christoph looked at me, pondered on it for a time, shrugged and replied, "Uh… no idea." I can always depend on my *Christoph* to provide me answers…

From inside our Lutheran group, others had also noticed the Katholische. One less timid person loudly asked *Herr Hess*, "What is going on? Is this a Lutheran Kirche or a Katholische Kirche?"

Herr Hess turned to us, and motioned with his hands to quiet down. Then he explained, "No need to be upset. In Büdingen, there is religious freedom and all groups get along well. This church was originally a Katholische Kirche, but now serves for both Katholische and Lutherans at different times on the Sabbath. Today, the Katholische went first to worship in their way. Next, you will be able to worship as Lutherans do. They call this Kirche the Marienkirche (St. Mary's Church) and the Liebfrauenkirche (Church of our Lady). Do we have any troubles here?"

Marienkirche and Liebfrauenkirche

Embarrassed, our group mumbled back almost as one voice, "No troubles, no troubles at all."

As the last Katholische left, we Lutherans entered. It was magnificent inside, and much more ornate than our former Katholische Kirche, but now Lutheran Kirche, in Heilbronn. I decided that was because part of the time this was still a Katholische Kirche. I was fine with that; I could still worship our LORD with all this extravagant grandeur around me.

The service was much like the one that *Christoph* and I grew up attending. It felt very comforting to be here with our faith. After the service, the Pastor announced that many of our group wished to married before leaving for the new lands, and so, he would marry all those couples in the church the next day.

I was shocked, and I looked around to see if I could recognize which couples were not actually married, and were living in sin.

Christoph must have realized what I was doing, and leaned over to me to sternly whisper, "*Jacobina*, stop that now! We are in the LORDs house. Let those without sin cast the first stone!" He was right.

Guilty as sin, I dropped my head and whispered back, "Sorry husband. I should know better." Only guilty for a moment, as I happily realized that if couples were going to marry tomorrow, we would not be traveling until the next day. Good, I was in no hurry to remount that oxen wagon.

As we left the church, the Pastor blessed us as had been done in our Heilbronn.

Herr Hess formed us up around him and announced, "You are free to stroll around the city for the rest of the day. Please make sure you make it back to the camp by supper or you will be on your own for the meal. Tomorrow, you may come back and visit the city and witness the marriages, or just stroll around. On the other hand, you may stay in the camp and rest or visit your fellow travelers. We will be back on the road traveling north towards the port on the day after. Be ready to leave on time."

We were now free to go anywhere we wanted, but which way? I asked *Christoph*, "Which way should we go?" I did not really expect an answer.

He looked around and then replied, "There is a castle over there. We will walk that way." I really did not care which way we went, it was just wonderful to not be herded around like swine. *Christoph* and I, with *Michael* following a ways back, strolled around the buildings, through the gardens, up and down the cobble streets; for just a while there was nowhere we had to be, and it felt good.

The day went by too quickly, and before we knew it, the sun was setting. We hurried back to the camp for supper. After eating, *Christoph* and I strolled around the camp, occasionally stopping to talk with the other travelers sitting at the campfires. Finally, it was time for bed.

For once, because of the relaxing day, sleep at first came easily to all of us. Again, my nightly despair ripped me from the blessing of sleep.

The next morn was another late wake-up and meal. *Christoph, Michael,* and I headed back into the village to witness the Lutheran marriages. About fifty Lutheran couples united, and about forty Katholische couples married. Much celebration occurred, and bier and wine appeared for all from somewhere. Towns' people and travelers like us were all merry.

Again, the day passed too quickly, and the sun was setting. We said our goodbyes and hurried back to the camp for supper. But on this night after eating, *Christoph* and *Michael* went to wash and cleanup in the men's area before tomorrow's travel.

I headed toward the women's area to do the same. I had thought that it would be empty, but many other women were there with the same thought as I had. The traveling was so dirty, and with little chance to wash up on the road, now was the time to get clean.

When I was again clean, and finished getting dressed, I headed back to our sleeping tent. *Christoph* and *Michael* were already there, and I thought about checking to see just how clean *Christoph* had gotten, but with all the other people around, that would have humiliated him. He would have gotten angry, so I decided however clean he was, would be good enough.... this time.

Like the night before, because of the relaxing day, sleep came easily to all of us. The wakeup call came early before the sunrise. After the morning meal, all the newly married couples moved to a nearby hillside and planted a sapling oak tree, as was the Büdingen tradition.

Once we were back on the road, the bumpy wagons, the mass of people, and the slow travel was a boring repeat of the days last week. One day and night vanished into another day and night and another day and night and on and on.

My nightly despair about leaving my family and my church plagued me a little less each night. That was the good news. The bad news was that there was no excitement or adventure left in this travel, and the fond memory of our few fun days in Büdingen, quickly faded to a dream.

Grünberg

Day by day, the villages of Wetzlar, Bad Salzhausen, and Grünberg slowly disappeared into the dusty distance behind us. By this time, not one of us really cared where we were.

More days slowly went by, and the villages of Alsfeld, Homberg, and Cassel shrunk in the dusty distance behind us.

Cassel

Still none really cared where we were, other than with each hour we were closer to the end of this damn road.

DAY AFTER DAY

♠CHRISTOPH KARL♠

On the road northeast of village Cassel

My poor *Jacobina*, she was so bored with riding on the wagon. Yet if she gave up her place to walk with me for a ways, she most likely would not have a place back on the wagon. Then, she too would learn how much fun it is to walk till the day's end.

While walking was tiring, at least I was doing something to keep my mind occupied. Of course, *Michael* and I would talk and joke, and occasionally have horseplay. The children, running in, around and between us, also were a good distraction.

I knew that *Jacobina* was distraught at leaving her family, and that she would often waken in the early morn and softly cry. I knew not how to comfort her and pretended to sleep, but I shared her pain as any husband would.

For me, the worst part of this trip was having no private nighttime with my dear wife, *Jacobina*. There were always crowds of people around, and there was nowhere to go where other people were not already there.

One cool evening, we decided to venture into the surrounding trees for a little husband-wife playtime, but found the forest was already alive with young couples playing our same game. While most of them paid no mind to us and continued their romp and play, some temporarily stopped and moved farther from sight.

My shy *Jacobina* was too uncomfortable at this public lovemaking and whispered to me, "I am too shy for this. We must leave and return to the camp."

What choice did I have but to take her back to the crowded camp? None at all! I had to remain content with holding her hand and stealing an occasional kiss. And there were the back rubs and foot rubs, but all in all, they were not very satisfying.

My hope is that soon things will somehow change and my wife and I will again be able to be as man and wife. I did not appreciate what we used to have when we had it. Those quiet times alone, with no one else around for a long ways, except my dear *Jacobina*.

I never imagined it would be like this. I was sure it would be an exciting adventure for all of us. I never realized how much pain she would be in if I took her away from her mother, father, and sisters. She always seemed so confident and independent of them as if she did not need them.

I pray to GOD that our promised future makes this all worth it. I dare not tell my dear wife, *Jacobina*, or even friend *Michael*, but I do sometimes wonder if it will be...

Göttingen

JACOBINA KARL▪

On the road outside of village Göttingen

Another week had passed, and the Sabbath was here again. This time we found ourselves on the eve of Sabbath in the village of Göttingen.

Before we arrived at the camp, I was certain that *Herr Hess* would tell us the same speech as last time.

Göttingen

Herr Hess did stand up and speak, "We have traveled well, and we are in Göttingen. Tomorrow is the Sabbath and we will all have some time to worship and a little time to rest, and for some of you, please for the sake of those traveling with you, clean yourselves up." This time no one was offended. We all knew we stunk, and were all looking forward to washing up.

He continued, "We will again have separate wash areas for the women and the men. There will not be enough time for your women to wash your clothes, so clean clothes will be available for all after washing."

His words were no surprise, and in fact, I do not think anybody cared what he was saying. The women wanted to get off this wagon; the men wanted to stop walking!

We were immediately taken to separate areas to wash, and as promised, were provided clean clothes for us to put on. It was still a madhouse as the women argued and tussled over the very same clothes. I made a quick choice of clothes, dressed, and moved outside to find my *Christoph* and friend *Michael.*

As before, I was so glad to be down off that wagon, and be washed and into clean clothes. It was still such a blessing. I found the common area where all would gather on the rows and rows of tables and benches. Eventually, *Christoph* and *Michael* arrived in clean, clothes. Just as before, I am not sure how clean they were, but neither stunk anymore. That too was such a blessing!

At supper, they announced that they would lead us into the town for Sabbath worship as we had in Büdingen, and that we would again have time for a stroll. This time, however, we learned would be traveling and back on the move north, the very next day.

Eventually, most all headed to their beds for a good night's rest. Too tired to think on what we might find tomorrow, *Christoph* and *Michael* were asleep and snoring in minutes. I fell asleep a short while later. I had bad dreams of being lost and alone, but did not wake this night.

The sun was already up when they woke us. It felt good to sleep in. Everyone hurried to clean up and get dressed, and to eat.

Once again, they divided us into the three groups, one our Lutherans, one of Katholische, and one small group of unbelievers who did not honor the Sabbath. They led our group to worship at the Kirche of St. Jacobi.

I was pleasantly surprised, as I too am named after the beloved St. Jacobi.

Kirche of St. Jacobi, Göttingen

After Kirche, they let us do as we pleased. Again, there was the same old warning about being back to camp for supper, and that we would be up very early on the morn to get back on the road. I commented to *Christoph*, "Even the Sabbath's were becoming the same.

He sighed and agreed and added, "You are just tired of traveling, as I am, but we have much longer to go."

In a moment of weakness, I asked him, "Do you ever think about our lives back home, or maybe about changing our minds and going back?"

Christoph looked deep into my eyes and slowly answered, "Yes, I often think of the good times that we had. No, I do not question our decision. I know that I made the right choice, and our lives will be better for it. We have many more good times ahead for us, but we must be patient and overcome these bad times."

I knew his answer before he replied, and felt foolish for even mentioning my thoughts…

Göttingen was beautiful, and we strolled around for a while… but we were tired of traveling and our hearts were not in it. We slowly walked back to the camp to sit and talk with all the other weary travelers. Supper, sleep, and up early back on the road.

More days and nights passed as the villages of Northeim, Einbeck, Alfeld, Elze, Pattensen, Hannover, and Langenhagen faded in the distance.

On the eve of the next Sabbath, we were near the village of Schwarmstedt. Same washing, same new clothes, same supper… only this time they told us that there were no churches nearby, and we would worship outside under the sky.

And on that Sabbath, we worshiped in the area set aside for our Lutherans. Instead of the ornate beauty of the Kirche, we basked in the beauty of the outdoors with the all

GODs creatures. Instead of sitting on pews, we sat on the ground. Instead of the organ, we had our own voices. Maybe it is better to worship our LORD outside.

After worship this time, we could not go to the village, and they only let us move about the camp. We rested, ate supper, talked with others, and went to bed.

Early morning rise, and I was back on the oxen wagon while *Christoph* and *Michael* were back on their two feet. I had come to hate this wagon…. But it was better than walking… at least a little better. My arsch (ass) hurt, but my feet did not!

More days and nights passed as the villages of Soltau, Falling-bostel, Tostedt, Buchholz, Hamburg, and Bad Oldesloe shrunk and finally vanished behind us.

Another week of days and nights had passed when *Herr Hess* stood up in the wagon and announced, "Congratulations all, we will be at the port city of Lübeck this evening. This part of your trip is almost finished."

Shouts of happiness came from all the men, women, and children. All in our group excitedly looked up the road for any glimpse of this Lübeck.

I said to the woman beside me, "Thanks be to the Lord for this blessing." The tired woman beside me simply answered, "Amen."

We camped that night on the outskirts of Lübeck. *Herr Hess* said that we must wait until sunup before we could enter the city. Only one more night sleeping on the ground next to the campfires; hopefully, only a short ride more and our time on this creaky wagon and bumpy road will end.

I was eagerly looking forward to being on a boat. Surely, sailing over the waves will be much more enjoyable.

9   The Port of Lübeck

♦CHRISTOPH KARL♦

A ways outside the gates to the Port of Lübeck

We were supposed to enter Lübeck on the morn of the Sabbath, but the weather the night before was not fit for man or animal. Torrents of rain from above pounded the tents, thunder boomed, and bolts of lightning streaked through the dark night sky. It was all we could do duck the leaks and stay dry. *Jacobina* and I huddled together to stay dry.

The Sabbath day was no better. The rain came down in buckets so fast that small rivers were running through our tents. Our planned entry into Lübeck would have to wait for a better day.

Just to eat, we had to scurry from tent to tent. Most of the time, *Jacobina* and I huddled under our oilcloth to keep warm and dry. The good part was that this was the closest I had been to my wife's soft body for a long time.

While *Jacobina* quietly scolded me, I was able to take some liberties without anyone noticing. She did not protest much, and when she did, only whispered 'nein' without meaning it.

That whole night our communal tent was quiet. It came to us that most of the couples were also under their oilcloths and staying warm in the same way. I felt sorry for poor *Michael*, he too was hiding under his own oilcloth, but there was no warm soft woman for him to play with.

We fell asleep all tangled up, and were still that way when *Herr Hess* woke the tent up. There was some embarrassment as the women quickly rearranged their clothing to cover themselves. The men just smiled, and gave knowing looks to each other. We men will be men!

Once we had gotten everything back to normal, we headed out to breakfast. The weather had turned clear with no clouds in sight, but it had turned noticeably cooler. By my guess, it must be around the first day of September…

Herr Hess formed us all together, got the women loaded on the oxen wagons, and started us toward Lübeck in quick time. He seemed to be more in a hurry than we were.

We were almost to the Lübeck city gate when *Herr Hess* stopped our oxen wagon, and announced, "This is as far as you women ride, and from here on, all walk. The city is much too crowded and busy for these wagons. I will lead the way, please pay attention and do not lose sight of me. My helpers will follow last to make sure no one is lost. Hold tight to your possessions and your money. Some living here may want to have your things much more than you."

As I clutched our packs tight to my body, *Jacobina* whispered, "What type of place is this? Do the thieves run free to threaten good and simple people like us?"

I shrugged and confidently replied, "I do not know, but my wife, you are safe. I will always protect you, you know that."

Jacobina quickly responded, "Yes, Oh good, but my dear husband, who will protect you?

Instantly I smiled and replied, "That would be *Michael.*" We both looked at *Michael,* and laughed, but he was not smiling or amused. I wondered why.

Herr Hess led us up and down the streets for about an hour. Eventually, after turning into a dark, narrow alley near the harbor, we stopped at a row of stone many-storied warehouses.

Here he turned to our group and announced, "The other warehouses here are filled to the brim. That is lucky for you as we are opening up a new one, just for all of you."

He unlocked and slowly pushed, as it groaned in protest, open the door, to our warehouse. He announced to all of us, "This will be your shelter until you are ready to board the ship. You will find cots and blankets, and a kitchen for your women to cook for you. Make yourselves comfortable as you may be here for two to three weeks. It looks dirty, but it is a strong building to cover you from the chill of the fog and rain of Lübeck. Mind yourselves; the upper floors are not as safe or strong as the ground level."

"If you have any problems, see your *Herr Balzer Barthuli* who we have appointed to be your Vorsteher (Leader). He will hand out to each of you daily allowances of eight groschen for men, five groschen for women, three groschen for children and one groschen for infants," he announced just before he left.

OUR NEW HOME?

◆JACOBINA KARL◆

Wulf Warehouse XXVI, An der Obertrave near Holstenbrücke (Holsten Bridge), Port of Lübeck

The night before we actually came in to Lübeck, the night of all the rains, the night that each of the couples slept under the oilcloth where no one could see what we were doing. That night, I let my *Christoph* have his way with me, as apparently all the other women had also done with their husbands. As it had been a long time since we had the opportunity, I expected my husband to quickly take me, fill my body as he fulfilled his needs, and then fall asleep.

To my shock, that is not what my *Christoph* did. He was slow, patient, and gentle, and took his time as fondled my body in ways that he had never done before. It was by far the most enjoyable night that we ever spent. While I was enjoying his skill much too much to really care at the time, I did wonder where he found these new nighttime skills.

As a loyal wife, I would never discuss my husband's nighttime abilities, but this new *Christoph* quickly sparked much more desire in me for him. He has been with me almost all the time, and when not actually next to me, he has been in my sight, so I know that he has not had time to sample and learn from the local whores. How then did he come to these new ways?

As I rode the waves of pleasure, it occurred to me that *Michael,* on the other hand, has been often away and he might have visited any number of loose women, and then talked about his techniques with my *Christoph.*

While still enjoying my husband's skillful use of my body, I decided *Michael* must be the answer. Silently, I laughed to myself because poor *Michael,* as close as he was to us, while he could not see, he certainly could hear the sounds our bodies were making. And since he did not have a woman with him right now, all he could do is be frustrated or tend to his needs himself; not quite the same as being with a real woman.

Again, silently to myself, I did thank *Michael* for teaching my *Christoph* all these new nighttime skills.

When we arrived at the warehouse, and all crowded inside it…. Our first sight in the dim shadowy and dusty light was that it was filthy with trash and rubbish all over, and with straw strewn on the floor. It smelled of the trash and fouled straw, and of a long closed up musty smell.

It was also cold because there was no stove anywhere. The warm clothes and blankets would have to be enough to keep us warm. They had piled the cots and blankets in a huge heap in the center of the room.

Looking at all the mess, I quickly chose where I wanted us to be, and told *Christoph* and *Michael,* "Go get what we need to be comfortable and stay warm, and bring put everything over there. We will claim that area and try to make it livable. I will go look at the kitchen area."

I went over to where the kitchen was supposed to be, and found instead, a rat infested room stinking of droppings and old decayed food. Without thinking, I exclaimed, "Mein Gott, what is this?" The smell was putrid and overwhelming, and made me feel faint, but I knew what we must do.

I immediately turned around and gathered round the other women in our group. It was important for us to make our areas livable, but even more important was for us to be able to cook and eat in the kitchen. We would all have to pitch in and clean. The other women had similar reactions to the rancid smell and nauseating sight, but also knew what we must do with this pigsty.

We cleaned and cleaned and cleaned some more, and after much hard work, were finally satisfied that it was safe to cook and eat in there.

By the time we were finished cleaning the kitchen, our men had arranged the beds in our living spaces. *Christoph* made one area for us, and *Michael* had his own area nearby. Since they had done everything I asked, they were just sitting there on the beds, talking and resting.

The women, including me, had two more simple tasks for our men. First, they needed to get all the rats, both the rodents and people, the vagabonds and beggars and such, out of the warehouse. Our men tackled the rodents with enthusiasm, and even seemed to be enjoying themselves. We never did see many rats after that. Our men were not quite as quick with the vagabonds and beggars, but those kinds never bothered us again.

The second task was a little harder for many of the men. We insisted that all the loose women, that seemed to draw to our men like flies to rancid meat, be escorted out of our warehouse. I was already happy with my husband's new night skills, and did want him to learn anymore at just this time. Many of the men were reluctant to remove these 'ladies' of the night, but as a group with one very loud voice, we married and proper women would not budge from this demand.

It is not that we really had anything against these women, and it may be a necessity of life that they do this 'work', but it is not appropriate for them to parade their 'work' in front of proper married women. These women could just offer their wares and talents elsewhere, away from us.

Michael did seem particularly attracted to one of them. I am absolutely certain that none of them met my dear *Christoph's* fancy.

It took some time, but after much cleaning and sweeping out of the dirt, and riffraff and scum, our warehouse areas almost made became livable. It was a relief to all the women, and after all the mud and dirt and dust on the roads coming here, this place almost made us happy. We could soon get back to a daily schedule, and life was good again.

We had to go out to shop for food every day. Luckily, the marktplatz was just up the street away from the harbor. As friendly as most of the villages along our travels had been, this port city of Lübeck was the extreme opposite. No greetings and the local women looked away when we were near them. We finally cornered one town's woman and bluntly asked her what was wrong.

With a sneer on her face and with her nose in the air, she tersely exclaimed, "We all know the rumors that you are the castoffs of good society, and most of you women are dirnen (prostitutes) and your men are dieben (thieves)! Good people of society do not mix with your type!" and then quickly rushed away.

I, along with the other proper women with me, of course, and at first, stood stunned and speechless. Quickly, we were embarrassed and ashamed, and then very, very angry. By that time, the 'nase in die luft' (nose in the air) woman was long gone, and we had no chance to retort. It mattered not; we could do nothing to change their minds about us.

Still, we were confused, this Lübeck was sinful with its own thieves and whores everywhere, and wickedness was flourishing on the streets around us. We too were good people, and yet they would not accept us as such. No matter, we would only be here a little while, and would make do. The sooner we left this Lübeck, the better it would be!

On a happier note, now that we were off the road, there was time to give daily thanks to our LORD and time for more marriages. Even better, the LORD blessed our group with births, and of course, baptisms. All joyous reasons give thanks to GOD, and wonderful reasons to celebrate.

Our Kirche was only a few streets from where we lived. It was a magnificent cathedral known as the Lübecker Dom. Like most extravagant Kirchen, it had first been Katholische, and so, was very beautiful and ornate inside.

With the Reformation, as in our Heilbronn, most of the people of Lübeck chose to leave the Katholische and follow our Friar Martin Luther, and so the Lübecker Dom became a Lutheran Kirche.

On the walls of the Kirche, the prior monks carved writings to inspire the worshipers. Of all that I found on the walls, I most liked this poem:

'Ye call Me Master and obey me not,

Ye call Me Light and see Me not,

Ye call Me Way and walk not,

Ye call Me Life and desire Me not,

Ye call Me wise and follow Me not,

Ye call Me fair and love Me not,

Ye call Me rich and ask Me not,

Ye call Me eternal and seek Me not,

Ye call Me gracious and trust Me not,

Ye call Me noble and serve Me not,

Ye call Me mighty and honor Me not,

Ye call Me just and fear Me not,

If I condemn you, blame me not.'

Along with regularly attending Kirche worship once more, I busy my time with keeping our temporary home clean. I have also made good friends with the other women, and we try to meet to just to talk and gossip every day.

Sadly, not all is rosy here. It is been many weeks now that we have been waiting to leave, far longer than what we were first told. The men have absolutely nothing to do, and are bored. They rest and sleep, but one can only do that so long. They go out on long walks just to settle down. It is not good; men must have labor to do to keep out of trouble.

More and more evident every day that went by, I noted that *Michael* was becoming more and more restless. My *Christoph* looked as if he was handling the boredom better, but could I really tell. One morning, I asked him, "Are you all right? I know there is not much for you to do. Maybe I can find something for you."

Christoph looked straight at me, frowned, and growled back, "Wife, I am fine! No, I do not need you, or anyone else, to find me something to do."

With that, *Christoph* abruptly got up and went out of the warehouse. I had been wrong, it was bothering him, and I was now worried about him, but what could I do?

It was shortly after, that one night he and *Michael* came home late. *Christoph* was stone drunk, and the only reason that he was standing up, was that *Michael* was propping him up. I had seen my *Christoph* drunk before so this was not new, but it was also not normal. This was not good!

I really was not that mad at *Christoph* for drinking, but was disappointed in him for what the other men alleged. They told their wives that *Michael* and *Christoph* went off with one of those loose women. I can understand why *Michael* needed that, but why did my dear *Christoph* break his vows and go off with her? It hurts so much I cannot endure thinking about it. How could he?

Michael swears that my *Christoph* only foolishly gambled away our money, and did not lie with another woman. He may be telling the truth, and if so, I am greatly relieved at this good news. A great weight is off my heart! Strange, here I am happy that my *Christoph* only lost some of our money. I should be furious about that! Men!

After finally about four weeks, *Herr Balzer Barthuli* announced that we were leaving in a few days. He said that it should be about a two-week voyage to Russland, and that we needed to go out and shop for food for our families to last at least that long, maybe longer. He gave what some called 'butter money' of forty-eight groschen for each family to buy brötchen, biscuits, pickled meat, beer, wine and French brandy for the trip.

I would do our shopping tomorrow, and in a few days, we would be on the ship to Russland. Life is getting better every day, and things are looking up again.

Before we leave though, I have one task to do. I must have a talk with our good friend, *Herr Michael Grün!*

OLD CHOICES

♦MICHAEL GRÜN♦

Wulf Warehouse XXVI

I was in the city again with the mass of people racing around chasing their dreams. The variety of aromas from the baking kuchen and brötchen (cakes and rolls) to the stench of the nachttopf (chamber pots) brought back many childhood memories, good and bad.

Ahh, I have returned to city life, and a port city at that. Everyone knows that a port city offers the widest excesses of life, so many choices to make on whether to sin or not. That is why there are so many churches... to serve all those repentant, but very bad sinners. My motto is always 'Sin heute und bitten um Vergebung morgen (sin tonight and repent tomorrow)!"

Herr Hess was absolutely correct when he warned everyone, "Hold tight to your possessions and your money. Some living here may want your things for themselves." In a previous time in a different city, I was one of those on the prowl to steal the valuables from stupid and careless people.

As much as I respect *Christoph*, he is not equipped to deal with these city low-lifes... While he and his wife laughed about who would protect them and jokingly mentioned me, I do have the skills and knowledge needed to protect them. Experiences, good and bad, ready you for many things in life. In my case, being a low-life shady character in my past, wholly prepared me for the here and now in Lübeck.

While I was happy to be off the road and no longer walking across the countryside, I was not impressed with the housing that our benefactors gave to us while we awaited transport to the new land. In fact, I was disappointed!

The harbor warehouses were overcrowded and filthy, infested with huge rats. While many of our fellow occupants were travelers like us, a large number of others were the people that *Herr Hess* had warned us of, scum just living here for any kind of frei shelter, and for the opportunity to take advantage of some of our careless travelers. Actually, I had better housing with a better class of scum while serving time in the jails.

It did not bother *Christoph* too much, but I could see that *Jacobina* was shocked and disappointed. This was way below her standards, but she gamely tried to arrange a temporary home for her *Christoph*, herself and me in a small corner of the filthy warehouse.

There was a communal kitchen on the floor of our warehouse. Here, the women of each family cooked their family's meals. I thought that *Jacobina* was going to faint when she saw the filth there.

I overheard her exclaim to herself, "Mein Gott, what is this" as *Jacobina* caught the putrid smell of the rat droppings everywhere mixed with the stink of old decayed food on the table and floor.

I saw her tremble for a second, and then recovering, *Jacobina* set out to talk with the other women about cleaning it up. Where just hours before was a pigsty, the women changed it into a useful and very clean kitchen area.

The men, including *Christoph* and myself, did have two important tasks. The first was to keep the rodent rats out and the second was to keep the human rats, the low-life scum of vagabonds and beggars, out! We easily rid the warehouse of both with enthusiasm, and soon we did not see many. Apparently, both type of rats decided to leave for easier living in filthier housing.

As for their second task, at first, we did not understand that our women felt that the local whores, who had followed us in, were not welcome. However, the family women insisted we throw out these 'Ladies' even if it was not to my liking. I actually had no stomach for doing this, but *Christoph* and the other married men supported it, at least in the presence of their unrelenting wives.

I mean these Ladies of the Night have to live also. I found it distasteful having to chase them out and tell them they were not welcome here. Many of them were quite pleasing to my eyes and very, very friendly! *Jacobina* and I did not share her opinion of these women, who knows what *Christoph* really thought. Whatever he thought, he wisely kept to himself.

After the women had cleaned up the area, and we cleaned out all the scum and less desirables, life returned almost to a normal level. All the women, including *Jacobina*, were much happier, and that meant the married men were happier, but to me, as a single man, this life was becoming boring.

Our benefactors appointed one man in each group as Vorsteher (Leader), depending on where we were eventually to settle. *Herr Balzer Barthuli*, a man we all respected from the village of Essen, led our group of families. He would inform us of what was going on, and how much longer we would be here. He also doled out a daily allowance to each of us. Every day, without fail and for doing absolutely nothing, I received eight groschen.

Christoph got eight groschen for himself and five groschen for *Jacobina*. This was supposed to be for daily food and drink, and necessities, but it was more than enough to live on and we always had money left over. Most of us just tucked it away for a 'rainy day' in our future travels.

We tried to be friendly with the locals of Lübeck, but the townspeople avoided us because someone had spread rumors that we were of the lowest social element of people. That was absolutely true in my case, but as for *Christoph* and *Jacobina* and the majority of the rest, they were all simple, good, virtuous GOD fearing people.

The days of waiting for transport turned into weeks of waiting. The women occupied their time with keeping their areas fit for living in spite of the environment. They cleaned and cooked from dawn to dusk, and sometimes longer. If they were not cleaning, they formed into little groups. That reminded me of the chicken-yard hens gathered together and clucking.

We did have an occasional break in our busy schedules, what with more marriages, more births, and more baptisms. These needed doing before we set off into the wilds of the new land. These were all good reasons for us to celebrate and enjoy life.

There was no real work for the men to do, and we were all bored out of our minds. That is just not right; men must have something to occupy their time. If not something good, then it will be something bad.

One can only sleep so long, or take so many walks outside. In fact, it was on one of those walks with *Christoph* and some of the other men that I recognized another way to occupy our time.

On one of our extended walks, I recognized one of the Ladies of the Night that I had personally escorted out of the warehouse. I had always thought about looking her up... and with GODs blessing, I now had the chance.

I made my excuses to break away from *Christoph* and the other men for a few minutes, and caught up with My Lady. She recognized me from the warehouse, but did not blame me for that. She asked, "How may I help you? Is there something on your mind?"

I replied, "You can help me, and yes, there are many things on my mind right now. But before we get to that, can you tell me where we might find some drink and maybe some gambling and whatever else?"

She looked surprised and said, "You are different from the rest of those men. Are you sure that you are one of them? I can show you everything you need, including where to find your drink and gambling, but are you sure that is really what you want?"

"Want, need, is there a difference?" I quickly replied.

She smiled widely and offered, "Just follow me, and we will find a place with all you want or need."

"I think some of my friends have wants and needs also. I would like to give them a chance to come with us," I added.

Again surprised, she replied, "I do not take them for that type.... yet maybe they will join us for some fun. Ask them." She remained where she was, while I returned to my fellow men.

I gathered my fellow men around and said, "This walk has made me thirsty. I have met someone who knows where we can get a refreshing bier or two. They also have some games for men. It is close by, who wants to join me?"

Some of the men, including *Christoph*, immediately said no and started to leave. Others indicated that they would come. It did take me a few minutes more to finally convince *Christoph* that it was only to have bier or two.

With me leading, *Christoph* and the others followed me to my Lady. When they saw her, they recognized her; almost all bolted and scurried back to their mommas at the warehouse.

Christoph started to leave, but hesitated and I assured him that it was only to have bier or two. Still wary, he came with us.

My Lady quickly led us to a building with a small Taverne sign outside. We entered into a large dark room filled with thick smoke and with the sounds of men heartily enjoying themselves. There were groups of men drinking and playing card games at the many tables, and other men drinking at the long bar. Occasionally over the noise of the men, we could hear the laughter of women. I nodded at My Lady, and motioned for her to give me a few minutes to settle my friends. She smiled and nodded back.

Christoph and I settled at the bar and ordered biers, and soon, we were quenching our thirst. After our long dry walk, the bier was delicious. We quickly finished those biers, and ordered two more. Thank GOD for that daily allowance that we had been squirreling away for a 'rainy day.' It was clear outside, but in here, it was definitely a 'rainy day.'

I told *Christoph*, "I have something to take care of by myself, and if he was alright, I would leave him here alone."

He was enjoying his bier, and said, "Go, do what you must. I will be just fine here, and will be so for a while."

With that, I was gone to join My Lady to... uhm... talk. We found a room in the back, and after moments of haggling, we worked out a mutual agreement on how to quench the rest of my needs. Soon I was much, much happier and slightly poorer, and she was slightly richer.

I am not sure how much time went by with My Lady, but when I eventually got back to the bar, *Christoph* had joined one of the card playing groups. While they were all friendly games, I noticed that there were groschen on the table.

Christoph must have had a few more biers. He was laughing and feeling happy. He also appeared to be losing all his groschen. A quick look around the table, and I knew he was being taken in by the local card scum.

I went over and whispered in his ear, "It is late and time for us to get back to *Jacobina*."

He pushed me away and said, "No, not yet." The others at the table frowned at me.

I ignored them and pulled *Christoph* up while whispering, "*Christoph*, now! We are leaving!" He looked at me, shrugged, and moved to leave.

The others at the table were not happy to see their sucker leave while he still had groschen, and rose to stop us. I stared at them, and in a low growl said, "Get out of our way! If you try to stop us, you will pay, and not in groschen."

The group hesitated, they were prepared to take a sucker for all he had, but they were not fighters. There would always be another game and another sucker.

We left quickly, and tried as best we could to walk back to the warehouse. There was no way that *Christoph* was going to sober up before getting back to *Jacobina*. We were in for it now.

Jacobina was waiting for us. The men who scurried back, told their wives who told the other men's wives. Humiliated in front of the other wives, *Jacobina* was furious with both of us.

She took *Christoph* and put him to bed. She gently whispered in his ear, "Sweet *Christoph*, you will pay later when you are sober enough to feel the pain!"

She then came to me and said, "I do not blame you. You are not a married man. You have not sworn a vow before GOD to be true to a wife. *Christoph* has, and now he has broken that vow." She began to cry; I hate it when they cry.

Thinking quickly, too quickly, I just said, "It was all my fault. I led *Christoph* there to drink, and encouraged him to stay." I hoped that this would stop her crying.

She just kept crying and between sobs said, "My *Christoph* broke his vow… he broke his vow. How could he?" Looking straight at me, she asked, "Did you force my *Christoph* to bed one of those whores?"

Dumbfounded, I realized that she was not upset about *Christoph* being drunk, but because she thought he had bedded down with one of the Ladies of the Night.

I quickly answered, "*Jacobina*, you are so wrong. Yes, *Christoph* went with me to the tavern and had some biers, but he never bedded another woman. I was the only one to do that. Honest truth, I was the only one. *Christoph* just drank some biers and played some card games."

Her crying instantly stopped. She believed me. Relief... I could relax now, as all was good. Good was short-lived.

Jacobina frowned at me and asked in low growl, "What kind of card games? How much did *Christoph* lose? Do we have any of our saved groschen left?"

How could I have been so dumb? I should not have mentioned the card games. We were both back in the fire now. Trying to squirm out of a bad situation, I calmly answered *Jacobina* with, "He only lost a little. In fact, since it was my fault leading him to this temptation, I will share all my savings with you and *Christoph*. We will just lump it together for all three of us."

Jacobina still frowned, but agreed my offer was fair. However, *Christoph* and I must promise never to go back there again. *Christoph* was unconscious, so he was not promising anything tonight. As for me, I was probably going back to My Lady again, especially if we stayed here for much longer.

To calm things down with *Jacobina*, I simply lied, '*Jacobina*, I promise!"

She accepted that, and went back to tend *Christoph*. I thought to myself, "These married women will believe anything."

The next morn was not a good time for *Christoph*. Not only did his head pound and his stomach cramp, his *Jacobina* was furious with him. One minute she was comforting him, the next she was yelling at him. He could do nothing other than lower his head, and take it.

When he finally felt a little better, *Jacobina* demanded to see how many of the saved groschen he had left. He brought out what he had, and she saw he had lost over half of their savings, grabbed the money away from him, and put the remainder in her bodice between her breasts for safekeeping. She would keep it all from now on. *Jacobina* came over to me and put out her hand. I just looked at her and pretended not to understand.

"*Michael*," she said sternly, "Give me your money as you promised last night. We will put it all together and share it for the three of us."

I resisted slightly, but realizing that she would never let up, reluctantly gave her all my groschen. My money, now our money, also went in her bodice for safekeeping. Satisfied, she went back to tending *Christoph*.

Eventually after a few days, life returned to normal with *Jacobina*. Even with all the trouble from that day, I still say it was worth it, at least my part of it. More boring days passed with nothing for us to do while we waited for transport to our future. It had been around five weeks, and was now the beginning of October.

Christoph did revisit the tavern occasionally for a bier, but never got drunk again. If *Jacobina* ever found out about his visits, she never mentioned it. I did break my promise to *Jacobina*. I am only a man, single at that, what else could you expect. I was just trying to make up for the next long dry spell. Besides, My Lady was really good looking, and very athletic, and a lot of fun.

Finally, *Herr Balzer Barthuli* came to us and announced, "We will be leaving in a few days. The voyage should take no more than two weeks, but if we encounter bad weather, it may take twice that long. I am giving you extra money to purchase enough food for your family's needs on this trip. Each person will receive 'butter money' of an extra sixteen groschen to buy food supplies such as brötchen, biscuits, pickled meat, beer, wine and French brandy for the fourteen-day sea voyage. You may want to buy extra food in case the trip is longer."

On the night before *Jacobina* was to go shopping for our food, she came over to me and said, "*Michael,* you try to be a good man and a good friend. However, you may not be cut out for our simple lives. Sadly, the old saying, 'In der Brut verdorbe' (It was spoiled in the brood or from the very start) may describe you."

She continued, "You do seem to fit better in the city. *Christoph* and I will welcome your company on the rest of the trip, but will not think ill of you if you choose to stay in Lübeck. If you do stay with us, you must promise me that you will not talk my *Christoph* into sinful things, and this time, I will expect you to keep your promise. Not like the last promise that you broke about seeing your whore. Please let us know tomorrow."

All this time I thought I had her fooled. I had a fitful nights' sleep trying to know what was best to do. It all came down to the one simple truth that *Jacobina* had said. I am really not cut out for their simple devout lives, and I am down deep a sinful city boy. Maybe I was spoiled from the start.

The next morn I sat with *Christoph* and *Jacobina* and told them I would not be traveling on with them. We all decided to keep this a secret from anyone else.

Jacobina took all the 'butter money' and some of the pooled money, and went out and bought enough for three people for twenty-one days. This would make all believe that they knew nothing, if any questions were asked after I was discovered gone.

The night before we were all to board the ship, I discreetly said my good-byes to *Jacobina* and *Christoph*. *Jacobina* gave me much of what was left of our pooled money to help me live on.

We all went to bed, and later that night while they were sleeping, I moved on. I really did not think anyone would come looking for me. I had made up the *Michael Grün* that signed the Contract, and as there was no real *Michael Grün*, there was no Contract. At least that is how I looked at it.

As I left the warehouse and walked down the cold dark street, I again became *Nobody*, just one of the many put out on the road by the forever wars, my fellow man's greed and jealousy, and fate. I never looked back.

Where I came from, who I am, and what drove me to this place I will never forget. It is the year of our LORD MDCCLXIV (1764) early in the month of October, and today, I now start a new life once again.

10 DEPARTURE

◆JACOBINA KARL◆

Wulf Warehouse XXVI

Herr Balzer Barthuli woke us up early this morning. This was the day for us to board the ship to Russland. To dispel any suspicion about *Christoph* and me knowing, I asked around if anyone had seen *Michael Grün* this morning. I even had *Christoph* report him missing to *Herr Balzer Barthuli*.

Loudly, so others could hear, I mentioned to *Christoph*, "I hope he did not get drunk with that woman again, or he may have gotten in trouble at those card games." Not a lie, but not the truth; I would pray for our LORD to forgive me later.

My words spread like wildfire, and soon everyone was sure that *Michael Grün* had run into some serious trouble and would not be able to make the transport. *Christoph* and I made sure that we appeared distressed and worried that he was missing. No one suspected anything.

After a quick but thorough search for him, everyone gave up looking and returned to preparing to leave. *Herr Balzer Barthuli* led us away from our horrible home in the warehouse, and down the streets to the harbor dock. One by one, we loaded on to the ship as they checked our names off a list.

Our ship, named 'Man and Woman' seemed so large while we were waiting on the dock. Now aboard, it was crowded with people and crew. Someone said that there were over one hundred of us aboard, all heading to Russland.

Even while tied to the dock, the ship rocked with the waves. Alarmed, all I wanted to do was get back on solid ground. That could not happen and I became frightened once more. I whispered to *Christoph*, "Husband, I am afraid. Please hold me until I feel better." Back in his strong and comforting arms, I felt protected and safe.

He smiled quietly said to me, "Im Dunkle is jeder stump a wolf (In the darkness, every stump is a wolf, imagining danger)!" He was right, and I laughed, and soon felt better.

It would have been even better if our friend *Michael Grün* was here with us, but our *Michael* is no more, and is only a fleeting memory for us now. Soon, we will not even remember his face.

DAMN THE BALTIC SEA

♦CHRISTOPH KARL♦

Aboard the ship 'Man and Woman' as it leaves the Port of Lübeck

Jacobina stayed in my arms as the ship left harbor. We walked the deck and watched the waves cross the water. We listened to the squawk of the gulls diving for food. At first, it was enjoyable, but eventually, the waves became worse and the crew ordered all of us below decks.

Down below decks, the air was moist and close and, with all of us crowded in, quickly became oppressive even with the cold wind above. Some of our fellow travelers had already become sick; many could not even stand up as the ship rolled in the waves.

Our only chance of good air was from the portholes, but the crew closed them to keep out the crashing water from the waves. This was not a good start for our trip. If all the following days are like this, many of us will not survive.

GOD or luck smiled on us, the strong waves left, and they again allowed us up on deck. While it was colder, the fresh air up there was so much better than the dank stale air below. We did have to stay out of the way of the working sailors, and *Jacobina* and I found a quiet out-of the-way place to settle in.

We remained up on the deck night and day, as long as we could; only going down below decks to the bad air when forced to either by order or bad weather, or when it was just too bitterly cold.

Many of our group chose to mostly stay down below, and soon became very weak and sick. When we had to be down below, we always found a small space away from those sick and just huddled together. Some of our fellow travelers had made it all this way only to die at sea, with only a few kind words said before the crew cast their bodies into the sea. *Jacobina* and I were lucky so far, and hoped to stay well.

Fourteen days had gone by and still we had not reached port. We walked that deck at least a thousand times. Many of our group was running out of food, and most of the water was becoming bad.

To make a bad situation even worse, the days and nights just kept getting colder as we sailed northward. All suffered from the gloomy and overcast days, and the cold north wind.

We both wished we had purchase some heavier clothes or coats back in Lübeck. We were not alone, as everyone felt cold and wished they had warmer clothes too.

The Captain told all of us that unfavorable winds slowed our arrival at port, but I wonder. Luckily, for those out of food, the Captain was willing to sell part of his cargo, which seemed to be mostly bread, biscuits, pickled meat, bier, wine and French brandy. Of course, since we were at sea, and he must profit, his prices were five times the cost back on land.

I thanked GOD that *Jacobina* had the good sense to purchase us extra food and drink. We had more than enough, and gave away some to our less prepared travelers.

On the evening of the twenty-first day, we were up on the freezing deck when the Captain announced that we would make the port of Кронштадт (Kronshtadt), Russland (Kronstadt, Russia) tomorrow.

Shivering from the bitter cold, *Jacobina* and I hugged each other in quiet celebration. Most everyone else was too weak or too sick to celebrate, or care, at all. The bitter north wind soon ended even our quiet celebration, and forced us back below decks again into our small space. Tonight though, the bitter cold tortured all of us even down here, and it was not going to be good night for getting any sleep.

I held my *Jacobina* close to warm and comfort her. I whispered into her ear, "Tomorrow we will reach solid land and we will be off this ship at last. We will be able to breathe fresh air again. We will be able to sleep in a warm bed, and get far from all these sick people. You will see that everything will be better tomorrow."

I hope she believes me, and I desperately hope I am right.

11 OUR NEW COUNTRY

♠CHRISTOPH KARL♠

Кронштадт (Kronshtadt) on Kotlin Island, Russland

Jacobina and I were almost hysterically overjoyed at the ship docking. As soon as the crew let us, we pushed our way through the crowd and scrambled to get up on the deck and see this new land.

We were surprised that there was snow on the deck, and even more surprised when we looked out at and saw nothing but snow and ice covered land as far as we could see. *Jacobina* and I turned and looked at each other, both suddenly understanding that we would need much, much warmer clothes than what we were wearing.

Our benefactors must have already known we would not come prepared for as we stepped on land, they wrapped each of us in thick fur coats. Still very cold, but quickly warming and so happy to be on solid ground and have some space to move.

Hurriedly, they grouped all of us together, encircled by men in uniforms armed with rifles. With wide eyes, *Jacobina*, held tightly to me and asked, "Who are these men? What is going to happen?"

Fortifications at Khronstadt on Kotlin Island

I had no idea, but did not want to scare her worse than she already was, and confidently answered, "They are here to make sure we do not fall or get lost." Not believing me, her forehead furrowed as she looked up at me, but did not say anything.

The armed soldiers formed us up two-by-two, and with soldiers on all sides, our rear and front, we walked for a few minutes up the icy and slippery road to a large stone building. Through a door, not knowing what to expect, we first encountered a blast of warm air.

We were so relieved to be warm again; we all relaxed and basked in the heat in spite of the soldiers surrounding us. We joined in a slowly moving line and once checked off the list, they led us to rows of long one story wooden barracks. These would be our new homes for a while. Mercifully, just like the larger building, a blazing hot stove also warmed each barracks. Thank the LORD, as the bitter cold and wind outside was unbearable.

Over the next few days, they carefully inspected our documents, and then inspected them again, and questioned and interrogated us, and examined and prodded to insure we were good and healthy people.

Those found sick, they quickly moved them away to a hospital in St. Petersburg. Those found to be criminals or unacceptable, they either them sent back or sent them to one of their military prisons. Luckily, we were neither sick, nor unacceptable, and not deemed criminals.

Just as we were beginning to enjoy living in our warm barracks, *Herr Balzer Barthuli* came in and announced that today, we would leave the island for the mainland.

Again, they grouped us all together, and encircled us with Russischen (Russian) soldiers armed with rifles. As before, the armed soldiers formed us up two-by-two and with soldiers on both sides, at our rear and front, we walked for a few minutes down the same icy and slippery road back to the docks.

They quickly loaded all of us onto ten small boats for the short ride to the mainland. We made good time in crossing and in only a short time, our boats docked on land.

Again, we stood in a slow moving line surrounded by soldiers. Once checked off another list, they led us to wagons driven by bearded Russischen teamsters. This next ride was to somewhere they called Oraniyenbaum (Oranienbaum).

Jacobina and I huddled together under the warm blankets they had given everybody. As we rode, we stared out at the strange buildings and the Russisch people we passed along the way.

The Russischen teamsters and other Russische men we saw, with their wild unkempt beards, immediately caught our notice. We all just stared.

Jacobina whispered to me, "They look so much like wild men."

She was right; they did look very much like wild men. Had we come to the end of civilized people? It was something to think on.

I saw one sign that read Ломоносов; I asked another traveler on the wagon what it said and he pronounced it as Oraniyenbaum. This Russische language made no sense at all.

I found that arriving in a new land with strange sights and customs is exciting, but not being able to read or speak their language, forced to make hand gestures and sounds like a child to let them know what you need, is unbearably frustrating and humiliating.

Ломоносов

♦CHRISTOPH KARL♦

Abandoned Army Camp, Ломоносов (Oraniyenbaum), one day ride west of Sankt-Peterburg, Russland

As we arrived in Ломоносов (Oraniyenbaum), they immediately took us to our temporary housing in rickety old wood barracks, formerly occupied by Russische Army soldiers.

Here we would stay as long as it took to sort out everything, and anything, needed by the Government. Typical as with anything our benefactors provided, this temporary housing was filthy. Either the standards our Deutschen parents taught us are much too high, or there are no standards of any kind for cleanliness in this country.

As our women had been through this before, they quickly began earnestly cleaning and arranging what little we had.

I overheard my *Jacobina* comment to one of the other women, "If this keeps up, we will have cleaned our way from Lübeck to the Volga River, one filthy hovel at a time, and this country will finally for once, be clean." The other women just grumbled and nodded in agreement.

More emigration paperwork had to be completed, and that meant an interpreter that spoke both our language and Russe, had to question each family... there were few interpreters and this process was slow and took much time... time we spent waiting in more lines.

Our benefactors gave tickets to *Herr Balzer Barthuli* to handout to obtain new much warmer Russische clothing. While it was much warmer, unfortunately, when we put on this Russische clothing, it was hard to tell our women from our men, or our men from our women! All those curves that we Deutsche men value in our women disappeared in a lumpy mass. We might as well have been looking at men... That is what our women looked like, like us, more ugly men! How enjoyable was that?

In fact, after changing into her new warmer Russische wear, *Jacobina* looked around at the other women and frowned, and said to me, "It is so nice to be warm again, but we look horrible! I wonder how Russische women even attract their men when they look like this. It is amazing they even have any children…"

I laughed, and replied too loudly, "Maybe most Russische women are so ugly that their men do not want to see them, and their children just come about because they are so cold they have to do something in bed together to just keep warm."

The other men and women overheard me, and much laughter erupted all around us. For a very short time, smiles replaced the frowns from the troubles we had gone through.

The days blurred into one another with more paperwork and more questions, we all wondered how long we must stay here. Finally, on day seventeen, *Herr Balzer Barthuli* came to us and said, "We have just a few more questions to answer and choices to make, and will most likely leave on our way tomorrow."

We all grumbled, and someone asked, "Questions, they have asked everything; what more could they want to know about us?"

Herr Barthuli shrugged and honestly replied, "I know not."

During the next questioning, the interpreter ever so slowly moved from family to family. When he got to us, he asked, "What trade do you want to perform in your new colony, and what colony do you want to live in?"

He showed us a map with names written in Russisch of an area that we did not recognize, and had no knowledge of. How could we choose? I brought this to his attention, but received only a bored and indifferent blank stare.

I knew what I had done all my life and was good at, and truthfully answered, "I would like to tend the vines, but I do not know where we should live."

He frowned and studied my face as if he did not understand, and then asked, "What is this tend the vines? Uh, it matters not. I do not have this tend the vines as a trade. As you do not know what you want to do, I will choose your trade and your colony for you. In your new colony, we only need one trade. You will be a Farmer. That is what we need you to be!"

Upset, I slowly replied, "No, not a Farmer... Grapes; I help the grape vines grow well and produce the best grapes of all. That is my trade!"

Already bored with this talk and ready to move on to the next family, he looked at me and rolled his eyes, and then slowly replied in a monotone voice, "Yes, I have put you down as a Farmer! That is what we need you to be in the colony I chose for you, and that is what you will be! We are finished."

He started to move away, but I was not finished and grabbed his arm. He jerked back with a startled look. Now that I had his attention again, I slowly repeated myself to him, "No! I am not a Farmer... I am a vine tender, my father was a vine tender, and my father's father was a vine tender. The *Karl* men will always tend the vines! I help the grape vines grow well and can produce the best grapes. That is my trade, and that is what I will do! Do you understand now? And what choice of colonies do we have?"

The interpreter slowly shook his head, deeply sighed and sternly replied, "We do not care what you used to be, and we do not really care what you want to be... We do not care what your father or father's father did in the past... We do not care what *Karl* men will always be... We only care what we want you to be! There is only one colony at this time to send you too, and all that go to this colony are Farmers. See, there is nothing on this form to mark except Farmers!" He pointed to the paper in his hand.

Not believing him, I did look at the paper, and as he said, there was only one trade listed and it read 'Farmers." Not really believing my eyes, I asked him, "All of us our going to be Farmers, and there is only one colony?"

He smiled widely, relieved that the dumb Deutscher finally understood, and replied, "Yes, all Farmers and the colony I chose for you... the only colony listed on this paper."

Angry, I asked him, "Why did you even ask us if we had no choice of colonies and if all will be Farmers no matter what we answer?"

He smiled widely again, then shrugged and replied, "Oh, that is easy. The regulation requires me to question you on your choice of trades and colony. I have now done that."

I quickly added, "But you have not recorded our answers of our choices!"

He chuckled and then answered, "Yes that is very true. The regulation only directs me to ask, it does not direct me to put your choice of colony down or to change what trades we need in your designated colony. One last time, as I have already tried to make you understand, you will be a Farmer in the colony I have chosen for you!" Completely satisfied with his explanations, and completely finished discussing this with me, he turned to question the next family.

His logic was sound, even if it was completely crazy. I was still not satisfied and started to reach for him to argue back, but *Jacobina* grabbed on to me and whispered a warning, "You are making a scene and the guards are now closely watching you! Do not get us in trouble with these Russen. We can change your trade later."

"Later when" I thought, but she was right, the Army Guards were frowning and now staring at me. I remained quiet.

The interpreter moved on to talk with the rest of the families, and eventually finished. He asked all to be quiet and with a wide smile, announced, "Congratulations new people, you are lucky that you have all been chosen as Farmers in the colony I have chosen for you. Good Luck!" With that, and again very satisfied with himself, he smiled widely, bowed to us, and hurried out of the room.

No one but the Farmers liked his words, but we all knew we could do nothing to change it. That night was not a good night to sleep, as everything that had gone on earlier that day was the cause of much arguing and discussion between each husband and wife.

THE CONTRACT

The next morning, they gathered us together for breakfast, and then moved us to a large building with many small tables with a man seated behind each table.

A Russische Army Officer came in the room and demanded for quiet. He continued and said, "People, there is one final requirement you complete before you leave on your journey. You must sign your contract with our Government." He pulled out a long paper and began reading it slowly and carefully in Deutsch to us:

"Each colonist will sign this Contract and Agreement that regulates all the goods and services already, or in the future, provided by, and due for reimbursement to, the Government of Imperial Russland, and all the resultant rights and duties of each signatory colonist."

"Each of you is already in debt to the Crown and Government of Imperial Russland for all the money already advanced to you, the cost of the food we have provided you, and the cost of the comfortable housing we have sheltered you in."

There was much snickering from our group at this point, but the Officer either did not care or ignored it. Without any reaction, he continued to drone on:

"Also, there is the cost of the clothes we have given you, and the cost of all the transportation we have provided from your meeting place."

Loud gasps of shock from our group, but again the Officer either did not care or ignored it. Without any reaction, he continued to drone on:

"We will also provide even more food and clothes, and transportation and shelter as you move farther on. At Saratov, each colonist will receive money on arrival for purchases; animals, implements, home, barn, and seed. All these costs and money and any payments you colonists, yours heirs and or successors have or will receive in Catherine II's Imperial Russland domain must be repaid to her after ten years in three installments. No interest is payable"

"Further, each colonist must then also pay a fifth of all his assets acquired in the first five years after arrival, to the Crown. If he leaves after only six to 10 years, then only a tenth is payable. Relief from all monetary taxation and obligatory rendering of good and/or services to the Russische Crown for the next 30 years is granted. The date on which debt repayment must begin will be determined later."

"In your colony, Russische law dictates that primogeniture applies where only one son, namely the oldest, becomes sole heir. This ensures that every father knowing this law will make every effort to teach all his children a trade from infancy."

The grumbling and discussion in our group rose in response to each word he now spoke. Finally, he became silent, lowered the paper and stood silent for a time as we continued to complain among ourselves.

Losing patience with us, he looked at the ceiling, then looked out at us and yelled, "Silence! I have had enough of your whining and complaining. You will all stand there and listen without any comment. Silence now!"

Not a sound was made in the building, and he smiled, satisfied that he had restored our attention to what he was reading to us, and continued slowly on:

"The obligations of the Russische Crown to each settler are hereby declared: Freedom of religion and construction of properly built state schools for every religion; Medical services are guaranteed; and Travel out of the country is permitted subject to conditions."

"Each family will receive thirty desjatines (about seventy-two acres) of land, fields, pastures, woods and the like of best arable quality suited to maintain the entire family on a hereditary leasehold basis. This land will not be split up, sold or mortgaged and remains municipal property. Use of the land assigned was to be fifteen desjatines for agriculture, five as pasture, five for dwelling and garden, plus five desjatines of woodland per family."

"Allocation of settlement areas on the Volga will be in circular areas with a diameter of sixty to seventy versts (forty to forty-six miles) in each of which one hundred families will be settled. The number of colonies to be founded is fifty-two on the mountain side and fifty-two on the pasture side of the river."

"In return, Colonists will behave as loyal subjects of the Crown and Catherine II of Russland. Each will adhere to Russische laws and customs, including those applying to the colonies."

"Each colony will have the right of self-government, and each colonist will swear on arrival that he or she will adhere to the laws of the area, and to any future provisions of Colonial Law."

He slowly lowered the paper, obviously finished reading, again smiled and asked, "Do you all understand?"

"As the contract is perfectly clear and precise in all explanations and requirements, I am sure there are no questions," he added.

Everyone looked around at each other. We all knew that none of this was on the Contracts we signed with the recruiters back in our homeland. But who would have the courage to defy this Government. I started to speak, but Jacobina put her hand over my mouth and whispered in my ear, "NEIN!"

Herr Balzer Barthuli, slowly made his way to the front to speak and said, "Respectfully, and we do not want it to seem like we are defying your wishes, but these requirements are all new to us. None of these requirements are written on the Contracts we signed at the start of the trip, and none of the recruiters representing your Empress ever mentioned these requirements. In truth, we were all told that all our travel costs and our new land and our new homes would all be free and cost us absolutely nothing."

As a group, everyone quietly agreed, and said, "Ja (Yes)!"

The Army Officer stared intently at *Herr Balzer Barthuli* for what seemed like minutes, then slowly looked around the room at all of us, and the said, "Very good. I see no hands and hear no questions! Good, each family must move to a table and sign your contract, and then you will be able to move on. If you choose not to sign, and understand there is no acceptable reason to not sign, your whole family will be taken into custody here by my soldiers until you repay back to the Crown all that we have so generously paid out on your behalf. If you do not have the money to pay back the Crown, you and your family will work in our prison for a long, long time! Now move to the tables and sign, if you so choose!"

Jacobina and I quickly moved to a table and looked down at the printed contract, but as neither of us could read, we had no idea what it actually stated. The seated man asked me my name and my wife's name, and wrote them down on the Contract.

He offered me a quill to sign my mark. I hesitated in signing, not sure what he wrote. I looked at *Jacobina* who was also confused. "What choice do we have at this point," I thought to myself.

If we refused to sign, we would be prisoners here until we could repay them for all they had already provided. How could we repay them if we were prisoners here? "No choice at all,' I said to *Jacobina* as I put my "x" next to where he indicated he had written my name. It looked like 'Карл Кристоф' and could have been anyone's name for all I knew.

I gave the quill to *Jacobina*, and the clerk pointed to where we hoped her name was. She put her "x" next to what looked like 'Карл Йацобина'.

The clerk dusted some powder on our signatures, and rolled up the Contract. He nodded to us and waved his hand, and a soldier quickly appeared to lead us outside to the wagons with the wild looking Russischen teamsters waiting to transport us.

Once all had finished signing, and all did, and loading on to the wagons, we proceeded back to the very dock we had previously arrived on not quite two weeks earlier.

Санкт-Петербург

We all boarded a small ship, and then were led below decks. We sailed east towards a large city that that a Russischer sailor called Санкт-Петербург, or in Deutsch, Sankt-Peterburg (St. Petersburg). As the ship rocked and wallowed in the waves, we worried about our future, but looked forward to when we again docked.

Everyone gathered up their few possessions and prepared to get off when an old white-haired Russische Army Officer with three younger soldiers came down below decks.

He stood before us and announced, "I am Подполковник (Lieutenant Colonel) *Chichelnitsky* of the Imperial Russische Army. You will all be staying down here on this ship temporarily while all your entry documents are rechecked and travel arrangements for going on are completed."

Herr Balzer Barthuli jumped forward and curtly asked *Lieutenant Colonel Chichelnitsky* of the Imperial Russische Army, "We are tired of all this processing and request you continue our travel on to our colony on the Volga River. If that is not possible, how long will we be here? If more than few hours, we insist you quickly provide food, water, blankets, and bedding. We demand these things!"

Lieutenant Colonel Chichelnitsky looked directly at *Herr Barthuli*, but seemed to stare right through him. He very slowly asked *Herr Barthuli*, "You are the leader of the group, yes? What is your name?"

Herr Barthuli straightened up proudly, and confidently answered for all to hear, "I am *Herr Balzer Barthuli*! Yes, I am the Vorsteher of this group!"

Lieutenant Colonel Chichelnitsky continued to stare intently at *Herr Barthuli*. With obvious contempt in his voice, he replied, "*Vorsteher Barthuli*, you and this group will be here as long as I want! None of you is in a position to insist or demand anything! You are no longer guests; you will all soon be subjects of the Crown. Subjects of the Crown demand nothing; Subjects of the Crown are always satisfied with what our benevolent Crown chooses to provide them. These are the rules of our society! As you are new to our ways, I will overlook your insolence this time. I will have what you asked for provided to you immediately."

He continued, "A word of caution to all; do not ever demand anything of me again. Your insolence will merit only swift and harsh punishment. You *Vorsteher,*

Barthuli they call you, you are only the leader as long as it suits me. Do you all understand my words and my warning?"

Shocked at what we all had heard, *Herr Barthuli* turned white and remained silent, and then slowly nodded his head up and down to answer yes. Like all the other men in the room, this insult to one of our fellow travelers and our leader, did not sit well with me.

I started to move towards this rude Russischen Officer, but *Jacobina* tightly clamped on to my arm and kept me from moving. I quickly looked at her to find out why she would not let me go. She silently, but vehemently shouted to me, "NEIN!"

I stopped, and did not move. She did not let go of my arm, and if anything, gripped it tighter. I could feel her fingernails cutting in to my skin.

Lieutenant Colonel Chichelnitsky looked around the room slowly at all of us, and then continued, "Do all of you understand that I make the rules and you must follow them without comment or argument? If you do not follow my instructions, you will not proceed on to your new homes, but will find a permanent home in our local тюрьмы (prison)! My soldiers here will be more than happy to escort you and your families away to that place right now!"

Another outright threat! Angry, I again started to move, but as before, *Jacobina* used all her strength to hold me back. Her fingernails were like little knives cutting in to my skin.

Finally finished with his announcement of his rules, *Lieutenant Colonel Chichelnitsky* turned, and followed by the three soldiers, returned up the steps to the main deck.

I was furious with my wife, but when I looked around, the same thing was happening with each of the couples. Each wife had prevented their husband from challenging the Officer and possibly finding out first hand if the horrors told about Russische prisons was true.

Jacobina had finally let go of my arm, and had her head down to accept whatever rebuke, physical or verbal, I might give her. I looked down at my arm and saw that she had actually drawn blood with her nails. I was angry at that and because she overridden my choice in public. She had challenges my male authority. However, as insulted as my pride was, I knew she was right.

I gently lifted her chin and whispered to her, "Thank you! I love you," and hugged her to me. Tears were in her eyes, and a smile was on her face.

We gathered around *Herr Barthuli* and offered our support and sympathy to let him know we supported him.

He said to all, "There is no problem. We must stand firm to get what we need, but it would be best if we ask, and not demand in the future, Ja?"

We all answered in one voice, "Ja."

Within minutes, as *Lieutenant Colonel Chichelnitsky* had said, all that we requested came down to us. We did the best to make this belly of the ship our new home. We settled in as best we could for who knew how long.

Cramped and packed together, angry from the insulting treatment, we began to bond into a group, united by this trouble, out of the individuals we were just hours ago. This may have been the very start of our Colony society, though we did not know this at the time.

Two weeks passed while the Russische Government delayed our moving on. One of our group became ill, and their whole family was taken away, never to be seen again.

When we asked about them, they told us that the ill and their families were under the care of a Dr. Prais in their хоспитал (hospital) near the Alexander Nevsky monastery, and might join us sometime in the future. We wondered to ourselves if this were true, or if we truly would ever see them again. Sadly, we never did.

They let us leave the ship during the day, but we were always required to be back on board well before sunset. On one of these walks on a bitterly cold, but clear, day with *Jacobina*, I said to her, "Dear wife, I am so sorry for what I have put you through these past few months. I was so wrong to drag you away from our life and home."

Jacobina looked up at me and said, "Shh, my dear *Christoph*. Stop this nonsense at once! This is an adventure. It has been both good and bad at times, but as long as we are together, all will be fine." We walked arm-in-arm, silent, nothing more needed to be said.

THESE DEUTSCHEN

◆LIEUTENANT COLONEL CHICHELNITSKY◆

Kontor of the Guardianship Chancery of Oversight of Foreigners

Official Report

19.11.1764

I hereby enter this report into the official record this 19th day of November in the year of our LORD one thousand seven hundred sixty-four.

The orientation of the group of Deutsche colonists brought here is complete. Oath and assignment to Lt. Von Ditmarr for transport remains.

The group consists of the following Colonists and families where shown: 12 families: 19 males, 19 females, 19 Reformed, 19 Lutheran, 11 farmers, 1 woodworker.

Colonist names: Balzer Barthuli 38, wife Anna Margarita 40, two daughters Elizabeth 12, Appollonia 10; Phillipp Decker 43, wife Jacobina 34, children Johannes two months, daughter Maria Katharina 2; Jakob Scheck 48, wife Katharina 43, son Jacob 11; Heinrich Heft 30, wife Katharina 23, with Heft: Valentine Haberman, 16; Leonhard Volz 33, wife Margarita 34, son George Thomas 15, Wilhelm 4, Elizabeth 9, Barbara 1; Ludwig Tehele, 32, wife Anna Barbara 33, son Johann Michael 7, daughter Eva Catharina Barbara 1; Christoph Karl 36, wife Jacobina 30; Georg Robertus 25, wife Appolina 33, daughters Katharina 6, Jacobina 2; Jacob Dittmer 61, wife Anna Maria 51, son Johan Martin 14, daughter Anna Elizabeth 11; Wagner, Heinrich 32, wife Dorothea 30; Weiss, Johann 41; and Bruckmann, Peter 21.

Our Medical Clinic examinations found all healthy and fit to continue. With the exception of Jacob Dittmer 61, wife Anna Maria 51, all appear to be young enough to have good chance to survive the expected harsh conditions.

The group still keeps the typical Deutsche arrogance towards us, and has yet to understand they are nothing more than Crown subjects that must do as we wish or command. Civil disobedience is not likely. In public exchange with their Vorsteher Balzer Barthuli, I reinforced that he served at our choice and that they all must obey as directed or suffer severe consequences.

Transport by riverboat and guided wagon (or sleigh if deep snow) caravan proceeds on 21 November in the year of our LORD one thousand seven hundred sixty-four (1764) for the Colony Голыи Карамыш or Goloi Karamysh.

Planned arrival date at their assigned Colony is late August of next year (1765).

Lt. Von Ditmarr from our Sankt-Peterburg detachment will assume control of the Colonists and with a squad of ten soldiers guide them to their new Colony.

Lt. Von Ditmarr from our Sankt-Peterburg detachment will provide to the Colonist group protection from any irate Russische peasants or robbers encountered along the way. He will also enforce good order and peace by the Deutschen at all times.

Written by me on this 19th day of November in the year of our LORD one thousand seven hundred sixty-four (1764) in the Kontor of the Guardianship Chancery of Oversight of Foreigners, Headquarters, Sankt-Peterburg.

Signed,

Ivan Chichelnitsky
Подполковник, Imperial Russische Army
Kontor of Guardianship Chancery
of Oversight of Foreigners
Headquarters, Sankt-Peterburg

THE OATH

◆JACOBINA KARL◆

Aboard ship docked on the reka Bol'shaya Neva along Admiralteyskaya Naberezhnaya (river Bol'shaya Neva along Admiralty Embankment Street), Sankt-Peterburg, Russland

Early one morning, *Lieutenant Colonel Chichelnitsky* and a squad of ten armed soldiers escorted us off the ship to a nearby Kirche. Strange, as it was not the Sabbath!

An interpreter arrived and explained that we would now all swear an oath to our new government, the Russische Crown, as required by the Law.

The interpreter continued and warned us, "The honorable *Lieutenant Colonel Chichelnitsky* and his soldiers will remain and be available to assist me with the swearing of the oath as needed, or to remove any that decline to swear their allegiance to Her Imperial Highness, most merciful great Lady, Empress Catherine Alexeevna, Autocrat of all Russland."

The meanings of his words were clear enough, and all understood his warning perfectly.

A man of the Kirche stood up to speak, and said, "I am Pastor Johann Christian König. I will say the words of this oath and you will each repeat after me all the words aloud. I say again, you will each repeat after me all the words aloud! Do you all understand?"

We all nodded our heads in agreement.

Pastor König replied, "Good then… We will start! He continued, "On this day the 20th Of November in the year of our LORD one thousand seven hundred sixty-four (1764), I do promise and bow to Almighty God before his Holy Gospel do promise and bow to Almighty God before his Holy Gospel and do declare that I desire and by duty to Her Imperial Highness, my most merciful great Lady, Empress Catherine Alexeevna, Autocrat of all Russland, and the most beloved son of Her Imperial Highness, Lord Tsarevich and Grand Prince Paul Petrovich, legal heir to the all-Russisch throne, to truly and without deceit serve and assume all duty, pledging my life to the last drop of my blood, and to the high autocracy of her Imperial Highness, all strength and power belonging there unto by right and prerogative legitimately and to be legitimized at least in thought power and possibility and to warn and defended by any measure to enable all that I may do in the service of Her Imperial Highness and for the use of the state in all cases. I will defend the interests of Her Majesty against harm and loss without report immediately, and will not only declare it immediately; will take all measures to prevent such and not allowed to be completed. All that is entrusted to me in secret I will strictly keep, and any rank placed upon me such as this, general or special, as determined from time to time in the name of Her Imperial Highness from those authorities appointed above me, all instructions, regulations, and decrees I will upon advice make correction, and for my profit, friendship, virtue will neither in enmity nor against my duty make any other oath; and will conduct myself as a good and faithful slave and subject of Her Imperial Highness that I am; and before God and His terrible judgment I may always give my reply that the LORD GOD will assist me in body and in soul. In conclusion of this solemn oath, I kiss the Word (Bible) and the Cross of my Savior. Amen."

We slowly repeated all the words as spoken by the Pastor, or at least I am sure that *Christoph* and I did. Some around us may have only moved their lips without saying the words aloud, thinking that an oath not actually spoken aloud was not an oath.

I knew better from my Lutheran teachings… An oath under GOD, said aloud or not, is still an oath binding us for our time on this world. Those that feel differently are fools or liars, and both should not be trusted.

At the completion of the oath, Pastor König passed the Holy Bible wrapped with the silver chain and covered with a silver Kreuz (Cross) from person to person to be kissed by all. I did so with sincere reverence as my Lutheran faith required.

One unmarried man in our group, who I knew not and had never noticed before, backed away and refused the Bible. He yelled out, "Nein, nein! I will not swear allegiance to this Empress Catherine Alexeevna! This is not what they promised to me when I agreed to come. I will not swear!"

Almost instantly, *Lieutenant Colonel Chichelnitsky* and two armed soldiers were at his side. The two soldiers violently grabbed the screaming man and dragged him off to somewhere. We never saw him again.

Christoph whispered to me, "Er ist verrückt (He is crazy)!"

Lieutenant Colonel Chichelnitsky looked around the room at our group, and with a strange smile calmly asked, "Anyone else wish to decline their oath?"

We all replied that we were more than happy to honor our oaths. No way to deny the truth, we all finally realized that we were now subjects of Empress Catherine Alexeevna, and return to Deutschland would be next to impossible, if not in fact, impossible.

Lieutenant Colonel Chichelnitsky and the remaining eight of his armed soldiers led us back to the ship. No one made any problems, as we remained quiet while all considered the oath and the fact that we were no longer citizens of our birthplace, but now, at least by Law, we were Russisch.

I turned to my husband *Christoph* and whispered, "I am a Russe by Law, but will always be Deutsch in my heart."

Christoph remained silent and said nothing, but nodded his head in agreement.

The next morning *Lieutenant Colonel Chichelnitsky* and four soldiers came down below decks. With the *Lieutenant Colonel* was a much younger Russische Army Officer that we had never seen before. Whoever he was, he remained well behind *Chichelnitsky*.

Lieutenant Colonel Chichelnitsky arrogantly spoke, "Where is your *Vorsteher?* No matter, I see him over there hiding in the corner. Leader, there is no need for you to come forward. I will handle this without your leadership. I have here the list of names of all authorized to continue on to your new colony. If your name is not on this list, then you will not be going on with the rest of this group to the designated colony south of Saratov and west of the Volga River, and you will be escorted off this ship and temporarily housed elsewhere."

He looked up, smiled and continued, "I will call off your names one by one, and you will come forward as a family. *Lt. Von Ditmarr* will give to each of you a brass token identifying you as part of this colony group. Safeguard this token and do not lose it as you travel from here on. Parents will keep and protect each child's token. The names of this colony group going with *Lt. Von Ditmarr* are:

1) *Herr Barthuli, Balzer* with *Frau Anna,* and two daughters *Elizabeth* and *Appollonia.*
2) *Herr Decker, Philipp* with *Frau Jacobina,* and son *Johannes* and daughter *Maria.*
3) *Herr Scheck, Jakob* with *Frau Katharina* and son *Jacob.*
4) *Herr Heft, Heinrich* with *Frau Katharina.*
5) *Herr Haberman, Valentine.*
6) *Herr Volz, Leonhard* with *Frau Margarita,* sons *George* and *Wilhelm,* and daughters *Elizabeth* and *Barbara.*
7) *Herr Tehele, Ludwig* with *Frau Anna,* and son *Johann* and daughter *Eva.*
8) *Herr Karl, Christoph* with *Frau Jacobina.*
9) *Herr Robertus, Georg* with *Frau Appolina* and daughters *Katharina* and *Jacobina.*
10) *Herr Dittmer, Jacob* with *Frau Anna,* son *Johan* and daughter *Anna.*
11) *Herr Wagner, Heinrich* with *Frau Dorothea.*
12) *Herr Weiss, Johann.*
13) *Herr Bruckmann, Peter.*

That is the complete list. Are there any here that were not called and now do not have tokens? If so, come forward, it will be better for you that we find out now then later!"

One family of a husband and wife, and a young boy slowly pushed through to the front to face the *Lieutenant Colonel.* Frowning, the *Lieutenant Colonel* said to them, "Your Names?"

The man was frightened and hesitated, but eventually so softly replied that it was hard to hear his words, "*Herr Johann Rupp* and wife *Eva*, and boy *George*."

The *Lieutenant Colonel* looked closely at the list again, and replied, "Your names are not on the list. Let me see all your papers now!"

Herr Johann Rupp pulled them out of his bag, gave him all the papers, and quietly replied, "Our papers are all in order, Ja?"

Lieutenant Colonel Chichelnitsky examined their papers and replied, "Nein, your papers are not in order. They are not correct. You will leave at once with two of my soldiers. You will be relocated until we discover why your papers are not in order." The *Lieutenant Colonel* motioned for the soldiers to come and escort them off the ship, and the soldiers quickly did just that. We never saw them again.

Lieutenant Colonel Chichelnitsky smiled and announced to the rest of us, "You are to be congratulated in your good fortune. You will be leaving today on this ship for your new homes. You will not see me again, but will be in the care of *Lt. Von Ditmarr* and his squad of soldiers. You will follow their orders without argument, and give him and his soldiers the same respect that you have learned to give to me. Failure to do so will end your travels and quickly place you in one of our enjoyable Army prisons as a danger to the Crown."

The *Lieutenant Colonel* turned to *Lt. Von Ditmarr* and shook his hand. *Lt. Von Ditmarr* saluted which the *Lieutenant Colonel* returned, and then old Russische Officer was gone up the steps. Thankfully, we never saw him again.

Lt. Von Ditmarr looked around at our group and said, "I am now the Leader of this movement. My soldiers and I are here to protect you from threats and the elements, and to keep you from wandering off to unauthorized areas. Your only authorized permanent area to settle is your designated colony. You will be of good conduct at all times, and avoid, at all costs, any conflict or argument with the locals"

He continued, "I will obtain transportation, food, shelter, and additional clothes or blankets as are required on this trip. All you need do is follow our orders, and stay healthy and alive. It will be cold and harsh, but GOD willing, we will all see Saratov. We will only be on this ship for a few hours today. The Neva River has completely frozen over upstream, as soon this part will be. We will move to covered wagons for our transport south to Velikly Novgorod near Lake Ilmen. If the winter weather is mild when we arrive there, we will continue on to Torzhok, but if the winter has set in, we will stay the winter there in Novgorod."

"You may all be wondering about your new colony, Goloi Karamysh. It is located in the Saratov Province, in the district of the city of Kamyshin, on the Bergseite (hilly western side) of the Volga River, along Goloi Karamysh Creek. The distance from the provincial city of Saratov is seventy-three versts (forty-eight miles). It is twelve versts (eight miles) from the Volga River Landing. The colony is unpopulated and has plentiful and bountiful lands for growing many crops. Woodlands and forests of oak, aspen, popular, birch, and linden are everywhere. There is plentiful water to grow your crops. The weather is pleasant during the summer, and much like the winters that you are familiar with in your homelands. As promised, homes will already be built for you by the time we arrive. All you have to do is cooperate with me and follow my orders, and soon you will all be safe and comfortable in your new homes. Questions?" asked *Lt. Von Ditmarr.*

No questions; no one said anything at all.

"Good, go prepare as we sail on the quarter-hour on this 21st day of November in the year of our LORD one thousand seven hundred sixty-four (1764)!" he announced.

We all went back to our cramped areas to check if we needed to do anything before we sailed. *Christoph* and I were satisfied the way we were, and settled down to wait for our leaving.

I whispered to *Christoph,* "I feel so sorry for the *Rupp* family. Thank our LORD that our papers were in order. I will feel so much better when we are gone from here and on our way."

Christoph whispered back, "I do not like this place either. I hope the rest of our trip to our promised Colony will be better."

I smiled and answered, "How can it not be better than this." *Christoph* started to answer, but I put my hand to his mouth, and shook my head. He just shrugged again.

We all heard much movement on the deck above us, and then we felt the ship begin to rock. We were on our way again.

Sankt-Peterburg

A voice from above yelled down, "You can come up on deck, and see the sights and get fresh air."

In an instant, we were all crowding up the steps to the deck. A cold breeze blew, but no one turned back to down below decks. I huddled with *Christoph* and watched as Sankt-Peterburg passed by our side. We sailed out of the city about thirty versts (twenty miles) up what they called the Neva River to a landing at Отрáдное (Otradnoye). As *Lt. Von Ditmarr* had told us, the Neva River had iced over a short distance further upstream.

We gathered all our belongings in preparation to load onto the covered wagons, and met more of the bearded Russischen teamsters that all looked alike. *Christoph* and I climbed up into a wagon, and found it partially filled with thick furs. The furs were to keep us as warm as possible during the bitter cold winter travel.

Our *Vorsteher Balzer Barthuli* and his *Frau Anna* and two daughters *Elizabeth* and *Appollonia,* and *Herr Heinrich Wagner* and *Frau Dorothea* climbed aboard the wagon to join us. We put a layer of furs on the wagon floor below us, and along the wagon insides, and then covered ourselves with those remaining.

All warm and toasty, soon we were moving south down a bumpy trail. Already, this reminded me of the long boring ride with strangers to Lübeck. This time, however, I already knew these people and I had my dear *Christoph* with me, holding me close.

12   OVERLAND TO OUR DREAM

♠CHRISTOPH KARL♠

Отра́дное (Otradnoye), thirty versts east of Sankt-Peterburg, Russland

There was snow on the ground, but it was not snowing. I could hear the wagon wheels crunching on the snow-covered road. It was brisk and cold outside, but we are all warm and snug riding in our fur-lined covered wagon.

I was sure the Russische teamster must have been very cold out there on the front of our wagon. Of course, it helps that he was most likely born to this Russische weather, not like us Deutsch.

Lt. Von Ditmarr had earlier given our *Vorsteher Balzer Barthuli* a rough map of our route to follow to our destination of Velikly Novgorod, and a list of our nightly stops along the way. He let his two daughters, *Elizabeth* and *Appollonia*, look at both map and list.

Schooled in Deutschland, they knew how to read and write in Deutsch. He had also given them a tablet to record the Deutsche and Russische names of all the villages we passed through on the way to our new colony.

Honestly, I thought it was a silly waste of time and whispered my thoughts about it to *Jacobina*.

She frowned and replied sternly, "Hush, it is good for all of us that they will have something to keep them out of mischief on this long trip."

Jacobina was, as usual, right. I had not thought about how bad it might be in this wagon for weeks with two giggly and silly young girls.

The road as far as you could see was flat. After some time, we passed the village of Покровскоые (Pokrovskoye) on our right side. A few run down and poorly kept wooden shacks along the reka Tosna (Tosna River) was all we saw.

We followed the reka Tosna road through tall forests and flat cleared land with no crops to the village of Никол'скоые (Nikolskoye). It was much like Pokrovskoye; there were even more of the run down and poorly kept wooden shacks that these Russische peasants called home. Instead of just a few wooden shacks as we saw before, there were many built in clusters on the east side of the river.

As we passed by, Russische peasant men, women, and children came out to stare at our caravan of wagons. We saw no waving, no smiles, or not even any reaction on their blank and emotionless faces.

The Russische peasants were a large coarse hardy people. Their winter dress was a high fur cap, sheep's skin, with the woolly side inward, that reached to the knee bound round the waist by a sash. Woolen or flannel cloth was round the leg instead of stockings.

I whispered to *Jacobina*, "Those are the faces of a beaten people with no hope or dreams."

She whispered back, "Ja, it makes one shiver. We are so lucky to still have our dreams and hopes."

We continued rolling along the river road and passed village of Пустынка (Pustynka). If I were not sure we had already passed the village of Pokrovskoye, I would have thought we were back in it. I saw the same run down and poorly kept wooden shacks with what I thought were the same Russische peasants.

As the day passed, we rolled down the river road through tall forests. As the sun was racing towards dusk in the west, we broke out on to another flat plain stretching as far as one could see. We crossed the river bridge and entered the village of Тосно (Tosno). Here in Tosno, we would spend the night.

While there were still many of the run down and poorly kept wooden shacks all over, here in Tosno there were also many well-kept large buildings and shops. While the locals still stared as we moved through, they did acknowledge our arrival. Women and men gathered in small groups to discuss who we were and what we might want. Even here in Tosno, having a caravan of wagons come through the village was not an everyday occurrence.

Lt. Von Ditmarr and his soldiers found the local мэр (Mayor) and asked for help in finding us lodging for the night. No one voiced any offers of food and lodging until *Lt. Von Ditmarr* produced a handful of silver coins, and reminded them of their duty to the Crown. Many volunteers suddenly changed their minds and opened their homes to us.

An older couple took in *Jacobina* and me, and the *Barthuli* family. We followed them to their home, this was no shack, but a large well-kept house built of rough round logs. It looked as if they piled whole trees one upon another, and then fastened somehow together.

Large stones supported the four corners of the house. They told me this is built so a current of air can flow under the floor to preserve the timbers from damp. In the winter, they pile up soil all round to exclude the cold, and stuff the cracks between the logs with clay and moss so no air can enter. The windows were openings of only a few inches square, closed with sliding frames located in the outside walls for light.

Heat for the room came from a peech (peclika) stove located in the center of the house. It worked so well that it made the room almost unbearably hot, but the Russen seemed to bask in the heat. There was no vent or chimney out of the house, and so the inside walls were as black with soot as the inside of the chimney that did not exist.

All the inside walls were smooth from an ax, but the outsides walls were left with their bark in their raw state. The roofs were usually made of the tree bark or shingles, sometimes covered with mold or grass.

We soon learned, as was the custom with the Russischen peasants, that instead of having a barn for their animals, their hogs, chickens and sheep lived inside their home with them. Their home was the barn, and typically smelled from the animals and the filthy conditions.

We were tired and hungry, so there were no complaints. Besides, we were guests in their home, and they were sharing all they had with us. Our Deutsche upbringing never would allow us to insult our hosts.

Their furniture consisted chiefly of a wooden table or dresser, and benches fastened to the sides of the room. We all sat down at a large table along with the old couple for uzhin (supper). Their utensils, platters, bowls, and spoons were all made of wood.

Our hosts offered no prayer of thanks to our LORD, so I spoke, "LORD, please bless our hosts and the food they have willingly shared with us. Bless each of us on our journey to our new home. Amen."

All, except for our hosts, prayed with me and waited until the end of the prayer to start eating. Our hosts completely ignored my blessing, and continued to eat paying us no attention.

Our supper was black-rye bread, eggs, cabbage soup seasoned with onions and garlic, and millet gruel, with fresh milk to drink.

While we were thankful for our supper fare, the sisters *Elizabeth* and *Appollonia* were not as happy with the food and voiced their discontent. The old Russisch couple paid no mind to them, but their mother *Anna* severely chastised them and made them eat every spoonful of their cabbage soup and every speck of their millet gruel. No fresh milk was wasted either.

After uzhin (supper), the old man led us first to the сортир (outhouse), then to where the drinking water was, and finally to our sleeping areas. There were no actual beds anywhere; they pointed to a bed of straw to sleep on. Exhausted, I lay down and *Jacobina* snuggled into my arms alongside me.

Last thing I remember was *Jacobina* saying, "Ich liebe dich (I love you)." Sleep came quickly that night for all of us, but did not last. Sometime during the night, the chickens pecking the grains of corn in the straw upon which *Jacobina* and I lay, pecked me hard, and I woke.

Early in the morning, a group of hogs roused both *Jacobina* and me by grunting close to our ears. Truly, we slept in a barn! Through the early dawn light, I could make out the Old Russische couple as they lay not far away sleeping flat on their backs on the bare floor.

It was still dark when the old man woke us. By candlelight, he motioned for us to gather up our things and come to завтрак (breakfast). This meal was just a repeat of supper.

Again, our hosts offered no prayer, so I again spoke, "LORD, please bless our hosts and this food they have willingly shared with us. Bless each of us on this day's journey to our new home. Amen."

Like earlier, the old couple paid us no mind and ate in silence. Our breakfast, like our previous night's supper, was again cabbage soup and millet gruel with fresh milk to drink. This time, the sisters *Elizabeth* and *Appollonia* did not show any unhappiness with the food.

Within the hour, we were back on our wagon rolling south out of Tosno. We had left the reka Tosna, and traveled for a time through more tall forests on both sides. Soon we passed through the village Строыениые (Stroyeniye). As before, nothing more than a few run down and poorly kept wooden shacks with a few Russische peasants in a clearing in the middle of the forests. A few hours later, we rolled through the village of Лисино-Корпус (Lisino-Corpus). All these small villages looked just the same, same clothing, same blank faces, and same wooden shacks.

As the day passed, we moved down the road over small hills and through forested valleys. By the time the sun dropped in the western sky, we reached our night's rest in the village Грисхкино (Grishkino). No big buildings here, but we saw smaller well-kept homes right alongside the run down and poorly kept wooden shacks.

Here there were not the blank faces, as the women and men gathered in small groups to discuss who we were and what we might want, or maybe how much money they could get from us.

Again, *Lt. Von Ditmarr* and his soldiers found the local leader and asked for help in finding us lodging for the night. Same as in Tosno, no one voiced any offers of food and lodging until *Lt. Von Ditmarr* produced his handful of silver coins and reminded them of their duty to the Crown. Again, many volunteers suddenly changed their minds and opened their homes to us.

A couple led our same group, *Jacobina* and me and the Barthuli family to their home. Not as nice a "barn" as the night before, but we were protected from the chill. Supper, sleep, and breakfast were just the same. Our hosts provided us all we needed, but paid us no mind and never actually spoke to us.

Soon we were back on our wagon rolling south out of Grishkino. We slowly rolled down the road through over small hills and through forested valleys towards the next villages of Каменка (Kamenka) and Еглино (Eglino). The day passed with a night in the village of Радифинниково (Radofinnikovo), and another day passed as we traveled through Огорел'е (Ogorel'e) with a night in the village of

Тесово-Нетыл'скиы (Tesovo-Netyl'skiy). The days and nights blurred into one Russisches village after another as Село Гора (Selo Gora), Татино (Tatino), and Выазхисхцхи (Vyazhischi) vanished in the distance.

Our Route from Санкт-Петербург (Sankt-Peterburg) to Вели́кии Но́вгород (Novgorod)

Finally, as the seventh night approached, we broke out of the forested hills. Before us, lay the city of Вели́кий Но́вгород (Velikiy Novgorod) along the reka Volkhov (Volkhov River). As we neared the end of this part of our trip, the sisters read to us what they recorded in their tablet:

21 November 1764   Leave from Отра́дное (Otradnoye)

Night 1 - 21 November 1764   Overnight in Тосно (Tosno)

Night 2 - 22 November 1764   Overnight in Грисхкино (Grishkino)

Night 3 - 23 November 1764   Overnight in Радифинниково (Radofinnikovo)

Night 4 - 24 November 1764   Overnight in Тесово-Нетыл'скиы (Tesovo-Netyl'skiy)

Night 5 - 25 November 1764   Overnight in Село Гора (Selo Gora)

Night 6 - 26 November 1764   Overnight in Выазхисхцхи (Vya- zhishchi)

Night 7 - 27 November 1764   Arrive in Вели́кий Но́вгород (Velikiy Novgorod)

Вели́кий Но́вгород

♦JACOBINA KARL♦

Вели́кий Но́вгород (Velikiy Novgorod), Russland

After traveling south from Sankt-Peterburg for seven days, we arrived in Вели́кий Но́вгород (Velikiy Novgorod) on the 27th day of November in the year of our LORD one thousand seven hundred sixty-four (1764).

We found Novgorod to be a bustling city; larger than any Deutsche or Russische city, other than Sankt-Peterburg, we had stopped at. Novgorod was a walled city built right on both banks of the reka Volkhov (Volkhov River).

Peasants living outside
Великий Но́вгород (Velikiy Novgorod)

We rolled into the walled city, our covered wagons scraping the roof of the entrance gate arches. Everyone was busy doing something or going somewhere, and paid no attention to our convoy at all... except to yell at the teamsters to move along faster.

Lt. Von Ditmarr and two of his soldiers went off to find the local мэр (Mayor) and officially request assistance in finding us long-term lodging. The approaching bad winter weather made any further travel towards the Volga impossible. This was the stop of our travels until the spring thaw; here in Novgorod we would stay.

The rest of our band of Russischen soldiers stayed with us to keep the locals away from us. Whether that was to protect them from us, or protect us from them, I do not know. However, more than once, one of the soldiers actually stopped a local from stealing supplies off our wagons.

I did not know what type of inducement *Lt. Von Ditmarr* and two of his soldiers used on the local мэр, but when he and his soldiers returned, there was with them a finely dressed man and ten workers.

We wondered what type of "barn" we would land up in, but that was not to be. They escorted us to what we would call in Deutschland, a 'Gasthaus or Wirtshaus.' Here, I think they called it a 'гостиница'.

We were the only guests staying there. I hoped not, but I am almost sure that whoever was staying here before we arrived found their possessions and themselves out into the weather so that we could all be boarded in the same place. For all in our group, along with *Lt. Von Ditmarr* and his soldiers, this was to be our new home till the spring thaw.

The гостиница staff and a soldier led each family to a room to stay in. When they showed me ours, I noticed it was very large and innocently asked, "How many others would we be sharing with?"

Puzzled looks on their faces. After some difficult translation, one of our soldiers laughed and said to me, "It is you and your husband's room, and yours only. No sharing." I was thrilled; *Christoph* and I had our own room. It was fine, and we were not sharing it with anyone else, or any pigs or chickens or sheep.

I looked at *Christoph* and smiled, he was already looking at me with a devilish look in his eyes. I quickly realized that, if he had his way, we would not be doing much sleeping tonight.

I slyly whispered to *Christoph*, "What is on your mind?"

He quickly replied, "You will see. We need to get cleaned up and eat our supper, and then it will be early to bed."

Mischievously acting as if I did not realize his plan, I innocently replied, "Oh no my *Christoph*, we have plenty of time. I am not at all sleepy, and I think we need to go out and look around at the city."

Christoph scrunched up his face and shot back, "No that is not what I mean.... Not sleeping. Uh...."

I smiled and put my hand to his mouth, and whispered, "I am teasing you. I know what you really mean and what you want."

One of our soldiers came by and announced that ужин (supper) was ready. We met our group downstairs already seated at long tables with benches. While the mid-day meal, обед (lunch), is normally the large one in Russland, our hosts added more food to this supper because we had been on the road so long.

While *Christoph's* plan was to eat a quick meal and then retire to our bed, once he saw the foods, I think he may have slightly changed his night's plans. On the tables were bowls of salads, along with bowls of noodle or vegetable soups. The main course of the второе блюдо (first dish) was a serving of fish with a side dish of vegetables and of kasha (wheat, rye or rice porridge). Hot tea was drink of the night.

Our entire group was stunned at how wonderful the food was, and ate like there was no tomorrow.

Christoph and I sat near *Lt. Von Ditmarr* and *Vorsteher Balzer Barthuli*. While I was enjoying myself with all the food, I was also able to overhear their talk.

Vorsteher Barthuli turned to *Lt. Von Ditmarr* and asked, "How much extra must we pay for all this?"

Lt. Von Ditmarr laughed and smiled, and then replied, "You pay nothing extra for this food and lodging while you are here. In fact, this is costing the Crown little or nothing."

He continued, "I just reminded the City Officials that this caravan and its travelers were traveling at the express desire of Her Imperial Highness, most merciful great Lady, Empress Catherine Alexeevna, Autocrat of all Russland; and that their enthusiastic cooperation or non-cooperation would be noted in my official report back to the Tsarina. They eagerly volunteered to house and feed all of you along with my soldiers and myself as long as we need such support. I told them that it would be till the spring thaw, and their reply was that was fine."

Vorsteher Barthuli sincerely replied, "Danke (Thank You) *Lt. Von Ditmarr*, I speak for our whole group when I say from my heart, Danke. We are at your Service."

Lt. Von Ditmarr nodded his head in agreement, and after a short moment replied, "Sie sind willkommen (You are welcome), and Ja, this is all very nice. Ja, truly you are at my service!"

After a long moment of silence, *Lt. Von Ditmarr* added, "It is good that everyone is happy and celebrating tonight. Tomorrow, after завтрак (breakfast) and in the harsh light of the day, we will all meet here. I will tell you and your entire group what contributions you will provide, and assign work the Crown expects from each person while we are here." The conversation finished, he turned to his plate of food and went back to busily filling his belly.

Vorsteher Balzer Barthuli started to reply, but did not. A few minutes before this his face was happy and smiling, now it was taut and serious. He remained silent.

Like me, he must have been wondering exactly what did *Lt. Von Ditmarr* mean by his cryptic comment 'about contributions and work the Crown expects from each person while we are here.' "Oh well, tonight we celebrate and on the morrow we will pay the bill!" I muttered to myself.

Full of much drink and good food, our group was happy with much talking and laughing. This went on till late as each family finally pushed away from the tables and retired to bed.

My *Christoph* and I did satisfy our other hungers that night, but it was far from an all-night event. In fact, what with our well-fed bellies, clean bed, and the quiet room, it was all we could do to stay awake for one spirited romp.

CALL FOR BREAKFAST

The sun was already up when we heard the call for завтрак (frühstück, breakfast). We arrived downstairs at the long tables to find plates of яичный омлет (ei omelett, egg omelet), more bowls of kasha, and чай (tee, tea) and кофе (kaffee, coffee). With more of all the food we could eat, we were all very happy and contented.

As we finished overfilling ourselves, *Lt. Von Ditmarr* stood and spoke, "Everyone, please be silent! It is good that I now find you all full and happy and healthy. We will be living here until the spring thaw arrives most likely in middle April. I trust that you have all found the lodging and food to be more than acceptable. Her Imperial Highness, most merciful great Lady, Empress Catherine Alexeevna, Autocrat of all Russland, desires that you be provided all you need while on your travels. In addition, from the time we left Санкт-Петербург (Sankt-Peterburg), each of you will be paid two groschen per day. This payment will continue until we arrive at your new colony. I hope you will each appreciate the dole of this money from the Crown."

He continued, "In return, as new subjects of the Crown, the following requirements will apply to each one of you. Until now, we treated all of you as guests in Russland. Now, each of you will become productive Russische citizens. Each of the women will do work, such as the cleaning and housekeeping and cooking of this lodging establishment. The staff will teach you what needs doing to keep life good here, and you will do it. The men will bring in firewood, carry in supplies we need, and any other work I choose. All children under sixteen years will attend a school here in this room to learn the Russische language and all they need to know about our ways. Simply put, everyone will become productive and busy. Anyone not able to keep up their share of the assigned work will be harshly dealt with by me!"

He added, "Also, you will not leave this building for any reason unless I approve. If you go out visiting the City, you will go out in groups of no less than four adults. You will eat all your meals with this group, and will sleep each night in this lodging. You will not carouse with the locals and will maintain a civility at all times. I will not tolerate heavy drinking or partying. You will not interact with the locals unless it is part of your duties or I have approved of it."

He went on, "The men may obtain employment for the time after their normal duties for extra money that you may keep if I approve. If there is doubt about what you are going to do, do not until you ask me! If for some reason, I am not here and cannot talk with me, you may at those times, ask *Vorsteher Balzer Barthuli*. Along with my giving him that authority, I will hold him personally responsible for any and all your actions. For any breaking of these rules, he and the rule breaker will both be punished."

He warned, "If anyone does not understand or agree to comply with these rules, speak now or by your silence I will assume your understanding and compliance." No one said anything at all.

Lt. Von Ditmarr continued to speak, "Good, we are all agreed. Your work will start on the morrow. For the rest of today, you may do as you wish… sleep, rest, or learn your way around the city. Remember though, you eat all your meals here with this group; do not miss the meals!" he added. With that, he walked out of the room.

His new rules and requirements were not to our liking. Voices discussing this dislike rose in the room. One thing we all agreed on, the rules were not fair or reasonable.

Vorsteher Balzer Barthuli, realizing that he would be personally accountable for any breaking of the rules, stood up and spoke, "Fellow colonists, these rules are as much a surprise to me as you. Whether we agree with the need for them or fairness of them does not matter. What is important to remember is that we have no choice in these events. We are at the mercy of the charity of the Crown and its representative, *Lt. Von Ditmarr*. We must closely follow the rules because we have no choice!"

"He was right, what choice was there at this point," I said to myself. If we refused to comply, we would be prisoners here until we who knows when. No choice at all, best to accept what we could not change.

THE CITY

♦JACOBINA KARL♦

On the streets of Великий Но́вгород (Novgorod), Russland

They gave us maps so that we could find our way back to our lodging.

Map of Великий Но́вгород
(Velikiy Novgorod)

We ventured out as group with *Herr Balzer Barthuli* and his wife and daughters, and *Herr Philipp Decker* and his wife. The city was crowded with people coming and going everywhere and all directions. There was constant noise from all the laughing, and yelling, and talking from the many people.

We made our way through the crowds and down the streets, stopping to look in the shops and businesses on both sides. Using the map, we slowly walked towards the river.

As we reached the river, we saw on the other bank the stonewalls of a detinet or kremlin (town castle) right in the heart of the city.

I was fascinated by it as it was like our Deutschen Castles, but still different with its twelve towers. I could see a silver dome crowning one of the towers. I turned to *Christoph*, and like a child, said, "I want to go there!"

A gate in Великий Новгород (Velikiy Novgorod)

Most of the group felt it was too far, but finally gave in to my wish. The tall stonewalls had fallen down in some places. Inside, we found the Kirche of Saint Sofia, one of five different Kirchen in this kremlin.

Herr Balzer Barthuli reminded us that we needed to get back for lunch. We would have another day to see more. We hurried back only getting lost a few times. In spite of our hurrying, we were still late to the group meal.

Five-Domed Kirche of St. Sofia

Lt. Von Ditmarr took notice of us as we came in late, but did not say anything. Having *Vorsteher Balzer Barthuli* with us may have saved us this time. We would have to pay more attention to the time in the future.

OLD FRIENDS

♦ℵOℬOⅅ𝒴 (MICℋ𝒜ℰL GRÜℵ) ♦

Somewhere on the road to Hamburg, Deutschland

A few months have passed since that early morning that I left my friends, *Christoph, Jacobina,* and the town of Lübeck. I wonder where they are now, and pray I did not cause trouble for them. They are good people, and certainly do not deserve any problems from me.

That morning I left, it was so early and still dark. I had not really thought about where to go, so I just naturally landed up at the door of My Lady. To my extreme disappointment and frustration, My Lady was already 'talking' with another of her friends. He apparently paid better than I, as she quickly shooed me away. What did I expect? She was not just My Lady, but also the My Lady of every other man in with any money to spend in Lübeck.

As I stood at the bar downstairs having my breakfast of hops, better than saying bier, I realized that it might be best if I left this town of Lübeck for someplace the former *Michael Grün* had never been. I doubted if someone might be looking for me, but there was always a chance.

No time better to leave this city than now, and as quickly as possible, I snuck out the nearest city gate going towards Hamburg. Once out of Lübeck, there was no chance of anyone recognizing me. What a relief!

Leaving Lübeck, I walked west, back on the same road I had traveled with *Christoph* and *Jacobina,* only then going east towards their future. As I slowly walked, I had lots of time to think about my two good friends, and the good time we had along the way. Their wide-eyed looks, especially those of *Jacobina*, each time they saw something new. They really were both country bumpkins and completely ignorant of the actual world.

I am going to miss that *Jacobina*. She was not too hard on the eyes, and those occasional glimpses of her unclothed body, those bountiful breasts with that small waist and trim legs, always stirred up my desire to have her. But she was the frau of *Christoph*, and while I would do almost anything once, I did have some scruples. Besides, she was just too damned Christian for my tastes. Had I actually taken her by force, she probably would have forgiven me. No, definitely, she was not my type. Still, I give good odds that she was a good romp in bed. *Christoph* is a lucky man!

My thoughts drifted back to when this all started. Whatever influenced *Christoph* to trust that *Recruiter* tale is beyond me? Anyone with the slightest knowledge of the actual world knew that this *Recruiter* was pure liar.

Yes, I fell for the line of the *Recruiter* too, but at least I got off the fishhook, and not eaten. I should have saved my two friends before I left, but I guess I am just a louse who thinks more of saving himself, before it is too late.

Oh well, I never said to anyone I was perfect, or for that matter even good. *Christoph* and *Jacobina* knew what I am, so they deserved what they got. If they really did not know what I am, they should have! As they say, "keine schreien uber versunken milch (do not cry over spilled milk)." On the other hand, they were good to me and were good people. Not my kind of people, you understand, but good people.

I hope they both get exactly what they were dreaming. My best wishes to *Christoph* and *Jacobina* for that. To their GOD, if any two deserve your blessings, these two do.

Enough unhappy and sobering thoughts, time to dream about all the fun with my new Ladies of the Night in Hamburg. It might be better this time to not fix my attention on just one, but to share my charms among many. I have to spend all the money *Jacobina* so foolishly gave me, and I cannot spend it all drinking, so I will spread a little cheer among the wonderful working Ladies of the Night.

Now that *Michael Grün* is no more, I wonder what name would best work for me now. I always liked 'Peter' and last time I used 'Grün' so maybe another color. I know, I shall be *Herr Peter Schwarze (Herr Peter Black)*. That should go well with all my new Ladies of the Night.

THE DAYS PASS

◆JACOBINA KARL◆

Gasthaus in Великий Новгород (Novgorod), Russland

There was not much chance to see more of the City. *Lt. Von Ditmarr* was serious when he said we would become productive Russische citizens. The lodging staff worked us like slaves so that they did not need to work.

Our women and older girls worked all day cleaning all the rooms, washing, or cooking, or sometimes all three. We never had time to leave the Gasthaus. In fact, the only time we had to ourselves was to rest at night.

Lt. Von Ditmarr also kept the men busy. They were always carrying in supplies for the Gasthaus, and if not, they were carrying supplies to other buildings. I wondered if *Lt. Von Ditmarr* had maybe hired out our men, and pocketing the money paid for their labor.

Cautiously, I only whispered this thought to *Christoph*, who upon hearing that, said, "*Jacobina*, best to not mention that again. If it is true, nothing good will come of making him angry. If it is not the truth, nothing good will come of insulting him. Best to forget those thoughts and not think on it again!"

The days quickly passed and before we realized it, we learned that Christmas was near. This would be our first Christmas in our new land. While *Christoph* and I always celebrated Christmas for three days around the 25th of December, here for some baffling reason the calendar was different, and Christmas was later here.

I asked one of the Gasthaus staff why they celebrated on the wrong day, and she answered, "No, Christmas is the same day as always." I tried and tried to explain to her that Christmas is on the 25th of December, but she just kept shaking her head.

Doing as they did, on their Christmas Eve most likely in the Deutsche early January, we made ready for the celebration. We learned how white tablecloths, symbolic of Christ's swaddling clothes, were to cover the tables. Our men brought in hay as a reminder of the poverty of the cave where Jesus was born. They placed tall white candles in the center of the tables, symbolic of Christ "the Light of the World." The Russen placed large round loaves of Lenten bread, "pagach," symbolic of Christ the Bread of Life, next to the candles.

We all sat down at a traditional Russische meal. By their custom, this is the 'Holy Supper' in honor of each of the twelve apostles. This 'Holy Supper' was of twelve different foods: Sauerkraut soup; Lenten bread (pagach); grated garlic; bowl of honey; baked cod; fresh apricots, oranges, figs and dates; nuts; kidney beans (slow cooked all day) seasoned with shredded potatoes, lots of garlic, and salt and pepper; peas; parsley potatoes (boiled new potatoes with chopped parsley and butter); bobal'ki (small biscuits combined with sauerkraut or poppy seed with honey); and red wine.

The meal began with the LORD's Prayer, led by *Lt. Von Ditmarr*. He also said a prayer of thanksgiving for all the blessings of the past year, and then offered prayers for the good things in the coming year. Following the prayer, everyone took of the pagach bread, dipping it first in honey, symbolic of the sweetness of life, and then in chopped garlic, symbolic of the bitterness of life.

Later that evening after our meal was finished, groups of people masked as manger animals visited our lodging and the surrounding houses.

They sang songs called kolyadki. These were pastoral carols to the baby Jesus, while others were homages to the ancient solar goddess Kolyada, who brings the lengthening days of sunlight through the winter. In return for their songs, the singers expected food and coins, which they gladly accepted, before moving on to the next charitable audience.

On Christmas Day, a day of both solemn ritual and joyous celebration, we sang hymns and carols. Christmas dinner included a variety of different meats, including goose and suckling pig. It was all wonderful; unfortunately, we women had to spend most of our time preparing it.

A week later, our Russischen hosts celebrated New Years on what must be mid-January in Deutschland. I still found these new dates very confusing. Like Christmas, our group celebrated as a large family with traditional meals, much singing, and celebratory drinking.

The days and weeks of January passed as we performed our daily chores from dawn to dusk. We slowly began to learn enough Russen to be able to communicate with the locals.

The weather of January was even colder and worse than December, and the spring thaw was still long off. February too passed with no change, as did most of March.

It was almost the first day of April when the weather started to become more favorable to travel. Our hopes were up that we would soon be on our way again, but were dashed by a late winter blizzard and ice storm that blanketed all with snow and ice.

Then on the 18ᵗʰ of April, *Lt. Von Ditmarr* called us all together and announced, "The weather is turning. Prepare yourselves for leaving in the next few days. It will still be a cold ride, but we best make progress before the roads thaw and become mud." We were ready to leave the very next day, but one last icy blast from 'old man winter' stopped us.

Finally, on the 21ˢᵗ of April 1765, we reloaded our all of our possessions and ourselves again onto the wagons, and slowly rolled through the streets of our home for the last five months, Великий Новгород (Novgorod), towards our Promised Land.

SPRING THAW

♠CHRISTOPH KARL♠

On the road heading east from Великий Новгород (Novgorod), Russland

We are finally on the road and traveling again. The relentless blizzards of snow and cold wind stopped about a week ago, and the sun finally appeared in the sky above.

The ground is still frozen, and we will make good use of this time before it thaws and becomes slush and mud.

It is the 21st day of April in the year of our LORD one thousand seven hundred sixty-five (1765) and our brave group of travelers, led by the honorable *Lt. Von Ditmarr* and his soldiers, are again on the move to our Promised Land.

We headed almost due east away from Novgorod along the lake flats. About mid-morning, we turned more to the south and passed through the small village of Волотово (Volotovo).

Like the small villages seen earlier, these were very poor people with crumbling and poorly kept wooden shacks. A few Russische peasants stopped from mending their fishing nets to look at us as we passed through their lives.

Russisches Village

A few hours later, we rolled through the villages of Броннитса (Bronnitsa) and Пролетарилы (Proletariy). By sunset, we entered the village of Красные Станки (Krasnye

Stanki). Here we stayed the night with another Russische family.

Early the next morning, we were back on our way towards the east. We rolled through the villages of Заытесво (Zaytesvo), Вины (Viny), Невскаыа (Nevskaya), and Долглы Мост (Dolgly Most) as the day passed.

Our Route from Великий Новгород
(Velikiy Novgorod) toТоржок (Torzhok)

We finally stopped moving, as darkness approached, in the village of Кресттсы (Krettsy). Another night with yet another Russische family. More meals with their tasteless cabbage soup and millet gruel, and milk to drink. I do so miss our Deutsches bier, and what I would give for one right now!

As the cold days and even colder nights blurred into one another, we rolled through village after village, all with what seemed like the very same run-down shacks with the very same peasants standing outside them.

The villages of Нов Ракино (Nov Rakino), Ыазхелбитсы (Yazhelbitsy), Варнитсы (Varnitsy), Валдаы (Valday), Зимогор'е (Zimogor'e), Едрово (Edrovo), Выползово (Vypolzovo), Макарово (Makarovo), Кузхенкино (Kuzhenkino), Коломно (Kolomno), Красномаыскиы (Krasnomayskiy), Афим'ино (Afim'ino), Выдропузхск (Vydropuzhsk), Будово (Budovo), and Зхитково (Zhitkovo) all slowly faded in the expanse behind us as we kept ever rolling east. As we neared our next stopover, the *Barthuli* sisters read what they had written:

"21 April 1765   Leave from Великий Новгород (Velikiy Novgorod)

Night 1 - 21 April 1765 (Krasnye Stanki)	Overnight in Красные Станки
Night 2 - 22 April 1765 (Kresttsy)	Overnight in Кресттсы
Night 3 - 23 April 1765	Overnight in Валдаы (Valday)
Night 4 - 24 April 1765	Overnight in Валдаы (Valday)
Night 5 - 25 April 1765	Overnight in Едрово (Edrovo)
Night 6 - 26 April 1765 (Kuzhenkino)	Overnight in Кузхенкино

Night 7 - 27 April 1765 (Krasnomayskiy)	Overnight in Красномаыскиы
Night 8 - 28 April 1765 (Krasnomayskiy)	Overnight in Красномаыскиы
Nacht 9 - 29 April 1765 (Afim'ino)	Overnight in Афим'ино
Night 10 - 30 April 1765 (Budovo)"	Overnight in Будово

We were almost to the city of Торжóк (Torzhok) and thankfully, some time away from being trapped day-after-day in this damned wagon. Here we planned to stay for almost a week to rest, change wagons, and obtain needed supplies.

Торжóк

We arrived in Торжóк on the 1st of May in the year of our LORD one thousand seven hundred sixty-five (1765).

As before, *Lt. Von Ditmarr* met with the City Officials and mentioned that his caravan and its travelers were traveling at the express desire of Her Imperial Highness, most merciful great Lady, Empress Catherine Alexeevna, Autocrat of all Russland; and that their enthusiastic cooperation or non-cooperation would be noted in his official report back to the Tsarina.

As in Novgorod, they eagerly volunteered to house and feed all of us as long as we chose to stay. Unlike our lodging in Novgorod, this lodging was not as nice. Here we both slept and ate in one large communal building.

Sadly, there were no separate room for *Jacobina* and me, however, on the good side, there were no sheep or pigs or chickens to share our bed with either.

The next morning at breakfast, *Lt. Von Ditmarr* reminded all of us, "The rules I previously set down in Novgorod still exist here in this city. As explained before, I will deal with any disobedience swiftly and harshly."

Торжо́к (Torzhok)

As with our stops before, there were more chores and work to do each day to help with the expense of our lodging and food. However, with the longer days and milder weather, we were able to visit the sites of the city.

Wandering around Torzhok, we found a huge marktplatz with all sorts of items for sale or trade. All around us, people of all races and in many languages talked of news, and haggled over prices and barters.

We learned that Torzhok was famous for the quality of their gold work embroidery... Not that any of us could afford it. Even so, our women were able to admire the beauty of this local folk craft and the skill of the local artisans.

We visited the breath-taking Monastery of Saints Boris and Gleb, founded in the year of our LORD one thousand eighty-three (1083), and dedicated to the earliest martyrs of the Russische Orthodox Kirche.

After about a week in Torzhok of gathering supplies and replacing our wagon drivers, *Lt. Von Ditmarr* called us all together and announced, "The weather is warming. The roads have thawed and are now mostly mud. This will make our travel slower as we push our way forward. Prepare yourselves for leaving tomorrow. With the warmer temperatures, all the men will walk, as much as possible, to ease the load on our draft animals."

Early the next morning on 7 May, we all gathered around the wagons ready to move on. Well, almost all; One of our group, a single man named *Johann Weiss*, did not show up.

We patiently waited while *Lt. Von Ditmarr* and his soldiers searched all the tavernen or таверн (taverns), and all the Hure Häuser or шлюха дома (whore houses) for any sign of him. They had no luck…

Lt. Von Ditmarr returned and questioned all of us; No one knew anything of his whereabouts, or if they did, they were not saying anything.

Lt. Von Ditmarr told *Vorsteher Balzer Barthuli* that he was leaving to meet the local Полиция or Polizei (Police). He would order them to arrest *Herr Weiss* on sight, and hold him indefinitely for punishment at the Crown's discretion.

When *Lt. Von Ditmarr* returned, he announced, "I have ordered the arrest of our missing *Herr Weiss*, and have offered a one hundred groschen reward to anyone for his capture. They will eventually find and capture him, and he will suffer terribly for a long time in our prison. Let this be a lesson to all of you that the Crown will not tolerate disobedience or deceit from its subjects at any time, and when discovered, will deal with it very harshly."

With that sober news, and with one less in our group, we re-boarded our wagon and rolled out of Торжок (Torzhok).

Time passed slowly as the days and nights faded into one. The only good change was most of the time I was out of that damned wagon, and able to breathe the fresh outside air as I walked along. *Jacobina* even joined me at times, but it was still too cold for her to stay out for long.

We rolled, and walked, through the villages of Думаново (Dumanovo), Мар'ино (Mar'ino), Медноые (Mednoye), Пуддубки (Puddubki), Схираыково (Shiraykovo), Николо-Малитса (Nikolo-Malitsa), and finally arrived in Твер (Tver). Here, one of our fellow colonists became sick, so we stayed a few nights in Твер for her to recover.

Soon we were back on the road, and the villages of Леново (Lenovo), Еммаусс (Emmauss), Голеникха (Golenikha), Готодныа (Gorodnya), Радцхенко (Radchenko), Староые Мелково (Staroye Melkovo), Моксхина (Mokshina), and Завидово (Zavidovo) faded in the western horizon.

More villages, those of Спас-Заулок (Spas-Zaulok), Ыамуга (Yamuga), Клин (Klin), Цхаыковского (Chaykovskogo), Козини (Kozini), Солнецхногорск

(Solnechnogorsk), Дубинино (Dubinino), Песхки (Peshki), Есипово (Esipovo), Радумиыа (Radumiya), Схходныа (Skhodnya), and Кхимки (Khimki) slowly vanished in the distance behind us.

As we neared Moscow, the *Barthuli* sisters read to us what they had recorded:

7 May 1765   Leave from Торжо́к (Torzhok).

Night 1 - 7 May 1765   Overnight in Мар'ино (Mar'ino)

Night 2 – 8 May 1765   Overnight in Медноые (Mednoye)

Night 3 – 9 May 1765   Overnight in Схираыково (Shiraykovo)

Night 4 – 10 May 1765   Overnight in Твер (Tver)

Night 5 – 11 May 1765   Overnight in Твер (Tver)

Night 6 – 12 May 1765   Overnight in Твер (Tver)

Night 7 – 13 May 1765   Overnight in Твер (Tver)

Night 8 – 14 May 1765   Overnight in Твер (Tver)

Night 9 – 15 May 1765   Overnight in Твер (Tver)

Night 10 – 16 May 1765   Overnight in Твер (Tver)

Night 11 – 17 May 1765   Overnight in Голеникха (Golenikha)

Night 12 – 18 May 1765   Overnight in Староые Мелково (Staroye Melkovo)

Night 13 – 19 May 1765   Overnight in Клин (Klin)

Night 14 – 20 May 1765   Overnight in Солнецхногорск (Solnechnogorsk)

Night 15 – 21 May 1765   Overnight in Солнецхногорск (Solnechnogorsk)

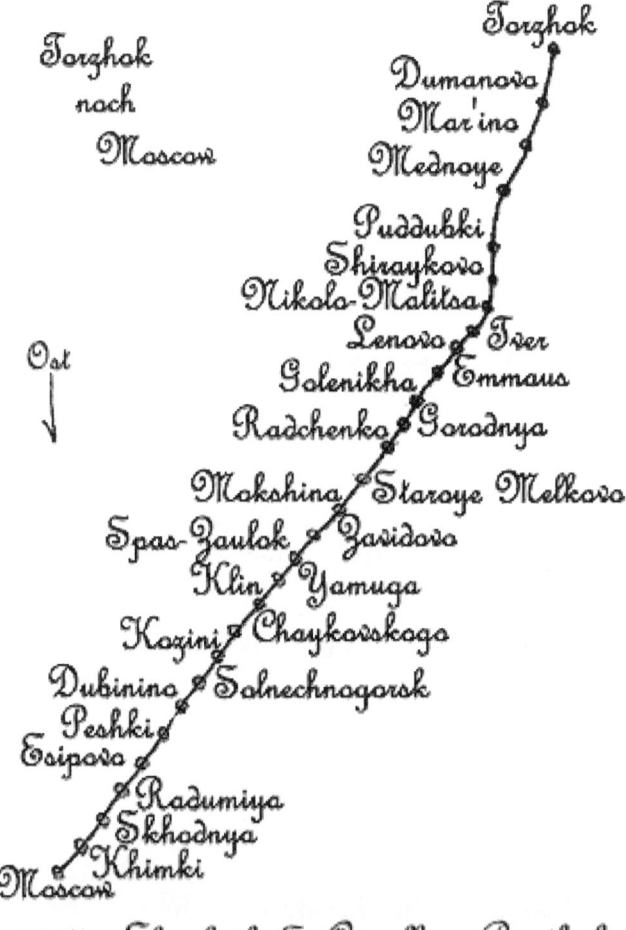

Torzhok
nach
Moscow

Torzhok
Dumanovo
Mar'ino
Mednoye
Puddubki
Shiraykovo
Nikolo-Malitsa
Lenovo *Tver*
Golenikha *Emmaus*
Radchenko *Gorodnya*
Mokshina *Staroye Melkovo*
Spas-Zaulok *Zavidovo*
Klin *Yamuga*
Kozini *Chaykovskogo*
Dubinino *Solnechnogorsk*
Peshki
Esipovo
Radumiya
Skhodnya
Khimki
Moscow

Ost

1765 - Elizabeth & Appollina Barthuli

Our Route from Торжо́к (Torzhok) to Москва́ (Moscow)

Night 16 – 22 May 1765 Overnight in Схходныа (Skhodnya)

Night 17 – 23 May 1765 Overnight in Схходныа (Skhodnya)

Night 18 – 24 May 1765 Overnight in Схходныа (Skhodnya)

Москва́

♦JACOBINA KARL♦

On the road entering Москва́, Russland

We arrived in the City of Москва́ (Moscow) on the 25th of May in the year of our LORD one thousand seven hundred sixty-five (1765).

Still very aware of the loss of one of his travelers, *Lt. Von Ditmarr* again reminded us, "The rules I set down in Novgorod also will be obeyed here in Москва́. As I stated before, I will deal with any disobedience swiftly and harshly. You are all aware that I have offered a one hundred groschen reward to anyone for the capture of *Herr Johann Weiss*. We will capture him and he will suffer terribly for a long time in in our prison. Anyone helping or hiding information for this type of treachery will also earn severely punishment. If this kind of incident happens again, your whole group may begin to suffer, either while on the road, or when you get to your new colony!"

I asked *Christoph*, "What does that mean? Why punish us if someone else breaks the rules? That is not fair!"

Christoph sighed, and then slowly answered, "We are no longer individuals or single families or even just couples, but are now part of a bigger group with the single goal of establishing our colony. I think it means that as our group gets smaller and smaller, our chances of success at building our colony lessen."

I thought about what *Lt. Von Ditmarr* and *Christoph* both said, and then replied to *Christoph*, "I felt that he was threatening us, but actually after thinking on it, he was probably just warning us. You are right that each person that leaves the group makes our group weaker, and makes our future success less likely."

Just as before, *Lt. Von Ditmarr* sought out and met with the City Officials to mention that his caravan and its travelers were traveling at the express desire of Her Imperial Highness, most merciful great Lady, Empress Catherine Alexeevna, Autocrat of all Russland; and that any cooperation or non-cooperation would be noted in his official report back to the Crown.

Like Novgorod and Torzhok, the city leaders enthusiastically scurried around to provide us adequate lodging and food. As in Novgorod, they guided us to a гостиница (gasthaus). The only difference was that this one was easily twice the size of the one in Novgorod.

Each family again had their own room. This time I was more experienced, and did not ask how many others we would be sharing it with. There were other guests also in the gasthaus, but they were all on another floor. Other than that, most everything else was about the same as in Novgorod.

One thing had changed, and that was here in Москва we did not have to do any chores. People actually waited on us, arranging our bed and covers, cleaning our room, and fixing our food. We had nothing to do, but rest and see the City. Everyone wondered why *Lt. Von Ditmarr* did not have us to chores, and so I asked our *Vorsteher Balzer Barthuli*.

Vorsteher Balzer Barthuli laughed and replied, "I wondered about that too, and asked the *Lieutenant*. He told me that he was worried about the general health of the group as more and more of us were getting sick. The last thing he needs is for some of our group getting seriously sick or dying. And it just looked bad to report into the Commander in Saratov with a bunch of sickly looking scarecrows. He needed our group to be, or at least look, strong and healthy."

When we told this to the rest of our group, everyone was happy and no one complained about no chores. We spent our nights sleeping well, and our days relaxing and eating well. This was my kind of traveling!

We had been in Москва́ two days when *£t. Von Ditmarr* called us all together. He announced, "We are going on a tour of the City. There are important sights that as new Russen, I have decided you must see. I will lead the group and two of my soldiers will follow to make sure you do not get lost. We leave now."

We followed as he led the way down one street and up another, left here, then right. We finally stopped on a wide street with all sorts of people hawking anything and everything. There were also street musicians playing songs for money, and artists with their paintings for sale. The crowds of people made our movement through them as a group difficult. We lost sight of our *£t. Von Ditmarr* a few times, but his soldiers following us always led us back to him.

We followed the *£ieutenant* up and down more streets. Eventually, he led us toward what he called the Kremlin, with its outer walls and towers standing over the busy streets of Москва́. He proudly told us, "All roads in Москва́ lead to the magnificent Kremlin. Its name means fortress or castle. The city of Москва́ was first founded within those very walls."

We entered a huge square many scores of sazhen (each sazhen is almost two yards) wide and hundreds of sazhen long called the Krasnaya Ploshchad. I noticed that many of the buildings were built of deep red bricks. Curious, I asked *Lt. Von Ditmarr*, "Is this place named after the red brick buildings?"

He laughed and replied, "Many people think it is, but actually, while the word Krasnaya does mean 'red', it also can mean 'beautiful', so it is really not the 'Red Square', but the 'Beautiful Square'. The more common 'red' meaning stuck with the ignorant peasants, and so we are now saddled with 'Red Square' forever."

Standing there in the square, *Lt. Von Ditmarr* pointed out the buildings all around, "To the south east are the brightly-domed Собор Покрова пресвятой Богородицы, что на Рву (Sobor Vasiliia Blazhennogo, St. Basil's Cathedral) and the palaces and cathedrals of the Кремль (Kremlin). On the eastern side of the square is the Kazan Cathedral. On the northwest are the Principal Medicine Store and the Воскресенские ворота (Иверские ворота, Resurrection or Iberian Gate), and the Chapel."

Lt. Von Ditmarr led us south, and stopped us at circular stone platform built. He called this the Лобное место (Lobnoye Mesto, Place of Skulls), and told us that the raised circular platform is for announcing the Tsar's ukases (Proclamations with force of Law) and for the public religious ceremonies that regularly takes place.

As he led us farther south in the square, we finally stood before St. Basil's Cathedral with each dome having a distinctive patterning and color, creating a stunning sight reminiscent of whipped meringue.

The *Lieutenant* told us that an old tale has it that Tsar Ivan IV was so impressed with the beauty of the St. Basil's Cathedral that he had the architects blinded, so that they could never build anything as beautiful again. I found the eight colorful domes so beautiful and breathtaking; I could almost believe the old tale.

Moving on, we passed vendors selling books on a stone bridge crossing the moat to the Spasskaya Tower Gate.

Sobor Vasiliia Blazhennogo (St. Basil's Cathedral)

The Spasskaya Tower Gate is the main front gate of the Kremlin and is normally only used for Crown use, but since *Lt. Von Ditmarr* was leading us, we also entered through it this one time. We found gardens to the left along the river, and many storied large buildings to the right.

Stone Bridge at the Spasskaya Tower Gate

Lt. Von Ditmarr led us into another square, and pointed out and talked about the Kolokolnia Ivana Velikogo (Ivan the Great Bell-Tower) standing higher than any other of the Kremlin's buildings; and the Blagoveshchenskii Sobor (Annunciation Cathedral); almost directly in front of us.

Kolokolnia Ivana Velikogo
(Ivan the Great Bell-Tower)

To the left he called out the Cathedral of the Archangel; and to the right, the Cathedral of Twelve Apostles, the golden-topped, the five-domed Uspenskii Sobor (Cathedral of the Assumption); the Church of the Deposition of the Virgin's Robe, and the Cathedral of the High Savior.

**Five-domed Uspenskii Sobor
(Cathedral of the Assumption)**

Our whole group was overwhelmed and speechless. Never before had any of us seen so many churches in any one place. Just as we had concluded in Lübeck with its half dozen churches, either the Москва locals were obsessed with GOD, or they needed that many churches to confess and repent for sin rampant in the streets.

I had *Christoph* ask the *Lieutenant*, "why are there so many Churches in Москва́?"

The *Lieutenant* scratched his beard for a minute, laughed, and replied, "I suppose that the official answer is that we Russen are a very GOD fearing people and wish to honor GOD as often as possible. The honest answer is likely that we Russen sample all that life has to offer, both good and sinful, sometimes in excess, and have much to repent for to GOD."

I was right all along.

Lt. Von Ditmarr led us back towards the river and soon we stopped to see the Bol'shoi Kremlevskii Dvorets (Great Kremlin Palace).

The *Lieutenant* turned to us, "It is time for us to make our way back to our lodging. Follow me closely so that you do not lose yourselves in the crowds of Москва́." We left the Kremlin out the nearby Borovitskaya Tower gate.

We were all exhausted, and were glad to be going back, though what we had seen today was as beautiful as anything we had ever seen in our whole lives.

These ornate and beautiful cathedrals were such a stark contrast from the Russische peasants' run-down wooden shacks that we had often seen in so many villages along our route.

I always knew that my family had been well off, not rich and not poor, and that there were both the very rich and very poor in my Deutschland, but here, the poor were so very, very poor and the rich looked very, very rich. Even our Deutsches Katholische Kirchen were not as ornate and fine as these Kirchen.

View of the Kremlin from the river

That night in bed, as I lay next to *Christoph*, I could not sleep as my head was spinning with all the beauty I had seen today; that overwhelming beauty, and the awareness of the enormous difference between the rich and poor in this country.

I wanted to talk about these thoughts with my *Christoph*, but he was sound asleep and softly snoring. Apparently, neither the beauty we saw today, nor the wide gap between poor and rich, bothered his sleep.

Kirche of St. Nicholas on the Ilyinka

The next day, we again rested all day. However, the day after, *Lt. Von Ditmarr* led us to another part of the city known as Китай-город (Kitay-Gorod).

We visited the Tserkov Troitsy v Nikitinkakh (Church of the Trinity in Nikitinov), the Cathedral of the Sign; the Церковь Всех Святых, что на Кулишках (Church of All Saints na Kulichkakh); St. George's Church on Pskov Hill; and St. Maksim's Church.

We also saw St. Anna's Church at the Corner, and the Church of St. Nicholas on the Ilyinka.

That night, at supper, *Lt. Von Ditmarr* announced that we would leave Москва́ early on the morrow. We all enjoyed ourselves here in Москва́, and realized we were reluctant to leave. Even so, all showed up that early morning of 2 June 1765 and soon we again rolled out on our way.

It was now much warmer, and when we left the City, almost everyone got out and walked. One couple in our group, *Herr Heinrich* and *Frau Dorothea Wagner*, had come down sick before we made it to Москва́, and were sick the whole time here. Still sick as we left, they rode all alone in one of the wagons. We all prayed for them to get better, but other than that, we could do nothing for them.

Over the next fourteen days and nights we rolled through the village of Лыубертсы (Lyubertsy), Токарево (Tokarevo), Вареыа (Vereya), Зхуковскиы (Zhukovskiy), Раменскоые (Ramenskoye), Ыурово (Yurovo), Бронитсы (Bronnitsy), Стамиково (Stamikovo), Никитскоые (Nikitskoye), Степансхцхино (Stepanshchino), Непетсино (Nepetsino), Никул'скоые (Nikul'skoye), Радузхныы (Raduzhnyy), and Коломна (Kolomna). We crossed the река Ока (reka Oka, river Oka) and passed through the villages of Коробцхеево (Korobcheevo), Лукховитсы (Lukhovitsy), Врацхово (Vrachovo), Гавриловскоые (Gavrilovskoye), Григор' евскоые (Grigor'evskoye), Высокоые (Vysokoye), and Тыусхево (Tyushevo).

Like so many times before, it was just day after day either riding inside the wagon bored crazy, or walking down the now dusty road in the hot sun. The nights were one strange silent Russische couple after another sharing their meal of cabbage soup and millet gruel and milk, and their home and barn, with us and their chickens and sheep and pigs.

The only thing that was different was our sick couple, *Herr Heinrich* and *Frau Dorothea Wagner*. They never got well, and day-by-day, just got worse. Nothing we gave them helped, and our prayers did not help either.

As we neared Ryazan, the *Barthuli* sisters read to us what they had written for our travels:

2 June 1765   Leave from Москва́ (Moscow).

Night 1 - 2 June 1765   Overnight in Токарево
(Tokarevo)

Night 2 – 3 June 1765   Overnight in Зхуковскиы
(Zhukovskiy)

Night 3 – 4 June 1765   Overnight in Ыурово (Yurovo)

Night 4 – 5 June 1765   Overnight in Бронитсы
(Bronnitsy)

Night 5 – 6 June 1765   Overnight in Никитскоые
(Nikitskoye)

Night 6 – 7 June 1765   Overnight in Непетсино
(Nepetsino)

Night 7 – 8 June 1765   Overnight in Коломна (Kolomna)

Night 8 – 9 June 1765   Overnight in Коробцхеево
(Korobcheevo)

Night 9 – 10 June 1765   Overnight in Лукховитсы

(Lukhovitsy)

Night 10 – 11 June 1765   Overnight in Врацхово
(Vrachovo)

Night 11 – 12 June 1765   Overnight in Григор'евскоые
(Grigor'evskoye)

Night 12 – 13 June 1765   Overnight in Григор'евскоые
(Grigor'evskoye)

1765 - Elizabeth & Appollina Barthuli

***Our Route from Москва́ (Moscow)
to Ряза́нь (Ryazan)***

Night 13 – 14 June 1765   Overnight in Тыусхево
(Tyushevo)

Night 14 – 15 June 1765   Overnight in Тыусхево
(Tyushevo)

Рязáнь

We arrived in Рязáнь (Ryazan) on 16 June in the year of our LORD one thousand seven hundred sixty-five (1765).

The plan was to stay here only overnight, but *Herr Heinrich* and *Frau Dorothea Wagner* had slipped into comas. They were both near death. The local doctor attended them, but could do nothing except wait for the inevitable. We could do nothing for them, but bow our heads and pray to the LORD for his mercy, and if he so chose, to take them to be at his side without any further suffering.

Our LORD must have heard our prayers, for on the 17th of June in the year of our LORD one thousand seven hundred sixty-five, they both passed minutes apart to a better place with our LORD in Heaven. Two more of our group were now gone.

Lt. Von Ditmarr made all the arrangements and paid all the costs for them, and decided they be buried according to Russische custom. As a group, we protested that they be buried in the Deutsche way, but he sternly overruled us with a few choice words, "You, and they, even when dead, are all now Russe!"

The *Barthuli* sisters wrote down the Russische burial traditions as performed, "First they washed the body. This prepares the dead for their meeting with GOD. They are dressed in all-white, handmade clothing left slightly unfinished since it belongs in not this world, but the other world of Heaven. The body must wear a belt, because the dead will need it when they resurrect in the Last Judgment."

The tradition continued, "After washing and dressing the body, the body was laid out for three days before it was laid in the coffin. For fear of waking the newly dead, mourning did not begin during the washing or dressing. The coffin is made like a bed, with a pillow stuffed with birch bark or wood shavings. The men carry the coffin on their backs to the cemetery, where the funeral will take place."

More of the tradition, "At the burial place, a priest performed the last ceremony, praying over the body and allowing mourners to throw dirt on the grave to symbolize merging the corpse into the earth. The mourners threw soil and coins into the grave, as the coins are to pay for transit to the Heaven. Once they bury the body, the soul can travel on to the better world of our LORD. After the burial, mourners sing laments, depicting the deceased leaving and the soul departing from the body."

While we did not know *Herr Heinrich* and *Frau Dorothea Wagner* well, we all prayed for the forgiveness of our LORD and the acceptance of their souls in Heaven.

A more somber group all boarded the covered wagons the next morning of 21 June 1765. Sadly, two of our group would never see their new home. As for us, soon the wagons again rolled closer and closer to our new home.

As time and our recent sorrow passed, almost everyone got out and walked. The fresh air felt good and made us feel stronger. Now and then, you could hear many in our group coughing and sneezing. I worried that our poor dead friends had somehow delivered their sickness to us before they passed.

As the days and nights came and went, more and more of us became sicker. Even the Russischen soldiers and teamsters came down with whatever this was, and *Lt. Von Ditmarr* was a pale figure of his normal self.

Our group continued to fall ill, weakened and could no longer walk, and one-by-one climbed into the wagons for rest. Some stubborn ones, refusing to concede they were sick, stumbled and fell, and were loaded in comatose. Now overloaded with the ill, the close quarters inside the wagons just made everyone even sicker.

We could only make it through a few villages each day, and each time we stopped for the night, we stayed at least two nights to gather strength.

The never-ending line of villages of Турлатово (Turlatovo), Мар'ино (Mar'ino), Александрово (Aleksandrovo), Протасово (Protasovo), Болосхнево (Boloshnevo), Подиково (Podikovo), Огородниково (Ogorodnikovo), Перкино (Perkino), Сусхки (Sushki), Мосолово (Mosolovo), Запол'е (Zapol'e), and Задубров'е (Zadubrov'e) faded into nothing in the distance behind us as we struggled to get closer to our final destination. Even though, as we became weaker and weaker and moved slower and slower each day, we were still closer and closer to our new colony.

Those that still had the strength to walk gladly did so as the smell in the wagons was foul from all the sick. There was no healthy place on any wagon, the sick were everywhere and outnumbered the well, five to one.

Christoph had somehow stayed well, maybe from all the walking outside alongside the wagons. I was not as lucky, as the fever and chills tormented me day and night, but I was not as sick as most, and could still eat a little food.

Christoph had moved me near the rear of our wagon for fresh air, and regularly looked in on me. He wanted to climb in and hold me, but I sternly told him, "You must keep away from me and stay well for both of us. If you get deathly sick, we and all our dreams are finished."

He frowned, but mostly did as I said. In spite of my warning, he maintained a watch over me, brought me water and food, and kept me as clean as he could.

By the time we reached the village of Сас'кино (Sas'kino), the sickness had overcome more than forty of our group and the soldiers and the teamsters. Even our strong *Lt. Von Ditmarr* had fallen very ill.

The locals of the village of Sas'kino stubbornly opposed a caravan of the sick in their village, but soon changed their mind, as they desperately wanted the silver coins that the *Lieutenant* tempted them with to take us in and care for us.

Food and blankets and good water quickly arrived along with good care for each of our sick. We stayed three days here, and most of our group, including me, gained strength and recovered slightly. Only one in our group, the single man *Herr Peter Bruckmann*, became weaker and worse off.

While I seemed to be recovering, my dear *Christoph* was also starting to show early signs of the sickness with the cough and the stuffed nose and the sore throat. I said a silent prayer to our LORD and begged that he keep my *Christoph* from this terrible illness.

We left Сас'кино (Sas'kino) on the 28th of June 1765, stronger and healthier, and with the villagers holding much more money than they had seen for a very long time, if ever. I prayed that they did not trade their health for our silver.

Our caravan rolled through Аводт'инка (Avdot'inka), Екатериновка (Ekaterinovka), Путыанино (Putyanino), Глебово (Glebovo), Карабукхино (Karabukhino), and Большая Екатериновка (Bol'shaya Ekaterinovka) over the next few days.

With most of us still weak from the sickness and the constantly traveling, *Lt. Von Ditmarr* ordered us again to stop for three nights in the village of Схатск (Shatsk).

Just as in Сас'кино (Sas'kino), the locals of the village also steadfastly opposed a caravan of the sick in their village. As before, they soon changed their mind when the *Lieutenant* tempted them with silver coins.

Russisches Home

Each day, the sick in our group, including my husband *Christoph* and me, gained back strength and became a little better. All except for our most sick, *Herr Peter Bruckmann*, he was not getting any better.

We rolled out and left early on the morn of the fourth day in Схатск (Shatsk). With more feeling stronger, walking outside, and getting fresh air, there was more room in the wagons for those still very sick. And there were now more of us to care for the sick.

Our caravan of wagons passed through the villages of Лесноые-Конобеево (Lesnoye-Konobeevo), Куцхас'ево (Kuchas'evo), Ыамбирно (Yambirno), Схафторка (Shaftorka), Салтыково (Saltykovo), Горбуновка (Gorbunovka), Умет (Umet), Зубова Полыана (Zubova Polyana), Цхапаев (Chapaev), and Новыые Выселки (Novyye Vyselki). As we neared Богдапово (Bogdanavo), the *Barthuli* sisters read to us what they had written:

21 June 1765   Leave from Рязáнь (Ryazan).

Night 1 - 21 June 1765   Overnight in Турлатово (Turlatovo)

Night 2 – 22 June 1765   Overnight in Болосхнево (Boloshnevo)

Night 3 – 23 June 1765   Overnight in Перкино (Perkino)

Night 4 – 24 June 1765   Overnight in Мосолово (Mosolovo)

Night 5 – 25 June 1765   Overnight in Сас'кино (Sas'kino)

Night 6 – 26 June 1765   Overnight in Сас'кино (Sas'kino)

Nacht 7 – 27 June 1765   Overnight in Сас'кино (Sas'kino)

Night 8 – 28 June 1765   Overnight in Путыанино (Putyanino)

Night 9 – 29 June 1765   Overnight in Большая Екатериновка (Bol'shaya Ekaterinovka)

Night 10 – 30 June 1765   Overnight in Схатск (Shatsk)

Night 11 – 31 June 1765   Overnight in Схатск (Shatsk)

Night 12 – 1 July 1765   Overnight in Схатск (Shatsk)

Night 13 – 2 July 1765   Overnight in Куцхас'ево (Kuchas'evo)

Night 14 – 3 July 1765   Overnight in Куцхас'ево (Kuchas'evo)

Night 15 – 4 July 1765   Overnight in Схафторка (Shaftorka)

Night 16 – 5 July 1765   Overnight in Схафторка (Shaftorka)

Night 17 – 6 July 1765   Overnight in Горбуновка (Gorbunovka)

Night 18 – 7 July 1765   Overnight in Горбуновка (Gorbunovka)

Night 19 – 8 July 1765   Overnight in Умет (Umet)

Night 20 – 9 July 1765   Overnight in Зубова Полыана (Zubova Polyana)

Night 21 – 10 July 1765   Overnight in Новыые Выселки (Novyye Vyselki)

Night 22 – 11 July 1765   Overnight in Новыые Выселки (Novyye Vyselki)

Богдапово

We arrived in Богдапово (Bogdanovo - now Spassk) on 12 July in the year of our LORD one thousand seven hundred sixty-five (1765), and spent one night there.

We would have stayed a few nights, but the locals would not have it. No amount of money the *Lieutenant* offered would sway their mind and allow "sick" in their village. Nothing he said about the wishes of the Crown and our being an "official" caravan mattered.

All they wanted was for us to leave their village, and leave quickly. As they vastly outnumbered our group and our soldiers, and acted as if they would move us out by force if needed, early the next morning we left along with an escort of many local villagers to make sure that we did not ever return.

Over the next few days, we rolled through the villages of Дубровки (Dubrovki), Кувак-Никол'скоые (Kuvak-Nikol'skoye), Низх Ломов (Nizh Lomov), Большая Кхутора (Bol'shaya Khutora), Атмис (Atmis) to finally stop for two days and nights in Вирга (Virga).

Most of us were well by this time, and while a few were still weak and recovering, our most ill member, *Herr Peter Bruckmann*, no longer reacted to anything and was near death. Again, as a group, we prayed for our LORD to have mercy.

And so, as was the will of the LORD, *Herr Peter Bruckmann* passed on in a deep sleep. We all prayed for the safe passage of his soul to Heaven.

Lt. Von Ditmarr, now eager to get our group to the new Saratov, did not even allow us time to bury poor *Peter*. Instead, he gave the locals extra money to give *Herr Peter,* a Christian but again Russen, burial.

We left the next morning, hoping that they would, in fact, actually give him a Christian burial, and not just pocket the money and dump his corpse in a hole in the ground. I suspect they did just dump his body…

Five days later, after having traveled through the villages of Ломовка (Lomovka), Микхаыловка (Mikhaylovka), Богородскове (Bogorodskoye), Моксхан (Mokshan), and Рамзаы (Ramzay), we were only hours from Пе́нза (Penza).

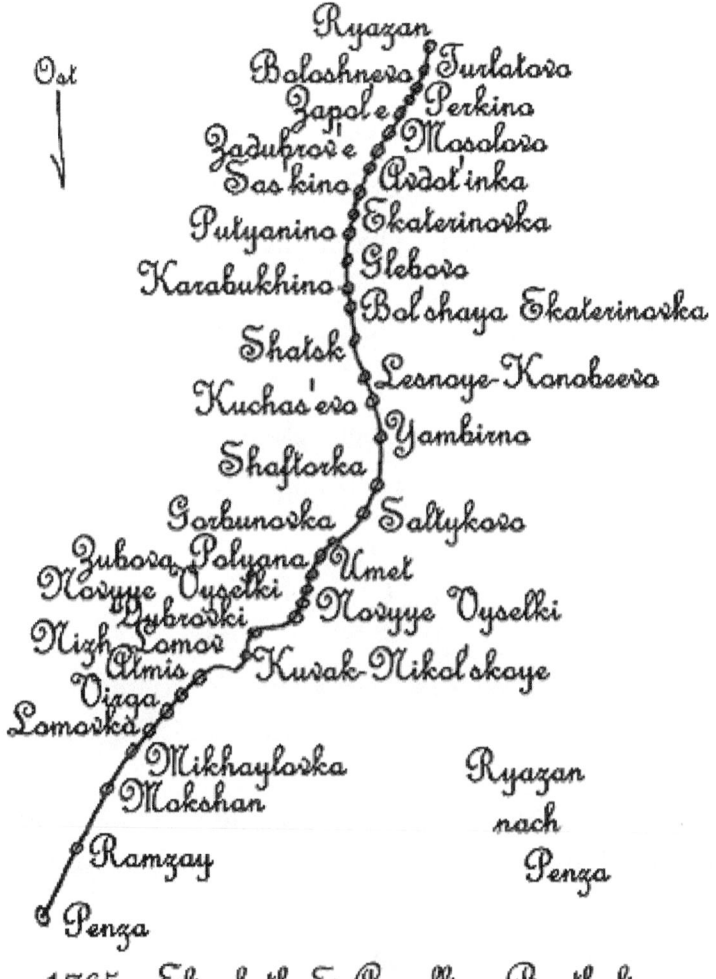

***Our Route from Ряза́нь (Ryazan)
to Пе́нза (Penza)***

As we neared Penza, our *Barthuli* sisters read to us what they had written for this part of our trip:

13 July 1765   Leave from Богдапово (Bogdanavo).

Night 1 - 13 July 1765   Overnight in Кувак-Никол'скоые (Kuvak-Nikol'skoye)

Night 2 – 14 July 1765   Overnight in Низх Ломов (Nizh Lomov)

Night 3 – 15 July 1765   Overnight in Вирга (Virga)

Night 4 – 16 July 1765   Overnight in Вирга (Virga)

Night 5 – 17 July 1765   Overnight in Микхаыловка (Mikhaylovka)

Night 6 – 18 July 1765   Overnight in Моксхан (Mokshan)

Night 7 – 19 July 1765   Overnight in Рамзаы (Ramzay)

Night 8 – 20 July 1765   Overnight in Рамзаы (Ramzay)

Пе́нза

◆LT. VON ÐITMARR◆

Entering Пе́нза (Penza), sixteen days north of Сара́тов (Saratov), Russland

After traveling east from Bogdanovo for nine days, we arrived in Пе́нза (Penza) on the 21st day of July in the year of our LORD one thousand seven hundred sixty-five (1765).

This group of Colonists, that I am completely responsible for, now numbers four less than what I started with on this mission. Each one lost, whether by death or desertion, lessens the odds of that their new Colony will succeed. It also will not reflect well on me, when I fail to deliver to the Military Command in Saratov, all they assigned to my care in St. Petersburg.

I have done my best, but this damn sickness destroyed all my travel plans. I know not what I could have done differently to change this outcome. Yet, maybe, I might have worked them too hard in Novgorod, or we might have left too soon after the winter storms ceased.

I must not lose anymore! Even if it means we are late reporting to Saratov, I must ensure that all stay healthy and fit, and above all, do not desert the group! I ordered my soldiers to double their attention and keep close eyes on the group, looking for anyone sickly or wanting to leave.

I ordered the Colonists to rest and get well while we stayed three nights in Пе́нза (Penza). I also had a long talk with *Vorsteher Balzer Barthuli* stressing the importance to all of us that everyone stays healthy, and that no one leave the group. I also brought to his attention that if his groups numbers continue to fall, at some point, the Crown may decide that there is no chance for the success of their Colony, and may reassign them all different colonies.

Early on the morning of the fourth day in Penza, I led the wagon caravan back out on the road heading south towards to the Volga River city of Сара́тов (Saratov). With some good fortune, something we have so far been lacking on this trip, we will arrive there in sixteen days on the 9th of August.

Moving according to my plan, we rolled south through the villages of Алфер'евка (Alfer'evka), Кныазевка (Knyazevka), Кондол (Kondol'), Клыуцхи (Klyuchi), Цхунаки (Chunaki), Маыскоые (Mayskoye), Петровск (Petrovsk), Новозакхаркино (Novozakharkino), Ыазыковка (Yazykovka), Озерки (Ozerki), Песцханка (Peschanka), Полцханиновка (Polchaninovka), Большая

Ивановка (Bol'shaya Ivanovka), Большая Каменка (Bol'shaya Kamenka), Схирокоые (Shirokoye), Сторозхевка (Storozhevka), and Елсханка (Elshanka).

One more day and we would be in Saratov, and I could hand responsibility for these Deutscher to the Officials of the Kontor of the Guardianship Chancery for Foreigners.

After over nine months, I am will be finally rid of them. None too soon and it will be a well-deserved celebration time for my men and me, with plenty of time off for good food and drink, and for time with the women of Saratov.

ALMOST TO SARATOV

◆CHRISTOPH KARL◆

A few hours north of Сара́тов (Saratov), Samara, Russland

Lt. Von Ditmarr announced that we would be in Saratov late today. Our traveling would soon be over, and we could get down to our real task, that of building our new Colony and our homes.

As we neared Saratov, the sisters read to us what they had written:

"24 July 1765   Leave from Пе́нза (Penza).

Night 1 - 24 July 1765   Overnight in Алфер'евка (Alfer'evka)

Night 2 – 25 July 1765   Overnight in Кныазевка (Knyazevka)

Night 3 – 26 July 1765   Overnight in Кондол (Kondol')

Night 4 – 27 July 1765   Overnight in Кондол (Kondol')

Night 5 – 28 July 1765   Overnight in Клыуцхи (Klyuchi)

Night 6 – 29 July 1765   Overnight in Клыуцхи (Klyuchi)

Night 7 – 30 July 1765   Overnight in Цхунаки (Chunaki)

Night 8 – 31 July 1765   Overnight in Петровск
(Petrovsk)

Our Route from Пе́нза (Penza)
to Сара́тов (Saratov)

Night 9 – 1 August 1765 (Petrovsk)   Overnight in Петровск

Night 10 – 2 August 1765 (Novozakharkino)   Overnight in Новозакхаркино

Night 11 – 3 August 1765 (Yazykovka)   Overnight in Ыазыковка

Night 12 – 4 August 1765 (Peschanka)   Overnight in Песцханка

Night 13 – 5 August 1765 (Polchaninovka)   Overnight in Полцханиновка

Night 14 – 6 August 1765 (Polchaninovka)   Overnight in Полцханиновка

Night 15 – 7 August 1765 (Bol'shaya Kamenka)   Overnight in Большая Каменка

Nacht 16 – 8 August 1765 (Elshanka)   Overnight in Елсханка

Сара́тов

▴LT. VON ÐITMᴙRR▴

Kontor of the Guardianship Chancery for Foreigners, Сара́тов (Saratov), Samara, Russland

After traveling south from Penza for sixteen days, we finally arrived in Сара́тов (Saratov) on the 9th day of August in the year of our LORD one thousand seven hundred sixty-five (1765).

It was early in the hot afternoon when we arrived at the walled compound of the 'Kontor of the Guardianship Chancery for Foreigners' subordinate office in Saratov. This was my delivery point for the Colonists.

I found the headquarters and reported in. The Kontor Official, a large Russischer Cossack, came out to process in the Colonists.

One by one, each Colonist's name checked off as they left my charge to become another's torment. He noted that four were missing!

"Yes, four names remain unchecked. One deserted along the way, three died along the way," I replied to the Kontor Officer.

"Yes, I know that I am responsible for their health and safety, and getting them here," I replied again to the Kontor Officer.

As the Kontor led my group of Deutsche away, with a happy heart, I said my last good-byes. Truthfully, they were all that bad, but they were, and would always be, still just Deutscher at heart.

"Yes, I know that I must turn in a complete report explaining how the one Colonist was 'lost', and how the other three became ill," I replied again to the Kontor Officer.

"Yes, I understand the importance of all the Colonists assigned to a location arriving intact and healthy," I replied again to the Kontor Officer.

"No, I dispute your assertion that I neglected my assigned duty! I do not feel that my men or I could have done any better in securing the Colonists or insuring their health. I doubt you could have done half as well!" I sarcastically answered the fat stupid Russischer Cossack Kontor Official.

"Good, you write your report that there are missing and dead! If we are now through here, then sign the release at once so my men and I can leave you to your important duties," I answered.

Thinking to myself, I wondered if this stupid Cossack knew how to sign his name. Well, the LORD protects us, this man does know how to sign his name, and has in fact signed his name on the release.

Yes, we are finally finished here! It will be good for my men and me to get back with our own people.

My new mission this moment is for my men and me to find good food, good drink, and loose women. Without another word, I turned and led my soldiers away from this damned place.

Heaven help those poor Colonists; they know not what they have signed on for, or are due to soon experience…

THE COMPOUND

♦JACOBINA KARL♦

A walled compound in Сара́тов (Saratov), Samara, Russland

On the outskirts of Сара́тов (Saratov), the *Lieutenant* led us into a large walled compound. There were armed Russischen soldiers guarding the entrance and checking all that came and went.

I glanced at *Christoph*, who was frowning and probably wondering the same thing, and thought to myself as I had before on this trip, "Are these guards to protect us from the locals or are they to protect us from escaping? Why would we even want to escape? Is there something more we need to know? Maybe, the guards are here to keep us from learning things from the locals that the Crown does not yet want us to know." I made up my mind to talk with *Christoph* about this later.

There were scores of long one-story log buildings like the run-down Army barracks we had stayed in before, but in much better shape; maybe even recently built.

The *Lieutenant* led us to a large three story building in the center of the compound, and went inside. A few minutes later, he returned with the largest Russen we had ever seen. This man was a good foot taller than my *Christoph*, and three times as thick around the middle. He had filthy hair halfway down his back, and a beard almost as long.

I pulled closer to *Christoph* for safety. I looked up at *Christoph*; who stunned by the size of this Russen, just stood there with his mouth open.

They called our names, and checked us off on a list. As they led us away, I could hear our *Lieutenant* loudly talking, and then arguing with the large Russen. The last I saw was that the *Lieutenants'* soldiers had moved closer to him and looked ready for a fight. I hope we did not get them in any trouble. They would never be my friends, but they did get us here, and I wished them no harm.

We followed our new guide to one of the long narrow log barracks buildings. The buildings looked to be maybe ten sazhen (sixty-five feet) long, and must be new as the cut logs still smelled.

Before we could enter the first one, one of the Russen guiding us spoke in poor Deutsch, "These five buildings are your buildings. Each building houses two families. Each family will get their own room. Stay in your room until I come back for you later. Do not leave your room or be found away from your room. We do not tolerate any insubordination or resistance to good order. Enter and follow me!"

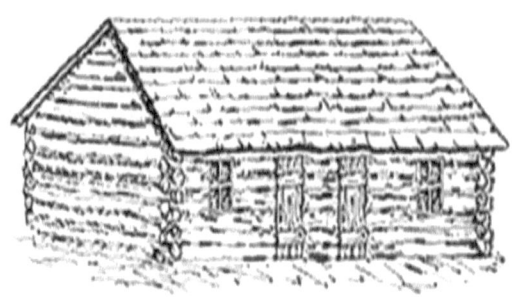

Once inside the door, I saw that there was a large room. It had a shared center wall that only went up maybe an arm's length past the top of my *Christoph's* head, but at least that provided some privacy.

Our room had a raised platform, I suppose it was for sleeping, and a bench, and a window of glass for light. There was a small wood stove, I suppose for heat. In the custom of most Russische houses, there was no chimney. When the stove was used, the smoke escaped through the roof, or if too smoky, through the open door.

Christoph closed the door and smiled a wide grin, and I already knew what he was thinking. Men! They only have one thing on their minds, or maybe they have nothing on their minds and it is not their mind they are following... We were finally alone, and *Christoph* sat on the bed and motioned me to come to him.

Almost in his arms, we heard a noise at the door, and thinking someone was coming in, I backed away. No one came in. "*Christoph*, what was that noise?" I asked.

Christoph got up, went to the door and pulled the handle to open it. It did not open. Thinking it was stuck, he pulled harder. Almost at the very same time, we both realized that they had just locked us in. As disturbing as that was, there was absolutely nothing that we could do about it.

Christoph shrugged, went back to the bed, and again motioned for me to come to him. Obviously, losing his freedom and being a prisoner in the building here, had little or no effect on his other more basic needs.

Reconciled with our situation and my fate at the hands of my *Christoph*, I came to him. One would think he had been in a monastery without a woman for years.

I lost track of time, and both *Christoph* and I had fell asleep after our romp. At the first loud bang on the door, we were instantly awake, up and dressing.

We could hear the door unlocked from the outside, and a voice that yelled in, "Outside now. We go to show you where water is, where food is, and where the сортир (outhouse) is."

A Russischen soldier led our group to a nearby large log building. This was the communal dining hall where we would eat all our meals while we were here.

The food was not as fine as what we were served in Moscow, but better than many of our village stops along the way. Bowls of salads, bowls of soups, and some type of fish waited our dining. Hot tea was again the drink of the night.

After our meal, they led us back to our lodging and locked us in; we were exhausted, early to bed and not to romp, but to sleep.

The next morning wakeup came a little after dawn. Breakfast completed, we followed our guide to another large building. On entry, I saw it filled with benches, like a Kirche, but with no religious items. They directed us to sit, and we did so.

A man I never seen before came and stood at the front of the room. He loudly announced, "I need your attention. I am господин (Mister) *Nicholai Paustovsky* of the Kontor of the Guardianship Chancery for Foreigners' subordinate office here in Саратов. If it is easier for you, you may address me as *Herr Paustovsky*. Today, I will tell you more about your future homes and land. I will also tell you, about Russische customs, and about what will happen during the next fourteen days you are here."

He continued, "First, all of you will be checked again to insure you are healthy before we send you to build your Colony. Those that are not healthy will stay here until you recover."

Herr Paustovsky continued with his talk about Russische customs and traditions. Few of us paid any attention to this, as we all knew we were still Deutscher, and would if possible; continue with our own ways and traditions.

He also told us that the 'Kontor of the Guardianship Chancery for Foreigners' office would issue to each family before we left the following: one horse, table, benches, bed, barrels, water buckets, boxes, iron skillet, wood plates, wood spoons, and a bread trough.

Over those fourteen days, *Herr Paustovsky* met with us often and told us more, "Keep a close watch on your money and anything you value while here and on the remainder of the trip. Others may want your things too."

Herr Paustovsky told us even more about our new lands, "The large river to the east is the Volga. It is the natural boundary between our planned Colonies. The Bergseite (hillside) Colonies or west side Colonies having land that climbs steeply from the Volga River to forested hills. This side has many deep creek gorges covered with tall grass and bushes. The Wiesenseite (meadow side) Colonies or east side Colonies will be located on the low and level grassy and tree-less plain that slopes gently towards the Volga, Here there are no deep gorges, but many small slow creeks. The land is flat as far as the eye can see."

"The steppes all around us were claimed by nomadic tribes many, many years ago were. The Crown has purchased these lands from the previous Russische landowners, so you, with our help, can build this 'New Russland.' This wonderful land now is idle awaiting your hard work and attention. While as I said, there is no one living there or tilling the land, you may occasionally have the opportunity to meet some of the nomadic tribes that previously claimed it for themselves. We have also set aside a small amount of land for any Russische peasant families that lived in this area for a long time. Most likely, you will have little to do with them."

"Your Colonies are planned areas of a specified diameter, with a good river or natural spring water source to be settled by up to one thousand families. Separate Colonies villages are located right next to each other so that as a group the Colonies will have mutual need and support. Our Kontor plan is to allocate thirty-four desyatines (eighty-one acres) of land per family to each colony. We have further planned the use of approximately half of this land or seventeen desyatines per family for farming. The remaining to be used for haying, natural forest, vegetable gardens, orchards, and finally, housing."

"We will give to each family one hundred fifty rubles (four thousand five hundred groschen) for you to buy your own livestock and additional farm tools or other things you really need. You will pay this loan of one hundred fifty rubles back to the Kontor over a period of years according to the contract. We will build your houses for you, but will charge those costs to your loan. You will also pay these costs to the Kontor over a period of years according to the contract."

"We are aware of the disagreements in your old country on your religious sects. To prevent this here, your Colony village religion is Lutheran and Reformed. The Kontor prohibits Catholics or other religions from settling in your Colony. This will preserve good order and maintain peace."

"Most of you were farmers in your previous lands. All of you will primarily be farmers now. Some of you were artisans and not farmers before, but as I said, you are all farmers now. You will provide your old crafts or skills after the farming is complete. These additional skills will make you even more valuable to the Colony and the rest of the people. They will need you, and appreciate your skills."

Herr Paustovsky finished with, "Do you have any questions? If not, I will give you some time to discuss all this as a group, and then come back for your questions." With that, he left the front and walked out the door.

Everyone had something to say, most of what he had said was not new to us, and much of it sounded fair, but the direction that all be farmers did not sit well with one of our group.

Herr Jakob Scheck, a handworker from Schweiz, angrily said to the group, "I was told by the *Recruiter* that I would be a wood worker here as the men of my family have always been. While I respect my fellow farmers, I do not enjoy farming and do not intend to become a farmer now. I will not ever follow a plow, and this I will tell to the Kontor man *Paustovsky* when he returns."

We all tried to reason with him but to no avail. Even his wife *Katharina*, and son *Jacob*, begged that he not make trouble. His mind was set. The only thing to do was to wait to see what happened.

Herr Paustovsky returned and asked for questions. Our group raised a few simple questions with simple answers as we all waited to see if our fellow traveler *Herr Scheck* would challenge the rules. We did not have to wait long.

Herr Jakob Scheck stood up, with some difficulty as his wife tried to pull him back down to the bench. He shook her off, and angrily repeated to *Herr Paustovsky* what he had already told us, "I am *Herr Jakob Scheck*, woodworker from Schweiz. The *Recruiter* told me that I would be a wood worker here as the men of my family have always been. While I respect my fellow farmers, I do not enjoy farming and do not intend to become a farmer now. I do not care what the Kontor orders. I will not take up the plow. I will be a woodworker!"

Herr Paustovsky of the Kontor Office of the Guardianship Chancery for Foreigners did not say anything at all for a while. In the dead silence, we all looked back and forth at *Herr Scheck* and then the Official waiting for something.

Herr Paustovsky finally responded, "*Jakob Scheck*. Yes, you are the woodworker that we have assigned to be part of this Colony so that it will grow and prosper. The farmers would have will need your skills in construction of their houses and buildings. You are a valuable member of this Colony."

He continued, "My sincere thanks to you for volunteering to be part of this great effort to build our 'New Russland.' However, let me be perfectly clear, we do not negotiate and you are a farmer now, you have no choice or alternative! And when your farmer work is completed, you will also be a woodworker! I expect your fellow Colonists to highly value your woodworker skills, and therefore possibly reduce your time behind the plow. However, with that said, you are, and will be, a farmer!"

Continuing on, "There will be no further discussion on this, and failure to cooperate and assist with the farming in your colony will be dealt with harshly and cause the removal of you and your family from the Colony for relocation to a less enjoyable, and drastically colder area such as Siberia. Have I made our position perfectly clear? The choice of whether you and your family live in the new Colony with your friends, or in Siberia as indentured workers is completely up to you. Answer me yes or no, *Herr Jakob Scheck*!"

Herr Jakob Scheck still stood, but did not speak.

Herr Paustovsky drew in a deep breath and sternly said, "*Frau* of *Jakob Scheck* and other Colonists, it is in all your best interests that this man, *Herr Jakob Scheck*, understand and agree with our rules. Disobedience is not choice and is a violation of good order and peace. Removal of the *Scheck* family for disobedience will be immediate if he does not agree. Since I am aware of this issue, the Kontor will regularly check if *Herr Jakob Scheck* does his farming. If he does not, removal of his family will quickly occur! I will leave and give you some time to persuade him to see the only choice. Be warned, my patience is running out. There will be no additional time! When I return, I expect this settled, and to hear *Herr Scheck* say to me only one word. That word is 'Yes'." With that, *Herr Paustovsky* stormed out the door.

The group swooped down on poor *Herr Jakob Scheck*. We told him that we needed his skills and, of course, while he must now be a farmer, we would make sure that he was more often a woodworker. He was still not convinced.

His wife, *Katerina*, crying, pleaded with him, "Dear husband, as always the choice is yours, but the alternative of Siberia that the Russen offer, that is horrible past even considering. We have no choice, but to agree and for you to answer 'Yes'. I beg you do this, my husband."

Realizing he had no choice, he deeply sighed and sat down, resigned to the understanding of what he must do. We all sighed in relief collectively, and returned to our benches.

Herr Paustovsky returned and looking directly at *Herr Scheck*, calmly said, "You have one word you wish to say to me?"

Without standing or even raising his head, *Herr Scheck* quietly answered back, "Yes."

Herr Paustovsky instantly yelled back to *Jakob Scheck*, "What did you say? Stand up *Scheck*! Do not whimper as a woman. Answer me loudly like a man, so all in this room can hear what you choice you have voluntarily made. Stand up now!"

Jakob Scheck stood up, and while angrily glaring at the Kontor Official, yelled back, "Yes, I will, but..."

Herr Paustovsky cut him off with, "Silence! I need hear no more from you on this. I only require your obedience. *Scheck*, be warned, do not force me to spend any more time now or in the future. This issue is now closed. Sit back down now and remain silent!"

Turning his attention to the rest of our group, the Kontor Official sighed and smiled widely, and said, "I expect that there are no more problems or questions. We will tell you more as you travel to, and after you arrive at, the new Colony. And regularly, after that, the Kontor will provide you information and rules that you will comply with out any protest. We do not negotiate, and as you now know, we demand good order and peace. Any and all disobedience will only result in harsh treatment."

Herr Paustovsky continued, "You will be leaving for your Colony in a day or so. Prepare yourself and insure you have all you need. Your guide and Officer-in-Charge is *Lt. Chernyshevsky*. Do not fail to do anything *Lt. Chernyshevsky* or his soldiers direct. Thank you for helping to create the 'New Russland' and good fortune in the growth of your Colony and village." With that, *Herr Paustovsky* left the front of the room and walked out the door. We were never to see him again. At least one, and probably most, in our group was very happy for that.

We spent the next day getting ready for our final travel. As we had been told, the Kontor gave us money, tools, and other things. Sellers brought into the Kontor compound sold us horses, and anything else we asked for, and could pay for.

We loaded all our possessions and tools onto ten wagons for the final trip the very next day. That night, it was early to bed, but I doubt many got much sleep. It was not that we were otherwise occupied, but the excitement of almost being at our new home, and memory of the past few days happenings would not allow sleep.

I could not stop talking, and when I did, I just tossed and turned in the bed. Even my *Christoph*, who can sleep anywhere at any time, lay awake next to me with his eyes wide open just staring at the roof above.

THE REPORT

♦OFFICIAL NICHOLAI PAUSTOVSKY♦

Kontor of the Guardianship Chancery for Foreigners, Сара́тов (Saratov), Samara, Russland

I hereby enter this report into the Kontor official record this 23rd day of August in the year of our LORD one thousand seven hundred sixty-five (1765).

The orientation of the group of Deutsche colonists brought here by Lt. Von Ditmarr on the 9th of August is now complete. The group consists of the following: 9 families / 16 male / 18 female / 18 Reformed/ 16 Lutheran/ 8 farmers/ 1 woodworker; Balzer Barthuli 38, wife Anna Margarita 40, two daughters Elizabeth 12, Appollonia 10; Phillipp Decker 43, wife Jacobina 34, children Johannes two months, daughter Maria Katharina 2; Jakob Scheck 48, wife Katharina 43, son Jacob 11; Heinrich Heft 30, wife Katharina 23, with Heft: Valentine Haberman 16; Leonhard Volz 33, wife Margarita 34, son George Thomas 15, Wilhelm 4, Elizabeth 9, Barbara 1; Ludwig Tehele, 32, wife Anna Barbara 33, son Johann Michael 7, daughter Eva Catharina Barbara 1; Christoph Karl 36, wife Jacobina 30; Georg Robertus 25, wife Appolina 33, daughters Katharina 6 Jacobina 2; Jacob Dittmer 61, wife Anna

Maria 51, son Johan Martin 14, daughter Anna Elizabeth 11.

It has been reported to me that Lt. Von Ditmarr failed to deliver four individuals transferred to his care. He reported that three of them, Heinrich Wagner and wife Dorothea, and Peter Bruckmann died of sickness along the way, and that Johann Weiss deserted on the 7th of May in Торжо́к.

Lt. Von Ditmarr's attitude and performance is not up to the high standards of a Russische Army Officer. When questioned about the loss of the four individuals in his care as required by regulation by one of my subordinates, he became surly and disrespectful to my man. Note for his Military record and suggest discipline to prevent happening again. His loss of the four people will lower the odds that the Colony start is a success. Suggest the reallocation and addition of more colonists to this group as soon as possible.

Overall, our Medical Clinic pronounced the group healthy and fit to continue. With the exception of Jacob Dittmer 61, wife Anna Maria 51, all appear to be young enough to have good chance to survive the expected harsh conditions.

The group appears to have developed the required kinship during the land journey. While they still keep the typical Deutsche arrogance towards us, they have come to accept that they are now nothing more than Russische subjects that must do as we wish or command. Note that Lt. Von Ditmarr may have been slack on discipline on them as they traveled here. Still, civil disobedience is not likely, with the exception of one Jakob Scheck, who seems to feel as a skilled woodworker, he is too good to be a farmer. Whether this arrogance affects his relationship with the other eight farmers bears watching. Another reason for bringing in more colonists to this Colony.

All equipment and funds have been disbursed to the Colonists according to regulation. Loan amounts have been transferred to their individual paper records and placed in their file.

We must be prepared for some protest and civil disobedience by the Colonist when they arrive at their new Colony and discover that no houses have been built. This is one of the Colonies that did not have the houses constructed because of the unforeseen delays caused by bad weather. Raw lumber has been delivered to their location, but they will be required to build their own houses. There may be some protest over our failure to provide already built houses as we have promised them.

Unfortunately, because this will require all the men to build shelters, no farming or soil preparation will be possible. If winter comes early, there may not be time to build any log houses, and the Colonists may need to build local Russe semlinken or semlyanka.

The shelters could be big enough for three or four families to live together in. This would allow them to survive during the harsh Russischen winter. Additional food will likely be required from us to carry them through the winter.

They leave by guided wagon caravan tomorrow on the 24th of August in the year of our LORD one thousand seven hundred sixty-five for the Colony Голыи Карамыш or Goloi Karamysh.

Planned arrival date at the Colony is 28th day of August. Lt. Viktor Chernyshevsky from our local Army detachment will assume control of the Colonists and with a squad of ten soldiers guide them to their new Colony.

They will also provide protection from any nomadic tribes, irate Russische peasants, or robbers in the area. In the event of protest by the Colonists upon arrival, they will use force to restore good order and peace, and prevent any desertions.

They will remain at the new location to maintain good order for a period of not less than one month and longer if Lt. Chernyshevsky deems necessary.

Written by me on this 23rd day of August in the year of our LORD one thousand seven hundred sixty-five in the Kontor of the Guardianship Chancery for Foreigners' subordinate office in Сара́тов.

Signed,

Nicholai Paustovsky

Nicholai Paustovsky
Kontor Сара́тов

ONLY A LITTLE LONGER

♦CHRISTOPH KARL♦

A walled compound in Сара́тов (Saratov), Samara, Russland

Early the morning of the 24th of August, our caravan of wagons with soldier escort rolled passed the armed soldiers and out of the compound of the 'Kontor of the Guardianship Chancery for Foreigners' subordinate office in Saratov.

Well, actually, most of the men in our group walked out leading our recently bought plow horses and cows. Our wives and young children rode in the wagons with the chickens. The older boys and girls herded along our recently acquired drift of hogs.

We headed southeast away from Saratov and by mid-day passed through the village of Каласхников (Kalashnikov). Continuing to roll southwest, our group reached the village of Ивановскиы (Ivanovskiy) by late afternoon.

We entered the village and received the icy stares of the local villagers. *Lt. Chernyshevsky* arranged both food and lodging for all of us, but wherever we were or we went, I sensed a feeling of intense loathing, and even hatred.

I thought I might just be imagining this, and asked *Jacobina*, "Do you feel anything strange or different with the people from the other villages we have stayed in?"

Jacobina frowned and was silent for a moment, and then quietly answered, "You feel it to? In the other villages, I felt they did not like us and they did not dislike us; they just did not care anything about us. I can understand that feeling as we are strange foreigners and not of this land. But here, they do intensely have feelings about us, only it is that they passionately hate us for something. I know not what we did to them."

She was right. Still trying to reason this out, I searched out *Lt. Chernyshevsky* and asked him if he had noticed the bad feeling here in Ivanovskiy.

He shrugged and answered, "They do not personally hate you or any of your group. They hate that the land promised to you had always been theirs to use before we gave it to you. You must know that the Crown gave you Deutsche, the best land to attract you to move here. The Kontor gives you horses, and tools, and even money to buy more of all you need. The Kontor even provides lumber for your homes. However, to their Russischen people, to these poor peasants that have lived here on this land for generations, the Crown gives nothing at all. Of course, they hate everything about you as each one of you remind them how little any of them matter to the Crown. I was able to buy our food and lodging with silver coin, and with the threat of reprisal from the Kontor, but there is not enough silver in all of Saratov to buy you welcome or their good feelings."

Stunned, I could not think of anything to say. I, like our entire group, assumed that we would be welcomed to this area, not hated. While I was not happy with his words, I thanked the *Lieutenant* for his honesty.

I later met with most of the men in our group and told them what I had learned from the *Lieutenant*. Like me, they became dismayed at the news. Now we all understood the cold icy stares. That night, for the very first time on this trip, we kept our own men awake to guard our party. Our wives and children kept close to their men, just in case of trouble.

Before dawn, we quickly assembled and moved out on our way due south. The men who stood guard last night slept in the wagons, while most of the group walked alongside. By early afternoon, we had reached our next overnight stop, the small Russen village of Сергиыевскиы (Sergiyevskiy). Our reception was the same as the day before, very unwelcome.

As in the village before, they provided us adequate food and lodging, but had obvious dislike and hatred for all of us. Like the night before, we kept our own men awake to guard our party, and again our wives and children did not wander, but stayed close to their men just in case of trouble. Few slept much, including both *Jacobina* and me.

Our group was up early, anxiously waiting to leave this village. *Lt. Chernyshevsky* informed us that one of the wagon axles needed repair before going on, and we would be here for the entire day and another night.

Not welcome news, we made sure that no children wandered off. We kept our entire group close. This night, I was part of the guard, and while I should have been sleepy, I was wide-awake all night long. Like the nights before, nothing happened, nothing at all. We worried for nothing.

Russisches Village Home

The next morning our wagon caravan left. As we moved away from the village, the group almost collectively signed and began to relax.

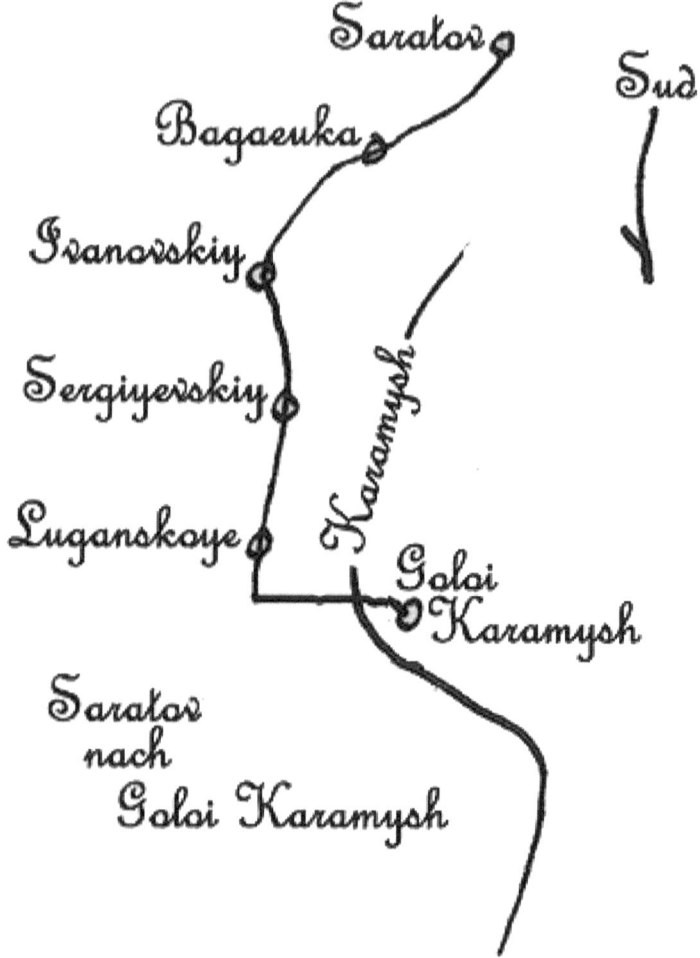

Saratov

Sud

Bagaeuka

Ivanovskiy

Sergiyevskiy

Karamysh

Luganskoye

Goloi
Karamysh

Saratov
nach
Goloi Karamysh

1765 - Elizabeth & Appollina Barthuli

Our Route from Сара́тов (Saratov) to
Голыи Карамыш (Goloi Karamysh)

We dreaded stopping at the next village, but with no choice, entered Луганскоые (Luganskoye) in late afternoon. We found the same understandable feelings as before, hatred on their faces. The only good part of being here was that this was the last night we must spend in a Russen village.

Tomorrow, we would be in our own village and sleep in our own new homes. Even though nothing had happened in the previous villages, we were still cautious and as on the previous nights, we kept our own men awake to guard our party, and kept the wives and children close to their men just in case of trouble. We quickly left the next morning; no one was slow now that we were so close to our new Colony. Our troubles would soon be just a bad memory.

This is the 28th day of August in the year of our LORD one thousand seven hundred sixty-five (1765), and today we would see our new lands.

As we neared our colony of Goloi Karamysh (Balzer), the *Barthuli* sisters read to us what they had written:

24 August 1765   Leave from Сара́тов (Saratov).

Night 1 - 24 August 1765   Overnight in Ивановскиы (Ivanovskiy)

Night 2 – 25 August 1765   Overnight in Сергиыевскиы (Sergiyevskiy)

Night 3 – 26 August 1765   Overnight in Сергиыевскиы (Sergiyevskiy)

Night 4 – 27 August 1765   Overnight in Луганскоые (Luganskoye)

13   HOME?

♦JACOBINA KARL♦

One day northwest of Colony Goloi Karamysh (Balzer)

I was overjoyed to be on the last leg of our long trip. Soon we would be at our new Colony and in our new homes. Like the rest of our group, I was certain that our numerous troubles and trials lay behind us, and this close to our Promised Land, what else could go wrong?

I walked that last hours of our trip alongside my *Christoph* as led our plow horse. It felt good to know that our LORD had blessed and protected us all this way.

Just after we had crossed a wide stream, all the wagons stopped. I supposed that maybe someone needed to rest for a moment, and then we would continue on to our new Colony. Looking around I saw that was a beautiful place with the grassy level land stretching from the banks of the creek as far as the eye could see. Abundant trees and tall green vegetation grew everywhere, obviously fed well by the water from the creek. Yes, a nice area that someday might be a good place for a future Colony.

Christoph had gone to the front of the wagons to learn why we stopped. Suddenly, I heard loud angry voices from there and started to go see, when four of the Russischen soldiers pushed by me and ran forward.

By the time I and the other women reached the front, the loud voices became much louder. Something had caused a serious argument. I looked for my *Christoph*, and to my surprise, he was right in the middle of the fray yelling in the face of *Lt. Chernyshevsky*.

Our men, very angry, looked almost out of control. The Russischen soldiers, worried looks on their faces, had their muskets down off their shoulders and leveled, appeared ready to use them on our men.

"What in the world is going on?" I said to myself. I and a few other women tried to push our way into the crowd of men and soldiers; they quickly and roughly forced us back out.

From all the yelling, we guessed that this was, in fact, our new Colony. Yes, this place that I was just thinking about how beautiful it was here with the grassy level land, the creek, and the forest of tall trees.

The only thing missing were the houses. "Where are the houses, which they had only days before in Saratov, promised to us?" I asked the woman beside me, not really expecting an answer.

She shook her head, and remarked, "There are no houses, there are no houses." She dropped to the ground, covered her face in her hands and began to cry and wail.

It was about then that one of the other women noticed the large pile of logs a little ways off. Like a flash, all of this made sense to me. Those logs were for our houses, only no one had put them together and built our houses.

With none already built, we would have to build our own houses. The question was whether there remained enough time before the winter cold set in to do just that. I was not the only one that just figured it all out. Already, several other women were also sitting on the ground weeping in despair.

ANOTHER LIE!

♠CHRISTOPH KARL♠

In the future Colony Goloi Karamysh (Balzer)

I went to the front of the wagons to find out why we had stopped. *Lt. Chernyshevsky* and several of his soldiers were already down off their horses. They were in a loud argument with several of our men, *Vorsteher Balzer Barthuli, Herr Jakob Scheck, Herr Jacob Dittmer*, and *Herr Phillipp Decker*.

As I got close enough to hear their words, I was shocked, and at first thought my ears must be hearing wrong. I swear I heard the *Lieutenant* say that this place, here where we stood, was our new Colony. Confused and scratching my head, I said aloud to no one at all, "How could that be? There is nothing here!"

Vorsteher Balzer Barthuli, angrily poking the *Lieutenant* in the chest, asked, "Where in GODs name were the houses we were promised by the Recruiters, and only a few days ago, by the Kontor?"

Lt. Chernyshevsky just shrugged, and then replied, "This is the correct location for the Colony of Голыи Карамыw (Goloi Karamysh).

He paused for a moment to weigh his next words, and then said, "As for your houses, because the recent bad weather on the Volga River delayed the delivery of the logs, there was no time to build your houses before you arrived."

Herr Jacob Dittmer loudly asked, "All right, we understand that the houses were not built because of bad weather, so where are the workers that are to build the houses? Were they also delayed by the bad weather on the Volga River?"

Other men joined in and yelled out as one, "Where are the workers? Tell us, where are the workers!"

The *Lieutenant* raised his arms to stop the yelling. His face fell blank with no emotion as he said, "Enough! You will build your own houses, and that is why it was so important that woodworker *Herr Scheck* be with you."

Herr Jacob Scheck instantly and angrily yelled back at the *Lieutenant*, "You mean that when that Kontor man was telling us that our houses were built and waiting for us, you both knew all along that was a lie."

Lt. Chernyshevsky closed his eyes and just stood there silent. He opened his eyes and looked at the men, and again shrugged and slowly replied, "Yes, we both knew he lied to you. The Kontor decided it would better to have you find out here in the wild then chance you making trouble in the Kontor compound. And what does it matter anyway? Accept your good fortune in making it here alive to your new lands, and get on with what you must do."

Several angry men started forward to seize the *Lieutenant* because of his last words, but *Lt. Chernyshevsky* quickly backed up so that his soldiers, with muskets leveled and ready to fire, covered him.

The two groups stood their ground staring at each other. While the soldiers were armed, several others of our men had gone back to the wagons and brought forward any sharp tool they could find to use to fight.

The numbers of soldiers and Colonist men were nearly the same, and in a close fight, the outcome was far from certain. The soldiers were trained regulars, but they did not really want to fight. Our men were farmers, but felt badly wronged and were eager to fight. The muskets at this range could not miss, but with only one shot, there would still be plenty of Colonist men hacking and slashing again and again at the *Lieutenant* and his soldiers. Yes, the outcome was far from certain.

Lt. Chernyshevsky thought to himself, "This is no good, no good at all. Even if my men put down the fight, many on both sides will be injured, if not killed. This would end the start of this new Colony, and I would have to return everyone back to the Kontor compound in Saratov. The Kontor would not accept any responsibility for this, and would blame me for the failure. This would be the end of my short military career at the best, to the stockades at the worst. No, this must somehow end now!

The *Lieutenant* said to his soldiers, "Lower your muskets and stand easy!" and they instantly complied.

He turned to our Colonist men and said, "I know your disappointment and frustration. You must realize I am under orders to use force, if necessary, to keep you here and to convince you to begin the building of your new Colony. My men and I will even help you in the building of your village. I can do nothing more than that, and if you choose to fight, this will end badly for all including your wives and children. Sadly, you have no choice but to accept this as it is and make the best of what our Crown has provided."

From the back of the crowd of men, someone yelled, "To the devil with the Crown." The soldiers again raised their muskets, and then started forward to answer this insult.

The *Lieutenant* raised his arm and again ordered, "Soldiers, lower your muskets and stand easy!" and again they instantly complied.

As angry and frustrated as we all were, his words rang true and made sense. We had compromised again and again on this trip so that we could reach our land here, what was one more compromise?

Seeing the truth of his words, each of the men dropped their sharp tools and turned to walk back to their wives and children. Each wondered how they would break the bad news to their families.

Everyone already knew. Each family group sat down where they were and vacantly stared out at the land. The women wept, and the men just sat, totally disillusioned and silent.

This was not the Paradise promised so long ago, and many including me, thought it best to quit this and return to our homelands. That choice was now not possible, and would be prevented by force.

That night all slept under the stars or in the wagons. There was an uneasy truce between the soldiers and our Colonists. The women did not cook, but fed their families fruits and dried meat. Many just continued to weep softly.

Other than the crying, it was so quiet that it was hard to imagine any people were here.

Jacobina and I had moved a ways from the others and down near the creek. The sound of the running water was relaxing and provided some small comfort to both of us. I held *Jacobina* all that night in my arms, nothing said between us. There were no words to describe what we felt. No way back, and only more pain forward.

It was a night of troubled sleep for all under the bright stars and on the hard ground in this our new Colony.

The dawn brought a cool light refreshing wind and a gently warming sun with the sky a clear light blue. The sounds of birds chirping in the trees echoed through the area. The leaves on the tree branches above fluttered and rustled in the breeze with dewdrops shimmering in the sunlight. The burbling of the stream as the water raced through the rocks provided pleasing sounds. Just lying there, without worrying about anything else, one might think they were in the Promised Land. Truly, today, at this very moment, this was wonderful place to be.

Jacobina must have felt the same as she rolled over and whispered to me, "Dear husband, is it not wonderful here this morning? The birds, the creek, the cool breeze and gentle sun, do you not think that maybe we should just accept what trials our LORD has set before us? While we should not forget the lies told, we must move forward and make the very best of what they provided here. I am willing to stand and work beside you to build our home and our village! If you feel as I do, we should talk with the others and let them know we are ready to move forward."

Of course, she was right, as usual. I pulled her close and hugged her, and simply whispered, "Yes, my wife, that is what we must, and will, do. We will not dwell on what should have been, but will set ourselves on what can be. We readily accept the trials our LORD has set before us just as our honorable and brave ancestors have always done. Today is the first day of our new life here in our new land! We must thank our LORD for this blessing."

DAWN OF THE NEW DAY

♦JACOBINA KARL♦

In the Colony Goloi Karamysh (Balzer)

As *Christoph* and I quietly continued to talk, we could hear sounds of the camp coming alive. We both slowly stretched and with some difficulty, rose from the hard ground.

To our great surprise, instead of the weeping women and broken men we had last seen as night came, there was the bustle of men hurrying to clear areas for cooking fires, children gathering wood, women bringing their pans and food to cook. Even the soldiers and *Lt. Chernyshevsky* had stacked their weapons, and were helping make ready.

The change from last night to this morning was astounding. Our GOD the HOLY SPIRIT must have visited and blessed all with a better understanding and hopeful attitude while we slept. Thanks be to GOD!

Christoph and I jumped right in and helped as needed. Before long, the smell of good food cooking made its way to each of our noses, and soon all realized how hungry they really were.

Soon, good food and plenty of water filled our bellies, and made this day even brighter. The children ran and played here and there, and their happy voices and laughter rang all around us. The women chatted, the men talked. Smiles outnumbered frowns almost all to none.

Vorsteher Balzer Barthuli asked for our attention, and said, "Dear friends, from what I see now, we must all have come to recognize what has happened, and what we must do. Our friend *Herr Christoph Karl* and I have talked, and I whole-heartedly agree with him that we must make the best we can of this situation. However, *Herr Karl* can say it better; *Herr Karl*, please stand and speak."

I was shocked. Never, in all my time with my dear husband, had I ever known him to speak to a crowd. He was a wonderful strong man, but a man of few words and most surely not a speaker. No, he would definitely not speak his mind today.

Christoph slowly stood and considered all the faces of the group looking towards him. He was, and looked uncomfortable with this new role.

Drawing on some here-to-unknown strength deep inside, *Christoph* took a deep breath and then said, "Friends, I am not a leader or speaker. I leave that to those that are better at it. I am but a simple vine-tender, and now a farmer. Our *Vorsteher Balzer Barthuli* has already told us what we all know. As my dear wife, *Frau Jacobina*, whispered to me this morning, look around, it is wonderful here this morning with sounds of the birds and the creek, and the cool breeze and gentle sun."

I was stunned, and thought to myself, "who was this man?" My dear husband had somehow changed before my very eyes. This must be more work of the GOD the HOLY GHOST!

Christoph continued, "Our LORD has blessed us by allowing us to be here. He has also apparently put trials for us to overcome just as he has always done for his faithful. We will readily accept the trials of our LORD just as our honorable ancestors have always done. While we will not forget the lies told, we must move forward and make the very best of what we have here. Today is the first day of our new life here in our new land! *Frau Jacobina* and I willingly pledge to this village to help develop the paradise we know it can be. We hope that you all will join with us in this quest. We must not forget who has generously provided all this; we must thank him, our LORD GOD for this blessing. Please bow your heads and join me now in giving thanks to our LORD GOD for all this."

Everyone joined my *Christoph* in prayer as he spoke, "LORD, we are eternally thankful for the sounds birds and the creek, for the gentle wind and warming sun, for our health and strength, for the laughter of our children, for the protection of the soldiers, for the very food we eat, and for all your other unspoken blessings. Thank you for the wisdom to recognize the trials that we now face as opportunities to grow and prosper, and not dwell on how difficult or unfair we might feel they be. Thank you for giving us the will and knowledge to move forward and make the very best of what we have. Thank you for this chance to demonstrate the strength of our faith in you and in the knowledge that we remain blessed by you. LORD, as always, our future in is your blessed hands. We humbly and willing accept your plans for each of us with no hesitation. Amen." The word 'Amen" rang out through the group.

Christoph quickly sat down, obviously drained. I looked at him, and now saw a much larger and stronger man than I had ever known. This was my husband, and I was so very proud of him. How lucky I am to be his wife!

Vorsteher Balzer Barthuli stood up again and said, "*Herr Christoph*, we thank you for your words. Now we must put those words in action for in one months' time, by the end of September, the fall cold will be here and we will need shelter to survive."

He went on, "Everyone, including the children, will need to work as a one team to build shelters for both our animals and us. If we do not succeed, many, if not all of us along with all of our animals, will not see the warmth of next spring. I, like almost all of you, am but a simple farmer. *Herr Jacob Scheck* is the man with the skills and the man we need to lead us now. *Herr Scheck*, I humbly ask you to lead us and tell us what we need to do. We will all follow your orders, everyone agree?"

All nodded or answered 'Ja'.

Herr Jacob Scheck stood and looked around at the faces of the group, remembering how these very same people had helped him in Saratov. He finally answered, "Yes, I will lead, and thank you for your trust in my knowledge and skills."

He continued speaking, "First, we must build a large Village House to shelter our families from the approaching winter cold and snow. It must be large enough to easily house all, as we may have to live in it for many months. Second, we must build a large Village Barn for all our animals. Our plow horses and other livestock must also survive the cold winter. We also need more chickens and hogs to carry us through the cold times, and maybe our *Lt. Chernyshevsky* and his men can somehow buy some from the neighboring Russen villages. New animals will need the shelter of the barn. If the winter cold holds off and there is still time, we will start building our single homes that our women so desperately want."

He continued, "I need four men to take horses and drag the cut logs near to where our Village House and Village Barn will be. *Herr Decker, Herr Heft, Herr Haberman*, and *Herr Robertus* will do that. I need three men to begin the clearing of stumps and rocks and other debris lying in our building footprints. *Herr Volz, Herr Dittmer*, and *Herr Tehele* will do that. *Vorsteher Balzer Barthuli, Herr Karl*, and I will draw the village plan, and start walking out and marking out our village and where our first buildings will go. Women and children, we need your help in also clearing the building sites of small debris, and raking the areas. The children also need to gather firewood for our future fires. We all now have something to do."

He turned to *Lt. Chernyshevsky* and said, "Yesterday, you offered the help of you and your men. I am now calling you on that and asking for that help. Please assign your men to assist us in our tasks as you see fit. We will sincerely appreciate any help."

Lt. Chernyshevsky said one word in reply, "Agreed."

Herr Scheck turned his attention back to us and said, "Why are you all still sitting there? You all know what we need done. Get moving!"

Almost instantly, everyone jumped to their feet. *Herr Scheck* was right; time was not waiting for us. The sun was already racing towards mid-day and we had built nothing!

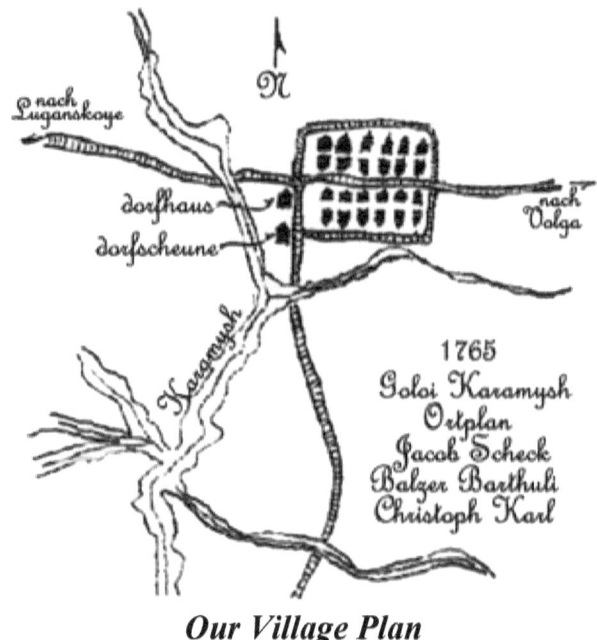

Our Village Plan

As the men quickly moved off to their work areas, the women formed together and quickly determined their duties. One woman assigned to watch over all the small children. Another woman tasked to take the older children to collect the needed firewood.

Others tasked to clean-up the morning cooking and prepare for the mid-day meal. The older girls tasked with carrying water to our hard working and thirsty men. The remaining women, including me, tasked to begin clearing and raking the building sites.

Lt. Chernyshevsky assigned two of his soldiers to remain at guard on the edges of our area. He assigned two more to help with the logs, two more to help with clearing of large debris from the building sites, and two more to escort the children as they gathered firewood. His remaining two he directed to rest, as they would be our night guards. He joined with my husband *Christoph, Vorsteher Balzer*

Barthuli, and *Herr Scheck* in the layout and stake of the building sites.

The day flew as we all did as told. By dusk, we had a large number of logs close to the now staked out, cleared, and raked building sites. Tomorrow, we would get new tasks. Exhausted, all slept soundly, except for our two Russischen soldiers standing guard through the night.

At dawn, our group was up and ready to go. *Herr Scheck* stood and said, "We all have done well. I have new tasks for some. I need four men to take a wagon and bring the largest rocks that you can handle back here to use as cornerstones for our buildings. *Herr Volz*, *Herr Dittmer*, *Herr Tehele*, and *Herr Karl* will do that. The children can scout the area to locate good size rocks so that you do not have to waste time searching. *Herr Decker*, *Herr Heft*, *Herr Haberman*, and *Herr Robertus* will continue to drag more logs to the site. *Vorsteher Balzer Barthuli* and I will begin digging out the soil for the corner stones. All the rest will continue as yesterday. Go!"

At the finish of the day, we had cornerstones placed at each corner of both buildings, and because the buildings are so large, stones placed mid-way down each wall. With more logs stacked, it looked like we might start the build tomorrow.

Another night passed under the stars in my *Christoph's* arms. Another wonderful dawn, and ready for new tasks.

Herr Scheck stood and said, "Again, we have made good progress. I have new tasks for some. I will need all the men to move the logs into position after we have trimmed them to fit. I need the children to scout the area for grasses that we can use to build the thatch bundles for the roof coverings. All right, go to work!"

While the men struggled with trimming and fitting the logs for the walls, I went out with the children to search for grasses good to make thatch. We soon located as much as we might ever need, and hurried back to tell the men.

Hearing what we had found, *Herr Scheck* told two of the older boys, *George Volz* and *Johann Dittmer*, to take a wagon and scythes, and follow us back to the good grasses. They were to cut the grasses as long as possible and gather and bring all of it back. Before they left, he warned them to be very careful with the scythes as they could easily injure anyone around them.

For their safety, we sent the children to a completely different area to find more firewood, while I accompanied *George* and *Johann*. The *Lieutenant* sent along one of his soldiers to help us and provide protection.

Cutting the wild grasses with the scythe wore all of us out in a short time. Use of the scythe was a skill I never learned, and soon my back ached from using it. Eventually, we had cut and gathered a wagon full of wild grasses and started back to our Colony.

I was amazed at the progress the men had made on the walls. Both buildings were going up at the same time causing *Herr Scheck* to scurry back and forth from one to the other to make sure all was right.

I helped the boys unload the wagon and spread the grasses out to dry. Tomorrow, we would begin tying the grasses into the thatch bundles. As the sun sank in the west, both our Village House and Village Barn buildings had walls up half a man's height.

Another night passed under the stars in my *Christoph's* arms. Another beautiful dawn, and ready for new tasks, or so I thought. This was not to be.

Dark black clouds raced in from somewhere and the sky opened up with buckets of rain and arcs of lightning. Everyone scrambled for the cover of the wagons. While we all made it, we packed in and under them with no room to move. It felt like it rained for hours, but more likely it lasted much less. Eventually as always, the rain did stop, and we all left our cover to resume our tasks. We did so much slower as the ground had become slick mud.

Vorsteher Balzer Barthuli and *Herr Scheck* decided that we would rest for the remainder of the day, and start fresh in the morn. While I valued time to rest with my husband, I worried that we are already short on days to the winter cold.

I told this to *Christoph*, but he reassured me with, "*Jacobina*, do not worry. We are making good progress and will have both of our large buildings done in time." Feeling better, I snuggled in his arms and went fast to sleep.

The next morn was clear and sunny. The men and older boys returned to the trimming and placement of the logs.

The wife of *Herr Jacob Scheck*, *Katharina*, and her son, *Jacob*, already knew how to make the thatch bundles for our roofs. They taught all the art, and I and five other women quickly learned the steps. A few failures at first, for sure, but eventually while we were not as fast as they were, we each made fine thatch bundles. As the day ended, we had many bundles, and even more grass to bundle.

The men now had the log walls up to man's height. They too had done so much, and still had so much more to do.

Another night passed under the stars in my *Christoph's* arms. Another clear dawn, and ready for new tasks.

For me and the other women, it was back to making thatch bundles. My hands and the others hands were already raw from yesterday, but no one complained. The day passed quickly with more progress everywhere.

Over the next week, we finished enough thatch bundles for the roofing of one of the buildings. The men had finished putting up the walls, but the work of cutting and setting the roof logs slowed their progress. With all the men needed at one building, there was no progress on the second.

We needed more thatch bundles made, and more grasses cut, gathered and hauled back. And still more for our own houses if we had time.

Another two weeks passed, and the weather had turned noticeably cooler. Most still slept out under the stars covered with blankets, but the children now slept in the warmer wagons.

Herr Scheck knew that soon we would need some type of heat for our building. He had studied the rock stoves used in the Russischen homes we had stayed in and found them good. We had no one skilled in the construction. The only solution was to try to find a Russisches pechniki (stone stove maker) close by that would be willing to build them for us.

Lt. Chernyshevsky was the man for this, and *Herr Scheck* sat down and asked for his help. The *Lieutenant* agreed to help, but said it would take hard rubles to convince a skilled pechniki to come and work with us.

Herr Scheck met with all the men of the village, and they all agreed to pay whatever he asked.

The outside of our Village House was finished, but lacked the thatch roof and a floor. The men were scrambling to finish the roof logs of the Village Barn, and worked non-stop from dawn to dusk.

Lt. Chernyshevsky and his men did convince a pechniki to come and build as many stone stoves as we wanted. What village he was from or how they actually convinced him, we did not care. His price was steep, thirty rubles (nine hundred groschen) plus food and shelter, and we would have to help in the building and haul in all the sand and stone.

With no choice, we gladly agreed to pay his price upon completion. We quickly hauled rock from all over our land, and sand and clay from the creek to the site, and our pechniki began to build the first stove.

Another week passed, and today our Village House is weather tight with a new thatched roof, and a split log floor. We pushed clay and moss into the cracks between the logs to seal out the cold wind. The pechniki had finished the stove, and it was working.

On this day, *Vorsteher Balzer Barthuli* called us all together and said, "You have all worked very hard. Tonight, on this 1st day of October in the year of our LORD one thousand seven hundred sixty-five (1765), we can all sleep warmly tonight."

Herr Scheck had planned well; there was more than enough room for all to live comfortably, and to store all our possessions. Our building was weather tight and warm.

Unfortunately, like all the Russischen peasant homes we had stayed in, the stove our pechniki built had no chimney and was usually very smoky. Thinking back, I remembered as a young girl watching my stonemason father build a chimney, and wondered if we could add one on to the Russischen stove.

I mentioned this to *Lt. Chernyshevsky*. He did not know why we could not add one, and asked the pechniki.

The pechniki scratched his head, and then answered the *Lieutenant*, "Это не построен таким образом. агреватель не нуждается в дымоходе, дым от пожара хорошо для здоровья и держать в тепле."

Lt. Chernyshevsky translated his words, "It is not built that way. The stove does not need chimney, smoke from fire good for health and keep warm."

I replied to the *Lieutenant* so that he could tell the pechniki my thoughts about this, "We women will not be happy with all this smoke, and will not pay your price unless we have a chimney through the roof to let the smoke out! You must build a chimney on top of it."

Lt. Chernyshevsky translated my words back to the pechniki, "Это женщин думает, что она знает лучше, чем вы. Но они не нравится дым и говорят, что они не будут платить свою цену, если вы строите трубу через крышу. Они Deutsche, что еще я могу сказать! (This woman thinks she knows better than you do. Nevertheless, they are not happy about the smoke and say they will not pay your price unless you build a chimney through the roof. They are Deutsche, what more can I say!)"

They both smiled and had a hearty laugh. My words should not have given them laughter, as nothing I said was funny. It dawned on me that the *Lieutenant* probably did not say what I said.

The pechniki looked at me and saw I was not smiling, but frowning. He scratched his untidy and scraggly Russischer beard, rubbed his hand across his mouth, and finally answered, "Нет, не правы. Большинство тепло пойдет в трубу, и в комнате будет холодно!"

Again, *Lt. Chernyshevsky* translated his words, "No, not right. Most of the heat will go up the chimney, and the room will be cold!"

Frustrated with this Russen, I took a deep breath and replied, "My father was a master stone mason. I know of what I say. I have helped build many a chimney as a young girl. If you are not skilled enough to build a chimney as we request, I, a woman, will build it myself!" I was bluffing, but they did not know that, and what did I have to lose.

Lt. Chernyshevsky stopped smiling and frowned for a time, and then translated my words for the pechniki, "Ее отец был каменщиком. Она помогла построить много дымоход, как молодая девушка. Она будет строить сама, если вы не достаточно опытный. (Her father was stonemason. She helped build many chimneys as young girl. She will build it herself if you are not skilled enough.)"

The face of the pechniki was no longer smiling, but was now frowning. I had implied he was not skilled in his trade.

He replied to the *Lieutenant*, "Я не мог терпеть оскорбления, такие как этого от человека, и задача любого человека, который говорит, что такие на бой. С женщиной, это оскорбление немыслимо. Не русская женщина осмелится вопрос мои навыки. Тем не менее, это не одна из наших женщин, но Deutscher. Я должен взять ее и избили ее за дерзость, но вы не позволили бы, что бы Вы? (I could not tolerate an insult such as this from a man, and challenge any man that said such to a fight. From a woman, this insult is unthinkable. No Russische woman dare question my skills. Yet, this is not a one of our woman, but a Deutscher. I should take her out and beat her for her insolence, but you would not allow that, would you?)"

The *Lieutenant* sternly replied to him, "Нет, я бы остановить вас и будет жестоко избили за попытку. Эти люди находятся под защитой Kontor. (No, I would stop you and would severely beat you for trying. These people are under Kontor protection.)"

The pechniki looked down at the floor and again scratched his untidy and scraggly Russischer beard, rubbed his hand across his mouth, and finally answered, "Я сделаю так, как они настаивают и строить дымоходы. Не от нее, я буду только делать, как сказал человек, а не женщина! И ей надо от меня, чтобы я мог строить свои трубы. Человек, я должен услышать это от человека. (I will do as they insist and build chimneys. Not from her, I will only do as told by a man, not a woman! And she must get away from me so that I can build their chimneys. A man, I must hear it from a man.)"

Lt. Chernyshevsky smiled, turned to me and translated his words, "He thanks you for your help. Russische women do not know anything about building, and he is not used to taking instructions from so skilled a woman. To make sure that this is what the entire group wants, he asks your husband to affirm it. And when that is done, he asks for you to let him build the chimney without interference."

He wants my husband, *Christoph*. I may have been too forceful. It is not our Lutheran way to insult another, but I was so frustrated, and they laughed at me. *Christoph* may not be too happy with my outspokenness.

"I will get my husband," I quickly replied. Some minutes later, I had found *Christoph*, and while hurrying back to the building, told him about what I had said and what happened.

Christoph knew I was right about the chimney, but was angry how I had talked to the *Lieutenant* and the pechniki. He too felt that it was not our Lutheran way to insult another, and was never proper for a woman to publicly insult or challenge any man.

Christoph stopped walking, grabbed my arm and turned me facing him, and in a stern voice said, "I will not have my wife arguing with other men. It is not acceptable ever. You will apologize to the *Lieutenant* and this Russe for this insult when we get there!"

I knew better than to argue with *Christoph*, and I knew he was right. I had overstepped the limits of a woman's place.

The *Lieutenant* and the pechniki stood just where I had left them. *Christoph* said to the *Lieutenant*, "Please tell him that I am *Herr Christoph Karl*, and this woman is my wife. Tell him I want chimneys on all the stoves. Also my wife has something to say to both of you. Please tell him what she says, also."

My husband turned towards me and frowned; my turn, and with my head lowered, I spoke, "I apologize for my words that questioned the skill of the pechniki. My husband has rightly rebuked me that it is never appropriate for a woman to insult or challenge a man. He of course, is right, and I beg your forgiveness."

The *Lieutenant* smiled, and spoke to the pechniki, "Это Кристоф Карл, несчастный муж этой женщины. Он спрашивает, что вы строите трубы на всех печах.Женщина была упрекал ее мужем для любого оскорбление ваших навыков. Она была напомнил, что женщина может никогда не оскорбление любого человека, и просит у вас прощения. (This is *Herr Christoph Karl*, unlucky husband of this woman. He asks that you build chimneys on all the stoves. The woman has been rebuked by her husband for any insult to your skills. She has been reminded that a woman may never ever insult any man, and begs your forgiveness.)"

The pechniki looked at *Christoph* and nodded. He smiled widely and replied, "Я даю ей меня прощения, и сказать ей, я начну трубы теперь, как он направлен. Его женщина должна уйти так, чтобы она не раздражает меня больше. (I give her my forgiveness, and tell her I will start the chimneys now as he has directed. His woman must go away so that she does not irritate me anymore.)"

Lt. Chernyshevsky smiled again, turned to *Christoph* and translated, "He will start on your chimneys now. He forgives her outburst, but insists she leave him alone so that he can properly build what you want."

I was fuming. I was absolutely right, and yet, I was being dismissed. I had no doubt that my *Christoph* would defend my honor, and not agree.

Christoph nodded and quickly replied, "Thank you. She will come with me and not bother him again."

What did I hear him just say?

Christoph grabbed my arm, turned me around, and pulled me outside. Seeing the lightning in my eyes, he knew I was very, very angry.

I expected him to apologize, but instead *Christoph* quietly said, "*Jacobina*, dear wife, you were wrong. Calm yourself and do not act unseemly in front of our neighbors. I know you are angry, and I know you are right about the chimneys. However, we will not get the chimneys made if you chase the pechniki off. Go for a walk by the creek and revel in the knowing that soon you will have what you wanted."

I began to speak, but did not, as I realized that he was right. I had won, and we would have chimneys. What the scraggly bearded pechniki thought about me was of no importance. I would have my chimneys!

By the end of the next week, the Village Barn was finished with its own thatched roof. Our animals now safely in their stalls and pens completely protected from the coming winter.

Late that evening, *Vorsteher Balzer Barthuli* again called us all together to tell us, "As you know, we are finished with our Village Barn. *Herr Scheck* and I have discussed what should be next, and we believe that there is still time to build four of your homes. Only four, if we are lucky, with the remaining seven waiting until next spring. To build those four, we will need all your help just as you did with our two Village House and Barn buildings. What say you?"

We enthusiastically answered 'Ja (Yes)'.

Vorsteher Barthuli continued to speak, "The problem is which families will get the first four houses. We could base it on age, or on family size, or on a group vote, or

I could just pick four. However, *Herr Jacob Scheck* and I feel the best way is to draw straws. Our LORD will decide who gets the first four houses. But enough on that, first the four houses must be built, and then we will draw straws. Tomorrow, we start."

THE FIRST FOUR & MORE

♦CHRISTOPH KARL♦

The new Colony of Balzer (Goloi Karamysh)

The next morning we were hard at it early. We had all gained skills in building the Village House and Village Barn, and knew what needed doing without asking.

Four more stoves, with chimneys, were requested from the pechniki. He did not ask for *Jacobina's* help, nor did she offer any.

One week later, on the 8th of October, 1765, we finished the walls, the roof, and the floors of four new log homes. That evening, we met in the Village House to take our chance along with the others for one of the new homes.

Vorsteher Balzer Barthuli stood and spoke, "We could not ask for more from all of you. Truly, we have become a village. I know that you each would like to have one of these first four homes, but I also know that you also wish the best for your fellow villagers. As I said before, we will draw straws. There are four long straws and five short straws in this cup. Each man of the family will draw a straw from this cup. I will go last. You will not look at your straw and will keep your straw hidden until all have drawn theirs. At my command, all will hold up their straws at the same time. The four with the long straws win the first four homes. We ask our LORD for his blessing in this difficult choice."

Lt. Chernyshevsky came around to each of the men and had them pull their straw from the cup. I was the fourth to draw. Honestly, I could not tell if it was long or short.

After *Vorsteher Barthuli* had drawn out the last one, he simply said to raise your arms and show your straws for all to see.

Four long straws and five short ones came in to sight.

Vorsteher Balzer Barthuli, a long one; *Herr Jacob Dittmer,* a long one; *Herr Leonhard Volz,* a long one, and I too, had a long one.

While we four had reason to rejoice, others were disappointed. All knew it was fair as it really was our LORD's decision, and no one complained.

We spent one last night in the Village House. The next day, *Jacobina* and I, would move in to our new home. Too excited, we did not sleep much that night. It was too bad that so many people were around us, I could not play either. Early that next morning, we did move our few possessions in to our new home. All moved in, we sat down in the middle of the one large room and just relaxed in knowing that this was all ours.

The only thing that was missing was that the pechniki had not yet finished our stove with its chimney. From my wife's previous words with the pechniki, we would probably be the last to have one.

That evening, *Vorsteher Balzer Barthuli* called for all the village men to meet in the Village House for a meeting.

When all were present, he spoke, "*Herr Scheck* has counted all the building materials including the logs and roofing thatch bundles that we already have on hand. He feels we have enough just barely to build three more homes. While it grows colder by the day, and the cold and weather will slow our progress, there is a chance that we might finish three more homes before old man winter forces us to stop. This will be cold, miserable work, and I ask for your support. What say each of you? Ja oder nein (Yes or no)?"

Three more homes for our families. That would bring the total to seven, with only two families forced to live in the Village House. We all said 'Ja'. Three more stoves, with chimneys, requested from the pechniki.

That night, without any heat, *Jacobina* and I slept in our warm clothes, and covered ourselves with furs and blankets. And we released some of our pent-up passion keeping us even warmer. After all these months with little or no privacy, we did make up for all lost time.

The next morning we started again on three more homes. Our women kept us with warm drinks, and hot food throughout the day. It was cold, but we were dressed well and our hard work made us even warmer. To insure none of us got too cold and sick, we rotated our time outside and warmed ourselves near the stove in the Village House.

One week later, we finished the three more homes for our fellow Villagers. Another drawing occurred, this time *Herr Scheck*, *Herr Decker*, and *Herr Robertus* were the blessed ones.

Our stove and chimney finished, that night was much warmer in our home, and as *Jacobina* had already observed, much less smoky. She was very satisfied with her new home.

I was very surprised when late that evening in bed, *Jacobina* snuggled next to me and said, "*Christoph*, I cannot stop thinking about our friends still living in the Village House. We have way too much room for us right now, can we not invite *Herr Heft* and his wife *Katharina* to share our home over the winter. I know we will not have as much privacy, but it seems to be the only fair thing to do. That would leave only the *Tehele* family living in the Village House. Do you agree?"

I did not want to give-up our privacy now that we just had it back again, but *Jacobina* was, as usual, right. It would be the Lutheran thing to do. I smiled and said to her, "Yes, tomorrow I will offer to them to stay with us if they so choose. But only tomorrow, as tonight I have other plans for you."

Jacobina felt so much better when *Herr Heinrich Heft* and his wife *Katharina* accepted our offer. Young *Valentine Haberman* who had traveled with them remained in the Village House. He was sixteen, almost a man, and would be fine on his own.

We divided our home into three areas, a private area for them to sleep, a private area for us to sleep, and a common area for all of us. *Katharina* and *Jacobina* easily became good friends, she was seven years younger, and I thought of her as a younger sister. We shared the daily chores and both worked every day at making our new home even better.

MUSKET PRACTICE

It was almost time for *Lt. Chernyshevsky* and his men to return to Saratov. He had one last mission to accomplish. His orders directed him to teach all the village men to load and shoot a musket.

Early one morning he called all of the men, and boys of at least fifteen years, to assemble a little ways outside the village.

With all men and older boys present, he began his lesson, "You will all learn to load and shoot a musket. This is necessary to ensure the defense of your village and help you repel any possible attack."

One of the men yelled out, "I am a farmer, not a soldier. I do not need to or want to learn how to use any weapon. Besides, they told us that there was no reason to worry out here because we had no enemies. If there are enemies we need to fear, keep the soldiers here to protect us until you capture or run-off all of them."

The *Lieutenant* took a deep breath, sighed and then replied, "There are no enemies here right now, but enemies may show up anytime in the future. There are different nomadic tribes that may not welcome you here, and some of their wilder members could cause troubles. They will not ask your trade or if you are a farmer or soldier before they kill you, and rape your women!"

Another man questioned, "What nomadic tribes, and why cannot you just go out and drive them away?"

The *Lieutenant* replied, "There are the nomadic tribes of the Kirghiz, Kazakh, and Kalmucks, and there are the robber bands that prowl the Astrakhan road that we came south on. We do regularly drive them away, but they return as they wish and our soldiers cannot be everywhere at the same time. In truth, the robber bands most likely watch us right now from the high Shishka ridge to the east, a ways before the Volga River. They have probably known of our arrival from the very first day, and are just trying to find our weak spot. You men will have to provide your Village defense once we are gone."

Several replied at the same time, "We are farmers, and no nothing about fighting. Our Christian faith even teaches us that we must always try and follow the way of brotherhood and peace."

The *Lieutenant* closed his eyes, again sighed deeply, and just thought for a moment. He opened his eyes and replied, "My faith too teaches the same thing. However, mine does not teach that you cannot learn how to defend yourself if peaceful ways fail through no fault of yours. Again, these are not Christians. They will not ask your trade before they kill you, and they will rape and then take or kill your women! *Vorsteher Barthuli*, does your faith teach you to not learn how to protect yourself and your families from danger?"

Herr Barthuli quickly answered, "No, it teaches us that we must be prepared for whatever is the will of our LORD. We still must learn how to protect our women and children, and ourselves, from any wild animal such as a wolf, or even men that wish to harm us. We must always do our best in any trial or task our LORD gives to us!"

The *Lieutenant* continued, "Good, that is settled. My orders are to teach you and that is what my men and I will do."

Holding up a мушкет, he continued, "This is a musket. It is a muzzle-loaded, smoothbore long gun and is fired from the shoulder. Used skillfully, it could hit a man's torso at up to one hundred steps, though it is only accurate to about fifty steps. We will pass one around so that you can hold it and look at it."

None of us had any experience and felt uncomfortable even handling it. In fact, we dropped it twice before a concerned soldier took it back.

The *Lieutenant* continued, "Before I leave, you will all be comfortable and skillful in using the musket. I hope that it will only take one day, but if takes seven that is what we will do. Each two of you will pair off with one of my soldiers. They will teach all you need to know. Give them your complete attention or we will be here doing this for much longer than needed. Move to your soldier!"

When we had done that, he continued, "Your musket has a flintlock firing mechanism. To quickly load and fire, you must learn and practice the following skills in this exact order each time. The musket will not fire if you do not always load and fire it the same correct way. In the military, we all follow the musket commands in order to lay down our fire in the most efficient way. You will learn by the commands, but in your lives, you will fire as individuals as needed."

He went on with the lesson, "First, on the command 'Prime and load' you will make a quarter turn to the right at the same time bringing the musket to the priming position. The pan would be open following the discharge of the previous shot, meaning that the frizzen would already be upward. Each of you practice this now!"

After all had successfully acquired and demonstrated at least some skill at this, the *Lieutenant* went on, "On the command 'Handle Cartridge', you draw out a cartridge. Cartridges contain a spherical lead bullet with gunpowder wrapped in a paper cartridge. The other end of the cartridge away from the ball is sealed closed with a twist of paper. You then rip off the paper end of the cartridge and throw it away, keeping the main end with the bullet in your right hand. Each of you practice this now!"

After some more practice time, he continued the lesson, "On the command 'Prime', you then pull the dogshead back to half-cock and pour a small pinch of the powder from the cartridge into the priming pan. You then close the frizzen so that the priming powder is trapped. Practice this now!"

Continuing, "On the command 'About', the butt of the musket is dropped to the ground and you pour the rest of the powder from the cartridge, followed by the ball and paper cartridge case into the barrel. The paper acts as wadding to stop the ball and powder from falling back out if the muzzle barrel is pointed downward. Practice now!"

After an extended time of doing everything possible wrong, we slowly made some progress with our skills.

Lt. Chernyshevsky continued, "On the command 'Draw ramrods', you take your ramrod from below the barrel, by first forcing it half out before seizing it backhanded in the middle, followed by drawing it entirely out. At the same time, you turn it to the front and place it one inch into the barrel. Practice this now!"

He went on, "On the command 'Ram down the cartridge' you use the ramrod to firmly ram the wadding, bullet, and powder down to the bottom of the barrel followed by tamping it down with two quick strokes. The ramrod is then returned to its hoops under the barrel. Practice!"

More to practice, he said, "On the command 'Present', you bring the butt back up to the shoulder. You pull the cock back and the musket is ready to fire, which you here with us today do only on hearing my command "Fire". Practice this now!"

We practiced all the steps for hours and hours. When we thought we had mastered all, we practiced all the steps again and again. The day was ending, and we never fired the musket.

The *Lieutenant* finally announced, "That is all for today. Early tomorrow you will all be back here to practice more. If you ever learn to do it right, you may even get to fire your musket. Go home now!"

That night over supper, *Heinrich* and I explained to our wives about our full day of practicing to use a musket. Both *Jacobina* and *Katharina* frowned and were not pleased. They felt, as many of the men had, that this was not in following our Christian ways.

I explained about the nomadic tribes and robber bands, and their raping and taking or killing women, and they both became frightened and concerned. *Heinrich* and I had our hands full getting them to settle down. While they remained not happy about our training, they reluctantly supported it as a necessary evil.

The next morning had all of us back practicing the steps from yesterday. It was just 'Prime and load', 'Handle Cartridge', 'Prime', 'About', 'Draw ramrods', 'Ram down the cartridge', and 'Present' again and again for hours.

Finally, in midafternoon, the *Lieutenant* announced, "This time, I will give you the command 'Fire'. You will aim your muskets at the short logs placed over there. You will not aim at anything else or fire your musket unless it is pointing at the short logs. We will do this until everyone can hit the logs. Once more, 'Prime and load', 'Handle Cartridge', 'Prime', 'About', 'Draw ramrods', 'Ram down the cartridge', and 'Present'. Aim at the logs, and 'Fire'."

We all fired... and no one hit anything except sky or grass. *Lt. Chernyshevsky* laughed and commented, "Good, no one was shot. Bad, no one hit any of the logs. More practice is what you all need! Your soldier will give you all the commands from now on."

We practiced, and practiced more, and then even more, the loading and firing the rest of the day. This was not easy, but eventually at least half of us hit the log pieces. Maybe not the ones we wanted to hit, but we at least hit some of them somewhere over there. At least I hope and think we did.

Feeling proud of our new skills, as the sun faded we headed home. Before we left, the *Lieutenant* ordered us to be back here tomorrow at same time, most likely to do more 'Practice'.

That night over supper, *Heinrich* and I proudly boasted of our new skills in firing the musket. We laughed together at all the stupid things we had done and the even dumber things we had seen the other men do. Our wives, *Jacobina* and *Katharina*, just sat quietly and listened to us talk foolish, and would occasionally whisper things to each other. We paid them no mind; we were men and we were having fun.

The next morn with all now having 'musket fever', we waited excitedly for our chance to fire again. We spent the whole rest of the day continuing to practice. With each shot, all got better, and did hit some of the logs they aimed at.

In midafternoon, the *Lieutenant* had us compete to identify the best shots in the village. While *Herr Heinrich* and I were good, three other men were much better. These three men would be our village expert shooters in case of attack.

The *Lieutenant* called us all together and said, "You are all trained now. I am leaving you ten muskets, along with barrels of gunpowder and cartridges. Guard them, as any stranger will quickly steal them to use against your village. My men and I will be leaving you on the early morn. We will return most likely in about a month with more food and supplies. You will be on your own to survive or not until that time. Remember; do not shoot each other or yourselves! Do not shoot your chicken, or cows, or children, and lastly, do not shoot your wives and mother-in-laws!" We laughed heartily for a good while on that.

The next morning, true to his word, he and his men rolled out leaving us with four wagons, and of course, our new muskets. As he and his men vanished from sight, we soon all realized that we men were the only thing that stood between the wild and our families. We would now need to have armed guards posted at each end of our village at night. We took them for granted, but those soldiers were more valuable then we realized.

From now on, most of us would be sleeping next to our wives, while always a few would be the soldiers guarding our village each night. We were no longer only farmers; we had become warriors!

THE REPORT

♦VIKTOR CHERNYSHEVSKY, LT.♦

Colony of Goloi Karamysh

I hereby enter this report into the Kontor official record this 7th day of November in the year of our LORD one thousand seven hundred sixty-five (1765).

The transportation of the group of Deutsche colonists assigned to me by Nicholai Paustovsky of the Kontor Саратов on the 23rd of August 1765 is now complete. They have been delivered to Голыи Карамыш or Goloi Karamysh.

Protest and the threat of civil disobedience did arise, as predicted, when we arrived at their new Colony and they realized that no houses have been built.

No actual disobedience occurred, and after one night, the colonists accepted this situation and voluntarily formed teams to build their own housing.

While they did complete the needed Village community house and barn, and all but two of the required houses, they were not able to do any land preparation. The soil remains unprepared. This will require us to provide additional food supplies to the Colony until they get their first crop seeded and harvested.

Additional Colonists need to be sent to this Village, however, I recommend that Russische labor be used to bring in the additional needed raw logs from the Volga River port and Russische woodworkers to build additional housing.

I provided musket training to all able men, and left ten muskets with gunpowder and cartridges for the Village safety.

No incidences of interference with the Colony from neighboring peasants, robbers, or nomadic peoples occurred. However, my soldiers did see unknown people numerous times apparently scouting out the Village. I did not notify the Colonists of this in order to prevent unneeded conflict.

I am scheduled to return to the Colony around 1 December with the needed supplies to get them through the winter, and will also guide any newly assigned Colonists at that time.

Written by me on this 7th day of November in the year of our LORD one thousand seven hundred sixty-five in the Kontor of the Guardianship Chancery for Foreigners' subordinate office in Саратов.

Signed,

Viktor Chernyshevsky
Lieutenant, Imp. Russische Army
Kontor Саратов

FIRST WINTER

♦JACOBINA KARL♦

Our Colony of Balzer (Goloi Karamysh)

The full force of our first Volga River winter was now here. The days never warmed above freezing with the nights much colder. It was already much colder than our coldest month back in Löwenstein which was always January, and here it was only November.

One early morning, walking the short distance with *Christoph* to the Village House, I turned and said to him through shivering teeth, "How much colder can it get?"

He looked at me and replied, "They say it will get much colder before it again turns warmer. Like home, January is the coldest month with February a close second. We can only hope for an early warm spring."

So far, our experience with the climate did not agree with our Recruiter's promises, and evidently, his promises on the climate were only more of his lies. It was much colder here with less rain, but more fog and clouds than where we grew up. I am not sure why I am surprised at this, nothing else the Recruiter said turned out to be true.

While I pray that life will be better here for *Christoph* and me and, hopefully someday, the children we have, I also pray that there is a special place in Hell for people such as the Recruiter with all his lies and broken promises. That my not following my Lutheran teachings, but it is as it is!

Our days passed with the village just trying to survive the cold. The men kept a steady supply of firewood and tended our animals in the Village Barn. We women concentrated on keeping the fires in the stoves going, and keeping all fed with warm food. This included thawing out all our water as it was well past freezing outside.

True to his word, *Lt. Chernyshevsky* and more soldiers arrived on the morn of 26 November. They were a cold exhausted group when they made it to us. We rushed them into the Village House and gave all blankets, warm tea and food. The soldiers eagerly and graciously accepted, and repeatedly thanked us.

Along with the welcome supplies, they also brought two new families for our Colony village. Looking haggard and exhausted from the yearlong trip here, as we had looked just months ago, the two cold families, like the soldiers, eagerly accepted our welcome of food, drink, and blankets.

I introduced myself, "Welcome to our Village. I am *Frau Jacobina*, wife of *Herr Christoph Karl*, and you are?" My being so forward startled both of the men of the two families. I was a Deutsche woman, and that was not expected.

Still being forward, I explained, "This is a new country, and we have no time to waste. Here we get right to the point needed."

Over in the corner, we could hear *Lt. Chernyshevsky* laughing loudly. I knew why he was laughing but just ignored him. I knew he thought I was crazy.

Puzzled by his laughing, but now recovered from my words, one of the men replied, "I am *Herr George Merkel,* Reformed blacksmith, with my wife *Frau Eva,* and my children, my son *Johann Georg,* and my three daughters *Catharina, Maria Magdalena,* and *Elisabeth.* We are from Switzerland."

As he spoke, both my husband *Christoph* and *Vorsteher Barthuli* arrived to greet the new comers.

The second man replied, "I am *Herr Jakob Herzog,* Reformed farmer, with my wife *Frau Anna Margaretha,* and my four sons *Johann Jacob, Leonhard, Johann Peter, Johann Heinrich,* and my three daughters *Anna Catharina, Elisabeth,* and *Jacobona.* We are of the Kurpfalz."

Vorsteher Barthuli stepped in and took control of our conversation and spoke, "I am the Vorsteher of the village. My name is *Herr Balzer Barthuli,* and this is *Herr Christoph Karl.* He is husband of *Frau Jacobina,* the woman you are talking with. Welcome to our Colony and village."

I was so irritated with *Herr Barthuli* for putting me down in front of these new people. If he was so important, why was he not to here to greet them right away? Men can be so useless at times, even my husband!

Both *Herr Merkel* and *Herr Herzog* did look more relieved talking to men. As I said before, Men can be so useless.

Herr Balzer continued, "*Herr George* and *Herr Jakob*, please come with *Herr Christoph* and me and we will make sure you meet all the other men and learn what is needed."

He turned to me and requested, "*Frau Jacobina*, please inform their women what women need to know in order to help their husbands and children, and to fit in our village society. Thank you."

Request, no, Order, yes. Of course, I replied as any proper Deutsche woman, "Yes, *Herr Balzer* as you wish." At the same time I flashed a look of anger at my *Christoph*, who seeing it, quickly looked away. Men!

With the men gone to do their important talking and meeting the other men, I now had the chance to converse with their women all about what was really important; how they felt, what they needed, how old their children were… The really important things to a family.

We did not have enough log houses built yet for even the last two of our original families, the *Tehele* and the *Heft* families, and now we had two more to shelter. We would make room for them as well as we could in the Village House.

With my and the other village women's help, the two new families fit right in to our village life. Before long, you could not tell them from us.

The fact that *Herr Merkel* was a blacksmith was great cause to welcome him in our Village. He had even brought thirty pub eisen (iron bars), four pub stahl (steel bars), and schmiedewerkzeuge (forging tools) with him. Plans were drawn up quickly to build a smith building with forge when the spring thaw arrived.

Of course, another farmer to help grow the crops for food on our tables was also very welcome. *Herr Herzog* had also brought more tools, pflugeisen (plowshare) and spitzhacken (picks).

Lt. Chernyshevsky and his men only stayed two nights before they left to return to Saratov. The seed and food they brought us was gladly accepted.

December was even colder than November, and day by day, it seemed to get colder with a bitter wind and more snow. The high during the day was colder than the coldest night back home.

The one bright spot in our cold survival was our celebration of Christmas. By homeland custom, we celebrated Christmas over three days ending on the 25th of December. While our men continued to do the everyday boring work, we village women enjoyed preparing for the celebration.

Our men went out and found a Christmas tree just right for our Village House. The younger children made small decorations of clay, shells, and wood and placed them on the tree. Candles were still in short supply, but I found a few for the tree.

Under the tree, we placed baskets filled with naschereien (sweets) and nuts and brötchen. In the old country, I would have put in fruits and apples, but sadly, we had none this year.

On the eve of Christmas, we had no Kirche or Kirche bell to ring, so instead one of the older boys went from house-to-house ringing a small ox bell to call all to our service in the Village House.

Together, we sang our songs of Christmas, as had our ancestors in the past. Our voices resounded into the night air with music never before heard in this area.

Our small ox bell rang a second time, and one honored older boy sang a song for all to hear and enjoy. All the children later joined him in singing more of our Holy songs.

With no minister, *Vorsteher Barthuli* stepped up and led us in prayer and a short devotion. More Christmas carols followed with the giving out of the Naschereien. Everyone shared blessings and hugs and kisses with all.

After all was finished, walking along with *Herr Heft* and wife *Frau Katharina*, and arm in arm with my dear *Christoph* to our home, I turned to him and said, "My husband, this was all so nice. Thank you for all you have provided."

Christoph did not say anything, just stopped walking and looked deep into my eyes for some time, and then ardently kissed me out in public. Right then in his strong arms, I knew that there could be no other place better. I basked in the good feeling.

My good feeling might have lasted longer but for the snickering of our friends, *Herr Heft* and wife *Frau*

Katharina. We had forgotten that we were still outside and not in the privacy of our home.

Blushing and embarrassed, I apologized to them. I looked at *Christoph* to see if he too was embarrassed, but he just had a wide stupid smile on his face. Men!

Herr Heft and wife *Frau Katharina* were not at all concerned, but agreed that it might be better if we continued after we got inside our home. The four of us hurried home, and separately continued our celebrations behind closed doors and curtains.

The next morn was Christmas. We awakened to the sound of singing as our village friends walked among the homes. Throughout the day, we shared much food and drink, and gave and received blessings from all. Good times for all to dim the memories of all the recent bad.

Six days later the Neue Jahr (New Year) with its traditional celebration arrived. Once that was over, the cold dreariness of January set in, and this winter, it was even colder outside than in December.

Never in our lives had we ever been so cold. Along with suffering from the cold, the frigid and windy weather forced us to stay inside our homes. When we did have to venture out, we bundled up like bears and we did it quickly.

I tried to keep myself busy, and heaven knows there was plenty of work for me, but often my mind would wander back to my former home, my Kirche, and my family.

The cold winter also brought sickness again, and while we did not have any die from it, we did have many sick and weak for a long time. January slowly moved on, and February arrived. I had hoped it might turn warmer, but that was not to be as this February stayed just as cold as January.

I, and everyone else in Balzer, prayed to our LORD to bless our Village with the quick end of end of winter and the warmth of an early spring.

FIRST SPRING

Our prayers were answered! It was an early spring this year. The winter had been fiercely cold, but left quickly.

It felt so good to be able to get out of the heavy Russische clothes and back into our much lighter and more womanly Deutsche wear. This is the first time for months that I have been happy about how I look. We lost much of our bright clothing on the trip, but our Village women quickly made the best of what they still had, and our Village is again now much more colorful.

The men, including my *Christoph*, have also noticed our improved looks and seem to have a little more 'spring' in their step. In fact, my *Christoph* has recently had only one thing on his 'mind' at bedtime, and I will honestly tell you, it is not sleeping.

I have gossiped with the other women as we always do, and this seems to be the new goal of all the men. Only Heaven knows, but we may have a large increase in our Village population in around nine months.

I may be helping with that increase. Last night, I dreamt that that our LORD had blessed us at last, and sent an Angel down from the Heavens to me. The Angel gently touched my belly and spoke gently to me, "You are now with your husband's child. Give thanks to our LORD."

With that, my Angel of Heaven vanished. I immediately awoke, wondering if it was real or a dream. Either way, I quickly gave thanks to the LORD. I pray that it was all real and that we are soon blessed with our own child.

The next few weeks and months passed slowly, and I hoped and patiently waited to see if my body told me I was with child. Sadly, I am not. I am thankful that I never mentioned to *Christoph* my dream of Angel of the LORD visit. I would not want to get his hopes up, and then have to tell him it was all not real, but just a silly dream of his wife.

MORE!

One morning a group of Russen with wagons and horses and a soldier escort arrived hauling in more logs from the river. All day long, more and more logs piled up until they totaled more than five times our original supply.

Eventually, *Vorsteher Barthuli* got the attention of one of the soldiers and asked him, "What are all these new logs for?" The Russischer soldier stared at him, and then motioned for him to wait right where he was.

A few minutes later, he returned with another soldier, who spoke to *Herr Barthuli*, "My friend does not talk Deutsches well like I. What need you?"

Vorsteher Barthuli repeated his question, "What are all these new logs for?"

The soldier scratched his head trying to understand, and then replied, "For log houses."

Puzzled, *Vorsteher Barthuli* replied, "We already have enough to build the four houses we still need logs for."

The soldier laughed and said, "More, many more houses needed. Many families coming, many men and women and children."

By this time, my husband *Christoph* had joined the two of them, and asked, "How many more families?"

The soldier struggled with that question, and then shook his head. Finally held up both hands as balled up and the spread his ten fingers, balled them up again and spread his ten fingers again.

Christoph spoke first, "You mean twenty families are coming here?"

The soldier nodded and smiled, "Yes, that right. Twenty and more."

Stunned, *Vorsteher Barthuli* and *Christoph* just stood silently as the soldier went back to his work.

Vorsteher Barthuli spoke first, as much to himself, as to *Christoph*, "Where in our LORDs name will we put twenty families? We cannot build that many log homes that fast. We do not have enough room in the Village House."

My *Christoph* did not reply, but just slowly shook his head in shock.

That night, all met in the Village House to discuss the news. No one had any idea what to do, but all decided to sleep on it and pray for our LORDs guidance. The next morning, the problem solved itself. Another group of twenty Russische men showed up with another soldier escort, and this time they had wagons loaded with tools.

One that spoke our language yelled out to no one in particular, "Where do you want the new log houses built?"

Our men hurried to mark where each new house would go and then stood back and watched the Russen go to work.

While the Russische men worked on the next twenty-five houses, our men began work on the houses for the families of *Herr Ludwig Tehele, Herr Heinrich Heft, Herr Georg Merkel,* and *Herr Jakob Herzog.*

A few days later, our pechniki (stone stove maker) arrived again, and immediately began to build his stoves and our chimneys. I avoided him so as not to interfere with is work.

All twenty-five log houses for new people, and the four log homes for our current villagers were finished except for the stoves in around four weeks. Strange though, as fast as they built the houses and used logs, even more logs arrived on wagons from the river.

The log homes were finished none too soon as two days later, on the day we were told was the 28th of March, a long caravan of wagons escorted by a score of soldiers arrived with twenty-two more families.

Our whole village turned out to welcome and help the new people. Like all that came here before them, including us, they were exhausted and tired from the yearlong travel.

We comforted and fed them as best we could in the Village House. Even though we had built it large, the large number of people in it now made it seem small.

After they ate and drank and rested for a short while, *Vorsteher Barthuli* stood up and spoke to all, "I am the Vorsteher of our village. My name is *Herr Balzer Barthuli.* Welcome to our Colony and village. I know that you are all tired from your trip and worried about what is in your future. All of us around you here have been in exactly the same place as you are now. You are not alone."

He continued on, "There are twenty-five new log homes ready. Each family can move into one right after this meeting. So that we can assign the homes and so that we all know who you are, I need each Man of the Family to stand, speak their name and religion and work, introduce their family members, and tell where they are from. Please start now."

The first man stood and spoke, "I am *Herr Jakob Borell*, Reformed farmer with my *Frau Elisabeth*, and my mother *Frau Anna Maria*. We are all from Baden-Durlach."

The second man stood and spoke, "I am *Herr Georg Borell*, Reformed farmer, brother to *Herr Jakob Borell* and son to *Frau Anna Maria*. With me is my *Frau Elisabeth*, and daughter *Susanna Catharina*. We are also from Baden-Durlach."

The third man stood and spoke, "I am *Herr Jakob Klein Senior*, Reformed farmer with my *Frau Dorothea*, son *Heinrich Peter*, and daughters *Susanna Margaretha, Maria Margaretha, Maria Catharina*. We are all from Baden-Baden."

The fourth man stood and spoke, "I am *Herr Jakob Klein*, Reformed farmer, son of *Herr Jakob Klein Senior*, and *Frau Dorothea*. With me is my *Frau Anna Barbara*. We are also from Baden-Baden."

The fifth man stood and spoke, "I am *Herr Georg Berg*, Lutheran farmer from Darmstadt, with my *Frau Elisabeth*."

The sixth man stood and spoke, "I am *Herr Michael Bär*, Lutheran farmer with my *Frau Anna Barbara*. We are also of Darmstadt."

The seventh man stood and spoke, "I am *Johannes Meier*, Reformed farmer with my *Frau Magdalena*, and stepdaughter *Catharina Barbara*. We are from Switzerland."

The eighth man stood and spoke, "I am *Jakob Späth*, Reformed farmer with my *Frau Maria Catharina*, and sons *Johann Diks*, *Johann Wilhelm*, *Johann Jacob*, and daughters *Juliana* and *Maria Margaretha*. We are all from Runkel."

One by one, they stood up and spoke, "I am *Herr Johannes Buseck*, Reformed farmer with my *Frau Margaretha* from the Kurpfalz."

"I am *Herr Philipp Eichner*, Reformed farmer, with my *Frau Catharina Margaretha*, and son *Johann Philipp*, and daughter *Anna Elisabeth* from the Kurpfalz."

"I am *Herr Peter Steinpreis*, Lutheran farmer with my *Frau Elisabeth*, also from the Kurpfalz."

"I am *Herr Wilhelm Kolb*, Reformed farmer with my *Frau Christina*. We are also of the Kurpfalz."

"I am *Herr Jakob Gropp*, Reformed farmer with my *Frau Elisabeth*, and my son *Johannes*, and my two daughters *Christina* and *Jacobina*, also all from the Kurpfalz area."

"I am *Herr Michael Heckmann*, Reformed farmer with my *Frau Anna Catharina*, and daughter *Jacobina*. We too are of the Kurpfalz."

"I am *Herr Johannes Bauer*, Reformed farmer with my *Frau Jacobina*, and daughter *Susanna Elisabeth* of the Kurpfalz."

"I am *Herr Adam Heckmann*, Reformed farmer with my *Frau Anna Maria*, and son *Georg Adam*. We too are from the Kurpfalz."

"I am *Herr Paul Stöhr*, Reformed farmer with my *Frau Anna Maria*, and sons *Johann Michael*, *Johann Jacob*, *Johann Peter*, and daughters *Susanna Elisabeth*, *Anna Catharina*, and *Maria Margaretha*, all from the Kurpfalz."

"I am *Herr Jakob Busch*, Reformed farmer with my *Frau Christina*, and sons *Philipp* and *Johann Jacob*, from the Kurpfalz."

"I am *Herr Ludwig Bauer*, Reformed farmer with my *Frau Eva Margaretha*, son *Johann Jacob*, and daughters *Susanna Catharina*, and *Christina*. We are from the Kurpfalz."

"I am *Herr Ludwig Huber*, Reformed farmer with wife *Frau Anna Catharina*, and sons *Martin* and *Christian*. We are all from the Kurpfalz."

"I am *Herr Valentin Hoffmann*, Reformed farmer, my *Frau Anna Barbara*, and daughters *Margaretha*, *Anna Catharina*, and *Susanna*, from Kurpfalz."

Finally, the 22nd man stood and said, "I am *Herr Mathias Kiselmann*, Lutheran farmer with my *Frau Elisabeth*, and sons *Johann Philipp*, and *Mathias*. We are from Wittenberg."

Vorsteher Barthuli stood up and spoke, "Thank you, and again, welcome to our village. I know you wish to get to your new homes. Please meet me outside and *Herr*

Karl and I will assign, and then lead each family to their new home."

Eager to get to their own homes, twenty-two families tried to exit the Village House at one time. Much patience was required by all, but eventually all safely made it outside.

They followed my husband *Christoph* and *Herr Barthuli* to the line of new homes. One by one, each family received their own log home.

Many of the women squealed in happiness, and a few even hugged my husband *Christoph*. A village woman stayed with each family to help them move-in and answer any questions they might have. By the end of the day, this 28th of March in the year 1766, our Colony village now had thirty-three families with sixty-two men and boys, sixty-nine women and girls for a total village of one hundred thirty-one.

FARMERS ALL

♦CHRISTOPH KARL♦

Our Colony of Balzer

Now that we all had homes, our highest need was to get our seeds into the ground for our future crops. The ground had warmed in the spring sun and thawed.

Our land was raw and never ever been cultivated or used to grow any crops. Stones and rocks lay everywhere, each one need be removed by hand from the fields so that we did not damage our plows. It would require the entire Village to work together to get our seeds in and growing before the summer heat arrived.

One of our problems was that we did not have any experience with the weather. When the rainy season was, how much it would rain, when the dry season was, and how hot would it get, were all just guesses for us. If lucky, we would have food; if not lucky, we would soon be hungry.

Our soil was like nothing we were used to, and was partly salty and sandy. To insure our seeds stayed protected from the harsh climate and strong dry winds, we plowed and sowed our seed deep, and prayed that enough warmth would get to it for growth.

We planted wheat, barley, watermelon, potatoes, flax and sunflowers, along with an herb known as woad (plant grown for blue dyestuff from its leaves), and watched and waited for any sign of new shoots.

As our seeds eventually did sprout from the ground, we fought the native weeds and hand carried water to keep our crops alive. Day after day, we struggled to tame the land and make it produce, as we desired.

Our plans and goals for our farming occasionally slowed and almost stopped, as even the best plans usually do. Many of our villagers kept coming down with an illness preventing them from helping in the village work. It was not just the new people that sickness struck, but many of the original group too. Some were stricken more than one or two times.

I was not immune, and spent much of my time in bed with a fever or chills. My dear *Jacobina* did not catch whatever it was, though I thought she would get it from caring for me.

Like most men, I am useless when I am sick, and that forced *Jacobina* to not only take care of me in addition to her normal work, but to finish my chores. I do not know how she kept up, but I thank the LORD that she did.

We had no doctor, so our women treated us as best they could with food, lots of water, rest, and prayer. The accepted idea was that it might be from the rigors of the long trip that we all went through. Or maybe it was from all the unexpected temperature ups and downs in this area with one day being cold and the next being hot. In truth, we were just not accustomed to this weather.

And then there was the water; *Jacobina* always took our water from the fast running part of our river. Some of our other women, too lazy to do that, took their water from the stagnant pond areas where the water was bad, and their families suffered greatly. Even so, life was not all sickness and work; eventually we recovered and still had time to enjoy our village friends and ourselves.

MY GARDEN

◆JACOBINA KARL◆

Our Colony of Balzer

The men were in the field much of the time, and most of my days, the chores never seemed to be finished. But one chore that gave me much pleasure was feeding and watching my chickens and roosters, and my garden down by the river.

I also enjoyed working in my part of the village gardens by the river. I came to feel that my plants are like children for me to protect, nurture and help grow. Some of the other women have said that tending the gardens is a chore that they do not like.

I have never feel that way, I see beauty in GODS bountiful blessing, and know it is an honor to let me help in this work. And my plants must feel this too, for my peas, and melons, and potatoes are plentiful and very tasty.

My feeling about my garden may be from that *Christoph* and I are still not blessed with children of our own. It is not for lack of trying, my *Christoph* sees to that! And I have prayed often, but it must be the wishes of our LORD that we not yet have children. I am disappointed, of course, as the other Village women seem to drop them out every nine months.

And while jealousy does not follow our Lutheran way, I admit that I do at times resent them. I have thought long and hard searching for what *Christoph* or I might have done to anger our LORD, but believe in my soul that it is not that. It must be that our LORD has decided that it is not yet our time.

No matter, I have my garden to mother, and to watch grow. For now, that will have to do. Still, I will continue to pray each morning, noon, and night that our LORD will allow me to give my *Christoph* a son to carry on his good name of *Karl.*

OSTERN

To prepare for unsere erste Ostern (Easter) on Saturday the 30th of March, we observed the Karfreitag (Good Friday) in memory of the resurrection of our JESUS. Our custom on this day was that erwachsene (adults) not eat anything. During the Karwoche (Holy Week), everyone would be extremely busy and working in the colonies. All in the house and yard must be clean for Easter, and much food prepared for the many special meals.

Our most important members of the village at this time were the Rätschebuwe, or oldest children not quite adults. Tradition set down that after our church service, our church bells were silent and only rung on the next Saturday again. We did not have any bells yet...

Our Rätschebuwe provided to the village what the bells normally did. They used a Rät, a wooden instrument provided with a crank, which made a ratcheting sharp clack when turned rapidly, to take the place of the bells.

I had taken my turn as a Rätschebuwe when I was a child, and I always enjoyed the sound that the Rät made. In fact, I was able to borrow one from the children, and I tormented poor *Christoph* with it in our home for several days. I especially enjoyed waking him up early in the morning with it. I would have continued playing it, but somehow it disappeared and no matter where I looked, I could not find it. *Christoph* must have really hid it well, or maybe he just buried it outside somewhere.

Following our custom, each day the Rätschebuwe walked all around the village; and at the same time, all cranked their Rät, and produced a loud noise. After they had cranked their Rät for about five minutes, the leader would raise his Rät to stop all the others. Of course, since we had no real Kirche or bells yet, our youngsters just cranked their Rät often. Continuing with our traditions, the children walked around our homes and sang in the morning, noon, and night to invite us to the Kirche for service.

Our Ostersonntag (Easter Sabbath) began at sunrise with a Choral sung by all. The village people met early at what we used for a Kirche, our Village House. Parents returned to their homes before their young kinder (children) woke, and hid colored eggs all around the village for them to find.

Finally, after all this fun and with the kinder exhausted along with their parents, we all went back to our Village House for our Oster service. Thanks be to our LORD for all his blessings!

NEW PEOPLE

About a month later on the 26th day of April, a group of Russischer soldiers, led by an Officer not seen before, delivered two more families to the Village House. We fed the new families and the soldiers. When the soldiers finished eating, they quickly left.

Vorsteher Barthuli, as usual, appeared out of nowhere and as before, stood up and spoke the exact same words as before, blah –blah-blah…"I am the Vorsteher of our village. My name is *Herr Balzer Barthuli* and welcome to our Colony and village. I know that you are all tired from your trip and worried about what is in your future. All of us around you here have been in exactly the same place as you are now. You are not alone. Please introduce yourselves and your families."

The first man stood and spoke, "I am *Herr Wilhelm Geist*, Reformed farmer, my *Frau Catharina,* and my son *Johann* and daughter *Magdelena.* We are all from the Kurpfalz."

The second man stood and spoke, "I am *Herr Konrad Ritter*, Reformed farmer. My wife died on the long trip getting here and I am now a witwer (widower). Also with me is my daughter *Maria.* We are also from Kurpfalz."

Vorsteher Barthuli again stood up and spoke, "Thank you, and again, welcome to our village. I know you wish to get to your new homes. Please meet me outside and I will assign and then lead each family to its new home."

The new people followed *Herr Barthuli* to the end of the line of new homes. Luckily, we still had three empty ones left. Each family received their own log home. Same as before, the women squealed in happiness.

By the end of the day, this 26th of April in the year 1766, our Colony village now had thirty-five families with sixty-five men and boys, seventy-one women and girls for a total village of one hundred thirty-six.

Our new people had arrived just in time for more of our traditional holiday celebrations. It was a good time for them to meet our entire Village.

Over the next few weeks, we celebrated 'The Battle Celebration' in recognition of the end of the harsh winter and the arrival of spring and better times. This day was a day of eating freshly slaughtered pigs, young bulls and sheep, and later of course, lying around relaxing from our stuffed bellies.

In reality, it was the men, including my *Christoph,* that ate and drank till they hurt, and then lay around as a group oinking and complaining. We women ate and drank well; we just did not make pigs of ourselves from eating the pigs. Nor did we have the time to lie around doing nothing!

I had reminded my *Christoph* just that morning, "Husband, do not eat like there was no tomorrow. There is no reason to make you sick. Show a little control and restraint."

Did he listen? Apparently not, for there he was with all the other Village men. I am not sure he even really heard me. I find it amazing that he can conveniently tune out my voice when he does not want to hear what I think he needs to hear, MEN!

All our men survived overeating, and a week later, we celebrated our Ascension Day. This day was in commemoration of the bodily Ascension of Jesus into Heaven forty days after his resurrection from the dead. This, of course, was cause for another great feast after a service at the friedhof. Like before, the Village men, including *Christoph*, ate as if there was no tomorrow.

Ten days later, we celebrated Pfingstfest. This is the celebration of the Holy Spirit and forms the end of the Ostern circle in the Kirche year. Pfingstfest occurs fifty days after Easter. As custom dictated, we celebrated the eve of Pfingstfest and through the whole night with songs and merriment, and of course, more eating.

BLAZING SUMMER

◆CHRISTOPH KARL◆

Our Colony of Balzer

Who knew that an early spring would also bring an early summer. The warmth of spring was appreciated was welcomed by all. We did not pray to our LORD for an early summer. This heat of summer, no, this blazing heat of our summer here was not welcome.

The weather had changed from the cool of spring with a light wind, sun mixed with cloudy skies and occasional showers to not a cloud in sight and dry winds and a blazing sun. It was as hot here as I had ever felt it in my valley near Löwenstein.

I, along with all the other men, carried water on our backs from our river to the fields just to save what crops we could save. Those areas that we did not get water to each day just shriveled up into brown stubble and died.

Jacobina, along with the other Village women, constantly watered our gardens near the river, and thankfully, since the river was so close they did not have to move the water far. Most of our garden crops not only were saved, but actually flourished in the hot summer sun.

While we will not have the harvest from our crops that we had planned for, we do have a good supply of watermelon, potatoes, cucumbers, sunflowers, gourds, cabbage, peas, beans, lettuce, parsley, parsnips, celery, pumpkins, or carrots. Obviously, we will not starve.

Our Goloi Karamysh River has lowered in this simmering heat, but still flows with plenty of good clear water. The river also provides us fish, though these Russische fish must be smarter than Deutsche fish and are harder to catch. Maybe we just are not using the right bait.

Our livestock of cows and pigs continues to grow without much help from us. Food, water, shade and they will do what nature intends. Our village chickens, turkeys, and geese have increased. However, it is always a balance that our women maintain of having enough eggs for our meals, and keeping our fowl numbers growing.

We occasionally also acquire Wild, but the ducks, pheasant, quail, gophers, and fox are wary, not easy to catch. We could catch more if we used our muskets, but have dedicated those supplies to the future safety of our Village.

On a positive side, the hotter it gets the less our women wear. Even outside where our women are traditionally very modest, the unending heat is allowing more of most of their ample bosoms to show. I dearly love my wife, *Jacobina*, but I also appreciate the sight of some of the other women's bountiful charms. Kind of keeps a man stirred up all day.

At night, alone in our home, my *Jacobina* and I try to stay as cool as possible, and wear even less. For me that is good, as she is a beautiful woman and I greatly enjoy her lack of cover. On the bad side, here I am all stirred up and it is just too darned hot to do anything about it. The very last thing she wants is for my hot body to be that close to hers... However, on those hot days with cool nights, she becomes much more receptive to my advances.

Near the end of June, around the 28th, another family arrived. They were *Herr Jakob Dorlosch*, and his *Frau Anna Maria*, both Reformed, of the village of Blanenbach, Hesse.

Herr Dorlosch was something we had never had here before; he was an experienced soldat (soldier). We immediately put him to work planning our Village defenses to insure our Colonies future safety.

At our request, he immediately began working on walls for our Village perimeter, and more training for our men. He was a welcome addition!

Finally, the heat of summer began to lessen, the nights were more often cool than the unbearable hot. *Jacobina* was much more receptive to my nighttime games, as I would guess all the other women in the village were with their husbands.

FALL AGAIN

The weather here is much more unpredictable and severe than back in our homeland. Frigid cold, blazing heat, parched dry, flooding wet; everything is extreme. It is taking every bit of our communal farming experience to figure out how best to adapt our planting and harvesting to this new area. Much of it is just trial an error, because what worked back home, does not work at all here. It may take years before we conquer this environment, but tame it we will! We are as a group of one mind, and determined in this goal.

With the cooler weather, our women have begun covering up more. No longer do I regularly get to regularly enjoy the nakedness of my *Jacobina*, who is now back to her more modest self. On the happier side, she is more and more receptive to my advances now that it is cooler.

This would seem to be just a trivia matter, but last evening in one of our regular Village men meetings, our discussion turned to this very subject. I suppose this is one of those issues that every man and wife confront.

COOLER WEATHER

◆JACOBINA KARL◆

Our Colony of Balzer

That damned summer heat has passed. The days were so bad, but the nights in our home were almost unbearable. Too hot to sleep, and no rest from my work.

And then, my dear *Christoph* is always getting worked up because I am almost or sometimes completely naked to fight the heat. He actually wants to have his way with me in that hot bed.

Each and every hot night I would have to sternly say to him, "My love, I am not naked not to seduce you. I am not, as you say 'flaunting my body' to stir up your passion, but only to stay as cool as possible. My answer is 'NEIN'!"

But men, it is no use talking to them when they get into that state. And I was in no mind to allow anything that was going to make me even hotter. And so every night following my say 'NEIN' I would have to follow it with, "Husband, go take a cold swim in the river to cool your body and your passion."

I think that one night he took five or six cold dips to calm himself down. At least I was comfortable.

Seems like such a trivial item, but in my talking with the other Village women, they all have the same problem with their menfolk. None of the men, including my *Christoph*, mentioned it, but we women guessed there were probably at least five or six of our husbands taking cold dips in the river at that very same time. Of course, they would never admit to any other man that their wife would ever say absolutely 'NEIN!'

I actually asked, "My *Christoph*, have you ever run into any other men at the river whose wives had declined their advances."

Christoph, with shoulders dropped and looking very disappointed, quickly replied with, "No my wife, all the other men have wives that remain willing to submit to their husband's needs."

I did not say anything, but thought to myself, "What a Liar! Good thing it is a small lie driven by his male pride, or I would be so upset. Our LORD does not allow any lying and our faith teaches us that pride is bad, but in this case I think even GOD must be laughing at this one. Men, and that includes my dear *Christoph*, are so foolish and funny at times!"

Now that it has turned cooler at night, I am much more receptive to my *Christoph's* needs. It is probably a good thing, because he was starting to grow fins and become part fish.

With the fall came the harvest of all that we had saved from the blazing summer. Not all that we wanted, but a start in our farming.

To celebrate what we had raised, our Village had their kirchweih. This is a traditional part religious and part 'old before' religion 'harvest thanks' parish fair to honor the bounty of the pastures and land. The celebration was an expression of unrestrained life and good times.

We, not the men but the women, began fourteen days before the actual celebration with the preparations. We women baked and roasted foods and special dishes.

Finally, when the actual day came, always on Sunday, *Christoph* and I dressed in our best, and met everyone else out if front of our Village House… I suppose you would call it our Village Platz, and enthusiastically celebrated for two whole days.

While dancing and drinking in public was not normally acceptable, *Christoph*, I, and all the other Villagers danced and laughed and filled our bellies with all the wonderful foods both days and much of the nights.

Even the young kinder danced, and ran, and ate, and played to their hearts content. And the older boys and girls, the almost adults, vanished as couples into the surrounding forest to learn about life and its rewards.

Some willing betrothals, along with some not so willing marriages, would soon follow this night over the next few months with an eventual rise in our Village population.

On the bad side, many of our husbands, normally good quiet dependable men including my *Christoph*, drank much too much.

With the drink, *Christoph* began to try to take liberties with me best reserved for our home. Many of the women faced this same problem, and had to take their husbands home to sober up and cool their passions.

Unfortunately, while our men seemed to get along well most of the time, their male pride and drink caused more than a few fistfights. No one actually hurt, but more than a few wore black eyes and bruises the next days.

And while we do not mention it out loud, a few of our Village women also fell to the drink, and in that state, accidentally slept with someone not their husband.

We hope that no kinder will spring from this night of transgression, but if they do, we pray that their husband will accept these 'kinder der kirchweih' as their own. Luckily, most of us are of dark hair and of the same stocky build, and no one would really be able to tell the difference. But there are a few that are light haired and of slight build, and that might raise some eyebrows and questions.

Instead of those other poor women having the 'kinder der kirchweih', I wish the LORD would instead bless me with a child. Maybe with much prayer he still will.

14   THE EARLY YEARS

♠CHRISTOPH KARL♠

Our Colony of Balzer

The first year here was a day-to-day struggle just to survive. We had no idea what to expect from the weather and climate, the soil, our neighbor Russen, or the robber bands and nomadic hordes.

Once past that year, we learned fast and began to plan for what needed done and when it needed to be done. Now, all was looking better for our future, or so we thought.

More and more families arrived to become members of our Village and Colony. On the 4th day of June 1766, a single man arrived here by alone: *Herr Jakob Herbel,* a Reformed handwerker from Hessen.

The morning of the 18th of June stared like any other morning. Chores to be done, animals to be fed, the remaining harvest to be brought in. forty more families arrived. The sameness of each day might be thought of as boring, and sometimes it was, but it was also very reassuring to know that new problems would not just pop up anymore, or so we thought.

It was afternoon when a large convoy of travelers crossed our river and arrived at our Village House. The escorting officer asked for the Village Leader, and *Vorsteher Barthuli* was located and arrived to meet him.

The officer handed *Herr Barthuli* a long list of names and explained that these were new people for our Village.

New Families List 18.6.1767

Herr Johannes Weil Becker, Reformed farmer, with *Frau Anna Margaretha*, and his wife's mother *Maria Elisabeth Ulrich*, all from Strotzbüsch.

Herr Just Bender, Reformed farmer, with *Frau Anna Margaretha*, and daughter *Anna Catharina*, along with brother of *Frau Anna Margaretha*, and *Herr Johann Peter Deckmann*, all from Düdelsheim, Isenburg.

Herr Wilhelm Bengel, Reformed farmer, with *Frau Anna Margaretha*, and daughter *Maria Catharina*, from Isenburg.

Herr Georg Blitz, Reformed farmer, with *Frau Maria Charlotta*, both from the Kurpfalz.

Herr Adam Eurich, Reformed farmer, with *Frau Anna Catharina*, and son *Johann Adam*, from Isenburg.

Herr Lorenz Eurich, Reformed handworker, with sons *Johann Heinrich*, *Johannes*, *Balthasar*, *Johann Conrad*, and daughter *Wilhelmina*, all from Düdelsheim, Isenburg.

Herr Hermann Fecht, Reformed farmer, with *Frau Elisabeth* and daughters *Anna Charlotta* and *Anna Catharina*, his *Schwiegervater Johannes Raab* and *Schwiegermutter Anna Maria*, all from Düdelsheim, Isenburg.

Herr Johannes Gerlach, Reformed farmer, with *Frau Anna Cunigunde*, from Isenburg.

Herr Konrad Grasmück, Reformed farmer, with *Frau Anna Maria*, and daughter *Anna Catharina*, from Isenburg.

Herr Jakob Grasmück, Reformed farmer, with *Frau Johanna Elisabeth*, and sons *Johannes*, *Conrad*, *Johann Georg*, and daughters *Elisabeth Margaretha*, *Catharina*, and *Eva*, all from Isenburg.

Herr Andreas Grün, Reformed farmer, with *Frau Apollonia*, and stepson *Johannes Gropp*, from Isenburg.

Herr Johann Georg Haupt, Reformed farmer, with *Frau Anna Maria*, daughter *Maria Elisabeth*, from the Kurpfalz.

Herr Christoph Heitzenröder, Reformed farmer, with *Frau Anna Margaretha*, and son *Johann Thomas*, from Isenburg.

Herr Heinrich Jackel, Reformed farmer, with *Frau Anna Catharina*, and sons *Johann Friedrich*, *Heinrich Peter*, and daughter *Anna Catharina*, all from Isenburg.

Herr Markus Kähm, Reformed farmer, with *Frau Anna Margaretha* from Isenburg.

Herr Philipp Kaiser, Reformed hosier, with *Frau Catharina*, daughter *Anna Elisabeth*, and his mother *Frau Anna Catharina*, all from Isenburg.

Herr Heinrich Kleinfelder, Reformed farmer, with *Frau Catharina*, and wife's brother *Johannes Ruckler* and sister *Elisabeth Ruckler*, all from Isenburg.

Herr Andreas Kling, Reformed farmer, with *Frau Julianna*, and daughter *Elisabeth*, along with his brother *Herr Johannes Kling*, all from Isenburg.

Herr Philipp Leichner, Reformed farmer, with *Frau Maria Margaretha*, and sons *Johann Christian and Johannes*, all from Lindheim, Isenburg.

Herr Just Lohrengel, Reformed farmer, with *Frau Magdalena*, and son *Johann Peter*, from Isenburg.

Herr Conrad Lutz, Reformed farmer, with *Frau Catharina*, sons *Jacob* and *Andreas*, and his *mutter Anna Elisabeth*, all from Isenburg.

Herr Heinrich Magel, Reformed farmer, with *Frau Anna Cunigunde*, son *Johannes* and daughter *Susanna Catharina*, all from Düdelsheim, Isenburg.

Herr Christian Mai, Reformed farmer, with *Frau Anna Maria*, from Isenburg.

Herr Johannes Meissinger, Reformed farmer, with *Frau Eva*, and son *Johann Heinrich*, from Isenburg.

Herr Ernst Müller, Reformed farmer, with *Frau Elisabeth*, from Isenburg.

Herr Heinrich Raab, Reformed farmer, with *Frau Magdalena* and their daughter *Margaretha*, from Isenburg.

Herr Johannes Reis, Reformed farmer, with *Frau Anna Elisabeth*, their two daughters, *Albertina* and *Apollonia*, and his wife's father, *Herr Johann Scheidt*, from Isenburg.

Herr Konrad Roth, Reformed farmer, with *Frau Elisabeth*, and his mother *Catharina*, from Isenburg.

Herr Karl Rutt, Reformed farmer, with *Frau Elisabeth*, from Isenburg.

Herr Konrad Schäfer, Reformed farmer, with *Frau Catharina*, from Isenburg.

Herr Heinrich Scheidt, Reformed farmer, with *Frau Margaretha*, from Isenburg.

Herr Philipp Scheidt, Reformed farmer, with *Frau Cathatina*, from Isenburg.

Herr Philipp Schlegel, Reformed farmer, with *Frau Maria Margaretha*, and brothers *Johann Martin Eiler* and *Johannes Eiler*, all from Isenburg.

Herr Heinrich Schneider, Reformed farmer, with *Frau Anna Catharina*, from Isenburg.

Herr Johannes Weisheim, Reformed farmer, with *Frau Anna Margaretha*, from Isenburg.

Herr Konrad Weisheim, Reformed farmer, with *Frau Anna Margaretha*, and son *Johann Heinrich*, from Isenburg.

Herr Heinrich Wuckert, Reformed farmer, with *Frau Anna Susanna*, and sons *Johann Heinrich* and *Johann Weil*, from Isenburg.

Frau Elisabeth Popp, Reformed widow farmer, with sons *Johann Heinrich*, *Johannes*, and daughters *Anna Barbara* and *Anna Betta*, all from Isenburg.

Frau Maria Sophie Weisheim, Reformed widow farmer, with son *Johann Adam Wilhelm* from Isenburg.

Vorsteher Barthuli looked over the list and then replied, "There must be a mistake. We have no houses for these families, and winter is coming, and we only have enough food for our old villagers. We cannot take them."

The officer curtly replied, "You have no choice. Provide for them as best you can. My only responsibility is to deliver them here, and since they are here, I have completed my orders." With that, he commanded his men to mount up, and shortly they rode off back towards Saratov.

The new arrivals totaled forty families. While they were relieved to finally be here, they were, as we were two years ago, confused that there were no houses or preparations for them. Someone had lied to them too, just as they lied to us.

Vorsteher Barthuli and I tried to reason with them and let them know that we would do all we could for them, but they became angry and blamed all of us for the lack of housing. After that, everything became a blur of angry voices and threats and yelling.

Each day became worse as fights broke out between the Villagers and the new arrivals. Our houses ransacked and our property stolen, with some Village families thrown out of their homes by force.

Our numbers and the new arrival numbers were almost equal, and while they had pitchforks and tools, we still had the ten muskets and powder for our protection. Being peaceful, we resisted the temptation to use them.

Thirteen days later on the 1st of July 1766, fourteen more families arrived to our troubled Village. The brand new arrivals quickly joined forces with the other new people against us, the original villagers.

By sheer numbers and force, the new arrivals took over the Village House and Village Barn. They confiscated all the food and animals for their own use, and even took the seed stock that we so carefully put away for next year plantings.

Many more fights took place, and many were hurt on both sides as we tried to protect our homes as best we could.

The original Villagers, including *Jacobina* and I, grouped ourselves in four homes across from the Village Barn and shared what little food we had in each house. Slowly, the new arrivals starved us out.

We hoped that now that they had almost all the houses and control of the Village that they would leave us alone, but that was not to be. The worst new arrivals wanted all.

Out of food and water, as a group with our men protecting our women and children, *Herr Dorlosch* led us as we fought our way across the open space to the Village Barn to reclaim anything that resembled food.

As the crazed mob of new arrivals charged, outnumbering us three to one, we fired our muskets directly into those closest to us. Many fell, and the crowd retreated. Our musket fire had not been very accurate, and the bodies of men, women, and even a child lay in front of us.

The horror of us having to kill to protect our own shocked all of us. Many of us retched at the awareness of what we had just done, and become. This was not like target practice at a tree, this was the end of a life.

The thought of reloading and firing again was not a choice that few of us could bring ourselves to make, and so we all retreated into the temporary safety of the Village Barn. All, but our brave *Herr Dorlosch*, who as a former soldat had settled these issues within his soul many years ago, and was now more hardened to this type of action; he remained on guard.

While many of the men still retched and had no stomach for food, the women and children searched, but found little to eat left in the barn. The mothers gave strips of leather to their children to chew, and this seemed to help some.

Many of our animals had not been cared for and ran away to find food. Those animals penned in had not been fed for a while and were not fit to eat, so we released them for a chance to live on.

All the men finally met together at one end of the barn, and *Herr Barthuli* quietly spoke, "Our future looks bad unless we can get the new arrivals to come to their senses and see reason, but I see no way for that to happen. Make the best of the time that you have with your loved ones."

With nowhere to go and no food to eat, each family settled into their own spots to await the eventual end. Women and children were crying, while their husbands felt guilty because they could do nothing more to protect them.

Jacobina and I settled down, leaning on the wall of one of the horse stalls. She whispered to me, "This makes no sense. Why do they hate us so? We are just like them."

I gently whispered back, "They are just like us, but they are angry at all the lies and scared that they may not survive the coming winter. They are jealous of what we had and blame us for all the evil things others have done to them. They cannot punish the others, and so we are the enemy to vanquish. And they have the craziness egging them on."

Jacobina whispered, "Is there no way to reason with them? What if we just give them everything and leave? Will that not satisfy them?"

I sighed, and whispered, "Maybe that is what we should have done before we killed some of them. We spilt their blood, and the mob will never let that pass. We must be prepared to kill more, or ourselves be killed. I am not sure that I can kill again, even to save you. I must pray for guidance and strength."

Jacobina squeezed my hand, and said, "I understand, dear husband. You have done all you can. Now it is time for us to pray to our LORD. Whatever is his plan, will be."

We prayed to our LORD for his guidance, protection, and forgiveness for all we have done in this conflict, but we all realized that it would take a miracle from him to save us now.

After a while, one by one, each man came to the same decision and stood up, and reloaded their muskets. Each having decided they must defend their families to the very end. More killing was to be, if that was the LORDs plan. Like the others, I too made that choice. As I left, I said to my *Jacobina*, "No matter what happens, I will be with you either here or in Heaven as our LORD chooses!" *Jacobina* did not answer, but just lowered her head and softly cried.

HIS ANSWER

◆CAPTAIN CHERNYSHEVSKY◆

One verst east of Colony Goloi Karamysh

It was the morning of the 8th of August 1767, and we were only a verst (less than a mile) or so from the Colony Goloi Karamysh. Now a капита́н (Captain), I was escorting fifteen new families for the Colony, and had not been back there for some time. I actually looked forward to seeing how the Deutschen had done while I was gone.

Suddenly, the unmistakable crack of many muskets firing at the same time echoed through the air. That did not sound right; ten of my men and me immediately left the caravan and galloped our horses to the Village to investigate.

I hoped that it was nothing more than musket target practice; I prayed that it was not Robbers. I found that it was nothing I ever expected.

As I entered the village, I saw before me, a battleground with dead and injured laying on the ground, and a mob of angry people surging towards the Village Barn.

When the crazed mob noticed my soldiers and me, they stopped for a moment, but then surged on towards the Village Barn.

My official report follows of that day, and the following day's events:

Official Report
15.8.1767

On the 8th of August, I arrived with my soldiers and fifteen families at Colony Goloi Karamysh. Upon arrival, I found that the Colony was in chaos with a complete breakdown of local leadership and control.

I immediately declared военное положение (Martial Law) and replaced the Village Leadership with myself as Military Commander.

While this action is not specifically authorized in my current orders, the necessity "to maintain good order and peace" is authorized. As "good order and peace" within the Village no longer existed, I assumed all Leadership responsibilities.

I immediately called out the Village population and announced the declaration the State of Martial Law and new laws supporting it. I stationed my soldiers at the Colony

Village limits, and as roving guards to police the Village and restore "good order and peace."

Some dissent and protest was immediately voiced, primarily from a faction of recent arrivals originally from the area of Isenburg. Notably, no protest was heard from the original founding colonists or their leadership that I delivered here about two years ago.

All protest and dissent was declared illegal and subject to arrest under this military declaration. All meetings and assemblies were also prohibited.

In conducting an investigation as to what led up to this breakdown in Village civil authority, I interviewed a number of the founding Villagers to include Vorsteher Balzer Barthuli, Herr Christoph Karl, and Herr Jacob Scheck. I also interviewed a number of the men from the new arrivals that arrived in the past forty-five days.

From their own accounts, I have pieced together the following chain of events leading to the breakdown of this Village authority and society:

18.6.1767 – Forty families, primarily Reformed Faith, and from one area of Deutschland, Isenburg, arrived without prior notice to the Village leadership. This increase basically doubled the Village population. Five recently built individual houses were unoccupied, and were assigned two families per house with thirty families housed in mass in the Village House until additional housing for all new families could be built.

The new arrivals were extremely unhappy that houses were not already built for all as their Recruiters had promised. The new arrivals blamed the current Villagers for not being prepared for their arrival, and insisted that all the current housing be assigned to two families per house including those houses occupied by the original colonists. The Village leadership did not support this request stating that the original colonists had already lived through months of temporary and shared housing two years ago.

With the doubled population, food and water shortages also began. The original Villagers had made great improvements in the yield from their gardens, and from their harvest, but it was insufficient to support a doubled population. While the new arrivals did bring more chickens, cows, and swine with them, no pens or coops were available for them. The new chickens had not started laying eggs, and quickly the supply of eggs from the original chickens was exhausted. Such was the newly arrived cows requiring care, but with little or no milk produced. Crime and theft, here to unknown in this Colony, of eggs and milk, and eventually personal property, began to occur.

With the great increase in children, the limited schooling that was available was overwhelmed, and children were left unsupervised without direction and resorted to prowling through the original Villager homes. Many were caught in the act, and were brought to the Village Leaders for punishment.

Punishment was issued as it has always been in accord with our Laws, but the new arrivals challenged the authority of the Village Leaders and by force removed their 'lawbreaker children' back into their own protection.

This challenge to the rule of law reinforced to the children the idea that it was all right to plunder the houses of the original Villagers, and crimes continued to escalate. The original Villagers were forced to spend their time protecting their homes instead of working around the Village and harvesting the remaining crops.

Slowly the Village society began to grind to a halt. While the Village Leaders attempted to assign communal tasks to continue the necessary work, the new arrivals refused to cooperate.

1.7.1767 – Fourteen more families, primarily Reformed Faith, again from one area of Deutschland, Isenburg, arrived without prior notice to the Village leadership. This new group reaction was the same as previous arrivals: with shock as they realized their housing was not yet ready.

These new arrivals naturally aligned with the others from Isenburg, and insisted on putting three families in each and every house. The Village Leaders refused, and with majority numbers, the new arrivals elected their own Village Leaders and attempted by force to remove the old Village leaders and enforce their three families per house ruling.

The new arrivals Village Leaders confiscated all foodstuffs, chickens, cows, garden crops, and seed stock for future planting throughout for only the new arrivals use. By sheer numbers, the new arrivals prevented the original Villagers from any source of food, and forced the original Villagers to survive on what little they had in their own homes. The new arrivals ate most of the seed stock so none is available for next year plantings.

In order to ensure their safety when the original village women went for water, they went in large groups of women with their men using the ten muskets that I previously issued to them for their protection. By this time, no harvesting was being done, no building of houses was being done, and no cultivation or gardening was done.

8.8.1767- In a final desperate act to find more food for their families, the original Villagers moved in an armed group and retook the Village Barn. The mob of new arrivals attacked, and the original Villagers used their loaded muskets and fired into the crowd.

I arrived shortly thereafter, and found two armed camps with the original Villagers in the Village Barn, while outnumbered three to one, were better equipped to fight with the ten muskets.

I found four new arrival men killed outright, as were two new arrival women, and one older male child. A few more new arrivals were less severely injured. No founding Villagers were seriously hurt in this fight, but some were injured in earlier disputes.

As noted above, I immediately declared a State of Martial Law and confiscated all weapons from both groups. I placed my soldiers with arms to protect all and maintain good order and peace.

There is no doubt that someone at the KONTOR in Сара́тов has been negligent in planning. To send sixty-nine families to a Colony without preparing housing and without notifying the existing Village Leadership to make ready for their arrival is criminal. All this only two months before winter sets in.

I will leave this to Higher Headquarters to investigate who is responsible for this travesty and to determine their punishment.

I have immediately instituted the following under my own authority:

1) I have suspended any Village self–governing indefinitely. I have selected the following original villagers to be on an advisory committee serving at my discretion: Herr Balzer Barthuli, Herr Christoph Karl, and Herr Jacob Scheck. I have also selected for this committee three men from the new arrivals. Additionally, I have formed another advisory committee reporting to me consisting of Frau Barthuli, Frau Karl, and Frau Scheck, and three women from the new arrivals. Both committees will advise me on Colony Village issues, while I will retain final decision authority.

2) I have assigned thirty of the men from the new group to begin working on more housing under the supervision of Herr Jacob Scheck. He will select and notify the men.

3) I have assigned the rest of the men to the breaking ground of new lands and cultivation for next year's harvest   under the supervision of Herr Christoph Karl. He will select and notify the men.

4) I have assigned the schooling and productive work of all children to Herr Barthuli and whoever he needs to assist. He will select and notify those needed.

5) I have assigned the enlargement of the river gardens to one third of all the Village women under the supervision of Frau Karl. She will select and notify the women.

6) I have assigned the care of the chickens and all their eggs, cows and milk, and swine to another third of all Village women under the supervision of Frau Scheck. She will select and notify the women.

7) I have assigned the preparation of daily food and bread to the final third of all Village women under the supervision of Frau Barthuli. She will select and notify the women.

8) All original Villagers housing will remain single family as it had been prior to the new groups' arrival. Any housing that has been taken over by the new arrivals will be immediately returned in a clean condition to the original owners.

9) While policing of the Colony Village area will remain primarily a military function, I have ordered that each soldier will be accompanied at night by an unarmed Village man. Rosters designating nightly guard duty will be posted immediately.

10) I have also ordered that any actions that disturb 'good peace and order' will be brought to my attention and will be severely punished. Theft or crimes by any member of a family, no matter the age, sex, or reason for such crime, will be met with either banishment of the entire family from this Colony or assignment of the entire family to a military confinement facility. Fighting, laziness or failure to perform assigned duties will likewise

cause severe treatment for all of the family members.

I know that the above will bring this Village back on track and over some time will allow them to restore self-government. I will remain here pending new orders or until there is a stable situation here.

Because of the extreme increase in population and the subsequent chaos, I request the following supplies immediately:

1) Re-supply of seed stock to insure crop yield to support one hundred families.
2) Additional Russischen labor to assist with house and barn building.
3) Additional supplies of logs from Volga River port or other colonies.
4) Additional chickens, swine, cows, sheep, goats, and horses.
5) Additional blankets to carry those without homes through winter.

Written by me on this 15th day of August in the year of our LORD one thousand seven hundred sixty-seven in Colony Goloi Karamysh.

Signed,

Viktor Chernyshevsky
капита́н, Imp. Russische Army
Kontor Сара́тов

New Families List 1.7.1767

Herr Jost Erth, Reformed farmer, with son *Philipp* from the Isenburg area.

Herr Johannes Heimbuch, a Reformed farmer with his *Frau Anna Maria*, and his son *Johann Heinrich*, all from the Isenburg area.

Herr Heinrich Heimbuch, a Reformed farmer from the area of Isenburg.

Herr Georg Idt, a Reformed farmer with his *Frau Catharina*, both from the area of Isenburg.

Herr Lorenz Kalbin, a Lutheran farmer with his *Frau Elisabeth*. Also with them were two brothers of his wife, *Herr Philipp Habermann* and *Herr Johann Ernst Habermann*, all four of them from the Hanau area.

Herr Stefan Klaus, a Reformed farmer with sons *Johannes, Johann Peter, Johann Adam*, and *daughter Susanna Catharina*, all from the Isenburg area.

Herr Caspar Köhler, a Reformed farmer with his *Frau Anna Barbara* and sons *Johann Caspar, Philipp, Johannes*, and daughter *Anna Christina*, all from the Isenburg area.

Herr Friedrich Kräuter, a Reformed farmer with his *Frau Anna Elisabeth*, and daughter *Maria Barbara* from the Isenburg area.

Herr Johannes Neuhard, a Reformed farmer with his *Frau Elisabeth*, his younger brother *Philipp*, and the sister of his wife, *Anna Maria*, all of them from the Isenburg area.

Herr Philipp Protsmann, a Reformed farmer with his *Frau Anna Gertrude*, and his brothers *Wilhelm Jacob* and *Johannes Jacob*, all from the Isenburg area.

Herr Konrad Schneider, a Reformed farmer with his *Frau Anna Barbara*, and stepmother *Margaretha* from the Isenburg area.

Herr Heinrich Tirol, a Reformed farmer with his *Frau Maria Eva*, both from the Isenburg area.

Herr Philipp Zieg, a Reformed farmer with his *Frau Helena*, son *Philipp*, his mother *Catharina*, his brother's son *Philipp*, all from the Isenburg area.

Frau Gertrude Schneider, a Reformed widow farmer with her two sons, *Johann Caspar* and *Johannes*, and her three daughters, *Margaretha*, *Anna Carolina*, and *Anna Maria*, all of them from the Isenburg area.

New Families List 8.8.1767

Herr Heinrich Bäcker, a Reformed farmer with his *Frau Wilhelmina*, his son *Johann Georg*, stepson *Johann Heinrich Junker* and stepdaughter *Elisabeth*, all from the Isenburg area.

Herr Heinrich Engel, a Reformed farmer with his *Frau Anna Margaretha*, his son *Conrad*, and the mother of his wife, *Frau Anna Catharina Heil*, all of them from the Isenburg area.

Herr Konrad Faust, a Reformed farmer with his *Frau Margaretha*, and their son *Herr Conrad* and his wife *Frau Margaretha*, all from the Isenburg area.

Herr Georg Frickel, a Reformed farmer with his *Frau Anna Margaretha*, and sons *Conrad* and *Friedrich*, and daughter *Anna Dorothea*, all from the Isenburg area.

Herr Konrad Heil, a Reformed farmer with his *Frau Eleonora* from the Isenburg area.

Herr Kaspar Kähm, a Reformed farmer with his *Frau Eleonora* from the Isenburg area.

Herr Johann Heinrich Keller, a Reformed farmer with his *Frau Anna Maria*, and his son *Johann Conrad*, from the Isenburg area.

Herr Philipp Röhrig, a Reformed farmer, with his *Frau Catharina* from the Isenburg area.

Herr Johannes Ross, a Reformed farmer with his *Frau Anna Elisabeth*, and son *Johann Heinrich*, and daughter *Wilhelmina*, from the Isenburg area.

Herr Heinrich Schleuger, a Reformed farmer with his *Frau Elisabeth*, stepson *Michael Kern* and stepdaughter *Maria Kern*, all from the Isenburg area.

Herr Johannes Schleuger, a Reformed farmer with his *Frau Anna Magdalena* from the Isenburg area.

Herr Johannes Stumpf, a Reformed farmer with his son *Wilhelm* and daughter *Anna Maria*, from the Isenburg area.

Frau Anna Maria Scheibel, a Reformed widow farmer with her three sons, *Johann Heinrich, Johannes, Johann Friedrich*, and *Heinrich Peter*, from the Isenburg area.

Frau Anna Maria Sinner, a Reformed widow farmer with sons, *Conrad, Georg, Johannes, Heinrich*, and daughter *Anna Margaretha*, all from the Isenburg area.

Frau Anna Margaretha Weber, a Reformed widow farmer with her son *Ludwig Karl*, and daughters *Anna Margaretha* and *Anna Maria*, all from the Isenburg area.

Official Report

29.8.1767

Good order and peace is restored here in the Village of Colony Goloi Karamysh. As in my previous report, local events required me to declare a State of Martial Law and under that control, much progress has been made:

1) With the help of Russischen laborers and the Villagers, twenty-five more houses are habitable. Work goes on until all new arrival families are housed individually.
2) Three additional Village Barns are nearly finished.
3) All harvesting complete, new fields cultivated, and the river gardens area is increased fourfold.
4) Food preparation is restored and all Villagers, new and old, receive adequate food to maintain health.
5) Tempers and feelings remain raw on both sides, but no fights have occurred. Some quarrels have occurred mostly between women, but teamwork from all has vastly improved. All crimes and thefts have stopped.

I remain confident that this Village is now back on track, and over some time will allow them to again have self-government. I will remain here pending new orders.

Written by me on this 31st day of August in the year of our LORD one thousand seven hundred sixty-seven in Colony Goloi Karamysh.

Signed,

Viktor Chernyshevsky
капита́н, Imp. Russische Army
Kontor Сара́тов

Official Report
30.9.1767

Good order and peace continues here in the Village of Colony Goloi Karamysh. As noted in my previous reports, local events required me to declare a State of Martial Law and take control of the Village. Martial Law continues indefinitely until further notice.

With the help of Russischen laborers, all Village families are now housed individually. The three additional Village Barns are completed and all animals are controlled and protected. New fields continue to be cultivated, and the river gardens area is ready for spring planting. All Villagers, new and old, receive adequate food to maintain health. No incidents of crimes or fights. Cooperation of all Villagers continues to get better with most wanting to put the terrible recent events behind them.

I remain confident that this Village is on its way to allow them to restore and return to self-government. I will remain here pending new orders, or until I see that they are ready.

Written by me on this 30th day of September in the year of our LORD one thousand seven hundred sixty-seven in Colony Goloi Karamysh.

Signed,

Viktor Chernyshevsky
капита́н, Imp. Russische Army
Kontor Сара́тов

Official Report
31.10.1767

I am no longer required to keep my full Command here and am returning to Saratov. However, I am leaving five of my soldiers here as a symbol of my authority, and continue Martial Law indefinitely.

Good order and peace will be maintained; all public meetings are prohibited.

My two advisory committees will continue to act in my absence. I have restored former Vorsteher Balzer Barthuli as acting Colony Leader with Herr Christoph Karl as his deputy in my absence.

In the event of any crime, they will act as judge and jury and mete out their punishment in my name.

Continued progress in preparations for the coming and improvement in the social interaction of all the members of Colony Goloi Karamysh is expected.

Written by me on this 31st day of October in the year of our LORD one thousand seven hundred sixty-seven in Colony Goloi Karamysh.

Signed,

Viktor Chernyshevsky
капита́н, Imp. Russische Army
Kontor Саратов

MY END

◆HERR PETER SCHWARZ (formerly MICHAEL GRÜN and NOBODY) ◆ Somewhere in Deutschland

It has been years since I thought of *Christoph* and *Jacobina Karl.* Probably would have been many more years, if at all, but that I ran into one of those vile Recruiters pitching 'all the gold at the end of the rainbow' crap to some poor peasant dupes.

Same old pitch, same old tale about frei land, choice of who to worship, be your own man and become rich, you know, never answer to anyone.

Same old hook where the Recruiter says, "This cannot last forever. Do not miss this once in a lifetime chance! Just sign your name here."

Their lies never change!

Back to my tale, I was just wandering through another of the villages making my way from tavern to tavern and woman to woman, equally sharing my charms among all.

One night, feeling no pain from my many biers, I happened to overhear two of these Recruiter's at the bar boasting about how they had fooled more dumb peasants into signing, and how much they were going to be paid.

I waited till one left, and then made friends with the other by buying him more biers. My plan was to loosen his tongue. He graciously drank the biers, but had enough sense left to stop talking about his recent suckers.

I succeeded in convincing him that the bier in the gasthaus around the corner was better, and we proceeded to together stagger out through the door and into a dark alley.

Here where no one could observe, I again asked him about his Recruiter job.

He resisted, but after I beat him severely about the head and body for a while, he began to talk. He did say that paid him for each fool that signed, but that there really was frei land and housing, and a good chance to make it rich in the Volga Colonies.

I beat him some more just to be sure that he was not lying, but he stuck to his words and apparently believed the frei land tale was true. I thought about beating him for all the pain he caused my friends, but no use wasting any more time on him, so one good kick to the ribs, and I was off to far more pleasant thoughts of my time with a woman, any woman.

Some months went by, I never gave any further thought of my actions that night, and all was well with me.

Like all the other nights, tonight had been a good night. Plenty of bier, plenty of loose women willing to share their bodies with me, I even won at cards. Did I mention there was plenty of bier?

As I was staggering down another dark alley in another unnamed village back to find somewhere to sleep, I again met that very same Recruiter, only this time he had friends with him.

Outnumbered, and too many to really fight, I took their punishment. As drunk as I already was, I felt little pain. They beat me unmercifully, but I guess that was not enough.

As they were turning to leave me in a ball moaning on the ground, the Recruiter I had beaten pulled out a long knife and ran it deep into my side. I screamed in pain, and then there was only the sound of them running away and laughing at my misfortune.

I lay there bleeding like a stuck pig, which I suppose I am. The pool on the ground of my lifeblood was growing, and I knew that this was to be my end. No more biers, worse no more women; no, maybe it was no more biers!

I should have been thinking about praying for GODs forgiveness, but I did not believe before, so what good would it do now? As the darkness slowly closed over me and Death stood at my side, my last thoughts were of dear friends *Christoph* and *Jacobina*.

If *Christoph* and *Jacobina* were here, they would pray for me. And if I had gone on with them, I too would now be a rich man, and if not rich, at least alive and well and not laying in this stinking alley, waiting for the black specter of death astride his pale horse!

ROBBERS

♦CHRISTOPH KARL♦

Our Colony of Balzer

If our recent problems with too many new people were not enough, we had many unwanted and uninvited visitors from outside Balzer. While our Village had not often been harassed by Robber Bands of deserters, vagabonds and escaped Russische serfs, the Army patrols brought news of their victims on the main road between Balzer and Saratov.

We knew that they observed our Village from the high Shishka, a mountain eighteen versts (twelve miles) to the east, and wondered why we were not attacked more often. Might they have felt we were too many and too strong?

Worse than the Robbers Bands, were those damned wanderers, those we knew as the Kirghiz and Kazakhs.

These were the nomadic horseman tribes claiming ownership to the Volga River steppes long ago.

First, we caught them stealing our animals and horses. Then, when we severely punished them for this, they returned in larger numbers for revenge on us.

Fight them we did, and many of our Villagers died in those first encounters, before we learned how to keep them out. They fought back and attacked our Village while our men where in the fields, taking from our homes our possessions, our wives, and even our children.

Each time they came, we followed and tracked them for days to get back our families and valuables. Sometimes all we found were the bodies of our loved ones, and these we carefully brought back to our Village for Christian burials. In a way, our dead were the lucky ones; rumors told that those never rescued are sold in the far south cities of Bukhara and Khiva in the slave markets.

Our patience gone, and frustrated by the scarcity and incompetence of the Russische Army patrols, our men of Balzer met in the Village House. To a man without any discord, we chose to act on our own authority. We formed armed hunting parties to track and scour the steppes for them, and then remove these vermin from our lives.

Choosing to follow the Old Testament words: "Wenn jemand seinen Nächsten Schaden zufügt, dem soll man thun, wie er gethan hat; Bruch um Bruch, Auge um Auge, Zahn um Zahn; derselbe Leibesschaden, den er einem andern zufügt, soll ihm zugefügt warden" (If anyone harms his fellow, the one should do what he has done; Breach for breach, eye for eye, tooth for tooth; the same physical harm he does to others is to be done to him. Lev.24:19-20), and obsessed with ending this terrorizing of our Village, our hunting parties used the Kirghiz and Kazakhs own unspeakable ways to ravage their camps.

As they had done to us, we too stole their women and children, and fired their camps. We hurt them worst by crippling or slaughtering their fine horses. They fought back and we fought back harder.

No quarter given, for us they were only cruel animals demanding death. We even put a bounty on the head on each Kirghiz and Kazakh man, his horse, and woman and child.

We learned to come and shield our Village at a moment's notice to defend without mercy. We also learned that while our LORD blesses us, we must always be willing to fight, and maybe die, to protect our Village and families from the many wicked unbelievers always around us.

MY FLOCK

◆JACOBINA KARL◆

Our Colony of Balzer

I had not grown up with hühnern (chickens) in my home village of Kirhart, so I had no idea what to expect from them. I never even thought about chickens, and if I had, would have thought you feed them and later they give you eggs, as they are just wild birds, nothing more, nothing less!

After just a short time observing my new flock, I soon learned that I was completely mistaken about chickens. They had so many rules that they lived by, their pecking order, their roosting order, and who ate first. I even learned hens furiously protected their young chicks from other hens, roosters, and any other enemies.

And like all good mothers, the hens made sure that their chicks had food to eat and grow. They taught their chicks how to survive, and how to find their prey and kill. They taught the chicks, when frightened, to find their mother hen to hide and under her spread wings.

The roosters had their own duties, much like our men. They visited the hens and protected all their flock. They also strutted around as if they were most important, much like our men, even if the hens, like we women, were actually of much more value.

I found that each hen and rooster had their own personalities and voices. Each rooster had different cries from long drawn out crows to rough, raspy ear-splitting crows. Some hens were social and noisy; others seemed to keep to themselves, independent and quiet.

I even named some of the roosters after the Village men that are around me. For one large rooster that is always crowing and strutting around, I called him "Balzer" after our Village Leader. For one that is handsome and has fantastic beautiful colors, I called him "Christoph" after my dear husband. For another that always seems to want to boss the others around, I called him "Jacob" after *Herr Scheck*, our Village know-it-all.

I have names for the hens, too, but not for specific women, just pleasant names like Maria, Sophia, and Katharina.

The hens and roosters soon learned that I am the bringer of seed. The roosters would beg for food and when I gave it to them, they immediately passed it to a nearby hen. Surprisingly, after some time getting used to me, both the hens and roosters came to me to be cuddled, held, and petted. When I stroked their feathers, they made sounds of thanks, just as we do when we are touched.

From all this, I learned to have a new respect for them. They were not just dumb things to use and eat, but part of the grand plan of our LORD. Yes, they are food for us, but they are more than that, and I now admire them. So much that I even ignored the old ways and customs that warned:

> If a chicken crows at you three times before noon, the death of a close family member can be expected within a fortnight. The chicken should be killed, but not eaten, as consuming it will bring about further misfortune.

My chickens crowed at me all the time, before noon, after noon…. And still we ate them when it was time for them to fill our hunger.

I never tire of watching them as they go about their daily business. I wonder if our LORD watches us this way as he sits on his throne in Heaven. Are we as fascinating as we scurry around doing our chores and chasing our dreams? Thank the LORD that he does not eat us…

Over the many months of watching them, I saw many funny happenings. On warm evenings, sitting on porch with some of my friends, I would tell the tales of my chickens to them.

The women always laughed, and sometimes, even some of the men laughed, too. One my favorite romantic chicken tales went like this:

Angel and the Bad Woman

"One afternoon a while back, two of the Village girls brought to me small feather bundles, two baby chicks that they had found wandering in the nearby field."

"Too small to survive without their mother hen to protect them, these little balls most certainly would have perished if out alone much longer, if not from the night cold, then certainly from the wolves of the night or hawks of the day."

"I gladly accepted them from Village girls. They were filthy from being all alone and I would need to clean them before introducing them into my flock. Cleaning them meant washing them and then drying them and then warming them, in other words, an all-day task. As I studied them, I realized that they looked somewhat unlike my normal chicks. Maybe they were just a different type chicken, or maybe they were not chickens at all. Oh well, I would let the flock decide if they were chickens or not."

"With some hesitation, I introduced them to the flock. The roosters quickly began chasing them; hens quickly pecked at them. The two poor chicks just cowered in fear and did not peck back. Terrified they would be gravely harmed, I decided that this was a mistake and went to save them from the flock. I was almost to them, when one of my hens, one I called 'Eva', suddenly jumped between the two chicks and the flock, and spread her wings to protect them. She also pecked back at the other hens and roosters, and when I tried to reach them, Eva even pecked at me. Apparently, she decided these two new, but slightly different, chicks were now hers and chose to save them from certain death. Her actions might be appropriate as her name 'Eva' means 'life'. As for the chicks being 'different, like any mother, I doubt she even noticed that they were not like the other chicks."

"From that time on, Eva was now their mother hen, and reluctantly the flock accepted the two chicks as hers and part of the flock, as long as Eva was around. Of course, she knew the nature of the other hens and roosters, and never ever left her two chicks alone by themselves."

"Over some weeks, it started to look like the two were not actually chickens. For one thing, they were already near twice as large their mother hen Eva. Now it was not Eva protecting them, they protected their mother hen. No one, not even the roosters, would bother the three of them as they moved about the yard."

"I quietly laughed many times at the ridiculous sight of the two much larger birds closely following their now much small mother hen, Eva. The size and shape or color of each one apparently did not matter at all, all that mattered was the feeling between a mother and her children and children to mother. Some things in all life never change, whether birds or beasts or people."

"A short time later, I realized I had actually had two female turkey hens that now thought they were chickens. As I did with all the others, I named them. For these two, it was 'Frik' and 'Frak'. I suppose that Frik and Frak, along with the real chickens, just thought they were very big chickens. No harm there as all settled down into normal daily chicken life and all went well, at least, for a little while."

"Unfortunately harsh misfortune came into my chicken yard one day, and Frak just died for no outward reason. That left poor Frik all alone, and she was distraught without her 'Frak'. She looked as if she had lost her best friend in the whole word, which actually is what happened. You do not think of chickens or turkeys showing that emotion."

"Anyway, Frik moped around for days. One of my many roosters, named 'Angel', eventually noticed her and began to follow her around. Angel had nothing in common with the much larger Frik other than both being birds and both having black and white colored plumage."

"Angel was not the top rooster; in fact, he was at the lower end of rooster status in my flock. He never had any luck with the hens, either they were not receptive or the older roosters claimed, sometimes quite violently, the right. Poor Angel was not a happy rooster."

"But now there was Frik. Yes, from his viewpoint, she was a rather a large, maybe even huge, hen, but the important facts were that first, she was a hen, and second, no other roosters were attracted to her. She was all his if he could convince her, and then solve the size issue."

"Being a rooster, a male no less, he could only handle one problem at a time. His problem right now was getting Frik to like him. He followed her around for some days, and what do you know, Frik eventually noticed this rooster half her size trying to always get near her."

"Well, as they say, misery loves company and Frik was pretty darn miserable and lonely. In her view, a small rooster was better than no rooster at all, and she responded positively to his attention."

'Now Angel had his own hen just for himself, and yes, Frik was a lot of hen to have, actually she was about equal to four hens to have. With loves blind eyes, Angel could only see that Frik was special, so special that he no longer wanted to have anything to do with the normal hens. However, Frik was huge! No matter, any problem can be overcome with patience and stubbornness, and roosters are born very stubborn."

"As they began their romantic liaison, they had many encounters attempting to mate, but the size difference made it physically difficult and possibly fairly hazardous for Angel. While they were both trying to work their differences out, Angel looked like a small rider on a big horse. It was so sad for them, but it was also so funny and I laughed many times at the spectacle. Of course, roosters were not intended to ride horses, or in this case, turkeys, so the odds of this relationship working out well were not very good."

"But as I said before, roosters are stubborn birds, and like all males, will not quit once in that state of mind. This went on for several weeks until Frik just became very frustrated with Angel's lack of success. Trying to urge poor Angel on to do better, Frik chased him around the yard while making yearning turkey sounds. Obviously, if chickens and turkeys can love and hate, this was a true love-hate turkey-chicken relationship."

"Even after all her encouraging yearning turkey sounds, Angel had no luck. They say size does not matter, in this case it did. Frik probably decided that being lonely was actually better than having this crazy cock riding around on her back all day."

"Realizing that nothing good could come out of this forbidden relationship, Frik just set on her unfertilized eggs. I would collect her eggs just as I would the other hens, and she would lay more. Apparently she did not need any rooster to help her lay eggs."

"In the end, she looked so unhappy that I eventually gave her to a family with a 'tom.' Last I heard, Frik was happy in her new relationship, and a more fulfilling turkey life, in her new home."

"Sadly, Angel never really recovered from his inability to satisfy Frik, and none of the normal hens could live up to the enviable size of his former love. Another male beaten down by the nature, or in this case, the size of a female!"

Another favorite chicken tale involved my dear *Christoph* and went like this:

The Hen

"A while after the first story happened, *Christoph*, trying to help me one day, went out to the coop to gather the eggs for me. On return, he said, "I got all the eggs, except the ones under the black and white hen that seemed to be soundly sleeping on the nest. I decided it be best not to bother her.""

I replied to *Christoph*, "Husband, that was very good of you, except that we do not have a black and white hen in our flock. Are you sure that it was a black and white hen?"

He stared up at the sky for a minute, thinking back, and then nodded 'Yes'.

Confused, we both went out the coop to see. *Christoph* opened the coop, and eagerly pointed to the black and white hen that was, in fact, soundly asleep on the nest of eggs, except, it was not a hen.

I immediately started laughing, and between laughs, blurted out, "Husband, see that red on its comb, that is not a hen, but is a rooster."

Christoph again looked at what he thought was a hen, and then countered, "But I assumed roosters never sat on eggs in the nest."

I nodded, and replied, 'Yes, normal roosters do not, but this is Angel. Remember, the story of the turkey hen Frik and the rooster Angel?"

Christoph rubbed his fingers across his mouth and his brow wrinkled in deep thought, and then exclaimed, "I remember now, Angel is that unfortunate rooster who could not satisfy the huge chicken hen that was actually a turkey."

"That is right, that is Angel right there in front of us. There we see our Angel, no longer the proud male rooster, crowing about everything and running about nothing, that he was before his failed encounter with Frik. Now Angel spends time sitting on other hens' eggs. Here we have a sad remnant of the male he proudly once was, and all because he could not keep the needs of his energetic, and quite large, mistress satisfied," I very solemnly answered.

The distressed look on the face of *Christoph* caused me to burst out laughing again. My *Christoph* however, did not think join me in laughter. In truth, he felt poor Angel's situation was terrible, and that my words were even worse; that made me laugh just that much harder!"

Everyone always laughed, including all the men, except for my *Christoph*. He always maintained a stern look, but from the twinkle in his eyes, I could see that he was laughing inside. [Chicken tales adapted from original writings of Elena Buchwitz.]

ANOTHER DREAM?

Last night, only some weeks after the terrible battles with the new families, I again dreamt that that our LORD sent one of his Angels down from the Heavens to me. As in the other dreams before, the LORDs Angel gently touched my belly and spoke the same words to me, "You are now with your husband's child. Give thanks to our LORD", and then vanished.

I quickly woke even though I wished not to wake. I so wanted it to all be real, and not just another dream! However, wide-awake I was, lying there next to my *Christoph* who was enjoying his deep slumber. Though tired, I could not sleep as the words of the LORDs Angel kept running through my mind. When dawn finally came some hours later, I was still hearing the words of the LORDs Angel, and still very wide-awake.

I knew this was just another wishful dream of a frustrated woman. I had no hope of being with child, even though each day I did pray to the LORD for his help. I cannot accept that I might never have another child, and so I most likely will pray each day to our LORD for a child for a long, long time.

Strangely, over the next few months, I seemed to tire more easily and often felt not quite right. It flashed into my mind that I might be with child, but I quickly dismissed that silly notion. I was still sure it was most likely some illness troubling me.

For a moment, I paused and thought back of my time before when I was with child, with the daily sickness each morning and all the weight I gained. All that for nothing as my dear baby soon died. All for nothing! This was so silly, I could not be with child. I had not gained any weight, and showed no other signs. No, I could not be with child. Having chores to do, I forced all this nonsense out of my mind. My life was too busy to just sit and idly think about wishful things that might never come true!

I did not give another moment to thinking about being with child until maybe a month later, one cold January evening, as I sat knitting in my chair near the warm fire. As usual, my dear *Christoph* was in his chair covered with a quilt. He was sound asleep, and he occasionally snored. This night, all was well, and as it should be, in the *Karl* house!

And then I felt it and knew something was different! But what was it? Bubbles in my belly, gas, the fluttering of a butterfly….almost as if I was again hungry, but not quite. I am ill again, yes, that is it, or maybe something I ate. No, being sick never felt like this. It was not uncomfortable, it did not pain, but was something else.

Like a thunderclap, it hit me. I knew; I knew that I was with child and these were the 'quickening' movements of my baby. This sensation of my baby moving inside my body was the sweetest feeling!

I wondered when did this happen. Counting back, I realized that it must have been right after the terrible battle with the newcomers. Yes, that must be it. Maybe this blessing from the LORD was his way of showing me that we did no wrong during those horrible times. I hope so. And also, my last dream of the Angel of the LORD visiting me was shortly after that time. Thanks be to our LORD, maybe that dream was for real!

I basked in my new awareness for a time, and knowing that this good news was my secret to keep. I would not tell my *Christoph* until I was absolutely sure!

The months went by slowly, and it became more and more difficult to keep my secret from *Christoph*. I had not gained more than a little weight, but I was in no mood to give in to my husband's desires. That was not normal for me, and confused, *Christoph* just retreated and sulked like a spanked puppy.

By early April, I knew what I must do. It was time to tell him the news. One evening at supper, I said, "My dear *Christoph*, I know that you are unhappy with my affection for you, and you are concerned why all seems to have changed with me."

Christoph, staring down at his food, slowly raised his head to look at me, sighed, and then spoke, "Yes, I have no idea what I have done. I would like to make you happy again as you used to be, but know not how."

I shook my head and replied, "Dear husband, you have done nothing wrong, and you are the best man any woman could ever want."

Christoph frowned and slowly asked, "What is the trouble, then?"

I quietly replied, "I am with your child. The LORD has blessed us again."

He froze for a moment, and then said, "With my child? You are with my child!" I nodded my head that I was.

He jumped up, came over to me, hugged and kissed me. He started for the door while happily saying, "I must tell everyone that you are with my child!"

I raised my arms and emphatically replied, "NEIN! We must tell no one until the birth. You must promise me! No one except for the Umfrau (Midwife), and she must also swear to keep my secret! If you do not agree, I will just not have our baby! Understand?"

SHE IS HERE!

We have a new daughter born on the 8th day of June in the year of our LORD one thousand seven hundred sixty eight (1768). She is already a sweet daughter and a joy to my heart and soul. We are finally blessed by our LORD again.

Christoph would have been happier with a son, but I can tell he already cherishes his new daughter. I must pray to our LORD for a son for my *Christoph* the next time. He is a good man of a good family line, and deserves a son to carry on his good family name of *Karl.*

I was in the fields working with *Christoph* when the first pains came. He, and the others there, quickly loaded me onto a wagon to carry me to our home, while another raced ahead to the Village to tell the Umfrau.

While I knew I was in my LORDs good hands, I was still afraid for my life. So many women seemed to die in childbirth, and while I wanted another child, I did not want to die. I had seen thirty-four winters now, and I was not as young as with my first child those many years ago. I knew many older women like me did die....

I do not remember much more, other than great pain for what seemed like forever and hearing distant voices inside my foggy head. When I finally awoke, my Umfrau was leaning above me, making the sign of the cross with her right hand over my belly and performing the forbidden Brauche (mystical practices with accepted religious sayings), "Im Namen Gottes des Vaters, des Sohnes, und des Heiligen Geistes (In the name of God the Father, the Son, and Holy Ghost)."

I was still groggy and in some pain, but I was awake enough to know I had heard these words before when other women gave birth, and that they were only used when something was very wrong.

I tried to focus and look around the room and saw, there in the arms of my dear friend *Katharina*, a baby crying and squirming. My baby, it was my baby!

With all the strength I had, I raised my arms toward my baby to show them I wanted to hold it, but the Umfrau pushed my arms back down and sternly said, "Nein, you are too weak and need rest. Sleep again!"

I wanted my baby much, but I was so, so tired, too tired to argue. The room faded from my sight as I again heard the Umfrau slowly repeating over and over, "Im Namen Gottes des Vaters, des Sohnes, und des Heiligen Geistes."

When I awoke some time later, I know not when, I was no longer in pain and felt much stronger. Instantly, I looked for my baby, and there it was, quietly sleeping in a crib near my bed. So beautiful, there in a gown with a pink edging, I knew then my baby was a girl.

I looked around the rest of the dark room, and saw my Umfrau fast asleep in a chair near my bed. As I moved slightly, she woke and seeing that I had come to, quickly came to my side.

She made the sign of the cross over my belly and recited once, "Im Namen Gottes des Vaters, des Sohnes, und des Heiligen Geistes" as she had done so many times before.

I tried to talk, but could only whisper, "Please Umfrau, let me hold my child."

She smiled, and went over to the crib and brought her back to me. As I held her close and felt the warmth of her small body, I knew that all I had endured was worth it. She was so beautiful and so perfect.

As I lay there, the Umfrau told me about my daughter and her birth, "You have a healthy and strong and beautiful daughter with ten fingers and ten toes. She is a stubborn one, and did not willingly leave her home for the last nine months. You were in great pain, and bled too much for quite a while. It would not stop and it seemed our LORD might take you, though after I recited the special prayer of the Trinity over you many, many times along with the sign of the Holy Cross, you slowly became stronger till now you are here awake."

My husband and our friends baptized our new daughter, and *Pastor Aloysius Jauch* announced her as *Anna Maria Karl* after my mother *Anna Maria Maurer*, hopefully still living back in the old land.

Still weak, I remained recovering in my bed. In truth, the Umfrau insisted I remain in bed for nine whole days and nights.

We did not have much to spare for a celebration, but our tradition required a Taufe schmaus (Baptism feast) with what food and drink we had, this for the future well-being of our *Anna Maria*. My *Christoph*, proud father that he was, would accept nothing less.

To celebrate the successful birth and to ensure that our daughter would prosper, as was the custom, my Umfrau wanted to prepare an 'absolutely sweet' liquor of Branntwein (Brandy wine) and burned sugar. But here, there was no Branntwein and very little sugar, and so she made do with our Village bier.

As tradition required, she passed a glass of this to our guests with each taking a sip, and then dropping a silver coin into the glass, if they had any. If not, they sincerely and heartily thanked my midwife for her work and skill in the successful delivery of our healthy baby.

Thank the LORD that in addition to taking care of my *Anna Maria* and me during the nine days I was in bed, the Umfrau also cooked and fed my dear *Christoph*. By the tenth day, I was up and strong enough to take care of both my new baby and my husband.

NEU VORSTEHER

◆CHRISTOPH KARL◆

Our Colony of Balzer

We have a new Village leader. It was bound to happen someday, but I did not think it would be so soon. After the disastrous happenings when the overwhelming mass of new people arrived and our normal Village life stopped, the Martial Law put into effect by *Captain Chernyshevsky* kept my good friend, *Herr Balzer Barthuli,* appointed as the acting Village Leader.

Now, it has been more than a year since that terrible time, and while not all the bad feelings have faded from our memories, at least all Villagers are now working together with the single goal of bettering the lives of all.

For that reason, that we are all now working together again, *Captain Chernyshevsky* rescinded Martial Law to reinstate the Village self-government.

The groups of newly arrived, with their greater numbers, quickly called for a meeting and vote of all Village males older than sixteen years. With their greater numbers, they elected one of their own as new Vorsteher, a *Herr Philipp Zieg*, and another of their own as one of our two Beisitzer (an Assessor and Treasurer), a *Herr Philipp Protsmann*. The second Beisitzer elected, *Herr Leonhard Voltz*, still came from our original group so we still had some representation.

We also elected a sheriff, and he too came from our original group, our former soldat, *Herr Dorlosch*. While there was still much bad feeling about his part in the killings during those terrible times, mutual respect of the entire Village for his leadership and soldier skills during the raids of, and battles with the wandering tribes, gave him the majority of votes.

Elected by the majority, to serve as friedensrichter (Magistrates), to sit in judgment of crimes or any infractions against good order and peace were: *Herr Philipp Zieg, Herr Philipp Protsmann, Herr Balzer Barthuli,* and myself, *Herr Christoph Karl.*

A Village proclamation of honor also passed that read:

"In honor of our former leader, *Herr Balzer Barthuli* and all he has done for us, from this day forward we of this Colony Goloi Karamysh now officially call, in honor of his service and for all time, our Village by the name of BALZER in recognition of our good friend, *Herr Balzer Barthuli.*"

A small gesture by the new majority to placate the original founding settlers, but at least they cared something about what we thought.

HE IS HERE!

♠JACOBINA KARL♠

Our Colony officially called Balzer

After years of waiting and praying, what seemed like forever to me, we have a son. Our son arrived on this 11th day of February in the year of our LORD one thousand seven hundred seventy (1770).

He is a strong stout baby boy, much like his father. I already can see *Christoph's* strong will along with my good sense in him. He is the best of the both of us.

I pray to our LORD that our new son prospers and grows to old age. Just in case, as the old ways warn, I will leave one light to always burn in our house, this to protect my new son from any bad spirits.

Proud father *Christoph* ran around our Village and announced to anyone that would listen, "Everyone, I have news. My wife and I are blessed with a son. Praise be to our LORD for this blessing! Please witness his baptism this Sunday. You are all welcome after Church to our home for Taufe schmaus."

On Sunday, our Umfrau dressed our son according to our custom in the white Kleidchen (gown) of the Taeuflings (person to be baptized) with a light blue edging around the Leibchen (camisole) and a silver Kreuz (Cross) presented by his Godfather *Philipp Kaiser.*

Godfather *Philipp,* accompanied with Godmother *Katharina Kaiser,* carried our new baby son to the holy baptism.

While I still remained in bed and could not attend the baptism, *Christoph* later told me that during the ceremony, *Pastor Aloysius Jauch* sprinkled Holy Water and placed the sign of the cross on our son's forehead. And that his Godparents accepted and swore to their duties as his Godfather and Godmother. And with a final prayer, our Pastor introduced our new son as *Wilhelm Philipp Karl,* the newest Church member.

This joyous day continued after they brought back my *Wilhelm Philipp Karl* to me. Of course, all came to our home for the Taufe schmaus (baptism feast). While our son lay fast asleep in his crib, all celebrated with much food and drink for the future well-being of our *Wilhelm Philipp.*

By custom, to celebrate the successful birth and to ensure that our boy will prosper, my Umfrau (midwife) prepared an 'absolutely sweet' liquor of Branntwein (brandy wine) and burned sugar. She passed one glass of this to the Godparents and other guests.

Continuing with tradition, each would sip the sweet liquor and drop a silver coin into it. The glass of sweet liquor passed from hand-to-hand to all guests and filled with coins.

After all the guests partook, the glass, now empty of liquor but filled with silver coins, was given back into the hands of the midwife. This acknowledged her work and skill in the successful delivery of our healthy baby.

Christoph and I had been through this before with our first son, but that child had soon crossed to dwell in Heaven with our LORD.

I could not bear to think that this might happen once more, and so I said a silent prayer begging GOD for his mercy and blessing of a long life for our new son, our *Wilhelm Philipp Karl*.

TEN YEARS

✦ANNA MARIA MAURER✦

Kirhart, Palatinate, Deutschland

It is the year of our LORD 1774, now ten whole years since we waved good-bye to daughter *Jacobina* and her husband *Christoph* that early morn in Heilbronn.

Just this morn at the table I said to my husband *Johann Jacob*, "I wonder how they are doing in their new land. They probably have a big house and lots of land with grapes. *Christoph* was so good at tending the vines. I am sure that he must be growing good ones there. Do you suppose the LORD blessed them with children? I hope so."

Johann Jacob looked at me, rubbed his chin, and replied, "Wife, they are long gone, and we will never know anything about them. It is a waste of good time wondering what happened to them or even talking about them. All we can do is keep praying to our LORD that he looks out for them."

I thought to myself, "Why do I even talk with him? After all these years, you would think I would have learned." In spite of how he feels, I do enjoy just sitting and dreaming about their lives and their family. I hope our LORD has blessed them with a family. I pray for them, I pray for them every day and all the time.

Enough dreaming, it is time to do my daily chores, sweep the floor and clean our home. Maybe I can sweep out husband *Johann Jacob*! That might be amusing!

BALZER 1774

♦JACOBINA KARL♦

My Colony Balzer

I wonder what my mother and father and sisters are doing right now. I doubt if *Christoph* even thinks about them. It has been ten years now, and I still think about them and pray for them all the time.

I remember a few weeks back, while talking about everything and nothing, *Christoph* did say, "I wonder if those two good looking sisters of yours ever found husbands. They were older than you were, but then they were quite good looking. They have both probably grown ugly and fat and are unmarried."

What a terrible thing to say I thought, and anger flashed inside me, but I saw he had a wide smile and could tell he was only having fun with me.

Christoph continued his teasing, "I do not really miss your mother. She was bossy and had no respect for me. Your father was good, but he was always threatening to beat me if I did not treat you right. Of course, I would always treat you right as long as you did everything I said."

Christoph was really needling me now. That was all it took, and he never saw the pillow that hit the back of his fat head.

All teasing aside, I do hope all is good with them. I still miss them so. I will say a special prayer to our LORD for all of them tonight.

15   TIME OF TERROR

▲CHRISTOPH KARL▲

Colony Balzer

It was in late March in the year of our LORD MDCCLXXIV (1774). All of the colonies had heard the horror stories. Most believed them just rumors passed from person to person or at the late night village fires where scary stories are told over and over.

No one really believed that nightmares like these actually could happen in the light of day. We had laws and we were all, well most of us, now civilized! The stories of hanging three hundred men, and raping the women and girls and of butchering the children in villages were just not believable.

We had endured and fought, and eventually overcome, all the swarms of robbers and bandits in our local area along with those tribes of Kirghiz and Kazakh and Kalmucks. In truth, what more could there be? All was better, and now we could live in Peace and our families and Village could prosper.

At night, we village men would talk about these wild rumors sometimes at our group meetings, but dismissed them as child's nightmares. We all felt there was nothing to worry about, and certainly not to waste our time preparing.

Early August arrives, and that is all about to change. Our worst evening fears will not be as bad as the daylight's reality. We heard from our village neighbors in the north that a massive army of several thousand Cossacks, serfs, peasants, and bandits led by a crazy Don Cossack named Emelian Ivanovich Pugachev, had overrun and ransacked the city of Saratov.

Faced with the size of his army, the cowardly Military garrison of Saratov mutinied and opened the gates to him. His army freed the criminals from the prison, and robbed the grain storage warehouses and the salt depots. They also tore down the liquor stores, plundered the houses, and hunted down any, and all, of noble family birth.

Those men, women, and children who had done nothing really wrong other than having the wealthy parents, were hunted down and captured, and immediately hanged, and then, even worse, left unburied to rot in the sun.

Even the simple people, the same as us, they were terrorized with the men killed or taken as slaves, and the women and girls raped and killed, or also put under ropes. Worse, the innocent small children, that could not work and were a burden to his Army, they butchered them on the spot with their bodies also left unburied to feed the birds or rot in the sun.

After hearing all that, terror raced through our Village like fire through a dry forest. People ran from place to place and around going nowhere. From one end to the other end of our village, frightened voices were heard yelling, "What can we do? Where will we go?" Children, too young to understand, cowered in the shadows, frightened by their parents' strange behavior and not knowing what to do.

We all realized that if the colossal Saratov, with its military garrison and many soldiers, could not stand before Pugachev, how would a simple village like ours could even hope to survive.

The village men quickly met together with our *Vorsteher* (leader) *Philip Zeig* to discuss all options.

Herr Thomas Berger yelled out, "We could all run away and hide, but where would we go that his army could not find us?"

"Wait! What about all we had worked for to build over the last nine years. Are we just to abandon that to these scum and criminals?" *Herr Jakob Busch* asked loudly.

Herr Georg Borel stood up and suggested, "Maybe we could come to an agreement with this leader, this Don Cossack Emelian Ivanovich Pugachev."

Herr Jakob Borel, his brother, agreed, "*Georg* is right. This Pugachev is a leader, surely he will be willing to negotiate if he can profit without fighting."

That seemed right to many and as they talked among themselves, "We could send as our emissary, *Beisitzer* (assessor) *Philip Brotzman,* to offer tribute and gifts in exchange for him leaving Balzer alone," *Herr Philipp Kaiser* suggested.

All, except for poor *Herr Philip Brotzman,* agreed that there was simple common sense to that idea. However, everyone also knew there was a good chance that *Herr Brotzman* would never come back to us alive, or that it might actually draw Pugachev to our Village.

Herr Jacob Klein added, "They say he openly claims to be the murdered Tsar Peter III come back from the dead to reclaim his throne. Maybe he is crazy and has no common sense." With that, everyone began talking at once as all had their own ideas about if was, or was not, crazy. After much arguing and discussion, we recognized that there was absolutely nothing at all that we could do. One by one, each man became quiet, and eventually the group just stood silent.

Sheriff Herr Dorlosch quietly said aloud what we were all now thinking, "This is out of our hands and in the hands of GOD. We must hide the women and children, and the food and grain and seed, as best we can. Our two hundred men and older boys stand and fight to protect our village. With GODs grace and blessing, and much luck, the main Army of Pugachev will miss us and plunder some other poor Colony, and we will only have to fight off any small roving bands of his followers. Most of all, we must pray for our LORDs protection, and if that is not to be, for merciful quick deaths and our eternal salvation."

I agreed with all he said; forlornly, I quietly said, "If we are not so blessed by our LORD, then the end of all of us and of our Balzer Colony is certain to be soon." My neighbor, standing near me, overheard my quiet words, just nodded his head that I was right...

We could not just stand there and do nothing, so we put our plans to action immediately. There were some river caves close by only known by a handful of the menfolk. To these caves, we sent all the women and children, along with food and our stores of grain and seed. We picked a few of our very best men to keep the caves hidden, and to guard the women and children from harm. And if the worst happened and we were defeated, to slay our loved ones before they were enslaved, tortured, or raped by the animals attacking us. As the old saying warns, "It is better to be dead and feel nothing than to be eaten alive and still feel!"

The rest of us dragged bales of hay, wagons, and anything else we could move to block both ends of the Village road. We gathered up all the pitchforks, scythes, mallets, poles, knives and hooks to use as weapons.

Jacobina did not want to leave me, but I insisted. We both knew that she was again with child. "You must go to protect the lives of our unborn child and son and daughter, our children. I could not live with myself if you or our children came to harm or took from me. I love you, but you must go now and hide. Pray for us all that we may rejoice together on the morrow. Go! Go now!" I said as I pushed her, and my son and daughter, away towards the caves.

"I will obey and go my husband, but only for our children. I too Love you. Fight bravely, but come back to us. I will pray for all of us," answered *Jacobina*. And then she was gone.

The next day came and went with no visit from his dreaded army, but friendly riders brought us the word that Pugachev had attacked and overrun both Norka Colony to the north-west, and Beideck Colony only three hours walk north.

The messenger warned us that Beideck had also prepared by hiding away their women and children, and food, grain and seed. The bastard Pugachev had them tortured to force them to tell where their loved ones were hiding. Those that he let live; he forced to become his slaves to transport his booty.

Later that same day, we heard that the main force of the army had ransacked Donhof Colony and murdered women and children, and set their houses and men on fire.

Then and there, all two hundred men and boys of Balzer swore a blood oath that we would fight to the death! We would not allow ourselves to be tortured and put our loved ones in jeopardy. And if any man or boy broke his sworn oath, their life and their family's lives would be forfeit to any of us that survived.

We armed ourselves as best we could with our score of muskets, pitchforks, scythes, mallets, poles, knives and hooks, and waited. With nothing to do but wait, the boys of our group quickly got restless and wandered about.

A group of them stopped to talk with me. Though they put on a brave front, I could see that they were worried, not of the enemy, but of what they would do when faced with almost certain death. To give them some strength, I said to them, "We are all in fear. If you were not, then you must be dead. Use that fear inside to be cautious, then you will not waste your lives. We all must live as long as possible to kill as many of the enemy as we can." Not sure if my words helped, they all still looked worried.

Just after dusk on that dark moonless night, we heard the sounds of many approaching horses from both ends of our village. With the sure knowledge that out time had come, we each prayed to our LORD for his forgiveness of the sins we were about to do to protect our families, for strength in this battle, for his blessing in our success, and for our eternal souls.

I said to my nearest man, "The best to you, may GOD bless you." He replied in like. We steeled ourselves for this inevitable fight. Inside each of us, we drew on all the hatred we could muster, building it into a crazed lust to increase our strength. We were ready to die, and to also send them all the way to Hell! They may overcome and defeat us, but they will pay dearly with their lives.

And instantly they were over and past the barricades and we were no longer waiting, but were fighting with our poles and axes against the enemy on horses and on foot.

It was to our good benefit that it was a moon-less night. We knew the Village ground and they did not. The clash of steel pitchforks against swords sang out in the night, as did the screams and moans of the injured and fallen.

We fought like wild men with no care to live, slashing and stabbing at anything and everything to kill and maim as many enemies as possible before we too would fall.

I enthusiastically stabbed my knife through the ribs of an enemy, and felt great happiness as his warm lifeblood ran out of his wound and down my arm. I was ecstatic to feel his body spasm and hear his screams as I twisted the blade with each thrust, and felt great satisfaction as he died on the end of my knife. Even the gasping sound of his very last breath of life was music to my ears.

Having killed with one beast, I moved to hunt down and kill another. I offered another monster the thrust of my sharp knife, and as it pierced his flesh and ground against bone, a feeling of great satisfaction overwhelmed me. Killing more of the devils was now my only goal. I called aloud to GOD, "Give me your strength and bless me so that I may kill many more before they kill me!"

The battle continued for what was probably minutes, but seemed like hours as time slowed. Kill one, kill one more, kill one more, kill one more…That is all there was.

The cowardly enemy, not prepared for such a crazed and vicious response from simple devout farmers, fell back to outside our village. During this lull, we took time to find and move our injured to a more defensible location, not to save their lives, but that they could continue to fight on to their death.

I found one of the boys I had talked with earlier. He was alive, but there was no chance for him to live long. He was sliced open like a hog with blood everywhere and bowel hanging out.

He reached up for me and pleaded, "Help me stand to fight more."

I held him down and told him, "My son, you have done enough for us today. You have driven them back and we are all very proud of you. Rest now and we will carry on the fight."

He smiled and then moaned, and then passed. I closed his eyes and picked him up from the ground. I said a prayer for his soul as I carried his body to where the other wounded were. He would fight no more, but others might use his body as a shield.

As our enemy ran away like the dogs they were to lick their wounds, the lull in battle also gave us time to finish off those of the enemy that had been injured, but not able to retreat.

One injured enemy that I came upon, looked up at me and ardently begged, "Please do not kill me. I will leave forever and not do this again. I beg you, have mercy on me."

Seeing in my mind only the sight of my dead friends nearby, I said nothing, but mercifully, at least in my mind, drove a pitchfork deep into the man straight through his heart. He screamed only once more, and then his body shook and he was dead. A feeling of great satisfaction and serenity flooded my body.

I would have just stood there and enjoyed the good feeling, but there were still more to help on their way to Hell. We enthusiastically and efficiently ended all their sorry lives. We treated them as we would any sick or diseased animal, quickly and mercifully ending their existence for the good of all other life! They would never trouble or terrorize anyone again. Pray GOD forgives us!

We had lost some of our own, but by count of the bodies, there were ten of theirs to every one of ours. We had made a good showing, but we knew that the next time our enemy would not be surprised by our resistance.

We treated our injured as best we could, and passed around drink and food to all that needed. And again, we patiently waited for our prey to come to us to die.

Again, we heard their approaching horses and their running feet as they attacked, and like before we steeled ourselves for this battle. Again, deep inside each of us, we found all the hatred and the horror of seeing our close friends slaughtered, and used that to build our courage and strength.

While they were more cautious and prepared for us this time, we slashed and stabbed, and cut and hacked at them from the dark shadows, and then moved to another hidden dark place to slash and stab, and cut and hack another of the enemy. We were as spiders are to the fly caught in their web.

Our band of men and boys kept moving from place to place, slashing, stabbing, killing in our dark village, keeping the vicious enemy confused and disorganized.

The clash of our steel pitchforks and scythes against their swords seemed to be everywhere, only outdone by the terrible screams and moans of the fallen of both sides.

We felt the sounds of the battle deep in the evil beyond our souls as we fell into a crazed blood-rage, slashing and stabbing again and again, to maim and, even better, kill all the enemy.

I had no past, I had no future; I had only now… and now was my time to kill these animals! No time to count those I dispatched to Hell, just to kill as many as I could.

Again, no longer a farmer, I became the hunter, and when I found my quest, I quickly and efficiently ended life. No longer men that I hunted: these were the hunt to find and slaughter.

Again and again, I killed with greater and greater enthusiasm and pleasure. One more down, more left to finish. Killing was now my only reason to exist; there was no wife, no children, no Village, no friends, no sworn oath, even no GOD; there was only Kill or be Killed!

We did not stop until, regrettably, we ran out of Pugachev's followers to kill. The few of the enemy that tried to retreat, we caught and without mercy put to death on the spot. Those enemies that surrendered, or were captured or injured, we also quickly slaughtered. I eagerly used my knife and enjoyed my share of revenge for my friend's deaths.

There would be no mercy given to insure there would be no one left to run back to tell Pugachev what had happened on this night in Balzer.

It was finally over…. And we slowly felt the blood-rage leave our minds and bodies. Exhausted and weary, we still found the strength to bury the bodies of the enemy in an unmarked mass grave and disguised its location to hide it from any other Pugachev scouts. We gathered up a treasure trove of knives, swords, and muskets and temporarily hid them in the caves with our families for safety and future use.

We had lost many brave men and boys, but by now had dispatched to Hell over two hundred of the enemy. All that survived were each wounded many times.

We moved the more seriously wounded back to the more defensible location so that, if attacked once more, they could continue to fight on to the death.

The rest of us did the best we could to stop the blood flowing from our wounds, and passed around drink and food to all that needed. And again, we waited for the next attack and daylight.

Daylight came, but the next attack did not. We remained at vigil till a fellow colonist arrived with the news that the Army of Pugachev had moved south last night after overrunning the Colonies of Bauer, Merkel, and Kratzke.

The messenger also said, "It has been reported that his Army is even now attacking the Colonies of Schuck, Vollmer, Husaren, and Kanenka. The messenger looked around at the bloody ground and our torn and bloody clothes and said, "It looks like you also have fought with them. How many did they take away as slaves?"

We all looked at each other, but I quickly replied, "No, we never did see them, thank the LORD. We just made it look this way in case some of his followers came by to terrorize us. They might be fooled by our sad appearance and just let us alone." It was only a little lie. I would ask our LORD for forgiveness later.

Not fooled by my lie, the messenger smiled and shook his head, and replied, "As you say it must be. Excellent idea to fool the animals. GOD bless you all." With that, he waved and rode off to tell another colony the news of the Armies movement south.

With care and stealth, we moved our most injured to the hidden caves for better care from our women. Some of the men remained on guard, while the rest of us repaired the damage to our village. It would be a few more days before our women and children, and the injured would return to our village. We would be sure that damned Pugachev and his Army were really long gone before we put our loved ones again in danger.

A day uneventfully went by, another day and another day, and village life in Balzer began to return to normal. All our men and boys were heroes, and we honored forever those that had given their lives as martyrs.

Some of our injured did not survive their mortal wounds. Infection came, and all one could do was wait for the inevitable end. When they felt their time was near, as custom dictated, they each asked for a white-covered table placed near their bed with two leuchter (candlesticks), a Bible and a gesangbuch (hymnal).

Our Pastor, *Herr Aloysius Jauch,* gave each their communion. As Death approached, all the family was there with them to face their passing. A 'chosen one' of the family said quiet prayers and cried parting tears for all the rest; all others remained silent and quiet. After the passing, their close friends came for one last visit until our LORD again reunites them in Heaven. Each friend knelt down and prayed for the soul and peace of their now departed friend.

We also remembered all our heroes that died in the recent battle. They also again received the blessing of our Pastor, and our prayers for these faithful departed trusting in God's mercy as they go to enter Eternal Life.

Our Pastor prayed aloud, "Oh GOD, Whose attribute it is always to have mercy and to spare, we humbly present our prayers to Thee for the soul of Thy servant which Thou has this day called out of this world, beseeching Thee not to deliver it into the hands of the enemy, nor to forget it for ever, but to command Thy holy angels to receive it, and to bear it into paradise; that as it has believed and hoped in Thee it may be delivered from the pains of hell and inherit eternal life through Christ our LORD. Amen."

On the third day, we buried all our dead after the funeral ceremony. We marked each of their graves with a cross of hard wood. After the ceremony, all the relatives and friends met for a mourning meal. Days later, on the seventh and thirtieth day, all the village folk met in a ceremony for all our recent dead. For a whole month, our Village focused only on the passing of all our good friends and brave men.

As for Pugachev and his beasts, it was as we had prayed for; his main Army had attacked and terrorized our sister Colonies, and missed Balzer. I was only a much smaller, but still deadly, group of maybe two hundred of his followers that attacked us, and with our LORDs blessing sent to dwell in Hell forever.

We were all guilty for praying for some other Colony to suffer, but we were all thankful that our Balzer survived. Each of us would pray for forgiveness, if we had not already done so.

A few days later, we were completely unprepared for an army of soldiers that surrounded our Village without any warning. As the soldiers on horse rode in to the hauptplatz (central square), our women and children ran to hide, while our men hastily grabbed any sharp tool and prepared to fight.

All was for naught as we learned that these were not our enemies, but the Russische Army chasing the Pugachev criminals. As soon as they determined that none of the criminals was still in our village, the Army quickly departed south to resume the chase.

The men of Balzer now sat around the village campfire each evening and talked about the battle, how brave each of them had been, and how many they had sent straight to Hell. We were all very proud of ourselves even though we each knew that pride is not good. Here all together, survivors still living, breathing, talking, and drinking; it did feel so good to brag about our hard-earned victory over evil. But later in the dark of late night when we were all alone to face our GOD, then the awful guilt would come and we would all ask for forgiveness for this and our other many sins.

As for me, *Jacobina* carefully and lovingly tended my wounds, and I slowly recovered. Our unborn child grew larger in her body and our son and daughter still lived.

I was blessed and no infection set in. My body slowly healed, but not so my soul. I had released that vicious animal hunger to kill from deep inside me; yes, it was to protect my family, but still once out that damned hunger would never go back in. As a devout Lutheran, I was not happy now knowing it had always been buried deep within me; I was more distressed knowing that now it would be with me forever, even after death as I dwell in Hell with the rest of the animals."

For a long time, I would revisit the battle in nightmares so violent that my thrashing and screams would wake up

Jacobina. She never asked what was wrong, but held me and said she would pray for me. What more could I ask?

Maybe two or three months went by when we heard that the damned Pugachev and his followers had been defeated and captured. Messengers reported Pugachev was in a very small and very strong iron cage on his way to Moscow to be beheaded, quartered, and burned. Straight to Hell, I hoped.

Pugachev in his Iron Cage

Surprisingly, when Pugachev was captured, over four hundred of our fellow Wolgadeutsche (Volga Germans) were captured as members of his army. We were not able to forgive them for their part in the violence; they all deserved any punishment they received. We were not able to forgive; maybe our LORD would forgive them. In any case, if not already, they would all soon be put to death and he would be able to sort them out!

As good Christians, we did pray for him and his followers; we prayed that the reports of their deaths are true.

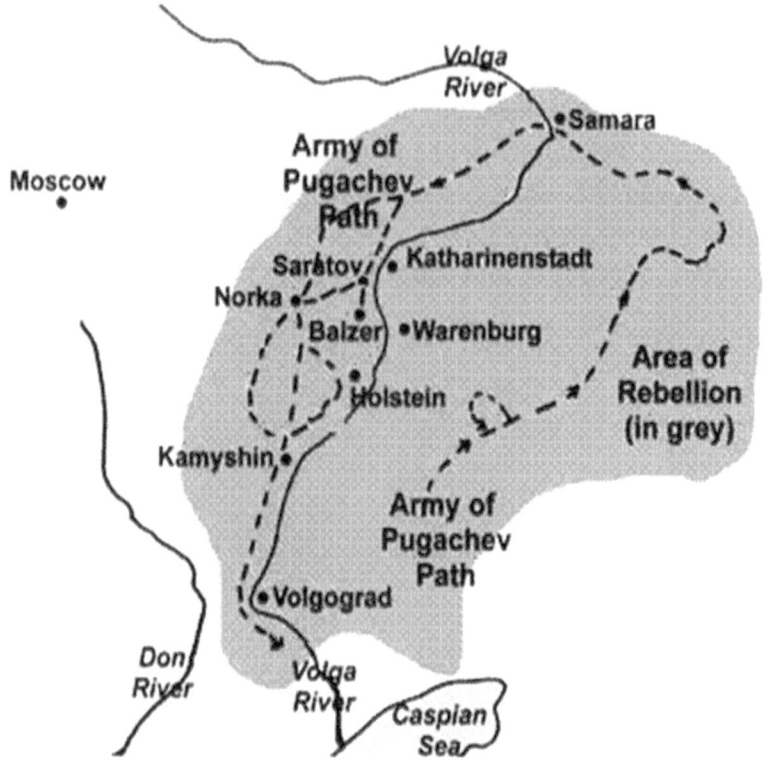

Path of the Army of Pugachev

So that all will remember what happened here for all time, mothers will tell their sons and daughters who will tell this story that we now call the *'TIME OF TERROR'* to their sons and daughters, and on and on, for all time.

MADNESS

◆JACOBINA KARL◆

My Colony Balzer

I will never forget that terrible night for as long as I live; that night I had to leave my dear husband *Christoph* and go hide, with my children and all the others, in that cave as those damned Pugachev soldiers attacked our Village.

While all the women, including myself, were afraid for our lives and the lives of our children, we were also out of our minds with worry for our husbands and young men.

I do not pretend to understand all that went on, and why we could not just hide or run, but to stand and fight as our men chose to do, seemed to ask for certain death.

My *Christoph* and the other men are simple farmers, not soldiers, and in this fight, they are sure to lose. Worse, the many experienced enemy fighting men outnumber them badly.

I grant that our men did well against the wandering nomads and eventually drove them away, but this is the Pugachev force that defeated the Russischer soldiers at the fort in Saratov. What hope do our men have of winning, or even surviving? Sadly, none, none at all!

It was not just me that was being driven out of my mind with worry, but all our Village women that had men and boys fighting for our Village. Thank the LORD that most of our children are too young to understand what might be in store for all of us.

I did not want to leave my *Christoph* back in the Village. If this was to be his time, then I wished it to be my time also. After all we have been through together getting here, I know there is no life without him!

He would not listen to my reason, and insisted I leave and hide in the caves with our son and daughter along with the other women and young boys, and girls.

And then, just as I had made up my mind to stay, *Christoph* looked into my eyes and said, "You must go to protect the life of our unborn child and our children. I would not be able to live with myself if you or our children came to harm. I love you, but you must go now and hide. Pray for us all that we may rejoice together on the morrow. Go!" and with that, he pushed me away.

He was right, of course. "I will obey and go my husband, for our children. I Love you. Fight bravely, but stay safe and come back for me. I will pray for all of us," I replied, and turned and hurried to the shelter of the hidden cave.

It seemed as days that we were in that cave with no word, making no sound to prevent discovery. We could not even let ourselves cry. We could only listen... and worry.

Suddenly without any warning, there was a commotion outside the cave and we all feared the worst. Surely, our men were vanquished and it was the enemy at the entrance.

I dropped to my knees and asked our LORD for a quick and merciful death for my children and myself, and for his blessing and forgiveness in this time of our passing.

But it was not the enemy, but our husbands who raced in to our arms, not all of them, as some were badly injured and carried in.

As soon as the injured were brought in, those men that still could, hurried back to our Village and brought more injured back to the cave for us to care for. From what little I overheard, our men had defeated, at least temporarily, the enemy. How could that be?

I looked for *Christoph,* but he was nowhere to be seen. When I asked about him, they told me that he had only minor injuries and was still on guard at the Village.

Relief swept through me from knowing that my *Christoph* had not been seriously hurt; almost instantly dread from knowing that he might still have to fight again, replaced it.

And then all the men, but for the seriously injured men and boys, were gone and our Cave entrance again was hidden from view. More time passed that seemed like many, many hours, but was probably much shorter, as we tried to make our injured as comfortable as possible.

Suddenly like before, there was a commotion outside the cave and again we all feared the worst. Surely this time, our brave men had been finally been defeated and it was the enemy at our door.

I again dropped to my knees, and repeated my earlier prayer, begging our LORD for a quick and merciful death for my children and myself, and for his blessing and forgiveness in this time of our passing.

A miracle! Not just a miracle, a miracle of our LORD! Thanks be to our LORD, I was again wrong! It was our husbands who came racing to our arms, fewer this time and with many more injured carried in.

As soon as those wounded were brought in, those men that still could walk hurried back to our Village and brought even more injured back to the cave for us to care for. One of the injured loudly proclaimed that we had won the battle and killed all of the enemy.

How could that be?

We stayed in the cave for another day, and then all moved back to our Village. While there was damage to the buildings, there were no dead bodies of the enemy anywhere to be seen. I later learned that they had all been buried in a mass grave hidden some ways away from the Village.

This terrible battle with the followers of Pugachev left many scars on our menfolk. Those wounds to their bodies healed slowly; other wounds would take a long time to heal, if ever.

My *Christoph* was wounded many times, but was blessed and no infection set in. I tended his wounds and nursed him, and his body quickly healed to almost as if he had never been hurt.

Other wounds I could not help with, as I quickly realized that my *Christoph* was changed by the terrible things he had to do. Sadly, I had to accept that my old *Christoph* was gone, and that this man, still my husband, was a new different *Christoph*. Still the same man outside, but somehow different deep inside. Not a better man, not a worse man, just a different man!

For a long time, *Christoph* had nightmares so violent with his arms flailing about and screams of agony from his throat. It was as if was reliving each moment of the fight in his nightmares, and that his soul was being torn apart piece by piece.

I never asked him what was wrong, but just held him and said I would pray for him. He never told me what he dreamed.

It was not just my *Christoph* that was tortured, but all the women talked of the same with their husbands. These changes in the behavior of the men revealed their hidden pain to their wives and village women. Their laughter that we heard so often in Balzer before Pugachev, was now more subdued if it happened at all.

Where once our men would joke and fool around each other at the evening Village campfire, now our men of Balzer talked in low whispers about the battle, how brave each of them had been, and how many they had sent straight to Hell. Their talk was more boastful, and they dwelled on the horrors of the battle. Their moods were much, much darker. As was my *Christoph*, they were all very proud of all the killing they had done.

And yet, when we women came around, they dropped their heads and became silent. They knew we women would not approve of this evil pride, and yet they still relished it.

I, as did all the women, tried to help our menfolk, but did not know how. None of us had fallen into the bottomless abyss of evil and hate that our men had seen. We desperately hoped our men would heal sometime in the future as their nightmares of the horrific battle faded in their memories.

Each night I prayed to our LORD, "Please GOD, forgive my dear husband *Christoph*, a good and devout man, for the sins he had to commit to protect me and my children, and heal his inner pain so that he may return to us as he was before this horrible event. Amen."

With time and our LORDs forgiveness and blessing, our suffering husbands may someday heal and return to us. If not, we will bear this change in them without fail or complaint, and continue to love and respect our men forever and ever. I beg you; pray with me each and every night for their eternal souls!

NO CROPS

♦CHRISTOPH KARL♦

Colony Balzer

If that damned Pugachev and his animals had not been bad enough, the next winter weather was brutally cold with the soil frozen well into March, and then the heat and drought of summer exploded. What seeds we did get into Mother Earth grew and broke through to shrivel up and die.

Each morning before the blazing sun would shine; I would get up from beside my *Jacobina*, and get ready to haul water to the fields. Each morning before leaving, I would bend down and kiss her sweet face, and say, "Sleep well my Love, and I will see you in the fields later."

And each day after the sun had been up for an hour, she would join me later with food to keep me going, and she hauled more than her share of the water.

It was not just us doing this, but every man, women, and child that walked did all they could to save our harvest. Even so, it was almost all in vain! There was little or no harvest, and we survived on our previous season's surplus. Eventually, we even had to eat some of our next year's seed stock to survive.

Each night, *Jacobina* and I knelt down and prayed, "LORD, in our time of need, please see fit to bring us some rain so that our crops may grow again. We look forward to your blessing of better days ahead. Amen." Throughout our Village, prayers for help from our LORD rang out every night. What else could we do, what else could go wrong, what else did we have left?

BETTER DAYS?

◆JACOBINA KARL◆

My Colony Balzer

A third daughter has arrived. After all that time in our birth land, here we are now blessed with one son and three daughters. That blessing makes all the pain we have endured worth every minute of it. I would not trade this life now for the world.

We baptized our new daughter and named her *Anna Cunigunde* after her Godmother *Anna Cunigunde Magel,* wife of our neighbor and her Godfather *Heinrich Magel.*

Following our custom and as with the previous baptism of our children, we celebrated the Taufe schmaus with much food and drink for the future well-being of our *Anna Cunigunde.*

As before, to celebrate the successful birth and to ensure that our daughter will prosper, my Umfrau prepared the Branntwein and burned sugar.

The glass of this went from the Godparents and all around to our other guests with each taking a sip, and then dropping a silver coin into it. The glass passed from hand-to-hand through all our guests and filled with coins.

Eventually, the glass now empty of liquor, but filled with silver coins, came back to the hands of our Umfrau to recognize her work and skill in the successful delivery of our healthy baby. Joyous events like this birth and baptism of our daughter helped counter the despair in our Colony.

Starvation, killing, drought, sickness…. In spite of the horrible things that have occurred in the past, our village was again able to prosper and grow.

From the almost the nothing *Christoph* and I started with, our family had done well with one son and three daughters, and two horses, three cows, one calf, and fifteen sheep.

We also owned two houses, one plow, one wagon, two pitchforks, two scythes, three sickles, two axes, one shovel, two horse collars, three bridles, one barn, one stable, and one granary.

COUNTING

♠CHRISTOPH KARL♠

Colony Balzer

In July 1775, a counting of all our numbers and all our property occurred.

Official Counting
31.07.1775

Recorded for the Kontor about the Colony of Goly Karamysh (Balzer):

1. The Colonists live fairly well, their work in the fields is adequate, but there are insufficient hay fields which they occupy on the Karamysh River, twenty versts from the village.

   They have spring grain, and they have received a small amount of rye for seed. In my opinion, if they have a good summer harvest, they can subsist and do not need spring seed from the state.

2. Houses and outbuildings are not adequately covered. They have been ordered to thatch roofs in the Deutschen manner.

3. Ploughed lands have been adequately divided by them into three fields. It remains only to help them with

haying, which they can in no wise accomplish. They will not be in a position to do this because they have too little adequate land.

They would like to receive an additional allocation of land, without which they will not be at all able to pay their state debts.

Without adequate meadows, they cannot raise stock as they would like, because feeding grain is too expensive.

The following items numbered:

Colonists

1. Family Heads 100
2. Male 276
3. Female 247

Livestock

4. Horses 212
5. Colts 74
6. Cows 219
7. Bullocks 2
8. Calves 168
9. Sheep 662
10. Swine 184

Farm Tools

11. Plows 98
12. Wagons 138
13. Pitchforks 160
14. Scythes 234
15. Sickles 247
16. Axes 201

17. Shovels 136
18. Horse Collars 227
19. Bridles 233

Buildings

20. Homes 98
21. Stables 154
22. Granaries 96
23. Barns 44

Written by me on this 31st day of July in the year of our LORD one thousand seven hundred seventy-five (1775) in Colony Goly Karamysh (Balzer).

Signed,

Michael Lodyzhinsky
Chief Justice
Kontora Сара́тов

OUR VILLAGE

♠JACOBINA KARL♠

My Colony Balzer

We are proud of our village and Colony, and of what we have all accomplished here! From the nothing that we found here ten years ago, we now have wide straight streets with perpendicular lanes, with each house on a lot measuring seven sazhen by twelve sazhen (fifteen yards by twenty-five yards). My haus (house), as are many of my neighbors, is fenced with many planted pretty flowers alongside it. We have long benches placed outside the front for our family to sit enjoying the evening air and talk on the day's happenings.

My haus has a front entrance, along with a rear entrance through the backyard on the road It is of white painted wood, and roofed with straw. Our front entry door is between two large windows with good glass, as is the back door entrance. Like our neighbors, we have a sign attached with a house number and our name.

On entering my house, a small entry gives way to the kitchen. I keep the floors always swept, the entrance covered with fresh sand. Inside, we have whitewashed rooms with the doors, windows and all the furniture brightly painted in different colors, mostly with my favorites, red and blue.

On one side is the opening to the our master bedroom with the most important furniture of any colony house; the high double bed with posts at the corners on a wooden frame marked with my *Christoph's* name and the year of our wedding. Over the bed is a colorful canopy, with a mass of feather pillows where *Christoph* and I rest each night.

In the front room, we have a large solid table with chairs, and a glass door cabinet holding our kitchen tools, cups, and spoons. Other furniture is a wardrobe, a clock, a mirror, and on the walls, I hang holy pictures.

In another room are the kinder beds with similar but simpler than ours. Most all is Deutsch, except for the primitive built-in oven I use for family cooking. We also built a backhaus (summer kitchen) for our family cooking outside, when it is too hot to be inside. All in all, the best home I have ever had.

KIRCHE

Our Kirche has always provided that bond back to the old country. Our strong belief in our LORD and our Lutheran and Reformed Faiths require us to practice our religion often and regularly.

The most important day of any week was always Sunday with the Sunday service being special in the church life of our Colony. The day before on Saturday, *Christoph* and I and our family would end our work and prepare for Sunday by making sure our yard and road were swept to clear the way for everyone to attend Kirche on-time.

Late each Saturday night or early each Sunday morning, all of us, even our men that rarely bathed on their own, would wash and scrub, and don clean clothes for the service. I do check that *Christoph* and my kinder do get clean.

Our tradition and our Society stress punctual on-time attendance at Kirche. There is no good reason to be late. This is the day of worship of our LORD, and work on Sunday by anyone is strictly forbidden.

Our Kirche is also our honored place for Baptisms, Funerals, Weddings, Confirmations, and religious holidays.

TWENTY YEARS

♦ANNA MARIA MAURER♦

Kirhart, Palatinate, Deutschland

It has now been twenty years, now the year of our LORD 1784, since that day when I last saw daughter *Jacobina* and her husband *Christoph*.

I was just saying to my husband *Johann Jacob* a few days ago about how I still missed them so. Was it a few days ago?

No, that could not be. *Johann Jacob* passed on last year from a bad sickness that struck down many. Some said the sickness came from the horses that sickened a few months earlier. I know not, but feel it was the work of Satan himself.

Now, I am alone here in my house. All three of my daughters have left me now. First my *Jacobina*, she left to some distant country, and the later both *Susanna Regina* and *Laudema Christiana* married and moved with their husbands away to... I think it was Heilbronn, but I am no longer sure.

Both have full lives with sons and daughters, and have no time for an old woman such as me, even if I am the mother carried them and who gave them life.

No matter, I can feel my time is near. I have lived a good life and I have no fear; a comforting verse keeps running through my mind:

"When your child is small

And their days are new,

You are their center of all,

Anything will you do.

And then they grow

In body and mind,

Each day farther away

Drawn by what they find.

Gone forever they are

And you are now old,

Fading memories afar

Remembrances now cold.

My mind is now slow

I have no wish or regret,

For one thing, I know

For all, our Sun does set."

(D. Philipp Kaiser)

♦JACOBINA KARL♦

My Colony Balzer

It has been twenty years since we left our homeland and my family. I often wonder what my two sisters have done with their lives. Did they marry and have children?

Or as my *Christoph* cruelly teases me, did they become old and fat and never find their true love? Did father let them marry at all, or did he chase them away believing them unworthy of his daughters' hands.

And my strong father, *Johann Jacob*, and my dear Mother, *Anna Maria,* I wonder what our LORD had in store for them.

Are they happy, are they sad, are they well, or are they sick as the old often become. Do they still walk this earth? And if not, are they with our LORD in Heaven?

I do pray so. It does not seem like twenty years have passed. I can still see all of them as clearly as yesterday, and I can still hear their voices in my mind.

But those long past times when I was a child, the times that we as a family would hike to the meadow by the creek and eat our mid-day meal, when father and mother would lay back and talk after filling our bellies, and we girls would chase the butterflies around till we dropped, the memories of those good times are no longer clear and have faded away into nothing.

I no longer have the sharp pictures of my childhood past in my mind, and am left with only the warm feeling from those long past good times.

THIRTY YEARS

♦SUSANNA REGINA MAURER♦

Heilbronn, Kingdom of Württemburg

It has now been thirty years, now the year of our LORD 1794, since that day when *Laudema* and I last saw dear sister *Jacobina* and her husband *Christoph Karl.* That day they left Heilbronn, that day back in 1764, I still remember how we all felt as we said our goodbyes. Thankfully, some memories never do fade.

As all life must end, our father *Johann Jacob* has passed, and our dear mother *Anna Maria* has joined with him and our LORD in eternal Heaven.

I pray that *Jacobina* and *Christoph* have done well, and have been blessed by our LORD with a large family of many sons and daughters.

Both *Laudema* and I are blessed with many sons and daughters, and now as we grow older, and our children have children, those little ones bring much pleasure to us as they run around and play and yell and laugh.

As I watch our little ones, I see myself and my sisters, as well as their mothers and fathers, playing the same games in on the same roads and in the same yards as we did in the long past. Some day after I am gone, my children will look upon all this, as I do now. That is the way of this life.

I hope *Jacobina* and *Christoph* have been blessed, and able to enjoy that also.

A SON!

♦WILHELM PHILIPP KARL♦

The Colony of Balzer

You may have already heard the news, but I will shout it out again. It is true! And if you do not believe me, listen to my father, *Herr Christoph Karl,* who is also proudly shouting the news to anyone that is around.

I have a son born this 30th day of August in the year of our LORD one thousand seven hundred ninety eight (1798). I could not be happier! My wife and my GOD have blessed me with my new boy, a son; yes, a son!

I am *Herr Wilhelm Philipp Karl,* proud son of *Herr Christoph Karl* and *Frau Jacobina Karl.* I was born here in Balzer back in the year of our LORD one thousand seven hundred seventy (1770).

I have three sisters here in Balzer: *Anna Maria, Anna Margaretha,* and *Anna Cunigunde.* Two years ago, I met and married my dear wife, *Anna Maria Margaretha Grün.*

She is the beautiful daughter of *Herr Andreas Grün* and *Frau Maria Appolonia Hartt* of Balzer, the granddaughter of *Herr Johannes Grün* and *Frau Anna Elisabetha Heylmann*, and *Herr Johannes Hart* and *Frau Dorothea Trieber*; the great granddaughter of *Herr Johann Jacob Grün* and *Frau Anna Appolonia*, and *Herr Conrad Heylmann*, and *Herr Philipp Hart*, and *Herr Johannes Trieber* and *Frau Anna Appolina* of the area near Büdingen, back in Deutschland.

My wife and I live in my parents' home along with our new baby son, *Johann Heinrich*, my brother *Johann Friedrich*, and my youngest sister, *Anna Cunigunde*.

My two older sisters, *Frau Anna Maria* and *Frau Anna Margaretha*, live with their husbands, *Herr Heinrich Bauer* and *Herr Kasper Weisheim* in homes nearby.

We go to baptize our new son in our Church. Pastor *Johannes S. Janet* will introduce him as *Johann Heinrich* after his Godfather *Johann Heinrich Engelmann*, stepson of my sister *Anna Maria's* father-in-law.

We will celebrate the Taufe schmaus with much food and drink, sip the sweet Branntwein and pass the glass filled with silver coins to the Umfrau.

What did you say, Father? Oh yes, my father *Herr Christoph Karl*, and his wife and my mother, *Frau Jacobina*, would like all of you to celebrate with us on this joyous event.

Please come so that we will see you there, and share our Branntwein with you! All our welcome!

16 COUNTING

◆WILHELM PHILIPP KARL◆

The Colony of Balzer

This is the year of our LORD one thousand seven hundred ninety eight (1798) and is the time of the Российская Империя (Imperial Russland) Census of the Colonies.

A group of Agents representing Deputy of the Chief Justice of the Kontora, Court Councilor Popov, travel from Colony to Colony and investigate and question everything and everyone.

They counted our families and all our individual possessions including how many homes and buildings, how many animals, how many tools we owned, how many desyatines we farmed, what crops we grew and what their yield was. All this they carefully recorded on paper.

After they counted and recorded each family and individual, they did the same for the Colony itself. They recorded and described the Colony assets and location, and the strengths and weaknesses of the Colony in the official record.

The Kontora Agents put down the following for our family:

Christoph Karl age: 66 M able to work: Yes

wife Jacobina Maurer age: 62   F

sons:

    1. Wilhelm Philipp age: 28 M able to work: Yes

       Wife Anna Maria Margaretha Grün age: 21 F

       son: Joh Heinrich age: 1/4 M able to work: No

    2. Johann Friedrich age: 16 M able to work: Yes

       daughter: Anna Cunigunde age: 23 F

For our animals, they recorded:

1. six horses
2. five cows
3. eighteen sheep
4. four pigs
5. three geese
6. fifteen chickens

For our 1796 growing season, planting:

1. 3 chetvert rye (866 lbs.)
2. 4 chetvert wheat (1155 lbs.)
3. 1 chetvert barley (289 lbs.)
4. 6 chetvert oats (1733 lbs.)

5. 1 chetverik millet (36 lbs.)
6. 1 chetverik peas (36 lbs.)
7. 3 chetvert potatoes (866 lbs.)

Harvest 1797:

1. 6 chetvert rye (1733 lbs.)
2. 9 chetvert wheat (2600 lbs.)
3. 5 chetvert barley (1444 lbs.)
4. 12 chetvert oats (3466 lbs.)
5. 2 chetvert millet (577 lbs.)
6. 2 chetverik peas (72 lbs.)
7. 4 chetvert potatoes (1155 lbs.)

As a colony, we were not happy with what they wrote about our Balzer. We had worked hard to make things better here, some of our friends had died helping, and yet, the Kontora Agents seemed to be overly critical.

The following comments about the colony come from the notes written on November 5, 1798 by Court Councilor Popov for the Census of 1798:

"This colony is located in the Saratov Province, in the district of the city of Kamyshin, on the Bergseite, along the Goly Karamysh Creek."

"The distance from the provincial city of Saratov: 73 versts: from the district city Kamyshin: 112 versts; from neighboring colonies of Beideck: 15 versts; from Messer: 12 versts; from Anton: 10 versts; from Kutter: 9 versts; Moor: 6 versts; from the Volga River and its boat landing: 12 versts. There are 402 male inhabitants and 379 females, totaling 781 souls comprising 111 families. All are of the Reformed faith. They belong to the parish of Messer, where there is a pastor, but the church is here. Young children are taught reading, writing, and religion by schoolmaster under the supervision of the pastor in a school building."

"The land of the colony is bordered by land belonging to the colonies mentioned above: Beideck, Messer, Anton, Kutter, Moor in the estates of the villages of Akhmat and Mordovo. In the previous land survey, the colony was allocated arable farmland of 8,356 desyatina 1,296 sazhen, hayfields of 95 desyatina 1,680 sazhen, woodlands of 634 desyatina 680 sazhen. In addition because of insufficient allocation of hayfields they were allocated 39 desyatina of vacant land some 20 versts from the colony along the Bolshoi Karaman River; allocation total of 9,025 desyatina 1,206 square sazhen. According to information from the inhabitants, of this quantity of land, 100 are taken by farmsteads, 50 by roads. Some 5,000 desyatina are marginally suitable for farming, remainder being Clay, Sandy, and Celine, which farming does not produce of the land is suitable only for pastoring livestock. A similar situation exists with hayfields, and they cannot be allocated any additional. Only about 50 desyatina are useful. The land set aside for their hay needs are inconvenient. Woodlands are sufficient as allocated. The forests are mostly birch with a few desyatina of Oak, Aspen, Linden, and such. It is good only for firewood. It has been preserved for about 12 years. They cut it only case of dire need."

"The colony has insufficiencies in almost all areas of economic importance, but most particularly in arable land and hay fields. As a result, all the inhabitants are engaged in farming on the aforementioned marginal lands and they purchase feed for livestock. They use dung for fuel. There is no relief from the insufficiencies, because as was stated above, the lands of the colony are bounded by limited state lands that cannot be allocated. The colony has no other insufficiencies except for flax and hemp, which will not grow here, even though they plant them."

"All are engaged in farming. As for trades, they have four blacksmiths, two wheelwrights, and five boot makers. They live in mediocre conditions. Buildings are mostly dilapidated. There are thirty new homes, one stone, and several stone outbuildings. Yards are fenced with boards and wattle. There are vegetable gardens near the colony, along the Karamysh River. There are no orchards or apiaries. There is one flourmill. The fields lie close to the farmsteads and as far away as eight versts. They farm with plows and horses. They do not fertilize the land. Harvests of grain are only mediocre. Gophers consume little crop here. In the course of the summer this year (1798), they consumed no more than 20 desyatina. They know no means of destroying the gophers, except flooding."

"The grain indicated above has up until now been harvested, then threshed on floors adjacent to the houses. They are only just now moving the threshing floors to a safe distance from the houses. The grain is sold in Saratov. While the local granary here is old, it is in good order and constructed in a safe place. In it are currently stored rye, wheat, and oats for each farmer. Only about half the quantity is held personally. The remainder is allocated communally to the inhabitants and will be collected in the next autumn."

Maybe the report did say the truth, maybe we did have those problems, but we were still all very proud of what we accomplished.

By the year of our LORD one thousand seven hundred ninety-eight (1798), our Village had many gardens, a flourmill, plenty of food to eat and even some to sell in Saratov.

Most of all and most important, we are all happy, and we bask in the knowledge that we have been blessed by our LORD!

A SECOND SON!

The news is true! I, *Wilhelm Philipp Karl,* now have a second son born on this 21st of April in the year of our LORD one thousand eight hundred one (1801).

I have a second son to help us tame this harsh land. I am a happy man. Bless GOD and bless my dear wife, *Anna Maria Margaretha.* My second son is *Johann Konrad Karl,* named after his Godfather *Konrad Keller,* husband to the sister of our good friend and former Vorsteher (leader) *Herr Balzer Barthuli.*

Join me and give thanks to our LORD for his blessing of my family!

17 THE MOVE

♠CHRISTOPH KARL♠

In the REFORMED FAITH Colony of Balzer

Balzer is changing all too fast! New people, mostly more of the Reformed, seem to be arriving here each day. They all have new ideas on what we should do and how we should do it. Worse yet, they have no respect at all for the old ways that we brought with us from Deutschland. Everything is changing and not for the better! I am no longer happy here in this colony.

After much thought and prayer, I have decided it is time to for us to move on to somewhere else. Yes, we will leave Balzer this year of our LORD one thousand eight hundred two (1802).

While we have grown and prospered here in Balzer over that last thirty-seven years, we are now well off enough to sell some our holdings here. I will purchase property in our new Colony, wherever I decide that is.

As soon as I make up my mind, *Jacobina* and I will move on. I will not make any others in our family leave Balzer, but will give all a choice to stay or go with my *Jacobina* and me. Of course, I would like all to go. I do feel that would be the best for all.

First though, I must talk this over with my dear wife, *Jacobina*. Thirty-eight years ago when I decided to move without talking to her, there was hell to pay, and I landed up paying all of it! I hope that we will not have to repeat that strained time again. I was right that time, and maybe now she will trust my judgement as a good wife should.

That night as *Jacobina* and I were outside on the front bench sitting and talking by ourselves, I spoke, "Dear wife, we Lutherans have always been outnumbered by those of the Reformed faith here in Balzer, and more and more those Reformed keeping coming in. While we have lived with them and many of them our close friends, I do not and have never shared their ideas and religious beliefs."

I went on, "Both of us have always strived to follow the ways of our Friar Martin Luther. We have raised our children as Lutherans and taught them our beliefs. Those dumb Kontora in Saratov did not care that Lutherans and Reformed worship differently, and so we were all lumped together. Assigned at the beginning to live here in this Reformed village, we have never been able to worship as we choose. Almost the first words out of that damned *Recruiter's* mouth were that they promised us our religious freedom, but that was one more promise they never kept, or even tried to keep. It is time for us to move to a Lutheran Colony so that our children will be brought up Lutheran, not this Reformed. After much thought and prayer, I have chosen the Colony Straub to be our new home."

Jacobina was silent for a while as she thought about all I had spoken, and then replied, "Dear *Christoph*, I have been your wife for over forty-five years. I have given you two strong sons, and three healthy daughters. I have walked beside you past the hills and valleys of two countries, and sailed with you on rivers and seas. I have tilled and seeded, and brought in the harvest with you on our land. You are right, I would be happier with our Lutheran ways, but you should know that I am happy living here in Balzer. Yet, if it your wish that we move on to Straub, then so it shall be."

She continued, and asked, "What if not all want to go to Straub? Our son *Johann Friedrich* has been for a while courting the sweet *Susanna Elisabeth*, daughter of *Herr Philipp Reichert* and *Frau Katharina geb Stöhr*. Assuming our son asks her to be his wife, *Susanna Elisabeth* may not want to leave Balzer as her family has been here almost as long as we have, and is Reformed! *Johann Friedrich* will most likely not move with us if *Susanna Elisabeth* does not go. If he chooses not to go with us, we must leave the house and some land for him to provide for a new family with her, if he so chooses."

I sighed, knowing well that she spoke the truth. Son *Johann Friedrich* was obviously quite fond of her and drawn to her charms, and would likely not come. This would make the move more difficult. While all we possessed belonged to me as head of the family, after my death it would by law pass to my eldest son, *Wilhelm Philipp*.

After some thought, I answered her, "Dear wife, you are always right. If son *Johann Friedrich* decides to stay and start a family with his *Susanna Elisabeth*, I will not oppose that. I will keep the house and some lands for them to live, but after I pass all this shall pass, as by law, to our eldest son *Wilhelm Philipp*. He can decide then if he chooses to pass the ownership of these lands to his younger brother or keep them for himself. That is fair!"

Jacobina nodded and replied, "Yes, husband, that is very fair of you."

I would break the news to the family at the morrow evening meal. This all went better than expected. Surprisingly, I had made my decision and I can still sleep in the bed of my dear wife, *Jacobina*. Much better than the last time…. I would sleep well this night.

The next day seemed to drag and felt longer than normal. When the evening meal was finished, I rose and requested their attention. With all eyes focused on me, I announced, "I have decided that we will move to Colony Straub very soon."

I looked around the room, and saw shock and concern on my family's faces. As customary, no one said anything out of respect as I was still standing and apparently had not finished talking.

I continued, "We need to rejoin our Lutheran brethren in Straub, and worship in the ways of our Friar Martin Luther. Here we cannot, but in Straub, we will be able to do that. I will not force anyone to come with your mutter and me, but we would like you all to move with us. We will start to prepare to move tomorrow. Who will join us?"

Neither of my sons said anything at all, so I asked them directly, "*Wilhelm Philipp*, will you and your wife, and my grandsons come with us?"

Wilhelm looked at his wife *Anna Maria*, who said nothing but lowered her head and eyes, and after a moment of silence, he answered, "Yes, my Vater and Mutter, we will join you in moving and building our new lives in Straub." His wife looked up at him, but as it was his decision as head of their family, remained silent.

"Good, good, my son," I replied. Then I asked my youngest son, "*Johann Friedrich*, will you join us?"

My youngest son looked up at me, and then looked at his mutter to see if she might help. Her face remained blank, and he realized that this was his choice to make. He squirmed in his chair and he looked around the table at his family, but still he said nothing.

After some time with no answer, I prodded, "Come now son, what will it be? Your bother has told us his decision. What say you, do you stay or do you go?"

Johann Friedrich looked directly at me and replied, "Nein, Vater, I cannot leave this place and go with you to Straub. My heart belongs here with my sweet *Susanna Elisabeth*, daughter of *Herr Philipp Reichert* and *Frau Katharina*. I mean on asking for her hand soon. She is of the Reformed faith as is her family, and I know she wants to remain close to her parents. So my answer must be, Nein!" He lowered his head waiting for my, most likely unpleasant, response.

No one said anything and the room remained quiet as a tomb. Only my *Jacobina*, who happened to be smiling, knew what I was about to say, and she was not saying anything.

I replied to my youngest son, "*Johann Friedrich*, raise your head and look at me. Your mother has already told me of your great affection for this *Susanna Elisabeth Reichert*. I am told it is your intention to ask her to be your wife, and if so, when?"

Johann Friedrich nodded yes and replied, "Soon, soon, when the good time arrives." At that, there were many soft snickers from around the table. *Johann Friedrich* frowned and squirmed in his chair.

I motioned for silence and quickly answered, "Son, the proper time may never arrive, so ask her now! If she agrees to be your wife, but does not want to move with us, then I will let you and her and your future children live in this house and work my lands when we move. I am not giving you all this as by our laws, it will pass after my death to your brother *Wilhelm*. He can at that time choose to keep ownership of all this or pass it to you and your family. What say you on this? It is fair, I believe."

Johann Friedrich looked over at his brother *Wilhelm*, who nodded in agreement.

With that, *Johann Friedrich* widely smiled and answered, "This is all more than fair. I would have never expected, as a second son, this chance to receive part of the family property. I respect that by custom it all goes to my elder brother *Wilhelm*. And if he chooses to give it on to me after your passing, I will be forever thankful. If he chooses not to, I will still love him as my brother forever. Father, as you advise, I will ask my *Susanna Elisabeth* on the morrow to wed."

Finally, I was able to sit down. The table immediately erupted with talking and laughing, and congratulations to son *Johann Friedrich*. I looked across the table to my dear wife *Jacobina*. She was not laughing or talking; she was staring deep into my eyes, on her face a wide smile.

It was good that I talked with her last night about this. This time I had her approval, so much better then when I not asked for her counsel and recommendations.

◆JACOBINA KARL◆

My Colony Balzer

My dear husband did very well this time. He has learned from his old mistakes. I am not sure that I agree with uprooting our life here and our moving to Straub. We have a good life and many friends, even if they are Reformed faith.

I know that as I approach my sixty-seventh winter, I to feel a need to be closer to our LORD as my end draws near. I am sure that *Christoph* feels much the same and wants to worship our GOD as our faith calls for. As my dear *Christoph* wishes, we will join our Lutheran brethren in Straub for our final years.

I am sad that my youngest son will not be coming with us, but I know he must start his own family. That is the way of life. And it is not as if he will be a country away from family as *Christoph* and I were when we started way back when, but will only be a day's walk and a boat ride.

◆WILHELM PHILIPP KARL◆

The Colony of Balzer

I was quite unaware of my father's plans to move. Neither father nor mother had hinted at such an idea. It was a difficult decision, as I knew my dear wife *Anna Maria* would like to remain near her sisters and brothers here in Balzer, but her older sister *Anna Margaretha* had married a *Herr Rudolph* and moved to Straub. So she was not moving away from some of them, but moving closer to *Anna Margaretha.*

As the eldest son, I knew that I had to go with them for whatever reason. They had given and sacrificed so much over the past years; I needed to be with them as their time passed.

And so I answered, "Ja." I was surprised when my brother said 'Nein.' I was proud that he stood his ground for his love. I was also surprised when my father so fairly allowed him to live on here in Balzer with his new wife. Of course I will, after father passes, Heaven forbid, give this land to my brother and his family.

✦ᗅNNᗅ MᗅRIᗅ KᗅRL geb GRÜN ✦

Balzer

My, all that was a shock! First, all this talk of moving, and then brother *Johann Friedrich* announces he is asking for the hand of *Susanna Elisabeth,* all much a surprise. I did not see any of this coming!

I am glad for how it turned out for brother *Johann Friedrich* who will be staying with his new wife. I am sad to think about leaving my sisters and brothers, but I do look forward to being close to older sister *Anna Margaretha.*

As for all the rest, I thought to myself, "All this talk about why we are moving, and who gets what is a waste of time. If we are to move, we move. Talk gets us not any closer to Straub!"

And I am sure who is going to have to do the majority of the work in this move; it will be my *Wilhelm* and me. I love his parents, but they are old! His father *Christoph* has seen sixty-eight winters, and *Frau Jacobina* has seen almost as many, at sixty-seven. Honestly, they are both old and cannot do much to help. *Johann Friedrich* will just have to help us move, even if he is not coming with us!

COLONY STRAUB

♦CHRISTOPH KARL♦

In the REFORMED FAITH Colony of Balzer

No matter what I wanted, it took more than a few days to pack our things and settle our affairs. In our Colonies, you cannot just up and leave one and move to another. The security and health of each Colony must take priority over personal freedom and choice. We understood that rule from the very first day of our arrival thirty-seven years ago, and so we knew that we would have to petition both Colony Balzer and Colony Straub for approval of this move. It was a formality at most, as both colonies readily approved.

With that and after time to say our good-byes, our family, all except for son *Johann Friedrich*, late one mid morn climbed up on our two wagons filled with all we would need, and slowly set out for our new home in Colony Straub.

Many of our old neighbors waved and blessed us as we left, and of course, all the women cried. After all these years of being married and having daughters, I still do not fathom why women cry at times like this, It is not like we died or were moving back to Deutschland; we were only moving to another colony across the Volga only about fifteen versts (ten miles) away.

I was glad when we were finally clear of our old village; that is when the sobbing and sniffling finally stopped. I felt excited, invigorated, and maybe even younger as this is a new beginning. I hoped all of the family would be happy given this opportunity.

It was a warm and still day as we moved along. The rhythmic sound of the hooves striking the ground as the horses slowly trod their way to the river mixed with the wagon rattles and squeaks brought back long put away memories of our last move, the one that brought my dear wife and I to Colony Balzer thirty-seven years ago. So much had changed during that time, and yet, here we were moving again to what we hoped was a better place. That very same desire again driving us forward, some things never change.

We had our midday meal along the side of the road, and by late afternoon, we reached the landing on the Volga. We would cross in the morning, and for this night, we would sleep under the stars.

Jacobina and I moved a little ways from our family, and snuggling together, talked about the old days, and how this move brought back those memories long forgotten of the many nights we slept together along the creek those first weeks in Balzer.

We talked of the early mornings at sunrise with the cool light refreshing wind and the gently warming sun and clear light blue sky. And the sounds of birds chirping in the trees with the leaves fluttering and rustling while their dewdrops shimmered in the sunlight. And of the burbling of the stream as the water raced through the rocks. We had forgotten all those wonderful memories in our daily rush of living.

Jacobina, whose recollection of those nights must have better than mine, said to me, "This is just as it was those many years ago. I will say what you said to me then; we will not dwell on what should have been, but will dwell on what can be. We will readily accept the trials our LORD has set before us just as our honorable ancestors have always done. Tomorrow is the first day of our new life here in our new land! We must thank our LORD for this blessing."

As usual, she was right and we must trust in our LORD. I had no problem with that, but how could she still remember what exactly what I said over thirty years ago. Amazing!

There under the open sky next to the wide Volga, having faith in what the good LORD planned for us, we both relaxed and fell deeply asleep.

The next morn we awoke late to the smell of food cooking over the fire. Our children had let us sleep while they prepared breakfast and loaded up everything back on our two wagons.

Daughter-in-law *Anna Maria* was a wonderful cook, and both *Jacobina* and I devoured what she prepared. Our son *Wilhelm* is lucky to have found such a wonderful woman. On the other hand, *Wilhelm* is a strong and fine man and father, and she is lucky to have him.

Before long, we were ready to cross the Volga. The river is wide and not really that deep, but it is not possible to ford it with wagons. We would pay our fare to load one wagon and horse onto the river raft and cross one at a time.

The crossings went smoothly, but took most of the morning before we were again ready to travel the last seven versts (bit over four miles) to Colony Straub.

The land on this side of the Volga is flatter and much less forested with cultivated farmland and pasture on both sides of the road. We made good time and by midafternoon approached Colony Straub.

Oak, Poplar and Willow trees welcomed us to the settlement. And there on a horse patiently waiting for our arrival was our new colony sponsor and old friend, *Herr Heinrich Rudolph*, husband of *Anna Margaretha* and brother-in-law of our *Anna Maria*.

OUR WELCOME

⋆WILHELM PHILIPP KARL⋆

Our new Colony of Straub

We were all tired and ready to there. When I saw the trees, houses, and the village Kirche, I silently thanked our LORD for bringing us here.

We were a dusty dirty group from traveling the dry road, and I am surprised that *Herr Rudolph* even recognized us at all. But he did, and before we even reached him, he waved and yelled out to us, "Welcome *Karl* family."

He already had realized that we were dead tired, and so, led us directly to an empty house. The former family had all sickened and died a few months back, but that mattered not to us. This would be our new home.

Mother and my wife immediately began to move everything in and set-up our new home. *Herr Rudolph's* wife *Anna Margaretha* and a few of the other village women also came over and helped. The house looked almost the same as what we had left in Balzer. I never took the time to think on it before, but I suppose most of the different colony houses were all built nearly the same.

With the women busy setting up the house, *Herr Rudolph,* father and I took a walk around the village while *Herr Rudolph* spoke about our new home, "About three hundred Lutherans live here in Colony Straub. We have four wind flourmills and one water flourmill, a public granary, many gardens, one blacksmith, one mill master, and one cobbler. We live well, but our buildings are old, except for one new home. As you see, our yards are all fenced with wattle fences. Behind the homes are vegetable gardens, and a ways distant too far to see now are melon, pumpkin, and cucumber patches and vegetable gardens. We worship at our Kirche; our congregation is led by our Pastor *Bernhard Wilhelm Litfass,* who we share with the Lutheran congregation in nearby Colony Warenburg. The Kirche and schoolhouse is just a short walk from our homes. Your new home is just behind mine."

He continued, "Our cemetery is a ways to the west of our village. Our closest field is out about two versts (a little more than a mile) away with the farthest some nine versts. Our farmland is divided into three fields which we till with plows. We do crop rotation to get as much out of the land as we can, but do not fertilize as some other areas. Sadly, our harvests of the grain rye, wheat, and oats are not that good. We sell our crops in Pokrovsk and our sister colonies."

It looked to me that our Straub was about the same size as Balzer, maybe a bit smaller. I mentioned this to *Herr Rudolph,* who nodded that it was so.

Strangely, father made no comment and was silent.

We made our way back to our new home. The wagons were all unloaded with the furniture inside. And the good smell of hot food was in the air. It was already like home.

Our women beckoned us in, set us down at the table, and plopped full plates before the three of us. One quick prayer thanking our LORD for these blessings, and we were all digging into our food. No time for more talk, just time to chew.

When we had filled our bellies, they ushered us outside onto benches to talk and relax. Now, the women had the table to themselves to eat at their own leisure. Many times, we heard their laughter through the open door.

As the end of the day drew near, the three of us talked about this and that and whatever, nothing of importance.

As dusk arrived, *Herr Rudolph* stood up and spoke, "I bid you a goodnight. I will come get you early morn as the sun rises, to lead you to the fields. With the help of your strong son *Wilhelm*, we will get much done tomorrow."

It was quickly to bed, and soon to sleep for our family.

◆ANNA MARIA KARL geb GRÜN◆

Our new Colony of Straub

I just knew that I would land up doing most of the work! Thanks be to our LORD for the help of my sister *Anna Margaretha* and the other village women.

The men, as usual, went off somewhere and were no help at all. I suppose they felt this was all women's work. What did they do? They walked around the village. At least Mother *Jacobina* tried to help, but she is so old and weak.

For me, it was work just like every other day since I married into this family. Come to think of it, it was like this before I married *Wilhelm*, back in my own family. Women work, men watch us work, that is how it always has been and always will be!

The good thing about this day is that after we fed the men and pushed them outside, my sister *Anna Margaretha* and I and the other women were able to relax and eat, talk, and laugh without our men around; at least for a while.

♦JACOBINA KARL♦

Colony Straub

We have a good house here in Colony Straub. I am thankful for all the other village women's help; I did all I could to help, but I do tire quickly and am not as strong as I used to be.

Luckily, my *Wilhelm's* wife, *Anna Maria,* is a strong woman; she was able to do much of my share of the work. That is as it has always been and will always be; the young must take the load for their elders. She feels as I felt when I was young, and did more than the old ones. She will feel different when she becomes, as we all someday do, old.

MORNING

♦CHRISTOPH KARL♦

Colony Straub

True to his word, *Herr Rudolph* came at sunrise to lead us to the fields. The work in the fields was much the same as we did in Balzer. That first day became many days, then many months, and then more than a year. With Colony Balzer only a memory, Colony Straub was now our home. Our fellow Lutherans opened their homes and hearts to us, and we all felt as we had always been here.

Our LORD had surely blessed us all.

A THIRD SON!

♠ANNA MARIA KARL geb GRÜN♠

Our Colony of Straub

I have given my husband, *Wilhelm Philipp*, a third son born on this 22nd of April in the year of our LORD one thousand eight hundred three (1803).

Our new boy will help us tame the land and produce much food. Now, there is no way that our family will not continue to prosper.

Our third son is *Johann Michael Karle*, named after his Godfather *Michael Rudolph*, uncle of our new son. Thanks to our LORD for his blessing!

Written record of the birth and baptism

[Author: Although the KARL family would only realize it many years later, the Official Recorder, in this birth and baptism record, changed forever the spelling of their family name from KARL to the current KARLE.]

FORTY YEARS

♠LAUDEMA CHRISTIANA MAURER♠

Heilbronn, Kingdom of Württemburg, Deutschland

It has been forty years, now the year of our LORD 1804, since that day when I last saw sister *Jacobina* and her husband *Christoph Karl.* So very many, many years ago.

Sister *Susanna Regina* passed on during the winter last year from a very bad illness. She was not alone as it ended the lives of many here in Heilbronn.

Everyone else from our family that waved good-bye to *Jacobina* and *Christoph* that day so long ago has passed on, and now walks with our GOD THE FATHER in Heaven. Pray they be blessed for all eternity.

I do find myself wondering where dear sister *Jacobina* and *Christoph* finally settled down, and what kind of life they could have had in the wilds of Russland. I wonder if the LORD ever blessed them with more children. Sister *Jacobina* always so wanted another of her own; her first died so soon.

I know I will never ever hear, but as always, my prayers are with *Jacobina* whether she is here or in heaven with the rest of the family.

♦JACOBINA KARL♦

Colony Straub

Forty years ago, *Christoph* and I said our goodbye's to my family in Heilbronn at the edge of the Neckar River. Today, I dedicate to remembering my mother and father and two sisters.

It was so long ago…. I is hard to remember their faces… they all merge into one. The feelings I felt that day, though, are as strong as ever. I do miss all of them so.

18 MY TIME

♦WILHELM PHILIPP KARL♦

Our Colony of Straub

It made no sense, there was no real reason, it just happened. No warning, no way I could have changed it. I suppose it was just my time.

My trusty old horse had been with me for many years and was like a friend to me. Neither of us saw that hole and when he stumbled, I fell off his back and hit the ground hard. Off balance, he followed me to the ground and with all his weight, crushed down on me hard.

It was not my fault, it was not his fault, it just was! Surprisingly, I felt little pain. My old friend did not move much either and for him too, this fall was apparently his end.

Not much I could do for either of us, pinned to the ground as I was. No pain, and while I always thought that dying would scare me... it was not at all like that.

I would miss my dear wife and sons, and I hoped the best for them, but I knew my time to leave this world rapidly approached. As my sight failed along with my hearing, my mind wandered through the memories of my life.... And then, I saw it, and I felt it.

Dim, at first, but slowly growing brighter.... A warm golden light, beautiful, alive and almost hypnotic, drawing me closer and closer to it. Reassuring and comforting me, letting me know that everything was just fine. Letting me know this is my time. There is no struggle as I surrender to the will of my LORD. All is well, and I am at Peace.

Suddenly, out of nowhere, unimaginable pain explodes through the light. My light is all gone, replaced by people pulling on me and yelling and screaming... and pain. And more pain. Voices, I hear voices that I know. I should answer them, but I care not. My light, where is my light?

Thank the LORD, the pain soon fades along with all the yelling and all the voices. My warm golden light, beautiful and alive again ever so slowly grows brighter, again drawing me, seducing me with its warmth towards it.... Willingly I surrender to it. This is my time, and everything is just fine.

SHADOW OF DEATH

♦ANNA MARIA KARL geb GRÜN♦

Our Colony of Straub

My dear husband, *Wilhelm Philipp Karl,* passed this night of 15 January in the year of our LORD one thousand eight hundred five (1805).

My nine years as the wife of *Wilhelm* passed much too fast. He was my life, and if not for the wonderful sons he gave me, I would not want to go on living. Thankfully, my sons will carry on the memory of my *Wilhelm* forever. I do miss him so, but I know that I will see him again when I too am called by our LORD.

Father *Christoph* is beside himself with grief. As a parent, I understand his pain as no parent ever wants to bury one of their own.

A parent always feels that they will go first, and their children will live on after their passing. But this was not to be in GODs plan, and my dear love, *Wilhelm Philipp*, has passed on to a better place.

It has only been a few days since we put our *Wilhelm* in the ground, and *Christoph* and *Jacobina* still grieve deeply.

Last night, *Christoph* spoke at family supper, "*Jacobina* and I are returning to Balzer to live with *Johann Friedrich,* wife *Susanna Elisabeth* and their son, also named *Johann Michael Karl.* We will also be closer to the families of daughters *Anna Maria, Anna Margaretha,* and *Anna Cunigunde* with our many grandchildren. We wish you and our grandsons, *Johann Heinrich, Johann Konrad,* and *Johann Michael* to return with us. You may also stay and continue to live here in Colony Straub if you so wish. While *Johann Heinrich* is only seven years, as eldest son, he inherits all of these properties here in Straub when I leave."

I was speechless, and knew not what to say. Nothing like this had ever been mentioned ever before tonight. I finally spoke, "Father *Christoph* and Mother *Jacobina,* are you sure that this is what you want? You are both still grieving and it may be better to decide in a few weeks or months. We can all still live here together."

I genuinely meant no harm in saying that grief may be clouding their choice, but *Christoph* was in no mood to have his decision questioned, or even inferred that he was unable to make the right choice.

Christoph glared at me and sternly spoke, "Daughter, do not assume that I am unable to choose my own way, and do not think that you are in any position to question any of my decisions, right or wrong. We, *Jacobina* and I, will begin packing on the morrow and will leave soon after that. That is my decision! Whether you and your sons remain here, or come with us, is actually the choice of your eldest son *Johann Heinrich* and not yours to make, but as I said before, he is young and will need your guidance. This discussion ends! No more will be said on this issue."

I remained silent, as I completely understood that when he made up his mind that was the way it would be. It had always been that way, and was the way of our people.

I also completely understood that now that my dear *Wilhelm* had passed, that all his possessions passed to my eldest son. I myself owned nothing, and now depended on the good will of my own seven-year-old son.

I looked over at Mother *Jacobina* to see if she felt the same way as Father *Christoph*, but she had lowered her head and would not look at me. So, whether she agreed to leave or not, they were leaving.

The rest of the supper, we ate in silence, and we all went to bed early. I had much to think about before the morning sun rose.

The next morning at breakfast, I politely asked Father *Christoph* if I could speak. He nodded, and I said, "Thank you for your generous offer to let us come with you back to Balzer, but I must say no as I have decided that my sons and I will remain here in Straub. It is not far between Balzer and Straub, and we will visit you and our cousins as often as possible."

Christoph frowned and sighed, and then with a harsh voice, replied, "As you wish, you stay! We will start packing today and we will leave tomorrow. You and *Jacobina* will start getting our things together to take. I will take your eldest son *Johann Heinrich* for a walk to talk with him about what I expect from him as the man of this *Karl* house. *Johann Heinrich*, follow me outside.

I began to object, but thought better of it. My seven-year-old eldest son, *Johann Heinrich,* is by custom and law now the man of this *Karl* house.

TO BE KARL

♦JOHANN HEINRICH KARLE♦

Village of Straub

I do not understand much that is going on. I know my father fell of his horse and was hurt badly. I know he has gone to live in Heaven with our LORD and that I will not see him again till I too pass when I am old. I know that my mother misses my father badly, and is upset at his going away. I know my *Opa* (grandfather) and *Oma* (grandmother) also miss my father, and cry much of the time.

I do not know why *Opa Christoph* and *Oma Jacobina* have to leave now for the Village of Balzer. Why can they not stay here with us?

I know that my mother wants to stay here in Straub because she is happy living here. My brothers and I are also happy living here, so why is *Opa Christoph* angry with my mother because we want to live here? Why is he trying to make us leave with them when we all do not want to go?

I do not know what difference it makes that I am the eldest of my brothers, and what this inheriting all our property means. I never owned it, my father and *Opa* owned everything, and that should mean that my mother and *Opa* now own all of it. None of this makes any sense to me!

Now *Opa Christoph* tells me that I have to go for a walk with him to talk about becoming the man of a *Karl* house…What does all this mean? The only times I have been ordered to go outside alone is when I needed switching for something bad I did. As far as I recollect, I have not done anything bad for quite a while.

Opa Christoph and I slowly walked for a while before he said anything. Eventually, he slowly spoke, "*Johann Heinrich*, I know that this is a hard time for you and that little of this will make any sense. Someday, you will understand all I am going to say."

I nodded that I understood, but I really did not.

He continued, "Our *Wilhelm Philipp* is now gone, and you understand that, yes?"

I nodded that I did, and this time, I really did.

Opa spoke again, "Your father was a good man true to our proud family name of *Karl*, as I believe I have also been, and as have been many generations of *Karl* gone before us. I know that you are young, but now it is time for you to quickly grow up and accept the responsibilities as the man of this *Karl* house. You are the eldest of my son's male offspring, and by custom, this is both your right and your duty. Do you understand so far?"

I had no idea what he was talking about, and replied, "Not at all, *Opa Christoph.*" I hoped this would not make him mad at me.

He went on, "Yes, this is much for you to take in. But, as I said earlier, much of this will become clearer as you become older. You must remember what I say now. This is important! Are you listening closely?"

"Yes *Opa Christoph,*" I answered.

"Good, now listen to my words and remember. All that your father owned, you now own and control. You, not your mother or brothers or anyone else. You, and only you, have the power to do with it as you wish, but have the duty to do with it only as you should. You are responsible for the well-being of both your mother and brothers. If you foolishly lose all you now have, you will harm your mother and brothers. You should listen and take counsel from your mother, as she is older and more experienced, but remember, she is a woman and as a woman is not the head of the house. There is only one person you must listen to and obey now, and that is me, as head of the *Karl* line. I will expect absolute obedience from you as I did from your father and everyone else in all our *Karl* families. But I will be away in Balzer, and you, my *Johann Heinrich*, are the head of this *Karl* family and home. Only you, do you follow?" he asked.

I thought to myself, no, I did not understand all this, but this was clearly important to *Opa* and I did not want to get him angry, so I lied and answered, "Yes *Opa Christoph*."

Opa continued, "Again good, good. Now you know that you always must do the best for those in your care, your mother and brothers. As I said before, many generations of our ancestors have kept our name of *Karl* true and respected by all. You must always remember that in anything you do, it must be to the highest standards to protect our *Karl* name. As you do, depending on your choices during your life, your sons and grandsons will either proudly wear our good name of *Karl,* respected by all, or in shame bear the brand of humiliation with the name of *Karl.* Each day, as head of this *Karl* house, you will have to make choices that your sons and grandsons, and even their sons will have to carry. That is why it is so important that you always make the right choice and do what is good. Look to our Bible and pray to our LORD for his guidance and counsel, and you will not go wrong. Do you understand? Do you have any questions?"

I thought deeply. He had talked of our LORD, and this time I knew I could not lie, but must tell only the truth. It is lucky I did now understand most of what he said. I answered, "I know that I am the man of my *Karl* home and own all, and must protect my mother and brothers so they are safe and have a place to live. I know that I have the proud name of *Karl,* and that I must always live in a way that keeps our *Karl* name good. I know that when mixed up, I should search the Bible and ask our LORD for his guidance and answers. I know all that now!"

I continued, "What bothers me is that you are trying to make my mother and brothers and I leave our home here and go with you back to Balzer. Why can we not all live here together as we always have?"

Opa Christoph answered, "It is enough that you understand what you must do. As for my reasons for what I do, they are my reasons and as head of our family, I do not explain them to anyone, not even you. You will understand when you are older, so we will leave this till then. This talk we have had is not to be told to anyone else, not your mother or brothers or even your *Oma*, but is just between two men of *Karl.* Come now, man of this *Karl* house, it is time to return and help us prepare for our leaving for the Village of Balzer. Our talk is now ended!"

"Yes *Opa Christoph*," I agreed. As we silently walked back home, I thought about all he had told me, and all that he had not told me. I still wanted more answers, but knew that this was neither the time nor place. I would just have to wait until I was older to learn what I wanted to know.

Opa Christoph and *Oma Jacobina* left early the next day on a horse-drawn wagon loaded with all their possessions. *Opa Christoph* said nothing more to me.

Softly crying, my dear *Oma Jacobina,* before leaving, did say to me, "We are so proud of you. Our love will be with you always no matter where we are or where we live. I know that you will grow to, and become a fine *Karl* and lead your own family here in Straub. GOD bless you always."

There we stood, my mother and brothers and me, now all alone, my father, *Opa* and *Oma,* all gone.

I am frightened, but cannot be, for I am now the *Karl* of this family. I took the hand of my mother and said, "Dear mother, all will be fine. I will make sure that you and my brothers are taken care of and safe always. I will grow and become a good man and earn our respected family name of *Karl*."

Looking down at me, my mother said nothing, but squeezed my hand and smiled, and began to cry. My brothers and I just stood there and held onto her for a long, long time.

MY NEW HUSBAND

♦ ANNA MARIA KARL geb GRÜN ♦

Our Colony of Straub

So much change so quickly. One day my dear *Wilhelm* is here with me, our sons, and *Christoph* and *Jacobina*, then just short days later my *Wilhelm* is in the ground and *Christoph* and *Jacobina* are gone back to Balzer.

Next, my seven-year-old son tells me that he is the man, the *Karl*, of this house and promises to take care and keep his brothers and me safe forever. Mein Gott, he is only seven years old!

My *Johann Heinrich* is growing up much too fast. Bless him for his strength and courage, but I must somehow find some way so that he is, for a short while longer, stay a child. I must do something!

But what? I am not strong enough to do a man's work in the fields each day and still do all my chores around the house. I cannot expect my young sons to work as the men do all day in the fields, not yet, but in a few more years, maybe *Johann Heinrich*. I cannot forever depend on the charity of my friends or the people of Straub to support our needs. But what else is there, I have three growing sons to feed and clothe. I can do with less food and make do with what I now wear, but my sons, they will always need more.

With no answers, I turned to our LORD and prayed, "Oh LORD, I beg you to hear my words. You have taken my man to be with you in Heaven. I am happy for his soul, but I am now without any way to feed and clothe my children. I know not what to do, and humbly ask you for help, or for a message to lead me to what I should next do. Your humble servant. Amen." It was in his hands, as it always was!

Within a few weeks, all my problems vanished. *Herr Nikolaus Schwind* came to my rescue and offered to help me in my time of grief. He was a family friend of the *Rudolph's*, both in Colony Norka and here, for many years before we arrived, and had quickly become one of my *Wilhelm's* best friends.

For no reason I will ever understand, *Nikolaus*, began to seriously court me. He quickly proposed, and I accepted. We married on 15 February of that same year with the blessing of our Lutheran Kirche and friends.

Nikolaus provided the father that my sons desperately needed and most all around our home became better. He also worked in the fields to earn our part of the communal harvest. Not all was well, as my courageous and brave *Johann Heinrich* did not easily adjust to another man in our house. Thankfully, my new husband did not seem to be bothered that *Johann Heinrich* always insisted that he was the *Karl* of the house. Actually, I am doubly blessed as I now have two men to care for me.

Apparently, our LORD also blessed my union with *Nikolaus* as he blessed us with a daughter, our *Anna Margareta*, born to us nine months later in November of 1805.

Written in the Colony Straub records for all time: *Anna Margareta* - baptized in our Lutheran Kirche by *Pastor Bernhard Wilhelm Litfass*; witnessed by his brother *Johanne Friedrich Schwind* and my dear sister, *Anna Margareta Rudolph geb Grün*.

19 BACK IN BALZER

ᴀCHRISTOPH KARLᴀ

Colony of Balzer

Life has disappointed me again. I honestly thought that when we got back to our familiar Balzer that all would be better. I was so wrong. Balzer had changed even more and faster while we were gone those three years, and by my thoughts, not for the better.

One day recently, nothing hurt and I felt good, the day was clear and fresh, the sun was warm, a good day to walk around and visit my old friends, the very founders of this Colony.

I searched long and hard, but I could not find most of them. I asked and asked many people I met, but most had never heard of my old friends. Of those few that remembered them, most times they only knew of their name. Best they could do was to tell me where someone with that name lived. When I asked those of that name living there, usually I learned that, sadly, my old friends had passed.

So, many of the old ones that built this Village and Colony with me are gone. Those few like me that still hang on are vastly outnumbered by those I think of as newcomers, not original settlers or the second and third generations of my old friends; but new people from who knows where with little or no respect or understanding of our old ways and customs.

It all feels so wrong, and almost makes it not worth living anymore. After all that we did to make this Village better, we, the elders, get no respect. Everyone is so busy, so fixed on their daily lives, that no one has the time or needs or wants to talk with an out of touch and boring old man.

No one even thinks to ask my for my advice or opinion for what would I know or what good ideas could I offer. No, no one at all, not even my own children or children's children, so here I sit alone on my porch, thinking about how and what it was, so many years ago.

Maybe, all that my old friends and I went through, was not worth the costs. Maybe we should have just given it all to that crazy Pugachev. Bleeding and dying, and all that horrible killing, for what? Apparently, for just nothing, nothing at all!

Nothing, except those horrible nightmares that plague me each and every night; where I again hear the screams of my friends as they are cut apart; where I face the memory of my own descent into becoming an animal with no soul just to survive... and the memory of the blood lust to kill and kill and kill. That is all I got for all my trouble, that, and most likely my ticket to eternal Hell.

Merciful GOD, you took my son *Wilhelm Philipp* before you took me. Why, if you in fact, are a merciful GOD, would you ever take a child before their parents? Why? I ask you again, Why? I need to know why!

No, there is never an answer, nothing but damned silence, and my own thoughts… I pray that my time for all this to end is near. Even eternal Hell would be better than this life, with this pain, that I now endure…

Maybe the LORD's blessing are the days that I remember nothing, those days that I get lost on my walks because I cannot remember the way back home, those days when I am again a young boy growing up and playing among the vines on the slopes below Löwenstein. Yes, those are the days I feel no regrets or pain.

Maybe the best I can hope for is that all my future days will be those where I fade into my long lost past, and am no longer aware of all the disappointments and pain that I endure today.

"LORD, I pray to you to be a merciful GOD and if this be so, let me live in the twilight of my long past until you finally call me to pay my dues in eternal Hell. Amen."

VATER FOLLOWS

◆JACOBINA KARL◆

Our Village of Balzer

My dear husband, *Christoph Karl*, passed on here in our Village of Balzer. He has followed his son and joined with him in Heaven, on this 4th day of January in the year of our LORD one thousand eight hundred eight (1808).

My *Christoph* is now free from the pain that has tortured his soul for these many years. May our LORD forgive him for the horrible sins he did, breaking our Ten Commandments. Truthfully, he had no choice but to sin here in this land, to protect our Village, our children and me.

I will pray for his soul each night, and look forward to my time soon when I will again walk with him, my dear son *Wilhelm Philipp*, and my mother and father in the realm of our LORD.

MUTTER PASSES

♠ANNA MARIA KARL SCHWINDT geb GRÜN♠

My Colony of Straub

My dear mother-in-law, *Frau Jacobina Maurer Karl*, has passed in the Village of Balzer, a little over two years after her *Christoph*, this 28th day of February in the year of our LORD one thousand eight hundred ten (1810).

We were all there at her side as her time drew near. She did not suffer, but went quietly with a smile on her face as if she had already found her departed loved ones, her *Christoph*, our *Wilhelm*, and her parents.

REMBERING

♠LAUDEMA CHRISTIANA MAURER♠

Heilbronn, Kingdom of Württemburg, Deutschland

It has now been fifty years, year of our LORD 1814, since that day when I last saw sister *Jacobina* and her husband *Christoph*. I am the only one left here, and I am quickly approaching my end. My husband is long gone, as our some of my children. I have outlived many of them.

My grandchildren are many, but they have no memory of *Jacobina* and *Christoph*. To them, *Jacobina* and *Christoph* are just faceless people in old stories that *Oma* tells over and over.

Bless all wherever they may be on this earth or in Heaven. Bless all our children and our children's children for eternity.

20 UNIONS

◆ ANNA MARIA KARL SCHWINDT geb GRÜN ◆

My Colony of Straub

It has been a time of celebration in our family with many marriages and births. My eldest son, *Johann Heinrich Karle*, my man of our house, married *Catharina Elisabeth Kukkus,* in our Lutheran Kirche in the year of our LORD one thousand eight hundred twenty (1820).

My second son, *Johann Conrad Karle*, married *Catharina Margaretha Becker* in our Lutheran Kirche in the year of our LORD one thousand eight hundred twenty two (1822).

My youngest son, *Johann Michael Karle*, married *Susanna Charlotte Ida Michel* in our Lutheran Kirche in the year of our LORD one thousand eight hundred twenty four (1824).

Join me as I pray, "May our LORD be merciful and see fit to bless their unions with the bounty of many healthy children. May their children, and their children's children, also have the bounty of many, many healthy children. Amen."

A DAUGHTER

◆SUSANNA CHARLOTTE KARLE geb MICHEL◆

Straub, Samara, Russland

I have given my husband, *Johann Michael Karle*, a daughter born on this 8th of May in the year of our LORD one thousand eight hundred twenty five (1825).

I am thankful for the birth of our healthy new daughter, but wish that I had first given my husband a son to carry on the *Karle* name. Our daughter is *Maria Margaretha Karle*, named after her father's mother and her sister. Thanks to our LORD for his blessing of this beautiful baby girl.

DAUGHTER TWO!

◆SUSANNA CHARLOTTE KARLE geb MICHEL◆

Straub, Samara, Russland

I have given my husband, *Johann Michael Karle*, a second daughter born on this 6th of January in the year of our LORD one thousand eight hundred twenty seven (1827).

I am again thankful for the birth of our healthy new daughter, but still wish that I had given my husband a son to carry on the *Karle* name. Our second daughter is

Catharina Elisabeth Karle, named after my mother. Thanks to our LORD for his blessing!

GROSSMUTTER

♠ANNA MARIA KARL SCHWINDT geb GRÜN♠

My Colony of Straub

Ja, I am Großmutter (Grandmother) of the many young children born into our family. My sons and daughters, as parents, are responsible for what their kinder do, both good and bad, along with reward and punishment. I and the other Großmütter devote our time and attention to the souls of our kinder.

We have the difficult task of teaching and tutoring them in our ways and customs and traditions so that they will be able to pass them on to their children. My work seems to never end as my children keep having more children for me to teach, but I would have it no other way, and I do cherish them all.

DAUGHTER THREE!

♠SUSANNA CHARLOTTE KARLE geb MICHEL♠

Straub, Samara, Russland

I have given my husband, *Johann Michael Karle*, a third daughter born on this 23rd of August in the year of our LORD one thousand eight hundred twenty-nine (1829).

I remain thankful for the birth of another healthy new daughter, but so wish that I had given my husband a son to carry on the *Karle* name. Our third daughter is

Catharina Margaretha Karle, named after my mother. Thanks to our LORD for his blessing!

DAUGHTER FOUR!

✦SUSANNA CHARLOTTE KARLE geb MICHEL✦

Straub, Samara, Russland

Ja, I have given my husband, *Johann Michael Karle*, a fourth daughter born on this 25th of April in the year of our LORD one thousand eight hundred thirty one (1831).

I remain thankful for the birth of another healthy new daughter. I will continue to try to give my husband a son to carry on the *Karle* name.

Our fourth daughter is *Maria Catharina Karle*, named after our mothers. Thanks to our LORD for his blessing!

A SON!!!

✦SUSANNA CHARLOTTE KARLE geb MICHEL✦

Straub, Samara, Russland

Finally, I have given my husband, *Johann Michael Karle*, a son born on this 12th of November in the year of our LORD one thousand eight hundred thirty two (1832).

My husband, who was always happy with each child I have brought, is even more overjoyed that he now has a son to carry on his family name of *Karle*. Our family will also continue to prosper with a strong boy to help us tame the land and produce much food. Our son is *Johann Conrad Karle*, named after my father. Thanks be to our LORD for this great and wonderful blessing!

SCHULE

♦MARIA MARGARETHA KARLE♦

Straub

Guten Tag, this beautiful day of May 8, 1833. I am *Maria Margaretha Karle*. *Maria* is my Christian name. My given name is *Margaretha*, everybody else calls me just that, and you can to! Today is my birthday and I am eight years old. You may give me a birthday gift.

My father is *Herr Karle* and my mother is *Frau Charlotte*, and I am their eldest daughter! I have three sisters, one brother, and one baby brother. *Oma Maria* is my Großmutter. I have many cousins living all around us her in Straub, and in nearby Warenburg.

I live here in Straub. I like living here. I like playing here. I do not like to go to schule (school) here. At schule, they are strict and mean, and have all sorts of rules that I must follow: not fun rules, but hard rules! And they punish you if you break the rules, no not me, mainly the boys.

The worst is that I have to go to schule every day. Even on the Sunday, I must go to Katechisation (religious instruction). I would rather play outside than be inside that schule room all day. I am not the only one that must go to schule. Many other girls also go, and then there are the boys, too. I like the other girls, but not the boys.

Our teacher is also the Pastor who speaks to us from the front of the Kirche every Sunday. He is no fun and frowns at us, and is always talking about being bad and sinning, and how GOD punishes us if we lie, cheat or steal, and some other things that I do not remember.

I should remember them as I had to repeat them many times in schule, but I do not. I wanted to ask our teacher how he knew GOD would punish us for lying, cheating and stealing. Maybe it was that GOD had already punished him for doing those things. I wanted to ask, but I was too afraid.

Very afraid, as he has taken the leather strap to some of the boys when they were bad, and they cried. I am afraid of the strap. Those boys were bad and earned the strap, but I will never earn it, as I am always very good.

Anyway, I have to go to school for a few more years until I am older. Then, I will be free from this boring schule and those horrible bad boys that sometimes chase me around, and be able to stay home and have fun working with my mother on all the household chores, or maybe help *Oma Maria*. That will be so much fun!

I dream about that time. It will be even better because my younger sisters and my brothers will still have to go to schule, and I will not. That is all I have to say, but maybe we might sit and talk again sometime. Auf Wiedersehen!

A SECOND SON!

♦SUSANNA CHARLOTTE KARLE geb MICHEL♦

Straub, Samara, Russland

I have given my husband, *Johann Michael Karle*, a second son born on this 16th of September in the year of our LORD one thousand eight hundred thirty four (1834). Our family will continue to prosper with even another strong boy to help us tame the land and produce much food. Our second son is *Johannes Karle*, named after his father. Thanks to our LORD for his blessing!

1834 COUNTING

♠JOHANN MICHAEL KARLE♠

Straub, Samara, Russland

This is the year of our LORD one thousand eight hundred thirty four (1834) and is the time of the Census of the Colonies. A group of Official Agents is traveling from Colony to Colony, and investigating and questioning everyone and everything.

They counted our families and all our individual possessions including how many homes and buildings, how many animals and what kind, how many tools we owned, how many desyatines we farmed, what crops we grew and what their yield was. All this they put in the Official books.

I never learned the results of the count, except that Straub had grown to now having five hundred ninety-four people. We, my wife and I, of course had done our best to add to the population by bringing our six into this world.

DAUGHTER FIVE

♠SUSANNA CHARLOTTE KARLE geb MICHEL♠

Straub, Samara, Russland

I have given my husband, *Johann Michael Karle*, a fifth daughter born on this 14th of February in the year of our LORD one thousand eight hundred thirty-six (1836).

I am so very thankful for the birth another healthy new daughter. We named her *Anna Margaretha Karle*. Thanks to our LORD for this blessing.

DAUGHTER SIX!

♠SUSANNA CHARLOTTE KARLE geb MICHEL♠

Straub, Samara, Russland

I have given my husband, *Johann Michael Karle*, another daughter, our sixth, born on this 24th of December in the year of our LORD one thousand eight hundred thirty-seven (1837).

I am so very thankful for the birth another healthy new daughter. We named her *Christina Elisabeth Karle*. Thanks to our LORD for more blessings.

DAUGHTER SEVEN!

♠SUSANNA CHARLOTTE KARLE geb MICHEL♠

Straub, Samara, Russland

I have given my husband, *Johann Michael Karle*, another daughter, now our seventh, born on this 16th of July in the year of our LORD one thousand eight hundred thirty-nine (1839).

I am so very thankful for the birth another healthy new daughter. Our seventh daughter is *Maria Elisabeth Karle*. Thanks to our LORD for his blessing!

THIRD SON!

♠SUSANNA CHARLOTTE KARLE geb MICHEL♠

Straub, Samara, Russland

I have given my husband, *Johann Michael Karle*, a third son born on this 8th of February in the year of our LORD one thousand eight hundred forty-three (1843). Our family will continue to prosper with a third strong boy to help us tame the land and produce much food. Our third son is *Johann Michael Karle*, named after his father. Thanks to our LORD!

FOURTH SON!

♠SUSANNA CHARLOTTE KARLE geb MICHEL♠

Straub, Samara, Russland

I have given my husband, *Johann Michael Karle*, a fourth son born on this 20th of May in the year of our LORD one thousand eight hundred forty-four (1844). Another son, with this fourth son our family will continue to prosper with another strong boy to join his three brothers and father to help us tame the land and produce much food. Our fourth son is *Johann Nicholaus Karle*. Thanks to the LORD.

DAUGHTER EIGHT!

♠SUSANNA CHARLOTTE KARLE geb MICHEL♠

Straub, Samara, Russland

I have given my husband, *Johann Michael Karle*, an eighth daughter born on this 3rd of November in the year of our LORD one thousand eight hundred forty-six (1846).

I am thankful for the birth an eighth daughter. Our eighth daughter is *Anna Katherina Karle*.

Thanks to our LORD for his special blessing! However, our LORD may choose to bless some other needy couple at any time. Our family is large enough, and I am tired.

21   1850

♠JOHANNES KARLE♠

Straub, Samara, Russland

I am *Johannes Karle*, the second son of *Herr Johann Michael* and *Frau Susanna Charlotte Michel Karle*. This is the year of our LORD one thousand eight hundred fifty (1850) and it is again the time of the Census of the Colonies.

A group of Official Agents traveled from Colony to Colony, and counted our families and all our individual possessions including how many homes and buildings, how many animals, how many tools we owned, how many desyatines we farmed, and what crops we grew.

All this they recorded in their many books. While our family had grown to fourteen, our Straub had grown to one thousand people with four hundred eighty-five men and sons, and five hundred fifteen women and daughters.

WEDDINGS

♦SUSANNA CHARLOTTE KARLE geb MICHEL♦

Straub, Samara, Russland

The year of our LORD one thousand eight hundred fifty-four (1854) was a good year for weddings in our family here in Straub.

Our second son, *Johannes Karle*, married *Christina Elisabeth Werner*, daughter of *Herr Johann Philipp* and *Frau Elizabeth Werner*, in our Lutheran Kirche. Our fifth daughter, *Anna Margaretha Karle*, married and became wife to *Herr Heinrich Philipp Adam Andreas*, son of *Herr Johann Christoph* and *Frau Christina Barbara Andreas*, in our Lutheran Kirche.

Join with me as I pray, "May our LORD be merciful and see fit to bless their unions with the bounty of as many healthy children as we were blessed with. Amen."

1857 COUNTING

♦JOHANNES KARLE♦

Straub, Samara, Russland

An unexpected census of the Colonies in the year of our LORD one thousand eight hundred fifty-seven (1857); we do not know why. Straub has continued to prosper and done well these years, and has continued to grow to a village population to over one thousand two hundred fifty souls.

FIRST SON!

♠ CHRISTINA ELISABETH KARLE geb WERNER ♠

Straub, Samara, Russland

I have given my husband, *Johannes Karle*, a son born on this 4th of December in the year of our LORD, 1855. Here is a son to carry on the *Karle* name. I have dreamed of a large family, and I hope that this is my first of many sons and daughters that I can provide my husband. Our son is *Johann Conrad Karle*; we call him *Conrad.* Thanks to our LORD for his blessing!

SECOND SON!

♠ CHRISTINA ELISABETH KARLE geb WERNER ♠

Straub, Samara, Russland

I have given my husband, *Johannes Karle*, a second son born on this 29th of March in the year of our LORD, 1858. We now have another son to make true my dream of a large family. Our son is *Johann Michael Karle*; we will call him *Michael.* Thanks to our LORD for his blessing!

A DAUGHTER

♠ CHRISTINA ELISABETH KARLE geb WERNER ♠

Straub, Samara, Russland

I have given my husband, *Johannes Karle*, a daughter born on this 31st of October in the year of our

LORD, 1860. I am thankful for our new daughter, *Maria Christina Karle*. Thanks to our LORD!

DAUGHTER TWO

♠CHRISTINA ELISABETH KARLE geb WERNER♠

Straub, Samara, Russland

I have given my husband, *Johannes Karle*, a second daughter born on this 22nd of February in the year of our LORD, 1863. I am again thankful for our new daughter, *Catharina Margaretha Karle*. Thanks to our LORD!

DAUGHTER THREE

♠CHRISTINA ELISABETH KARLE geb WERNER♠

Straub, Samara, Russland

I have given my husband, *Johannes Karle*, a third daughter born on this 1st of October in the year of our LORD, 1865. I am again thankful for our new daughter, *Christina Elisabeth Karle*. Thanks to our LORD for his generous blessing!

DAUGHTER FOUR

♠CHRISTINA ELISABETH KARLE geb WERNER♠

Straub, Samara, Russland

I have given my husband, *Johannes Karle*, a fourth daughter born on this 24th of February in the year of our LORD, 1869. I am again thankful for our new daughter,

Catharine Elisabeth Karle. Thanks to our LORD for his blessing!

THIRD SON!

♦CHRISTINA ELISABETH KARLE geb WERNER♦

Straub, Samara, Russland

I have given my husband, *Johannes Karle*, a third son born on this 21st of December 1871. My dream of a large family has come true.

This third son of ours is *Johann August Karle*; we will call him *August*. Thanks to our LORD!

DAUGHTER FIVE!

♦CHRISTINA ELISABETH KARLE geb WERNER♦

Straub, Samara, Russland

I have given my husband, *Johannes Karle*, a fifth daughter born on this 1st of September 1875. I am thankful for our new daughter, *Catharine Karle*.

Thanks to our LORD for all his blessings, however, I now have my large family, and I am tired. Our LORD may bless some other woman if he so chooses…

22   FOUL WINDS

◆JOHANNES KARLE◆

Straub, Samara, Russland

It is late October 1875. While we in the Colonies have prospered, Russland has not. As each year goes by, more and more regulations and policies come to us from far away Moscow.

My father, *Johann Michael,* just yesterday said to me, "For as long as I can remember, no one from Moscow paid much attention to us as long as we did not make trouble. Now it seems that has all changed, and not for our better."

I listened intently as my father described how it used to be, and, by his words, it did seem to be changing for the worse. Only a few years back in 1867, we were all told of a "Colonial Statute" that Moscow directed.

Strange men from outside our Colonies appeared with the titles of "Sheriffs and Deputies" enforcing new work rules and enforcing limits on how extravagant our funerals, weddings, and baptisms could be. Those that questioned these new "Sheriffs and Deputies" were themselves immediately questioned, and risked losing their property and imprisonment.

Yes, I answered my father, "These changes are not for our better."

Father went on, "Remember back four years ago, when Moscow ended our original right to self-govern our Colonies. The Tsarina granted our ancestors that right when they first came to Russland, and now it taken away. I say again, this is not for our better."

I agreed with everything he was saying, and replied, "Father, you are right, but what can we do? Without waiting for his answer, I said, "Nothing, nothing at all." He nodded in agreement.

An even worse change than taking away our right to govern ourselves had an effect on many of our lives. The Russische Army needed fresh recruits to replace all their soldiers dying in their many conflicts around country, and so, the young men of the Colonies were now subject to mandatory military service of six years active duty beginning at age nineteen. Not all young men, but most, as first-born sons were exempt.

Almost as soon as we heard of this new obligation, most of the men of Straub attended a secret meeting to discuss what to do. From everyone there we heard the same thing, "Our families have never had to serve in the Russische Army. It is not fair! We will not join! We will never fight for Russland!"

And, it was not just the young men that were upset, but all the men and women were disgusted with Moscow. But what could we do against the mighty Tsar? Nothing, nothing at all. We could only wait until they came to take us.

A UNION

♦CHRISTINA ELISABETH KARLE geb WERNER♦

Straub, Samara, Russland

In spite of all the bad news and bad laws from Moscow, for most of us, our lives here in Straub still move on. For our family, we have another happy event, a wedding.

Our second-born, but now eldest son now, *Michael*, has found a woman to love and has asked for her hand. Her name is *Christina Elisabeth Andreas*; we call her *Lisget*. She is the daughter of *Herr Heinrich Philipp Andreas* and *Frau Anna Margaretha Karle*, who is my husband's younger sister.

Michael and *Lisget* married in our Lutheran Kirche this year of 1879. Join me as I pray, "May our LORD be merciful and see fit to bless the union of our *Michael* and *Lisget* with the bounty of as many healthy children as we were blessed with. Amen."

LEAVE?

♦JOHANNES KARLE♦

Straub, Samara, Russland

As our lives here in the Colonies slowly worsened day-by-day, wild rumors of free land in a country far away, called America, spread throughout all the Colonies, including here in Straub. Some talked of running and leaving all we built here, some talked of staying and fighting to the very end, and some just hid in their homes like scared puppies hoping that all this would just go away. The teamwork, the foundation and very strength that made the Colonies prosper thru all the earlier hard times, was beginning to crack and crumble under Moscow's unrelenting pressure.

Thank the LORD that my father, *Johann Michael Karle,* passed away on 20 January 1879, and that my mother had passed on some years earlier. Luckily, they did not live to see this; it would have broken their hearts.

We frequently heard rumors of horrific treatment and severe punishment by the Russische Army on our young men forced to serve. Tales that our sons were always sent in first to fight and soften up the enemy because they were only Wolgadeutsche, and therefore better for them to die than real Russischer soldiers. No surprise, this did not sit well with anyone here.

At fifty-two years old, I was probably too old for the Russische Army to want. My eldest living and by the law, first-born son *Michael,* was exempt from this military service, but *August,* my younger son was moving toward the conscription age. I did not want him to serve the Russische Army ever in a way.

Late one night, I met secretly with both my sons while everyone else slept. No one, including their mother or *Michael's* wife, would know of what we said here tonight.

I spoke first, "My sons, I only see that we have two choices, and they are to accept these harsh treatments and new rules every day, or we leave this land just as our ancestors left their homelands when they were oppressed over a century ago. If we stay, *August* most likely will be taken by the Army, and if the rumors be true, will die in some battle in a foreign land. I will not and cannot accept that. The only choice I see is to take our families and leave. What say you?'

Both my sons were silent for a while. Finally, eldest son *Michael* spoke his mind, "Father, I do not want to leave here. Everything we know is here, but to allow the Russen to take August away… No, I could not live knowing that he was suffering and maybe dying, while I was here safe and enjoying life. Yet, where would we go, and how would we do it in secret so that the Army does not catch my brother?"

I replied, "It will be difficult and risky, we may all be caught. It will take money to make it happen, and will take careful planning and some time. As for where, I hear of a place called America where land is free and one can live as they choose. That is where we would go. And my younger son, this most affects you, what say you?"

Younger son *August* answered, "I am not afraid to serve in the Russische Army! If I must be a Russischer soldier so that all of you can be safe, then it is my duty to become one. I understand that neither of you want me to serve the Russen, nor do I want to, but I will if I must. Running away never solves anything, and so my answer is, I will serve in the Russische Army!"

I thought to myself, such a brash and foolish young man willing to give up his most valuable possession, his life, for nothing, nothing at all but pride and duty. I should be proud of him, but this is too important.

I said to him, "*August*, do not be a young fool! We are not running away, as our honored ancestors did not run away from their homeland. We, like them, are searching for a better place for us and all our descendants to live their lives. You have no duty to the Russische Army; we are Deutsch, we will always be Deutsch, and we will never be Russen! It may be that you are still too young to think on this clearly, so as your father, I will make the decision for you! Understand this *August*, I do not take your choice away lightly, but I cannot and will not stand by and let you make this wrong, and most likely fatal, decision. We go, and we go soon!"

August frowned at my words, and looked as if he would argue. After a moment though, he relaxed and looked to calm down. I could tell he was weighing each of my words and thinking about all I had said.

Finally, he replied, "Father, I do not know if you and my brother are right. I do not know if I share your views on whether I have a duty to go and serve in the Russische Army. I am not sure what it is to be Deutsch, as all I know is this Russland. I am not even sure where our homeland, this Deutschland is. If it were only my choice, then I would join the Army. But, you are my father, and I am your son. I must follow and support your decisions, and so I willingly agree and go with you and *Michael.* That question is now settled and we all agree. Now, we must make our plans, so how do we do this?"

"First we tell no one until the very last moment. *Michael,* you are the eldest son and as such are exempt from military service. However, you and your family will be the first to go and will get everything ready for us when we arrive later. We will pool all our money and send you off as soon as we can," I answered.

I continued, "*August*, you will not be conscription age for some years and will be safe till then. You and your family will go as soon your elder brother and his family is settled in America, and we have enough money to pay your passage. He will send back what money he can spare to help us get you out sooner. You must be away from here before you are nineteen. Once you are also settled with your brother, both of you will send what money you can spare to help get your mother and I to America."

"I will arrange and pay for everything. It will be some risk, but I will meet with the elders of our other *Karle* and *Rudolph* and *Andreas* families to discuss my concern. We owe our brothers, sister, and cousins that, but I will not reveal our exact plans to anyone as to when we will do all this."

"*Michael*, we must not raise any suspicion that anyone in our family wishes to leave here. You must slowly start sneaking your valuable property and possessions to your brother and I. You and your family will only be able to carry possessions in a sack with each of you, as we may have to provide the excuse that your family has only left for a short time to care for another sick family in a border Colony. This will give you enough time to clear the Russische territory. We will quietly sell off the possessions that you give us to raise the money for you to leave that much faster," I said.

Michael responded, "Father, my wife *Lisget* will ask why. If I do not provide a reasonable answer, she will still do as I say, but will become very suspicious. If she is worried and suspicious, she will discuss her worries with all the other women and may somehow discover our plans."

Quickly, I answered, "Yes, you are so right. We cannot have our women begin openly talking about this change. Tell *Lisget* that you need the money to cover "gambling" debts. Tell her you lost control and will never do it again, but that you must have money now. Tell her that you are sneaking it to your brother and me for us to quietly sell in order to save face and maintain your family's good reputation. This should keep her from saying anything to the other women for a while; she will not want to embarrass you. You will eventually have to tell *Lisget* the truth and swear her to secrecy at the very risk of imprisonment of her whole family. But not yet, as every day that we can maintain this secret is another day closer to getting you out."

"I will tell your mother exactly the same story about your "gambling" if she becomes suspicious. She too will keep this horrible information too herself as she will not want to sully our family name. Yes, she will be furious with us for not sharing our actual plans and for lying to her, but the risk of discovery by the Sheriff's is too great to allow us any other choice," I cautioned.

No one said anything. After some time for all to ponder, I asked, "Do we all still agree? Yes or no; let me hear it now!"

As if with one voice, we all vigorously said, "Yes!"

"Good, tomorrow I start the preparations. Now, quietly go to your homes and to your beds. Remember; tell no one of our plans. We must act and be as we always have been to not raise any suspicions," I cautioned.

Both nodded in agreement and quietly left. So it was decided, our *Karle* family would bravely march into the unknown to obtain a better future for our families, just as my great grandparents, *Christoph* and *Jacobina,* did over a century ago.

Tomorrow, I would meet with the elders of our other *Karle* and *Rudolph* and *Andreas* families one at a time to talk about my worries and concerns for all our young men. Enough for today, my last task before sleep is quietly slipping into bed without awakening my wife, and maybe raising her questions. I was successful, my wife never woke, and for the first night in many, I slept well.

The next day, I talked alone with each of the elders of our close families, and surprisingly discovered that each of them had come to the same choice. We all agreed that each elder would keep all of us generally informed, but would keep the exact details on who was leaving to themselves.

This secrecy provides some protection for the rest of the group in case any one family is found out. All agreed that secrecy is required, and the "gambling" story is most plausible. In fact, we set up a false gambling place to cover what we were doing. Our plans would move forward, both as separate families and as a whole group of families.

As the days and months passed, we did as we planned. *Michael* was right; our women became immediately suspicious and constantly questioned us until finally, and with much reluctance, we admitted to the disgraceful "gambling" and money problems in our family. As predicted, they were first shocked, and then disappointed in this bad behavior. Also, as I expected, they kept this problem to themselves for the sake of our family name.

As *Michael* secretly moved his valuables to us for sale, we secretly moved worthless substitutes back to his home. We sold much of what he brought us in the nearby colonies of Warenburg, Dinkel, Laub, and Jost. This avoided any suspicion in our Straub. Day by day, we gathered more money to pay for our plans.

Finally, at last, late one night I again met secretly with my sons and told them, "As for how much money for our plans, I was able to realize how much we need for each husband and wife. We need fifty rubles (twenty-five American dollars) for food, transportation, lodging, and maybe bribes to get one family out of Russland territory. We need another fifty rubles for boat or train to the countries of England, France, Belgium, or of course, Deutschland along with food and lodging. We will need two hundred fifty rubles (one hundred twenty-five American dollars) for a ship ticket across the Atlantic Ocean along with food. We will need one hundred fifty rubles (seventy-five American dollars) for the train ride to our new homes along with food, and we will need one hundred rubles to survive at your new village until you find work for money. All comes to around six hundred rubles per man or women, or twelve hundred rubles (six hundred American dollars) per couple, almost two year's earnings."

Both of my sons gasped and shook their heads, but I continued, "That is the bad news. The good news is that when we pooled our money we already had over six hundred rubles, and after selling off all we could without raising any questions, we raised another seven hundred rubles. Yes, we have enough to send off *Michael* and *Lisget*. It is time for them to prepare to leave."

Both sons let out a quiet, but enthusiastic, "Ja!"

I spoke directly to *Michael*, "Son, it is time for you to admit your lies and share our plans with *Lisget*, but only with your wife. This is very important; she must not tell anyone at all, even your children must think that you are all going on a short trip and will be coming back here soon. You must not change any of your normal habits so that you do not raise any suspicions. Prepare to leave within days. I will let you know how and when very soon."

I sighed deeply. This next was the hard part to explain to my sons. As a married man of over twenty years, I fully understood what was about to happen. I spoke again, "*Michael*, this will not be easy. You must be patient with your wife and show her much understanding and compassion. I will also tell your mother of our plans tonight. For a good reason we lied to both of them; but no matter what the reason is, good or bad, we did lie to them. They will be furious with us for not talking this over with them. They will be hurt because we did not trust them. Be ready for those first responses; there is nothing you can do to prevent them. And they must get angry and hurt, for if they become silent and quiet, then the wounds we have caused will never heal. But with our truth, patience and some time, they will forgive us and support this decision to move. We must be strong men and calmly accept punishment for the wrong we have done. It will not be easy, and I do not look forward to the wrath of your mother. Her tongue is a mighty and hurtful weapon at times. *August* is the lucky one tonight, as he has no wife to admit our plans to."

Looking at both my sons, I asked, "Are we all agreed to do this? Yes or no; let me hear it now."

Like before, as if with one voice, we all emphatically said, "Ja!"

"Sons, may GOD go with each of us tonight!"

THE TRUTH

◆MICHAEL KARLE◆

Straub on the Volga, Samara Province, Russland

That night I told my *Lisget* the truth. As predicted, she was upset and angry and hurt, more so than I had ever seen her before tonight. My father was so right.

"Husband, what are you saying? Are you telling me that you lied to me about gambling and owing money? What nonsense is this about us moving from here in a few days? I am furious that you did not tell me the truth and you obviously do not trust me. What other things have you not told me?" yelled *Lisget*.

Not waiting for any words from me, and between sobbing and yelling, she managed to continue, "So you and your father and brother have decided this is best for all of us without asking any of the women. You are the men of the family and we will always follow, but we may not be happy about it and you and the others will have to live with our wrath and unhappiness! Tell me now the details of who, why, when, where and how this will all take place."

I gently answered and told her all I knew, and cautioned her about secrecy. That was a stupid mistake.

Warning her about the need for secrecy made her even angrier, and *Lisget* yelled back, "Damn you, *Michael*! Do not treat me like a stupid child. I am your wife and I understand what is at risk here. You will promise to be completely honest with me from this moment on! Swear to me now on our Marriage Oath."

I quickly and solemnly answered, "*Lisget*, I so swear."

Content with my reply, she slowly calmed down. She sat silent for what seemed hours, but was probably only many moments. Finally she again spoke, this time softly with a slight tremble in her voice, "Husband, I am hesitant to leave my life here; I am afraid of what we might find out there in the strange new lands."

I went to her, held her tight, and told her, "We will be fine. We will, as our great-great grandparents *Christoph* and *Jacobina,* did over a century ago. We will both survive and prosper in the new lands. We must be as strong as they were so long ago as they left their homeland, as there is nothing good in our future here."

Holding tightly to me, *Lisget* softly replied, "Yes, I know you are right. There is nothing left here for us; We must be strong, and we must go."

◆JOHANNES KARLE◆

Straub, Samara, Russland

That night I told their mother and my wife, my *Christina Elisabeth*, the truth. Hell hath no fury like an angry wife! This very night in this *Karle* home, Hell raged without any limits! I had known it would be bad, but I misjudged the passion of her feelings. I sincerely hoped that son *Michael* was doing better in his *Karle* home, next door. Truly, my son *August* is the lucky one tonight with no wife.

Visibly upset, but not yelling, she sternly rebuked me, "*Johannes*, I am not angry for your lies. I am not silly enough to think you always tell me the truth! I know you have lied to me before and I accept that weakness in you. I am distressed for your lack of trust in me, and for not discussing this with me. You know from our long past, that things work out better for us when we both find the best answer to our problems. Of course, I will support your decision, and I forgive you for all this as you only had our best interests in mind. But, and take heed, I am deeply hurt and will be so for some time. Now tell me all that you and my sons have planned."

I told her all.

She was silent for a time, and then said, "It is a good plan. You have made many wise decisions. How soon will *Michael* and *Lisget* leave?"

"Soon, very soon," I quickly replied.

She sighed, and then spoke, "I will meet secretly with *Lisget* early tomorrow. She may not accept this news as well as me. Understanding, patience, and forgiveness of husbands are things learned only after many, many years of marriage."

All I could say was, "Thank you, my wife."

She frowned again, and quickly replied, "*Johannes*, you are so welcome, and by the way, you will be sleeping somewhere else other than our bed, until I no longer feel the hurt of your lies and distrust."

It would be cold nights on the floor for me in this *Karle* home for a while…

23   LEAVING

♦MICHAEL KARLE♦

Straub on the Volga, Samara Province, Russland

The best-laid plans are often wrong and must change with time, and so it was with us. Almost at the last day, our "secret" plans changed. Father found out that no one, not the Army, not the Sheriffs, really cared if the first-born son of a family left. They were only concerned with where all the other sons were.

Instead of leaving in the dead of night, we boarded a wagon during the light of day for the trip to Saratov. All our close friends, my brother, *Lisget's* family, and my parents crowded around us to give their blessing and say their good-byes. There was much crying and hugging among the women, and joking and backslapping among the men.

Lisget's father, *Herr Johan Peter Steitz*, blessed us, "Children, we will all miss you so, but remember that you must let us know where you settle, for if we can, we will all join you there. May GOD be with you."

My father spoke last to us, "Travel safe and the LORD keep you both safe. Find us a good place for our new homes. Your brother, *August,* will join you first. Remember, he must leave before his nineteenth birthday or we will lose him to the Russische Army. Mother and I will join you after that. We will all be together again soon."

As we rode the wagon out of Straub for the last time on that 30th day of October 1887, my dear *Lisget* was sobbing. Our friends all continued to wave good-bye until we could see them no more.

Between sobs, *Lisget* pulled close to me and asked, "Are we doing best for us by moving?"

I held her tightly in my arms, and gently replied, "Yes, my love. This is all for the best. Trust me and you will see."

I was not that certain we were making the best choice, but I could never let her know that. As the *Karle* of our family, I must be strong enough for the two of us.

The distance to Saratov was about fifty versts (about seventy-five miles) as the road turned. We would cross the Volga, go west, and then turn north back toward Saratov. It would take four days.

To us, the city of Saratov was both amazing and frightening. It was so much bigger than anything we ever saw before. *Lisget* tightly clamped on to my arm, so tightly that I worried she might cut off the blood.

After wandering around confused and lost for some hours, we at last found the railroad station, and purchased our tickets taking us all the way to America from an Official Agent a Bremen, Deutschland Travel Agency. Our tickets cost us seven hundred rubles (three hundred fifty America dollars), only leaving us another seven hundred rubles for everything else. I hoped my father was right and that it would be enough to get us safely to our new land. Where that was, I had no idea, yet.

The train was crowded, but we finally found two seats and squeezed into them. This was fine for *Lisget,* as she was trembling, probably as much from the excitement as the fear.

We rode the rails west through the cities of Smolensk and Vitebsk and St. Petersburg, and then south across the border to the port city of Libau, Latvia. By this time, *Lisget* was no longer fearful and afraid. Now, she acted like a wild-eyed child wanting to see and watch everything and everyone.

Full of comments and questions about everything, she whispered, "*Michael,* see how strangely that man dresses. *Michael,* do you think she is prettier than I am? *Michael,* how much longer will we be riding the train? *Michael,* where are we going after we get there? *Michael,* the land here is so is different from our old home. *Michael,* are you still sure that we have done the right thing by leaving our Straub?"

As soon as I answered one question, she would whisper out another. It was maddening, but I must say that it did help pass the time.

On arrival in Libau, we joined up with others with tickets like ours. *Herr Jacob Bretzer* and his family, *Herr Friedrich Bopp* and his family, and *Herr Jacob Bauer* and his family, were all there waiting with us.

Another Official Agent of the Travel Agency took our group to the waterfront to board a ship. We would sail on this ship south-west across the sea to Bremen, Deutschland. There we would board a larger ship for the Atlantic Ocean voyage to America. Here, they also told us that no one could enter America if they showed signs of a sickness called trachoma or other eye diseases, or with a hair disease. By our LORDs grace, as far as we knew, no one on our groups had either.

As we began to board our ship, *Lisget* became frightened of all the water as far as she could see, and just would not get on. After trying to reason with her and convince her, I finally just picked her up and carried her on. Her objecting screams and angry words just made all the other passengers laugh.

Once she calmed down, my *Lisget* was terribly embarrassed. *Frau Bopp*, not at all frightened by the water or ship, came over and offered comforting conversation and reassurance, and soon my *Lisget* was back to her normal happy self.

Lisget remained happy, at least for a while, until a few hours after our ship left the port. The large waves rocking the ship, first this way and then that way, made us both sick as well as many others. We spent much of our time leaning over the ships rail and retching. As best we could, eventually we slumped down right where we were and just held on to each other. We spent that first night on deck feeding the fish all we had eaten. Thankfully, the next morning it was calmer and we were much better.

Our next stop was the Port of Bremen, in our Deutschland. Some also called this place 'Bremerhaven' but no one could ever tell me why. I was glad we had stopped here, as this was my very first time being a Deutscher in my

Deutschland. We stayed in billets like the ones in Libau for a few days until our ship, the America, that would carry us to New York City in America, was ready to leave.

From Bremerhaven, we sailed out across the Atlantic Ocean. For over a week, all we could see on all sides was water and more water. Usually it was fairly calm, but once in a while it became like the North and Baltic Seas with large waves crashing against the ship and rocking it back and forth.

We soon learned that it was not a pleasant experience to endure a long ocean voyage. The trip seemed to take forever. We could do nothing, but walk the decks around and around, or just sit and wait to get to somewhere else.

From all we had heard back in Straub, we had planned to try our luck in a place called the Lincoln of Nebraska. However, while on the voyage we heard the story of others that recently went farther west to a place called Fresno in the California. Good land was rumored to be cheap, the climate was mild, and the railroad paid well for workers to lay track. I was a farmer, but if paid enough, I would lay track, whatever that was.

We talked about where to go with the *Bretzer*, *Bopp*, and *Bauer* families, and others. At first, it was just a way to pass the time, nothing more than idle talk when we had nothing else to do. At some point, this Fresno place began to sound better than the Lincoln place did, and by the time we approached the coast of America, our family, the *Bopp* family, the *Bauer* family, and the *Bretzer* family decided to the Fresno we would go.

Early the next morning, we could see land. Soon, almost everyone was on deck to see for themselves. As we sailed into a large bay, our excitement quickly rose. Exactly where we were or when we would get there, no one had any idea. We all knew that soon we would be in America, as our ship turned and headed north to towards the mouth of a much smaller bay. Two small boats approached; they hooked onto our ship with long ropes and helped guide us up the narrow water.

There I saw a large green statue of a woman standing and holding a torch. They told us that it was the Statue of Liberty welcoming all of us to America. I am not sure why anyone would build a large green statue holding a torch to welcome us, but it was a nice gesture. These people of America must be nice, but also must be strange.

After a while, our ship stopped and dropped its anchors. Every one began pushing and shoving with many, many hundreds of people all wanting to get off the ship as soon as they could, to all step on their new land. I held tightly on to *Lisget*; I was afraid the jostling of the crowd might pull her away from me.

I looked around at the others, like us, that had made the voyage and were patiently waiting. Many were too excited to stand still and were constantly moving and shifting, the colors of their clothes creating an always-changing display.

Some stood quietly at the rail looking out at the strange new horizon desperately looking for anything familiar and in awe of the sheer size of the city. Worried and afraid, they wondered what all this will bring, praying to GOD that it will be a blessing, and not the other. Yet, a few others stood or sat, appearing to care not one way or another, no excitement, no expression, confident they could handle anything that comes, as if they were above all the chaos surrounding them.

Me... I was all those things; awed, wondering and scared, but confident that I will conquer any trial or challenge.

Tired of being on the road, the train, or one ship after another, just wanting it to be over, the anxious crowd surged toward where they thought the first exit would be.

The ship's crew had been through this many times before, and knew just what to do. They knew that if they let the people all leave at one time, pushing and shoving as if leaving a building on fire, that someone would be hurt, and most likely, it would be children or the women. They knew that it is not that the crowd wanted anyone hurt; but that none was aware of the danger they might put others in.

The ship's crew and officials slowly began to separate the men from the women and children, to let the latter get off first. This set off a frantic search for all the excited children that were everywhere. Mothers frantically searched for their young, as the children being children, earnestly made it a game and hid. Tempers flared as mothers ended the game with rebukes and well-placed spanks to their bottoms, setting off a new chorus of the sound not of music, but of loud crying. Seeing the strain and stress on the parent's faces, even though *Lisget* and I always wanted a child, at this very moment I was grateful that we did not have one, or two, or three!

The women and children slowly moved onto the tender boat for transport over the last small distance over the water. We could see them as they walked down the gangplank off the tender to land with great bundles of all they possessed balanced on their heads with their babies clutched tightly in their arms, and with the younger children hanging on for their very lives to their mother's skirts. Closely following their mothers were the older children stumbling, carrying, dragging, pushing, and sometimes all four at the same time, more of those valuable possessions that have come so far with each family. Finally triumphant in making it to the land with all they had, they collapsed in small groups waiting for their men to rejoin them.

It was my *Lisget's* turn, but she and the other women in our group did not want to leave us for fear that they would never find us again among the crowds. Leave us they did, and within an hour on this 30th day of November 1887, we were all back together on the land of our America, waiting again in line at what someone called, the Castle Garden's Immigration Building.

One family at a time, we slowly moved up the corridor inside the building. Our boxes and baggage, almost all of our personal possessions, were taken away to be inspected and stored somewhere else. More than a few violently resisted giving up their valuables, but luckily, the officials had been all through this many times before and always had someone there that could speak the different languages and explain what was going on.

An Official came to our larger group and explained in both Russ and Deutscher, "Listen carefully! You will each be given two brass tickets marked with the same letter of the English alphabet from A to F and with the same number from 1 to 600. One you will attach on your baggage, the other you will keep safe on you so that you can reclaim your baggage later after you are processed. We will take your now identified and ticketed baggage to our protected baggage room. This room has six bins, marked with the letters A, B, C, D, E, F, and each bin has six hundred numbers so we will be able to find and give you back your own baggage. After processing and your approval to leave, when you show your ticket to us, our baggage man at once goes to the bin indicated by the letter and number on your ticket, and returns your baggage to you. Lose your brass ticket or have no brass ticket to show, you have no baggage that you can pick-up. Do not let anyone steal your brass ticket! Keep it safe and close, as you do with your wives and children!"

Baggage Inspection

Much laughter erupted at his last words, but his point was taken and everyone tightly clenched their brass tickets in their hands. With hands still clenched around the brass tickets, they guided us to an area of hundreds of seats and benches where we all waited to be registered, one family at a time. *Lisget* and I patiently waited, along with our larger group.

The men sat silent and serious, the women, including my *Lisget*, almost immediately began quietly chatting among themselves about all that had happened so far.

Our turn finally came, and a clerk sitting behind a desk carefully looked at us and our clothing, and then asked me,

"What is your full name?"

"Johann Michael Karle," I quickly answered.

"What is your place of birth?" he asked.

"Straub near Saratov, Russland," I replied.

"Where is your former place of residence?" he asked.

"Straub near Saratov, Russland," I replied.

"Where are you going?" he asked.

"Fresno in California," I answered.

Having written my information in a large book on the desk and apparently satisfied with my answers, he turned his attention to my *Lisget* and asked her the same questions.

She quickly answered in order of his questions:

"Christina Elisabeth Karle."

"Warenburg near Saratov, Russland."

"Straub near Saratov, Russland."

"Fresno in California."

Again satisfied, and having entered all in his big book, he motioned for us to move to the next area. With much relief, we quickly did so, and found ourselves in line waiting for medical inspection.

The examination was to discover if any sick had somehow passed the health authorities, and since we both had no sickness, they directed us into the main rotunda, a huge circular space with separate areas for English-speaking and Deutsch-speaking and Russisch-speaking peoples.

There our group settled down to patiently wait for whatever next they had planned for us.

Castle Gardens Rotunda

After some time, an Immigration Officer stood on a platform and announced, one language at a time that I did not understand, and finally in our Deutsch, "Your attention all. Those of you sitting in this room have passed the all our requirements and are now registered. You may turn in your brass tickets and pick-up your baggage now, or when you choose during daytime hours and you may leave when you choose. If you do not yet have anywhere to go or have your lodging reserved outside or are waiting to board a train for other cities, you may stay in this building under this roof for free for as long as you need to."

He continued, "If you need to purchase tickets on the railroads, official agents are ready to help you here in this building. They will help you with choosing your correct route, handling your baggage, and providing tickets to all parts of the United States and Canada, all without the risk of fraud or extortion. Money exchange into dollars is also available at government set exchange rates at the Bureau of Exchange in this building. Be warned, if you buy your tickets for travel or lodging, or exchange your money with someone outside Castle Gardens, you will be at risk of fraud or extortion. There are people out there that live off cheating new immigrants. Do all your business here in this building! Good luck!"

A crowd of men, including others and me from our group, moved quickly and swamped the railroad agents. Again, we had to patiently wait our turn, and by luck or the LORDs blessing, all in our group were able to get train tickets on the early tomorrow morning train for somewhere called the Chicago, then the Omaha, then the Sacramento, and finally into the Fresno. We triumphantly returned to our waiting and anxious families where we each gave them our good news.

By the time we purchased our train tickets and returned with the good news, it was late in the afternoon, almost early evening. Only one more night left, and we would be on the last leg of our long trip.

Many of the other immigrants had left for the local areas around New York City, and there was now some room to stretch out. At first glance, I thought that they seated us in no special order. My *Lisget* noticed that everyone around us was just like us: Russischer, Deutscher, and Russischer Deutscher. People from other countries were located in other areas of the big building.

We settled down for the night as best we could, the building lit up with gaslights providing a more cheerful mood. It was then that *Lisget* also noticed the two large coal fed iron stoves at each end of our area, each giving off considerable heat.

It was about that time that another Official came by. He gently suggested to all that the women and children move to one end near one stove and the men move to the opposite end near the other stove. He did not order anyone to move, but from his voice, we all understood that it was much more than a suggestion, and if not followed, would soon be an order.

Quickly, we all complied with his suggestion. I could still see *Lisget* only a short ways from me. She looked back and seeing me, waved as she was arranging her sleeping area.

I began to try and make my space comfortable for sleep, but was disturbed when my belly growled that it was very hungry. In all the excitement, we both had forgotten to eat. I looked around and saw there was a food area nearby.

Lisget must have been hungry too, for she waved to get my attention and motioned to me to meet her. Together we slowly made our way through all the people to the food. There they had water at no cost at all. They also had coffee, a roll, and cheese or butter for fifteen or twenty cents.

She whispered to me, "I know we do not want to spend our money, but I do so want to buy coffee and rolls for the celebration of our first night in America. I also have some food from our ship to eat."

I was now starving, and quickly agreed with her suggestion. We celebrated with our rolls and coffee and other food, and were able to quench the emptiness in our bellies.

After our celebration feast, and as late night drew near, we both returned to our allotted sleep areas. It was good to settle down, but it was like sleeping on a floor of hard wood boards, because that is exactly what we were doing. In honesty, the sleep on our ship was much better than this. I could tolerate this minor discomfort, as this was our only night here.

I noticed that two Official Watchmen roamed the room all night, making sure that all was safe and quiet under their watchful eyes. Trying to relax, trying not to be excited, I finally fell to sleep.

Early the next morning, we were all up and ready to go. No one slept well that night, and like me, probably counted every minute until the dawn of this first day of December.

Our train was to leave at what they said was 8:00 AM. Our whole group, not sure exactly when 8:00 AM was, made sure we were on the platform, ready to board a short time after sunrise. We did wait patiently for some time.

As all good things come to he who waits, our time came to board and we did so. Sitting down next to my *Lisget*, I gave her a quick kiss on the cheek, and whispered, "We are on our way now to our new lives. Thank the LORD for his blessing."

Lisget smiled, and then whispered back, "Yes, thank the LORD, and thank you for convincing me to come!"

A short time later, our train was racing up the tracks towards the Chicago, then the Omaha, and eventually the Sacramento.

We watched through the windows as the land changed from city to farmland to steppes to forests to high mountains to desert, and finally to the San Joaquin Valley farmlands.

The days and nights blurred into one another and flashed by, as did the miles of track. Our only reminder of passing time was the rhythmic clickety-clack of the wheels on the rails. It was the same as before, all we wanted to do was get off this train and be home!

On nights when the train stopped at a town depot, we slept inside the depot on the floor. Some nights when it did not stop, we slept in our seats. It was always uncomfortable, but we knew that every moment and every mile we traveled, we were that much closer to Fresno.

At Sacramento, we changed trains and then rode south through more San Joaquin Valley lands of wild grass to arrive in Fresno on 8 December 1887. It was just seventeen days before we celebrated our first Christmas in Fresno.

Sacramento Railroad Depot

Within days, I was able to find work as a farm laborer. There was so much good land ready here for farming. All the land needed was water, plowing and seeding, and you could sit back and watch your harvest grow.

My *Lisget,* also found paid work as a midwife helping the local doctor, Doctor Chester Rowell, deliver babies.

Fresno 1887

Now that we had arrived, our task now was to reunite with my brother and my parents, along with *Lisget's* mother and my aunt, *Anna Margaretha (Karle) Andreas.*

Even with us sending much money back home to bring brother *August* out, we were able to prosper and enjoy our lives here in Fresno. We soon learned there was much to enjoy here in Fresno that cost absolutely nothing.

AUGUST'S TIME

♦AUGUST KARLE♦

Straub on the Volga, Samara Province, Russland

My time to leave was fast approaching. We again made our secret plans for how and when I would leave, but this time we included my mother in our group.

Unlike the great crowd of friends that said their farewells to brother *Michael* and his wife, I would have to leave in the dead of night so that the Sheriffs and deputies could not catch me and turn me in to the Russische Army.

No one had cared if my eldest brother and his wife left, but no such military exemption existed for a younger son. As I was one of those, they would all be on the lookout for me.

Just after midnight on a moonless night, my mother and father and a few close trusted friends met in secret and prayed with me for GODs blessing, and wished me the best of luck. As usual, there was much crying and hugging among the women, and more joking and backslapping among the men.

My mother packed me food for the road, and my father gave me the huge sum of eight hundred rubles (four hundred American dollars) for my tickets, more food, and possibly for bribes to get me out of Russischer territory.

My mother gave me one last kiss goodbye as my father pulled me aside, and whispered, "August, you must be careful, and do not trust anyone, anyone at all, until you are outside Russland. Travel safe and the LORD be with you. Your brother, *Michael,* is waiting for you in a village called Fresno in the California. You already have all the instructions on how to get there. Guard them, and guard your money. Again, do not trust anyone as there will be a reward for your capture very quickly! Mother and I will join you and *Michael* as soon as we can raise the money, but it will probably be a few more years. Stay in contact with us. Whatever money you and *Michael* can spare, send us so that we may all be together again soon."

He gave me a hearty bear hug, and then pushed me out the door and closed it, his way of telling me to leave on this early morning of 20 November 1891.

I just stood there in the crisp cold air, not moving at all for a moment or two, thinking how unfair this was. Why did I have to leave? Why was I not exempt from military service? Why me, I mean, what had I done to deserve this? It was all so unfair!

Father had bought a good horse a few months back for seventy-five rubles, supposedly to help in the fields. He was a typical chestnut colored Russische Don Steppe horse. He was about sixteen hands high with a thick skin and a dense fur coat to keep out the cold. We had fed him quite well to build his reserves, and had carefully ridden him and worked him to build his strength and endurance. He will need all of that strength to carry me quickly to Saratov.

I must get there and get on the train before the Sheriffs and deputies realize that I am gone. They will quickly send a search party, and will eventually get word out of a reward on me all the way to Saratov.

People will notice tomorrow that I am missing, and shortly the Sheriffs will come snooping around asking questions. Mother and Father will say that I am sick, but that excuse will be good for only a few days.

Within a week of no one seeing me, the Sheriffs will become more insistent about where I am. Mother and Father will say that I must have been fooling them all this time, because just last night I slipped out and stole their best horse. Of course, they had no idea where I was or why I would do such a strange thing. That story might give me a couple of more days head start.

I tied cloth sacks on the horse hooves to quiet his sound, and slowly walked out between the houses into the fields. I skirted the road until I had ridden quite a ways from the village. I would be safe traveling the road until daybreak when I would have to move back into the pasture fields and trees. The less people that see me will be the better, and the harder for the Sheriffs to catch my direction and trail.

A light snow fell and made me cold and uncomfortable, but also quickly covered my tracks. I hoped to find the Volga frozen over solid, so that I could cross without anyone seeing me. Crossing the Volga River in winter is always risky though, many of have fallen through bad ice and drowned.

GOD must have blessed my trip, as the Volga River ice was solid as rock. Before the dawn came, I had made it across and a good ways toward the Astrakhan Road that ran north to Saratov.

As the sun rose, I spotted an abandoned building away from any roads where my stallion and I could rest out of sight. Yes, to me he was no longer just a horse, now he was a stallion carrying me to freedom. It was sad that I would have to sell him in Saratov, but I needed the extra money just in case I met trouble along the way. I pray that I find him a kind owner.

We rested most of the day; he ate the hay that I found and I my mother's food. Strength restored, we left shortly before sunset, again heading west all the time.

We cautiously avoided any occupied homes or buildings we passed, and by early morning we were heading north on the Astrakhan Road. We made good time, and after one more day hidden, we would make Saratov.

We were out of the Colonies area, and now were skirting the native Russen lands. It was more dangerous here than back near the Colonies for me. There had always been bad blood between the native Russen and the Colonies from the start, and these people would gladly turn me in for a reward. Luckily, it was cold and harsh outside this time of the year with no one out to notice me. Just the same, I remained very careful and quiet.

Luck was again with us, and as happened the day before, I spotted an abandoned barn away from any roads. Exhausted, we both ate and rested the whole day. At sunset, we again left. Both horse and man still tired from the long difficult and cold ride the previous night, my stallion moved a bit slower up the road toward Saratov.

At next sunrise, we were near Saratov and my stallion, exhausted, began to falter. Feeling sorry for him, I got off and led him the last five versts (less than four miles) to Saratov. Many people saw me, but no one took notice, as this area was apparently always full of strangers coming and going.

My brother had told me precisely how to find the train station in Saratov, and within an hour, I was standing in front of it. Even at this early hour, people were milling about, some waiting for the next train, some wanting to sell almost everything, and some wanting to steal anything you had of value.

I had to get rid of my horse; I could just tie him up and eventually someone would steal him, but I could really use the extra money. I noticed a hauler with a nice wagon pulled by four healthy, and obviously well cared for, horses.

Hoping the LORD was with me; I approached the hauler, and after some small talk, I spoke bluntly, "Friend, I noticed your four fine and healthy horses. You obviously care well for your animals. I am soon leaving on the train, and wonder if you might be interested in my horse for a fair price."

He frowned, squinted at me, and then replied, "Is he stolen? Looks like you rode him hard for the last few days, but otherwise seems a strong horse. Good breeding, a Russische Don I think. Again, is he stolen and are you on the run?"

Damn, what do I say now? Thinking quickly, I replied as sincerely as I could with not a complete lie, but a half-truth, "No, not stolen and not on the run. My brother and his wife live far from here. He wrote me and asked me to come quickly without writing why. With all the bad weather and the cold, that did not sit well with me, but how could I refuse. He is blood; he is my brother, so here I am! My horse is a good horse, healthy and strong, and you are right, I did ride him hard to get here. See for yourself, and if you think he is not a good horse, I will bother you no longer and go away."

He scrunched up his face, rubbed his mitten hand over his mouth and beard, and then got down from his wagon to look closer at my horse. After a few minutes of looking at both ends and the middle, he turned to me and said, "All right, in truth he is a good horse, but you have ridden him too hard and he will need some care before he is up to strength again. I will have to house and feed him extra before he will be of any value to me. How much do you want for him?"

I relaxed, for now my horse was as good as sold, we were now just haggling over price. I slowly replied, "Friend, I am in a bad way and you have me at a disadvantage. He has been a good horse and I want him to go to someone that will treat him fairly, as you apparently will. You are right that he needs extra feed and care, and as I know you are fair to your animals, I trust that you will be fair with me. You name your price, and I will gladly accept it."

My words startled and confused him, and his eyes opened wide for a moment. He scrunched up his face as before, and rubbed his mitten hand over his mouth and beard again, sighed a few times, and then spoke, "Never heard anyone say that before! Never heard of anyone ever letting me set my own price: what a strange idea, not bad, but very strange. I like you, young man, and I like your ways. You offered your trust in me to be fair with you, and I will be."

With that, he pulled out his money purse from beneath his coat, opened it, and counted out many rubles. Smiling, he offered them to me, and said, "Here is one hundred rubles (fifty American dollars), count them if you want to, and take them and we will have a trade."

I took the money from his hand and put it safely away, and replied, "Friend, I have no need to count it, as however much it is, you have treated me fairly. Thank you for helping me out. I pray our LORD blesses you and all your family."

Still smiling, he replied, "Son, may you always be in his blessing and may he keep you safe on your way to help your brother and his wife. Good meeting you, friend!"

I gave him the line to his new horse, gave a soft pat to my old stallion, and walked away toward the station and my future. As I walked, I congratulated myself on my luck. Not only had I sold my horse, but also I had made twenty-five more rubles than he originally cost us. Our LORD must be watching out for me. I now had nine hundred rubles to get me to my brother. I had plenty of money now. My only worry now is discovery, capture, and the Russische Army.

Just as my brother had described, I found the Official Agent of the Travel Agency of Bremen, Deutschland. I inquired of the price of one ticket to America.

The agent, a short old balding man with thick glasses, studied me hard for a minute, and then asked, "Son, you are how old? Let me see your Passport!"

I had no Passport, and when I did not answer, he said, "Hmm, no Passport. I suspect you must have forgotten to bring yours, or maybe you did not have time to get one. Are either of those, what happened?"

Scratching my head, trying to understand just what he meant, it finally dawned on me what he was saying. Quickly, I answered with the half-truth story again, "Yes, that is just what happened. My brother and his wife who live far away wrote me and asked me to come to them quickly. They did not write why, and with all the bad weather and the cold, that did not sit well with me, but how could I refuse. He is blood; he is my brother, so here I am! In the rush to answer his call, I forgot my passport. What can I do now?"

He grinned widely and said, "Young man, do not trouble yourself. The ticket from here to America for those who have their passport is a mere four hundred rubles (two hundred American dollars), for those that need a passport and a ticket it is a little more at six hundred rubles (three hundred American dollars). If you have the six hundred rubles, I can provide you a Passport and ticket on the next train leaving in about a half hour. Do you want the ticket and Passport?"

I was sure he was lying and cheating me, as my brother had paid only three hundred fifty rubles for one ticket, and he was quoting fifty rubles more. His six hundred rubles price only left me three hundred rubles for the rest of the trip. What choice did I have, if I said no, he might turn me over to the Sheriffs. I was in a bad way now, as he might even turn me over to the Sheriffs or soldiers even if I did pay him the six hundred rubles. Yes, I was sure that he was cheating me, but did I have any choice here? No, none at all, and he knew it!

Losing patience with my indecision, he sternly spoke, "Come now, boy. Make up your mind and show me the money. I am a busy man, and others are waiting to purchase their tickets to America!"

I looked around, and I was the only one anywhere near him. I did not see anyone else wanting to buy tickets from him to America. No matter, I would pay his price. I did however see a couple of soldiers watching the area and talking together, a little ways off.

"Yes, I do want the tickets and the Passport, and here is the six hundred rubles," I said, and handing them to him.

He slowly counted each one, and satisfied all six hundred rubles were there; he again widely grinned and replied, "Good choice. I was about to turn you over to the soldiers for a reward, but I make more this way. Here are your tickets taking you all the way to America. By the way, what is your name for the Passport?"

My name, he wanted my name. No choice but to tell him, and I replied, "It is *August Karle*."

He scribbled something on several pages in the passport, handed it to me and said, "You are welcome, *Karle*. This is your new approved and signed Official Passport. I wrote in it that you are the eldest son of your family and are exempt from all military service, and of course, are free to leave Russland as you wish. Have no worry, it is good and will get you out, as long as you do not delay. Have a safe trip; you may board your train now. It will soon leave, and I would not want to miss it, if I were you."

I understood his meaning, and found my train, boarded it, and quickly found a seat in the crowded car. Paying no attention to who was sitting around me, I scrunched down and tried looking like I was just one of many trying to get some sleep. So scared of capture, I silently prayed to our LORD that the Agent was a good man, and would not change his mind and call the Sheriffs or soldiers down on me.

Those few moments waiting for the train to leave were like hours to me. With each noise, I imagined it signaled my discovery; each movement became their reaching to grab me. Suddenly, the train car lurched and we were moving. The LORD was still blessing my trip, and I was still on my way to freedom.

I tried to look like I was soundly sleeping, but twice two different soldiers' woke me and asked for my Passport. Both times, they studied the pages intently, and then returned it back to me and moved away to check someone else.

It took me some hours to relax, and to decide to wake from my pretend sleep. By that time, the others in the car had settled down, and become used to traveling with one another.

When I cautiously looked around the car, to my great surprise, I saw people I knew, and that knew me. There, a few rows over on the left side, was *Herr August Rudolf* with *Frau Catharina* and their family.

A row farther on sat *Herr Jacob Schafer* and *Frau Catharine* and his family, both families from Straub and all my cousins.

I also saw, sitting three rows in front on the right side, *Herr George Bier* and *Frau Maria* along with *Christoph, Philipp,* and *Johan Bier,* and *Herr David Andreas* and wife *Frau Marie,* all from Warenburg and also all my cousins. Directly across from me sat *Herr George Roth* and *Frau Anna* with their two daughters.

I had not known that any of my cousins might be leaving on this train, and of course, they surely did not know I would be here.

For a moment, it felt good being among family again, even if it was just cousins. Then I suddenly realized that I was in more danger now than ever. These people knew me by sight, and knew I was the younger son; they knew I could not have a military exemption. Very soon, if not already, they would realize I was unlawfully leaving.

"What if they said something to the soldiers?" I thought to myself.

Just then, I noticed one of the younger *Roth* girls pointing her finger in my direction, and pulling at her sister's sleeve. Soon, both of them were looking at me, and pulling on their mothers dress. *Frau Anna* took one look and recognized me; I could see it in her face. I am recognized; this is the end of my trip and a soldier's life is soon. It is now just a matter of time before certain discovery, and no words written in any Passport can save me.

Frau Anna sternly told the girls to be quiet and stop pointing, then leaned over and whispered something to husband, *George*. He looked up at me and then quickly looked away. Again, even in that short time, I saw in his face that he knew me. My goose was cooked!

George Roth got up from his seat, and began making his way to the soldier at the rear of the car. Nowhere to run, nowhere to hide, I was trapped in a railcar cage.

Suddenly he stopped, leaned over, and whispered to my cousin *Herr August Rudolf*. I saw *August's* head jerk for a second, but he did not look in my direction. *George Roth* stood back up straight and stretched, and then turned around and went back to his seat next to his wife.

I did not know what was going on. Some time went by and then cousin *August* slowly got up, and walked in my direction. Reaching my row and seat, he motioned for me to move over and then just sat down.

After a few moments of just sitting there in silence, he casually turned to me and whispered, "Cousin, you will never get away with this if you keep hiding under that blanket. You look damned guilty. Now, stretch and act as if you are actually waking up, and then sit up straight and look like you do belong here. No one in our group will give you away, and in fact, we can make the soldiers believe you are part of our group, which is not actually a lie, as you are a cousin of most of us. Do not talk or argue, just do as I say!"

It just seemed the wrong thing to do as he said, but what choice did I have? None, none at all!

I did as my cousin had said, and after some time went by with the soldiers' paying no attention to me, whispered to my cousin, "Thank you for helping me. I was sure I was discovered."

He smiled, and whispered back, "No thanks needed; you are part of our family. How far are you going?"

"To join my brother *Michael* and his wife in a place called Fresno," I answered.

He smiled again, and quietly laughed, "We are all going there. You stay close to us all the way and I will make sure you get to your brother *Michael.*"

As my brother had written, we rode the rails west through the cities of Smolensk and Vitebsk and St. Petersburg, and then south across the border to the port city of Libau, Latvia.

It took four days to travel the over one thousand five hundred versts (one thousand miles) to the northwest all the way through Russland. I saw many pine forests and valleys; I had never seen tall forests like these. No longer worried about being discovered, I actually enjoyed riding the train.

We did sometimes stop in large towns to change trains, and had to sleep on the floor when we stopped overnight. Each time we stopped, the locals were very helpful, that is they tried to pickpocket and help separate us from our money. One of us always had to stay awake on guard. Still, all was good for every day farther from Saratov, was a day closer to safety until finally, I was out of Russland!

On arrival in Libau, I traveled as part of our larger group heading to Fresno. Another Travel Agency Official Agent greeted us and arranged billets for us to stay in for a few days until our ship out was ready to leave. The lodgings were small, crowded, and dirty, but still I was out of Russland and everything was fine now.

Soon another Agent came by and guided our group back to the waterfront to board the ship. Just as with my brother, we would sail on this ship south west across the sea to Bremen, Deutschland, and there we would board a larger ship for the Atlantic Ocean voyage to America.

My brother had also written that I would get sick on the voyage, and he was right, many others and I did get sick. For four uncomfortable days, the choppy waters of the Baltic and North Sea kept the boat swaying and rocking, making almost all of us seasick.

Our next stop was in a port known as Bremerhaven. Here we rested until our bigger ship to England was ready to leave. A few days later we steamed out on a ship called the EMS. We traveled in the steerage class, where each family had a small room.

Our boat sailed south to the port of Southampton in England. Upon our arrival, they guided us off the ship and led us to a huge immigration hall where they gave us bread with meat and cheese, and coffee. I think they called these 'sandwiches'.

Here in England, we also underwent more examinations for smallpox, typhus, and yellow fever. Again, we were in luck as no one had any signs of these. Eventually, we again boarded our same ship, EMS, and went back to the steerage class for our travel to America.

As they warned us is usual during this time of the year, a terrific storm came up as we crossed the Atlantic, and again we were not only sick, but also this time, actually frightened. Looking out at the ocean, all I could see was wave after wave of angry water and more angry water.

I had seen the wide Volga River when storms whipped it up and created angry waves, but those were small compared with what was tossing our ship around. Many of the people worried the ship was going down, and prayed and sang songs to our LORD. Some, sure that this was the end, wanted to go up and see the blue sky just one more time, but they could not, as all the hatches were closed down tight.

Eventually, the weather changed and the ocean became calmer. Some loudly praised, others sang songs to our LORD for his mercy in protecting us. I chose to say a silent prayer of my sincere thanks.

After ten days, rumors spread through the ship that we were finally approaching America, and by tomorrow might arrive. Spirits were high, and all were genuinely excited. Children, who had become bored and depressed from being on the ship, again ran and played, and yelled and laughed. Their happiness was felt by all, and for all, life was better.

At the break of dawn, we were close to the bay of New York, and we could see the many hundreds of tall buildings on the horizon. Everyone was out on the decks, and excitement rose as we passed between two spits of land on either side, and entered a huge bay. After a few minutes, our ship turned again, someone said north, and we headed towards the mouth of a much smaller bay.

As we continued slowly sailing on, I could see large buildings in front of us, on both sides, and to the rear of the ship. We must be deep in the center of the city, in awe, we just watched. No one could ever expect all of this.

Two small boats approached, 'tug boats' someone called them, and they helped guide us further up the waters.

I noticed a large statue of a woman standing with some book in her arms and holding a torch. Much discussion about her began, but we finally learned that this was the Statue of Liberty welcoming all to America. As we passed this Statue of Liberty on the left side of the ship, our ship began moving even more slowly, almost not at all.

I asked one of the friends I had made on the voyage who spoke both Deutsches and English what was happening, and he said, "There, in front of us to the right, is the Barge Office where we will first step on America. We are almost there."

Barge Office... my brother had written that we would land at something called Castle Gardens. Was I going to the wrong place? I asked my friend, "I was told we must land at Castle Gardens? Is that not the right place instead of some barge office?"

He scratched his head, and motioned for me to stay while he went asking. A few minutes later, he returned with a big smile on his face, and replied, "Castle Gardens is the old place and is no longer used; we now go to the Barge Office to be processed."

Immigration Barge Office
Whitehall Street in the Battery

Relieved, I hugged him in joy. Together we laughed and laughed until we both cried. It was finally coming true, after all the perils, I had made it to America. All I had left to worry about was if they would let me in.

There had been much talk on the voyage over about how some did not get in to America, and quickly sent back to England or Deutschland, or I suppose, Russland. No one ever told us why they were sent back, some guessed that they were sick with something, but no one really knew. I said a silent prayer to our LORD for just one more blessing allowing me in to America. I suppose that most all on the deck that morning were asking the same thing of our LORD!

After a few minutes, our ship stopped and dropped its anchors. There were hundreds of us waiting to get on to land, so it took a while for my turn. First, the women and children made their way on to the boat tenders to carry them across the water to the Barge Office pier.

I patiently waited, my turn came, and before long on this 22nd day of December 1891, I was finally in America.

The immigration process was much like my brother had written to expect. Waiting in this line, and then that line, and maybe one more line for many questions and then even more questions. Inspections of everything including what little baggage I carried, and even of me.

The good news is that our entire group passed all the inspections and questions in only one day. The bad news was that there were no trains going towards Fresno until the morning of the day after tomorrow.

Nothing to do, but to walk around and watch as time slowly goes by. The nights were even worse as no one could possibly sleep on those hard wood floors with all the racket and noise of the crying children, the people constantly moving around, and even the boats in the harbor.

On the morning of the 24 December, we boarded a train for Fresno. Still with me, or me still with them, were cousins *David Andreas* and his wife *Christina*, and *George Bier* and his wife *Christina*, and the single woman *Catharina Andreas*, along with *Alex Will.*

Also getting on the same train were more people from Straub and the other colonies. *Carl Wolf*, his wife and family, and *Heinrich Steitz* and his wife *Catharina* and *Peter, Elisabeth, Margaret*, and *Carl*, along with his niece, a rather nice looking single young woman about my age named *Anna Steitz*, also boarded.

Apparently, their group had arrived back on 4 December, but could not actually enter America because one of the children was sick, and had to be well. The group decided to stay until all could leave at once, and so, now we all rode the train to Fresno together.

I had seen this *Anna Steitz* from afar back in Straub, but had never actually talked with her. Luckily, it was much easier to get near her here on the train, and so I made my plans to meet her. The LORD was still blessing me, as I was able to sit and talk with her many times during the train trip to Fresno.

Anna was not only very comely, but she was smart and witty, and most important, she seemed to enjoy my attention and my time with her. I remember her saying to me on more than one occasion in her soft and very pleasant voice, "I do think that you are so brave and courageous for striking out on your own on this trip." Yes indeed, she was a very smart young woman!

I hoped that she would still enjoy my attention when we finally arrived in Fresno and got off the train. I knew in my heart that I had found my future wife; how could I convince her that I was to be her future husband?

We traveled a route always west through Chicago, then Omaha, and eventually to Sacramento at the western edge of America. We then rode south into the San Joaquin Valley and arrived in Fresno on 29 December 1891.

While *Anna* and I did part on arrival in Fresno, where my brother *Michael* and wife *Lisget* met me, I never forgot how I felt when I was around *Anna*. I still knew that she would someday be my wife. I did not know how or when, just someday!

At the station in Fresno, my *Anna Steitz* went off with her uncles family, and I with *Michael* and *Lisget*. Luckily, Fresno was a small town and the German-Rooshin community even smaller. A few months later in mid-March 1892, my brother and I helped organize the Evangelical Lutheran Cross Church with Jacob Legler as our Pastor.

Many times over the next year, as we both attended church services and functions, I ran into, and walked and talked with, my future wife, my *Anna Steitz*.

It was there in the Evangelical Lutheran Cross Church, that *Anna Steitz* became my wife, *Mrs. Johann August Karle*, on 2 December 1892, less than one year after our arrival.

JOHN AUGUST KARLE & ANNA STEITZ
December 2, 1892

24   MORE

◆ CHRISTINA ELISABETH KARLE geb WERNER ◆

Straub, Samara, Russland

When my son *August* left in the night, all Hell eventually broke loose around us. We successfully delayed from the officials, the discovery of his leaving for a whole week, but they eventually, as we knew they would, realized that he was gone.

Of course, we did tell a small half-truth, not a lie, to cover our part in all this. In truth, we did report to the Sheriffs and file charges that he took our horse, though the report was some days later and not right way. We truthfully said we did not know where he was right now. As for the half of the truth, but not a lie, we only said that we did not know what *August* was planning and did in no way at any time help him.

I lay wide-awake on many nights, unable to get good sleep, worried sick for his safety. Many tears have I shed as horrible fears about him torture my mind; not knowing if he made it safely to *Michael* and *Lisget*, or if even if he is still alive, or if he had been caught by the Army and might now be fighting for the Russen in some foreign country, or if he was lying in some alley half-beaten to death, or if he was already dead and buried. All these nightmares visited me over and over. I prayed to our LORD for strength and faith that *August* was safe, still the bad dreams came.

Husband *Johannes* worries too, but he will never own up it. He would say to me, "Our *August* is a strong and smart and brave man. I have no doubt that he is with his brother in America. There is no reason to worry and we will soon hear he is safe and well!" Still, I knew he too, was worried.

It was early in March 1892 that we received a letter with more money from our eldest *Michael.* Husband *Johannes* tore it open and the money fell out on the ground. Instead of picking it up, he intently studied the letter. For a moment, he just stood there, and then with a yell, raced to me on the stoop. He excitedly yelled to me, "He made it; our *August* made it to America and is safe with *Michael* and *Lisget*. I knew he would do it and was never worried at all."

He hugged me in his arms, while we both laughed and cried with happiness and relief, for a long time.

After we settled down, I said to him, "Even though you were always so sure of his safety, we should say a prayer of thanks to our LORD for this blessing."

He replied quickly, "Yes, you are right. Join me in prayer."

Johannes dropped to his knees, and with bent head and clasped hands, prayed aloud, "Merciful LORD, thank you for watching over our son *August* and keeping him safe. Thank you for blessing him with the success of his trip to the home of his brother. Thank you for all the blessings you continue to shower on this *Karle* family, and as your humble servants, we remain forever and ever. Amen."

Johannes stood back up, and again took up the letter, carefully rereading each word aloud to me, a wide happy smile across his face.

I whispered in his ear, "Do you not think it might be wise to go pick up the money off the ground before the wind blows it away to someone else?"

Husband frowned and looked at me in shock, and then yelled back to me, "I completely forgot about the money," as he quickly raced to where the money had fallen.

I thought to myself, "That is a first, as my husband has never ever forgotten about money!"

The next year was very hard on all of the village, and even harder on us. *Johannes* had no sons to help work the fields and bring in the harvests, and while he was a strong man, he was getting older and was now almost fifty-eight years old. I watched him struggle to keep up with the younger men of our village with never a complaint, but I knew how hard it was for him.

Making our lives even worse, a terrible famine swept through all of Russland, including our area. *Johannes* and I had gone through famines before, as recently as a few year back, but we remembered none as severe as this one. Never in the memories of anyone had a famine like this occurred before.

There had been poor harvests of almost everything for the last six years. Some said this was caused by bad weather and not enough rain at the right time, or too much rain at the wrong time, or too much hot dry wind, or too early or later of the winter and spring cold. That might be, or might it be it was our LORDs wrath for something we did wrong. No matter and for whatever reason, the harvests were poor in spite of everything my *Johannes* and the others did.

In truth, a very dry autumn in 1891, delayed our seeding of the fields, Then the winter cold began early and was more severe than usual, with only a bad or light snowfall. Where a heavy snow will protect the new seedlings from the cold, a light snowfall lets them freeze and die. A heavy snowfall also melts in the spring and causes the good Volga River spring floods that spread over the plains to grow the grass that we use as fodder for our animals.

This year another bad snow, the small amount of snow only caused the ground to freeze. Like the year before, a delay in seeding and late planting did not give the young plants time to root, and the freeze killed off all of them. The bad weather wiped out all the sources of feed for our animals, whose well-being was crucial as they provided the power to plow the fields. No young plants, no food for the animals, no way to plow the fields; a perfect bad storm!

The terrible cold weather lasted until well into April, and then quickly turned hot and dry for five rainless months. If anything had lived through the winter cold, it died in this searing dry summer heat.

Our men did all they could, but it was of no help. Food was scarce, and many of our animals died. I prayed that we might be able to leave this place soon before, like everything around us, husband *Johannes* and I both perished too. It was as if our LORD had left us.

We somehow survived that year, but were able to save no money for our trip to America. In truth, just in order to survive, we spent some of the money, which our sons Michael and August regularly sent to us, on food to eat.

By mid-summer of 1893, we knew we finally had enough money saved, and made our plans to leave Straub in July. We sold or gave away all we could not take, and on the morning of 24 July 1893, with all our friends blessing us and waving goodbye, we rode the wagon out of Straub for the very last time, toward a new life with our sons in America.

As we left, I took husband *Johannes*' hand in mine, and asked him, "*Johannes*, dear husband, are we too old to be starting over? Are we too old to begin this adventure to a new land?"

Johannes gently squeezed my hand and replied, "Never, we are still young enough and strong enough to make our lives better and rejoin our sons. Wife, we will not worry and we will enjoy this trip. We are, as we have always been, in the hands of our merciful and just LORD."

And so it was as he said, we did not worry, and we sat back and enjoyed our time traveling together.

Our wagon ride was without any problems, and we stayed a day with our cousins in Balzer. A days ride north and we were in the city of Saratov. We easily found the train station and the Travel Agent who was happy to sell each of us a ticket to America for three hundred fifty rubles (one hundred seventy-five American dollars).

Upon boarding the rail car, we found that our friends *Herr Jacob Klamm* and wife *Maria* and daughters, *Herr George Scharton* and wife *Anna* and daughters, *Herr George Steitz* with wife *Catharine* with sons

August and *Michael,* and daughters *Anna* and *Catharine,* and *Herr Rath Schwabenland* were all riding with us. This was not only an adventure, now it was a celebration!

As our sons had written, our trip took us west through the cities of Smolensk and Vitebsk and St. Petersburg, and then south across the Russischer border to the port city of Libau, Latvia.

There, after a short wait of a few days for our next ship, we enjoyed strolling the city and seeing the sights and visiting the shops. Time to continue and we boarded our ship to take us west to the port of Bremen in our ancestral homeland, Deutschland.

True to the strong warnings of both our sons, we did not easily take to the rolling of the ship, and like most others, became very seasick for a short while. All bad things pass, and while I felt better first and had to hold my *Johannes* head as he emptied his belly one last time over the ships rails, eventually we both recovered. *Johannes* had always been the healthier one of the two of us, always getting well sooner, but this time it took him much longer to regain his strength. Puzzled, I wondered to myself why.

Each day the weather was cold, but clear, and we enjoyed each other's company as we strolled the deck and talked about what are future might be like with our sons in Fresno.

We soon reached the port of Bremen, and guided off the ship. Another three days delay again gave us the chance to take in the sights of this place called Bremerhaven, not Bremen, and to visit and sample some of the fine Deutschen foods.

All this time, I thought I was cooking Deutsche food for my family, but the Deutsche food here is different. Not only are the foods different, but the words are not always the same. Here, 'kuchen' is any cake, but back on the Volga as 'kuga,' it is a low pie-like pastry, with a thick crust and sweet filling.

As we were eating at a gasthaus one evening, I remarked to *Johannes*, "This food is nothing like what we grew up with, and all this time I thought we were eating food from our old homeland, but in fact, we must have been eating Russische food all the time. I like this Deutsche food better, and I could stay a few more days and just enjoy eating."

Johannes laughed and replied, "Ja, I could too, but they would probably charge us for another ticket for all the weight we would gain." We both laughed so hard that soon tears ran down our cheeks.

The next day, along with the rest of our group, we boarded our ship the ELBE to sail to Southampton, England, and then on to America. Much of both trips were in calm weather. Yes, there were a few bad days when we hid in our steerage room. Most days though, *Johannes* and I spent enjoying the fresh sea air and the plentiful sun. Many hours of slow casual strolls, we happily spent going around on those decks. There was nowhere to go and no rush to be anywhere, nothing to do but enjoy what we had this day. This was the first real time away from our work and chores in our entire lives, and it was all good.

We arrived in America on 30 August 1893, and first set foot on our new land at Ellis Island, in the City of New York.

Waiting in the long line slowly moving towards the immigration building, I thought back on all that *Johannes* and I had been able to see and do since leaving our Straub. Not that it was all enjoyable; some of it I would never want to do again, but much of it was amazing and wonderful.

For the very first time in our marriage, it was just the two of us, *Johannes* and I, together talking about everything and about nothing, remembering about the old times and all our old friends with no worry about the harvest or too much or too little rain, or the hot dry winds, or even the evil Moscow government. No matter how this all turns out, just being here with my *Johannes,* has made the trip worth everything to me.

We, as was everyone else in line, were both very tired. My *Johannes* did not look as strong as just a few years ago, not that he looked ill, but maybe this hard life and his age were finally catching up. I hoped not, as I had plans for him in Fresno.

As we finally made it to the front of the line, they took our baggage from us and inspected it, and temporarily stored it elsewhere. Next, Inspectors examined us for any sign of sickness. We both looked healthy, but old, and passed. Then on to another desk where they asked our names, our age, our birthplace, our last homes, how much money we had, where we were going, what we did for a living, and about our future plans. They even asked who would be meeting us and taking responsibility for us at our final destination. We gave them our sons' names, but honestly, we had taken care of ourselves for years, so why would anyone have to take responsibility for us?

Thankfully, we passed all their inspections and questions, and they approved us to enter America and travel on to Fresno. Our entire group also passed, and together we purchased our railroad tickets to Fresno. While some other groups had to stay overnight, we were lucky enough get tickets for everyone on a train leaving that very day.

Once on board, I turned to *Johannes*, and said, "Once again we are on our way with little trouble. Join me, husband, in a quiet prayer thanking our LORD." Holding hands, with head bowed, I said, "LORD, our merciful father, our sincere thanks to you for all the blessings you provided on this trip, as well as all the blessings that you have provided our sons, *Michael* and *August*, along with all the others that travel with us. Amen."

After a seven-day rail ride through large cities and small towns, past one horse-stops, through fields of wheat and grain, tall forests and green valleys, over high snow covered mountains, through bushy deserts, and finally into this bountiful valley, we arrived in Fresno.

We stepped off the rail car on 6 September 1893, greeted by son, *Michael* and wife *Lisget,* and son *August* along with, to our surprise, his new wife *Anna.*

Now here together with them, we all settled in to living in Fresno and enjoying the freedoms of America. May the LORD continue to bless us and help us to grow and prosper!

NEW CENTURY

CHRISTINA ELISABETH KARLE geb WERNER

Fresno, California, United States of America

It is the first day of the first month of a new century, January 1, 1900! Our LORD continues to bless our families.

Johannes and I joined the Free Evangelical Lutheran Cross Church here in Fresno, so that we will always make time and remember to thank our LORD for his many gifts.

My *Michael* and his wife, *Lisget*, are now the owners of a store selling food; they call it a 'grocery store'. Now who would have believed that anyone in our poor family would ever own a store; certainly, no one in Straub ever would have thought such a thing! *Michael* was also the first Moderator of our church for a time, and still is a church officer. Sadly, our LORD never blessed them with children of their own.

FREE EVANGELICAL LUTHERAN CROSS CHURCH
Fresno 1895

My *August* and his wife, *Anna*, have been very blessed in the few short years since they married. They now have three strong sons, *Michael*, *August*, and *John Peter Karle*, and one beautiful daughter, *Katie*, and one more child on the way, which they are sure will be a boy and named

Alexander! My *August* is also a storeowner along with being a successful farmer and partner with his cousin, *David Andreas*.

Not every story can be a happy one, and sadly, a few years back on 13 June, 1896, my husband of more than forty years, my *Johannes Karle*, who had loved and comforted and kept me safe for all that time, passed on and is now sits alongside our LORD in Heaven. As I suspected, he never did recover from all that hard work during those terrible years of '91 and '92; his strength just slowly left him.

I have no regrets for all we went through together. Our families have prospered here in our new land, and I will be ready, without any hesitation, when my LORD finally calls me to be with him, and my *Johannes*.

My only wish, my last request, is the same as that I pray each and every night, "Merciful LORD, please continue to shower your blessings on my children, their children, and children's children forever and ever wherever they are. Guide them as you have guided us in our faith and our lives, and keep a place for them with you in eternal Heaven. Amen."

25   ALL ENDS

All are now gone; only fading memories kept alive in the stories handed down from mother to child, and on the pages of this book. Each lived their life as they chose and as best they could. As with all things, each came to an eventual end.

That end, good or bad, is chronicled for posterity and history. Some of their deaths are on earlier pages; the others are below in order of the date of their passing (Fact where available; otherwise fictional):

♠KONRAD HESS♠

Brutally murdered in 1768 trying to stop a recruited traveler under contract from running away.

♠JOHANN WEISS♠

Successfully evaded capture until 1768; hung by local Russians, then executed by Russian Army.

♠ LT. VON DITMARR ♠
Later suspected of cheating those in his care, and not returning monies owed to the Crown. No charges, but disappeared with no trace in 1769.

♠ NICHOLAI PAUSTOVSKY ♠
Killed fighting a huge Cossack in 1771; crushed in a bear hug.

♠ RUSSISCHES PECHNIKI ♠
Died in 1773; crushed under a falling stone chimney that he had poorly built some years earlier.

♠ LT. VIKTOR CHERNYSHEVSKY ♠
Promoted to Captain, died in 1774 in the battle for Saratov fighting the Pugachev Army.

♠ JAKOB SCHECK ♠
Woodworker, Head Carpenter in Balzer; Died in 1774 of mortal wounds in 'Time of Terror' with the Pugachev Army.

♠ JAKOB DORLOSCH ♠
Soldier by trade, originally from Blanenbach, Germany, he fought bravely with the Original Settlers in the battle between them and the New Arrivals. Elected as Sheriff of Balzer in 1768. Died in early 1774 of mortal wounds in 'Time of Terror' with the Pugachev Army.

♠ RECRUITER for Johann Facius ♠
In 1774, they hanged him in Germany for illegal recruiting and lying, and sent his body to St. Petersburg.

♠ LT. COLONEL IVAN CHICHELNITSKY ♠
Stabbed another officer in a fight over cards; thrown out of the Army a broken man. Died 1781 of cold and hunger in a back alley of St. Petersburg, Russia.

♠ LUTHERAN PASTOR in Heilbronn ♠
He died in 1785 having succumbed to the grippe he caught from giving 'last rites' to the dying.

♠BALZER BARTHULI♠
Colony of Balzer named after him; Reformed faith farmer and one of the leaders of the original settlers. Died in 1810 in Balzer.

♠LAUDEMA CHRISTIANA MAURER♠
Died March 1815 of old age in Heilbronn, Germany.

♠ANNA MARIA KARL SCHWIND geb GRÜN♠
Daughter of Andreas Grün and Anna Maria Grün geb Hartt, she was born in 1777 in Balzer, Russia. After her husband, Wilhelm died in 1805; she married Nikolaus Schwind, and had at least one more daughter. She died in 1820 in Straub.

♠MARIA MARGARETHA KARLE♠
Only 9 years old when she died of the grippe in Straub in 1834.

♠JOHANN FRIEDRICH KARL♠
Married Elisabeth Reichert in Balzer and had five sons; Died June 12, 1841 in Balzer.

♠SUSANNA CHARLOTTE IDA KARLE geb MICHEL♠
Daughter of Konrad Michel and Anna Katharina Michel geb Iskam, she was born in 1805 in Moor, Russia. Married John Michael Karle in 1823 with many sons and daughters. She died in 1863 in Straub in childbirth.

♠JOHANN HEINRICH KARLE♠
Married Catharina Elisabeth Kukkus and had at least one daughter. Died January 27, 1875 in Straub.

♠JOHANN MICHAEL KARLE♠
Farm laborer, Grocery store owner, Church official, and part-time agent for Holland American Steamship line; Husband of Elisabeth Andreas; Mike died January 22, 1917 in Fresno, California.

♠KATIE KARLE♠
Born in 1894 in Fresno, California, Katie grew up in Fresno's 'Roosian' town on G Street. She married Alex Adolph in

1920, and died shortly thereafter, on June 25, 1921 in Fresno, California.

♦CHRISTINA ELISABETH KARLE geb WERNER♦

Daughter of Johann Philipp Werner and Elisabeth Werner geb Geringer, she was born March 14, 1833 in Warenburg, Russia. Married to Johannes (John) Karle. After her husband, John died in 1896, she lived with their son Mike and Lisget in their home, first on E Street, and then on G Street. She died January 17, 1922 in Fresno, California, and is buried in Mountain View Cemetery, Fresno, California.

♦ANNA KARLE geb STEITZ♦

Daughter of Johann Peter Steitz and Maria Elisabeth Steitz geb Scherer, she was born April 21, 1872 in Straub, Russia. Married to John Karle and had five sons and one daughter. She died July 17, 1925 in Fresno, California, and is buried in Mountain View Cemetery, Fresno, California.

♦CHRISTINA ELISABETH KARLE geb ANDREAS♦

Daughter of Heinrich Philipp Andreas and Anna Margaretha Andreas geb Karle, she was born August 9, 1856 in Warenburg, Russia. Married Mike Karle in 1879; Midwife for Dr. Chester Rowell. After her husband died in 1917, Lisget married again to August Lung. Lisget died May 13, 1927 and is buried in Mountain View Cemetery, Fresno, California.

♦AUGUST KARLE♦

Born August 30, 1893, in Fresno, California, August grew up in Fresno's 'Roosian' town on G Street. He married Alvina Gable. In 1930, he was a Manager for an Insurance Company, and lived at 3902 Platt Avenue, Fresno. August died December 18, 1936 in Fresno, California.

♦JOHN (JOHANN) AUGUST KARLE♦

Remembered as a wonderful grandfather, and for his handle bar mustache, John was in the construction business and helped build the City Hall in Fresno. Married to Anna Steitz and had five sons and one daughter. After his wife, Anna, died in 1925, he married for the second time at age 57. John died February 20, 1950 in Fresno, California.

♠ JOHN PETER KARLE ♠

Born September 2, 1896, in Fresno, California, JP grew up in Fresno's 'Roosian' town on G Street. He married Katherine Will(s) from Sanger, California in 1917. Over the years, they had two sons and three daughters. He worked at a variety of jobs, clerk, meter man and finally for the Fresno City Water Works. JP died March 5, 1958 in Fresno, California, and is buried in Belmont Memorial Park Cemetery, Fresno, California. Their sons and daughters had many children, with their children having children, living around the Fresno area.

♠ MICHAEL KARLE ♠

Born July 9, 1898 in Fresno, California, Mike grew up in Fresno's 'Roosian' town on G Street. He married Rosie Ginder. Over the years, they had three daughters. While continuing to live in Fresno for many years, by 1930, he and his family lived in Hayward, California at 219 C Street. Both he and Rosie worked as Grocery workers in the Food Preserve. Mike died Jul 1973 in Hayward, California.

♠ ALEXANDER KARLE ♠

Born February 26, 1900 in Fresno, California, Alex grew up in Fresno's 'Roosian' town on G Street. He married Annie Bopp in 1924. They had one daughter. Alex died September 10, 1984 in Fresno, California.

26   EPILOG

♦D. PHILIPP KAISER♦
Green Mountain, Huntsville, Alabama

The year 2012, nearly two hundred and fifty years after the start of this story, over a century since the end: Eight generations later, a grandson writes a tale about his brave ancestors for all to read. Maybe this will insure we will never ever forget what they accomplished for all of us.

A Forgotten Volga German Grave
Warenburg Cemetery
(Sharon White 2003)

After fighting to get to this Promised Land, the Germans from the Volga Colonies found that they were different from earlier German immigrants. They had spent over one hundred twenty-five years among the Russians, and their speech and customs had changed much while in Russia. The German-Americans that arrived much earlier felt these new immigrants were different and not real Germans, and did not readily accept them into their society and culture. Along with their English-speaking neighbors, the earlier German-Americans referred to the Volga Germans as "Roosians" and to their settlements as "Roosian town."

As all newcomers do, they started at the bottom of the social ladder and in order to survive, accepted the jobs that others avoided. Women were domestics; men worked on railroad construction, farmed, or dug ditches. Industrious and determined they moved forward, all who encountered them admired their ability and passion to work.

While many of Volga German ancestors eventually traveled to the San Joaquin Valley (around Fresno and Visalia) in California, many of their brothers, sisters, uncles, aunts, and cousins and other relatives settled in the German areas of the states of Colorado, Idaho, Illinois, Kansas, Maryland, Michigan, Minnesota, Montana, Nebraska, New York, North Dakota, Oklahoma, Oregon, Washington, Wisconsin, and Wyoming. Volga Germans became closely tied to the sugar beet industry in Colorado and western Nebraska, others became wheat growers in the Dakotas and in Canada; and orchard and grape growers in California. No matter where they settled, they always prospered and improved the area they finally called their home.

May GOD bless them for all they did, for without their faith, courage and determination, I would not exist, and their story might never be written.

Remembrance

They left a land of pain and strife,
And gave up all for a better life.
North over hill, valley they rode, they walked,
On boat and ship until at last, they docked.

To a cold mother Russland they had come,
The end of their lives for not all, but some.
Closer, closer to the Promised Land each day,
Too many of their dead left along the way.

South, always south, was the way to go,
Saratov was the only city to know.
So near, yet so far, to our land at last,
Months more than a year had passed.

At last finally here, but what is this?

Nothing, no homes, only a broken promise.
In spite of all those damned recruiter's lies,
Out of this nothing, their villages would rise.

They overcame, and paid the ultimate fee,
So their descendants would always be free.
Truly, we owe them our very existence,
Humbly, we give them eternal remembrance.

D. Philipp Kaiser 2011

And now a special excerpt from
D. Philipp KAISER's newest novel

Dreams on the Volga

Always available at DarrelKaiserBooks.com

1   THE BEGINNING

◆MARGARETHA MÜLLER◆

A days ride north of stadt Frankfurt, Reichsstadt (Imperial City) of the Holy Roman Empire

It was a bitterly cold and stormy night, much worse than the usual in January around our village of Nauborn. Wind-driven ice pellets peppered my face like stinging bees. The falling snow covering all in white blanket, so thick and blinding our eyes, we could barely make out our horse pulling our sleigh. For my husband and I, or any man or beast, this night in this year of our LORD one thousand seven hundred thirty-seven (1737), is not a time to be to be out.

Our benevolent patron of over twenty years, *Herr Heinrich Köhler,* along with the rest of the *Köhler* family, had fallen gravely ill with the grippe (influenza). They desperately needed healing goods from the apotheke (pharmacy) some distance away in stadt Wetzlar.

My valiant, but rash husband, *Herr Andreas Müller*, knew the way to stadt Wetzlar best and offered to go alone. My *Andreas* is a sturdy and strong man, but having seen more than forty of the Neu Jahr (New Year), he is far from his best, and too old for this.

Alas, no one else offered, and my *Andreas* meant to go out alone. This I could not agree to, and so this night, I joined him on this sleigh ride out in this dreadful weather.

On any other normal winter night, I would have relished an outing thru the hills and meadows on the sleigh with him. We would be snuggling together beneath the thick warm pelts, and laughing about much of nothing while nipping on our home made cider, but not this night, not this terrible night.

Earlier, I feared for his life if he went out alone; now as I look up at his face with his beard frozen in ice as he struggles to keep our sleigh moving, now I fear for both our lives.

In spite of all my fears, he did guide us down into the lower valley and stadt Wetzlar. It took more time than usual and by the time we arrived, we were already cold and wet, and our horse already tired. Here in the village, the storm was not as bad, with only a light snow falling that covered all. Not a person or creature moved about, the streets deserted and buildings all closed up. We quickly sleighed thru the stadt and soon arrived at the apotheke.

Andreas leaped off the sleigh, ran to the shop door, and began pounding on it. In the silence of the dead of night, his pounding resounded, it was so loud I was sure we would rouse the dead in their graves. Even so, no one came to open the door.

As he continued beating the door with his fists, *Andreas* yelled as loudly as he could, "Open up! Open up,

I say. We have urgent need of your help. Open up now, or I swear, I, *Andreas Müller*, will beat this door down!"

I believed him, and apparently so did those inside behind the door, for the apotheker pulled open the door, and angrily demanded, "Quiet! What is wrong with you people? Quiet or I will send for the authorities to silence you!"

Andreas quickly told him of the grippe, and our needs. The apotheker knew of the good *Köhler* family, and quickly turned to gather medicines and supplies. Together, he and my *Andreas* began loading and packing them into the sleigh.

Finished loading, the apotheker squinted out into the stormy night, frowned and shook his head, and cautioned *Andreas*, "Your patron, *Herr Köhler*, is my old friend and I admire your faithfulness to him and his family, but only the very foolish would go back out this night! A sensible man would stop, and stay the night right here. Neither of you will do the sick any good if you freeze to death on the way back!"

Did I say that my brave husband, *Herr Andreas Müller*, is not always "a sensible" man? *Andreas* said nothing back to the apotheker, but reached out his hand to shake the apothekers in thanks for all his help.

The apotheker, shivering in the cold, frowned again and slowly shook his head from side to side, but took my husband's hand and tightly gripped it in a firm shake. Then, with a quick wave good night, he closed the door and returned inside to his warm and toasty home.

The weather was getting worse, and fearful of what we might meet on the way back, I desperately pleaded with *Andreas*, "My husband, I am afraid for us. I do love the *Köhlers* and they have given us so much all these years, but I fear that our own lives will end this night if we again travel that road. I know that '*Andreas*' is for 'brave', but please; I beg that we stay the night here in shelter."

Andreas looked at me and said nothing, but shook his head 'no.' 'Please," I softly begged.

He finished tying down the supplies, and moved to our horse to adjust his blanket, and give him some dry grain to eat. While the horse chewed, *Andreas* slowly walked back to me. He gently took my hand, and spoke, "Wife, you are right; you must stay the night here. I must go back; I will do all I can to get these medicines back to the *Köhler* family. I have no choice, it is what as a man I must do! It is what I would expect any other man to do for you, if you were deathly ill. In my own eyes, if I do not go, I will never be a man again! Stay, but I must go now!"

I knew that I could not let him go back alone, no matter what words he uses. If he continues back, then I too will be there at his side till death, or hopefully with our LORDs blessing, till we safely arrive back home.

I quickly replied to him, "*Andreas Müller*! I am your wife, and you will not tell me where and when I will be with you! If you foolishly choose to risk your life, then you choose to risk both our lives, as I will be at your side the whole way back." Very frustrated, I screamed at him, "You will not leave me here, do you understand? I will not be left! I will not be left!"

Startled by my outburst, he just looked at me for a time, shrugged, and agreeing, nodded his head. My *Andreas*, always a man of few words, no matter, I would have my way and return with him. A small voice back in the depths of my mind yelled out, "Fine, you won and you will now die alongside him in this terrible storm. How lucky you are!"

I answered back to my own self, "Shush, I am his wife and it is my place to be at his side, and that is the end of it!" The small irritating voice, back in the depths of my mind, stayed silent.

As *Andreas* busied himself with our horse, adjusting and tightening the horses blanket, and hand feeding him more food and warmed water, I silently said a prayer, "LORD, please protect all the fools that are out this night, including us. I beg you to end this storm, but if you choose not to, at least safely guide our horse and us back to our home. We ask this not only for ourselves, but also for our *Köhler* family, so sick. If this cannot be and we must perish this night, please be merciful and end our lives with little pain. Thank you for all your blessings, LORD. Amen."

All packed up and ready, *Andreas* climbed on and sat down. I snuggled next to him, and he turned and said to me, "Are you sure?"

I quickly, and forcefully, replied, "Yes, my husband!"

He slowly shook his head, but then leaned over and gently kissed my lips. After that sweet moment, we slowly sleighed over the snow and out of the still sleeping village towards home. Even knowing the road, and being all bundled up, the ride was cold and hard to bear. We huddled together as best we could under the many pelts on the sleigh bench, and prayed that our horse would not falter.

I could see *Andreas* was as worried as I was, and I asked him, "Will our horse be able to stand this cold? What if he falters?"

Andreas looked at me, and solemnly spoke, "Pray that he does not fall, for if he does, we will surely perish this night."

I knew he was right... we could never survive out here for long. I softly said to him, "It is all in the hands of our LORD. He will decide what will be for us." *Andreas* slowly nodded in agreement, as he concentrated on keeping our horse moving.

It seemed like many hours, but likely not more than two and we were just past the village of Nauborn and almost to *Köhler* land, when I noticed something strange at the side of the road, a large odd shaped mound all covered with snow. "*Andreas*, Stop!" I yelled. I could feel in my soul that something was not right about here.

Puzzled, and hearing me, but not understanding, he looked at me, but did not stop and continued urging our horse on thru the deep snow.

I grabbed his arm, and again yelled as loud as I could, "Stop! Stop now!" I just knew I must act now. I struggled out from under the pelts and jumped off the sleigh, and fell on my face into the deep snow. Pushing myself back up on my feet, slipping and sliding, I ran back to the odd shaped mound as fast as my unsteady feet could move.

Andreas, still confused, jumped off when the sleigh stopped moving, and quickly followed while yelling, "*Margaretha*, have you lost your mind? What is wrong with you? Come back here, and get back on the sleigh or we will both freeze to death!"

I had reached the snow-covered mound and was pushing off the snow, while he was desperately pulling at me to get me back to the sleigh. As I finally uncovered the mound, we both stopped in astonishment and then, shock. There before us, the bodies of a young couple, man and a woman held in each other's arms, frozen to death on the side of this road.

Stunned, we both just stood there, time seemed to stop and for just an instant there was no storm, no cold, no snow nor ice, no danger for us; only the terrible awareness that the young couple before us had recently perished, and that it was such a waste! I moved to my *Andreas* and grabbed on to him for strength, and burying my face in his chest, sobbed.

The young couple was long passed, and there was nothing we could do for them in this storm. *Andreas* promised to come back and bury them when the storm cleared. I said a prayer to our LORD as I covered them again. *Andreas* again began desperately pulling at me to get me back to the sleigh.

We had only covered a few steps back to the sleigh, when we heard the soft sound of a baby's whimper and cry. Most likely the wind, yet we both stopped and carefully listened for that cry again. There, that faint cry again; and it is not the wind. At the exact same time, we both grasped that there was still a life back in that snow-covered mound.

Slipping and sliding, we raced back to the frozen couple and searched for a baby. It was a baby boy that we found, very hungry and cold, but still alive, barely. The poor coupled had died shielding their child from the terrible storm.

We hurried to the sleigh, placed the baby boy between our bodies, and covered all with pelts to warm him. Throwing all caution to the wind, *Andreas* drove our poor horse without mercy, as we raced home as fast as he could pull the sleigh. Not a sound I heard, other than the crack of the whip, as *Andreas* drove us faster and faster.

Even as our horse began to weaken and falter, *Andreas* did not let up. Exhausted, our horse finally slipped and fell to the ground, both horse and sleigh sliding down the snow covered road.

Andreas leaped out, and somehow got our unsteady horse up, and standing again. Soon, we were once more racing over the snow-covered road, praying that our horse would last just a little longer. As we crested the last hill and could see the *Köhler* Family house, our horse fell for his final time, loudly snorted once, and died. He would never run again, his own life sacrificed in an effort to save the boy.

Without speaking, we both knew that the life of the baby was almost gone. Without a word, *Andreas* grabbed the baby, and madly took off through the deep snow towards our home.

I followed *Andreas* as best I could, but there was no way I could keep up as he raced home with the boy. Moving as fast as I could, slipping and sliding, and falling, all the while praying aloud again and again, "LORD, please have mercy on this innocent baby. I pledge that if you save him, we will devote our lives to caring for him as if he were of our own bodies. Amen."

<><><><><><><><><><><><>

The baby boy did survive, and Andreas Mueller and Margaretha named him, Daniel Andreas.

<><><><><><><><><><><><>

An excerpt from

Dreams on the Volga

A story of the life of Daniel Andreas,
and the lives of many of his descendants,
by

D. Philipp Kaiser

DarrelKaiserBooks.com

www.ingramcontent.com/pod-product-compliance
Lightning Source LLC
Chambersburg PA
CBHW020244030726

47499CB00001B/55